**ALSO BY LAURIE ELIZABETH FLYNN**

*The Girls Are All So Nice Here*

# Till Death Do Us Part

**LAURIE ELIZABETH FLYNN**

**SIMON & SCHUSTER**

NEW YORK   LONDON   TORONTO   SYDNEY   NEW DELHI

1230 Avenue of the Americas
New York, NY 10020

First Simon & Schuster hardcover edition August 2024

SIMON & SCHUSTER and colophon are registered trademarks of Simon & Schuster, LLC

Simon & Schuster: Celebrating 100 Years of Publishing in 2024

For information about special discounts for bulk purchases,
please contact Simon & Schuster Special Sales
at 1-866-506-1949 or business@simonandschuster.com.

The Simon & Schuster Speakers Bureau can bring authors to your live event.
For more information or to book an event, contact the
Simon & Schuster Speakers Bureau at 1-866-248-3049 or
visit our website at www.simonspeakers.com.

*Interior design by Ruth Lee-Mui*

Manufactured in the United States of America

1   3   5   7   9   10   8   6   4   2

Library of Congress Cataloging-in-Publication Data has been applied for.

ISBN 978-1-9821-4466-1
ISBN 978-1-9821-4470-8 (ebook)

*For Astrid, Cullen, Delilah, and Briar:*
*For deepening my writing, and my heart*
*For your creative souls, your unconditional love,*
*and your limitless imaginations*
*For absolutely everything.*

The past is never dead. It's not even past.
—William Faulkner


In vino veritas.
In wine, there is truth.
—Pliny the Elder

# Prologue

September 2012

HE STEPPED OUT OF THE SEA, the ocean pooling under his feet like a fallen cape, waves packing the sand into brown sugar. *My husband*, a phrase that still seemed foreign to me. Nobody had thought we would last beyond a month, *maybe* two, once the lust started to flatline. *You barely know him*, friends had warned me after a diamond ring encircled my finger so much sooner than anyone expected.

Everyone would hate that we eloped, but our spontaneous ceremony on the beach in Santa Barbara had been perfect. I'd worn a simple linen dress and held red-mouthed hibiscus flowers. Humidity had curled the ends of our hair, the crown of my head beginning to bleach from the sun. A day later, we had yet to tell our loved ones. We wanted it to be only us for a little bit longer.

"You should come in next time," Josh said as he sat down and toweled off beside me.

I straddled his lap, my fingers resting on his damp shoulders. "You swim too far. It stresses me out when I can't see you anymore."

He kissed me, long and hard, his thumbs hooked into my hips. When he pulled away, his eyes were playful. "I love you for worrying about me,

June Kelly." My new name felt like a novelty. "But you don't need to. Nothing bad is going to happen."

I believed him. After all, he had been right about everything else.

But seven days after I was pronounced his wife, I became Josh Kelly's widow.

# PART I

# The Harvest

Harvesting—or picking—is the first step in winemaking. Ultimate precision must be used, and harvesting by hand ensures that only the best-quality grapes make it to the next stage of the process. The harvest is all about the when. Pick too soon, and the physiology of the grapes will be all wrong, the acids too high and sugars too low. Missing the ideal window tips the scale the other way, the acids skyrocketing while sugars plummet.

On the vineyard, as in life, timing is everything.

# One

## June

Prospect Heights, Brooklyn

August 2022

**I KNOW IT'S COMING** before it actually happens. We're underneath a sprawling elm in Prospect Park, eating a picnic lunch Kyle packed—baguette and sliced pears and Comté cheese the shade of caramelized butter, paired with a notoriously hard-to-find Australian bottle that I'd mentioned was one of the best orange wines I'd ever tasted. It's the wine that tips me off, from a small husband-and-wife-operated natural winery in Victoria, too special for a regular lunch.

He doesn't get down on one knee, because I told him I didn't want him to. I wanted casual, just us. No dimly lit restaurant, no audience of family and friends. His hand reaches behind his back, where he must have been hiding the ring box in his pocket all morning. The ring itself is not a surprise: we picked it out together, a one-carat oval diamond on a thin gold band. Its design is simple and classic, something I knew I wouldn't question in five or ten or thirty years.

"June Emery, you know how much I love you. You're my best friend and the person I want to spend the rest of my life with. I've never been so sure about anything, and I'll do whatever it takes to make you as happy and loved as you make me feel. Do you think . . . will you marry me?" he says, his smile almost sheepish, as though he's afraid I'm going to respond with anything other than a resounding *yes*. We've been together for six years, and marriage has been on the table for at least two of them. It was a conversation Kyle was ready to have long before I was. Now, in the warm late-summer air, his question lingers between us.

I pause for only a second. "Yes. Yes! Of course I will." My hand extends, and he slides the ring onto my finger. It's a perfect fit. My nails are buffed and polished a neutral pink. I suspected, when he asked me yesterday if I wanted to spend Sunday afternoon at the park, that he had something planned, and the minute I saw the wine, I was certain that this was it. That we'd leave engaged.

Kyle embraces me tightly, my face embedded in his soft flannel shirt, which is his weekend-casual uniform when he's not in suits for work. Tears burn my eyes, and when I pull away, he notices.

"I didn't think I'd cry," I say, holding my smile steady. "They're happy tears, I promise. This just feels so *right*."

And it does feel right, me and Kyle. But the tears aren't simply those of happiness. My intense emotion in this moment has nothing to do with Kyle and everything to do with a past he isn't part of, a version of me that preceded him. The other ring, the one I wore before, a tiny cluster of diamonds I'd thought was the most beautiful piece of jewelry I'd ever seen. The one I continued to wear for years after Josh was gone.

"Hey," Kyle says, brushing his thumb under my eye. "This is different for you than it is for me, and I get it. You don't have to pretend otherwise."

I nestle under his arm, grateful beyond words that he's this understanding, this forgiving. A lot of men in Kyle's situation might feel like they were perpetually competing against a ghost, locked in a comparison game they had no chance of winning. I half-heartedly dated a few guys in the years after Josh, but they never stuck around, either because they sensed my hesitation or because they didn't want to live under the weight of my trauma. Kyle has only ever been thoughtful and patient. He's so good to me that sometimes I fear I don't deserve him.

"You absolutely deserve him," my best friend, Phoebe, has repeated more than once. "You of all people deserve to find love again."

*Again*, because this isn't my first time feeling that I've found the one. This won't be my first wedding. The happiest day of my life was followed a week later by the worst day imaginable. Until Kyle, I didn't think I'd get that second chance at passionate, true love.

Kyle tips up my chin to kiss me, his lips soft and yielding. *My fiancé*. This time will be different, because everything is different, including me. I'm thirty-nine now, Kyle forty in November. We're more established—I own a natural wine bar; he's a vice president at a private equity firm—we've lived together in our Prospect Heights apartment ever since the start of the pandemic when our individual leases expired; and we've talked extensively about the future, mapping out what our lives might look like next year, five years, a decade from now. We discussed a short engagement, mostly because we both want kids. I've been off the pill for six months: we're not actively trying, but we're not being careful either, though so far, my period has still shown up every month like clockwork.

From our spot in Long Meadow, we FaceTime Phoebe and then my parents, who still live in Connecticut, along with Kyle's parents in Pasadena. Pam and Richard, my future in-laws, are gray-haired but tanned and fit from years of hiking in the canyons. Pam has become like a second mother to me, perpetually warm and welcoming—the opposite of Josh's mother, so many years ago, whom I barely got to know.

My own parents are thrilled, but not surprised. Kyle lets me know that he secretly asked them for their blessing weeks ago. "It was really important for me to do things right," he says with a little shrug, and my love for him swells. My mom has tears in her eyes as I show her the ring. We keep the calls short, a flurry of gleeful congratulations. It was hard for my parents, after Josh. They didn't know what to say or how to act around me, my grief as raw as an exposed nerve. Every time I tried to tell them his death hadn't been an accident, they'd exchange a look, a quick flicker of their eyes that told me they thought I was letting the sadness destroy me. I knew they wanted me to find a way to move on.

A stranger offers to take our picture, and I hold up my hand while

Kyle swings his arm reassuringly across my shoulders, *I said yes*, I'll type underneath it later before posting on social media, and there will be so many comments from friends and coworkers and clients, people who have supported and loved us, who genuinely want the best for us both.

"I have one more surprise," Kyle says as we leave the park. "You now have the night off work, and we have a reservation at a place I know you're going to love."

"But how?" I say. "The bar's going to be busy—"

He smiles, laugh lines creasing around his glasses. "I might have told Trish about this and sworn her to secrecy, and she made it happen."

"Seriously? I can't believe Trish could keep that secret."

Trish is the manager at Grape Juice, my wine bar. Even though she and the rest of my staff are very capable, I still find it difficult not to be there to oversee everything. I knew when I began to pursue the idea of opening my own bar that I'd need to pour all of myself into it to even have a chance at succeeding. It's notoriously easy for bars to fail in their first year, especially in Brooklyn, where patrons have seemingly infinite options to choose from. People advised me against it—Phoebe, my parents—just like they'd warned me against getting engaged to Josh so quickly. But I *wanted* the bar to consume me. In the absence of Josh, I ached for a distraction from my sadness. And I knew failure wasn't the worst thing that could happen.

There was interest in Grape Juice from the start because of my existing connections through the wine bar I'd previously managed and increasing curiosity about natural wine. After the uncertainty of lockdowns and closures during the pandemic, business has picked up again, and I'm grateful to my small but loyal staff for sticking with me. Grape Juice is now a popular weekend destination for twenty- and thirtysomethings and a favorite dinner spot for couples, thanks to our careful recommendations for pairing natural wines with locally sourced food choices.

"You really thought of everything." I touch the stubbly skin on his cheeks. Tomorrow morning, he'll be clean-shaven for the office, but I like him this way best.

We dress up for dinner and our Lyft takes us to Modern Love, a cozy vegan restaurant where we'd had one of our first dates. Kyle's eyes meet mine, both of us doing a bad job at suppressing grins. Shortly after we'd started dating, I'd told Kyle I was a vegetarian, and he'd said he wanted to surprise me with the next restaurant we went to. I tried to act impressed when we arrived at Modern Love, but when the waitstaff greeted me by name and he realized I was already a regular there, we both burst into laughter. Even funnier was watching Kyle—a red-meat lover—pretend to be enthralled by the menu options. But he grew to like the food, even teaching himself a few vegetarian recipes to prepare at home.

After dinner, when it's just us in our apartment, Kyle undresses me carefully, trailing kisses down my body. He uses his mouth to make me come before he enters me, moving slowly, deliberately, taking cues for what I want. Our sex life has always been great, and I know how lucky I am that Kyle has my pleasure at the forefront of his mind. Some of my friends are married to men who do the bare minimum, men who expect them to be turned on after a long day without doing the work to get them there.

After, he quickly falls asleep, his arm slung loosely across my chest. He doesn't notice when I get up and shrug into an oversize hoodie and retreat to the living room, tiptoeing across the parquet floor. I sink onto the sofa and, with a shuddering breath, stare at my ring finger. It's everything I wanted, the ring and the man who gave it to me. I have a beautiful life.

And yet—there's a life running parallel to it, threaded somewhere beneath the surface like an unfinished seam. A life where I'm celebrating my tenth wedding anniversary next month, where I already have children. We'd be living outside the city by now, on a property with a bit of acreage where the kids could run free, the kind of idyllic country childhood Josh had always wanted for our future children. He'd probably be graying by now, his dimples creased more sharply into his face, the skin around his slate-blue eyes feathering. Would we still love each other as much as we did back then?

Maybe we would have crashed abruptly after entering the *real world* together. Maybe we would have gotten on each other's nerves in that tiny studio walk-up. Maybe he would have hated how I crunched my cereal and I would have hated how he left his clothes in a growing pile on the floor.

I could imagine that. But in my heart, I know we would have still loved each other. That when we said *till death do us part* in our vows, we both meant it.

*Till death do us part.* I'd smiled when I said those words at the beach-side altar, my hands knotted with Josh's, both of us jittery with anticipation that we were actually doing this—the elopement had been his idea, but I loved the romance of it and had been more than eager to be carried along with his excitement.

But a week later, death *would* do us part, and now our love story is just that: a story, suspended like an insect in amber, embalmed forever.

I reach into my purse on the coffee table, pull out my phone, and open my texts to scroll past the new congratulations and well wishes to the very bottom of my message history, to a phone number that will never contact me again. I click on Josh's name and stare at the last text he ever sent me.

**Decided to go for a quick swim first, be back soon ❤**

I've lost track of how many people I showed the message to after Josh didn't come back to our Airbnb that day. The police, the same officers who collected his belongings from the beach. His mom, his friends, my parents, my friends. My body twitching with sleeplessness, my eyes manic, my voice a feverish staccato. I told them how Josh hated emojis; he thought they were a lazy substitute for words and never used them. And how he was supposed to be getting us breakfast that morning, not going for a swim.

I made everyone look at the message, but the general reaction was pity. Everyone just told me they were sorry for my loss and tried to change the subject. I wasn't ever able to convince a single person of the thing that was so obvious to me.

That the text hadn't come from Josh at all.

# Two

## *Bev*

St. Helena, Napa County, California
September 1999

**ROWS OF GRAPES STRETCHED INTO THE DISTANCE,** vines full and clustered under a bronze sunrise that inched toward the western foothills. There was a bite in the air that hadn't been around a week ago, a chill imperceptible to someone without our bone-deep knowledge of the environment. It was harvest season, the chance to correct last year's mistakes and have a fresh start, a do-over.

I crouched down in my rubber boots and held a plump green grape between my thumb and forefinger. Its skin was dusty and warm, its texture soft but firm. Most of the family-owned wineries around us—and they appeared so often lately, people with big dreams who craved a different lifestyle—used machines for the harvest, machines that shook the fruit from the vines and cut out the human element of the work. They prioritized quantity, but not us, never us. Last year, David suggested bringing in a machine—*We can get the grapes chilling so much faster*—but I refused.

The physical part of the process was what I enjoyed most. The touch, the precision that a machine would never be able to achieve. We clipped the grapes by hand and let plump bunches fall into buckets. A machine would take everything—even the inferior grapes, blistered and sunburned and rotted—shearing bits of leaves and branches in the process. Every morning during the harvest I was outside with the pickers, choosing only the best fruit. There was no substitution for human care, and our wines reflected the attention we put into them.

David had disagreed but hadn't pushed; lately, his mind wasn't fully on the harvest. He had been distracted, a vacant quality behind his dark blue eyes. When I'd asked him what was wrong, he'd responded without looking at me: *Nothing. Just trying to get everything done before the wedding.*

The wedding that night wasn't ours. Our wedding was nearly twenty years ago, a ceremony and reception at this very vineyard. The location had been an obvious choice. We'd been in the process of taking over the Golden Grape from David's parents, and what better way to start the next chapter of our life together? I remembered David's hand, reassuring on my back, the heat of it radiating through my dress. I'd thought about how lucky I was. Our friends at UC Davis had all said from the start that we'd end up married; David had told me after he proposed that he knew from the night we met that he'd ask me to marry him one day.

Tonight, we were attending the wedding of a friend's daughter who was from another family of vintners down the St. Helena Highway, a corridor punctuated by wineries. There would be talk about this year's harvest, about how all of us have been obsessively following the weather reports, checking sugars and pH and acid levels. Every day in September mattered: the pick date chosen is a winemaker's most crucial decision. Wine, like people, is notoriously unforgiving.

To an inexperienced eye, the grape in my hand looked ready to eat. It was green and bulbous, straining with flavor. But I knew it would be too bitter. That it wasn't yet time. Of all people, I understood that appearances could be deceiving.

David drove us to the wedding. In the back seat of our Escalade, our son Josh and his girlfriend, Michelle, were having a hard time not touching each other. I watched in the rearview mirror as his hand darted in and out of the lap of her short pink dress, a smile twitching at her lips as she crossed her legs and swatted him away. David and I had been like that, so many years ago: we'd driven from our off-campus housing at UC Davis to Napa in his beat-up Oldsmobile, our meager possessions bundled into the trunk, his fingers lazily drumming on my thigh.

As an only child, he was the heir to the Golden Grape, and our move here was inevitable. The winery had been in his family for over a century, passed down from generation to generation. He had learned the day-to-day operations as a teenager, never needing to find a part-time job of his own. His parents had been looking to retire, and David and I had freshly graduated, David from the viticulture and enology program and I with a degree in art history that I was never quite sure what to do with. It was time. David had been forthcoming from the start that the winery was his future—a future he wanted me in too.

"Forty-five acres," he'd said when he first told me about the Golden Grape, casting his hands in the air. "With a house on the edge of the property. So it's a bit dated, but we can renovate. A huge vineyard, right in our own backyard. Imagine all the space for our kids to run around, and for us to just—be a family. What more could you possibly want?" His palm had migrated to my back, his grin as infectious as his perpetual optimism. He'd looked so hopeful and sure of himself, like he was when we first met. We'd been dating for less than two weeks when he confessed he was already falling in love with me. He had pulled me out of the most uncertain time of my life and had given me the one thing I was starved for: a feeling of safety.

I loved the way he talked about parts of our life that hadn't yet happened: his certainty, the way his eyes fixated on me and only me. His enthusiasm was contagious.

"Only if you're sure, though," David kept saying. "I know you wanted to work in a gallery—this is a different lifestyle."

"I can handle it," I assured him, brushing his floppy hair off his forehead, relishing how soft it felt in my hand. The handsome face underneath it, blue eyes and long lashes and strong cheekbones. *We'd make beautiful babies*, I found myself thinking out of nowhere.

"We'll still travel all the time," he promised me. We'd recently returned from Europe, where we'd stayed at hostels in Italy and Spain, and I itched to see even more of the world, to press colorful pushpins into the world map we'd tacked on the wall of our apartment.

I loved the Golden Grape the same way I would later love our children: without trying to, without even truly meaning to, memorizing and marveling over every inch of rolling skin. I pictured myself in the screened-in sunroom of the old house, working in a sketchbook as sun seared the vines. I didn't know much about wine at first, but David was a good teacher, and in those early days, our teeth stained with cabernet sauvignon, we couldn't get enough of our new land—all of it, ours—and each other—all of him, mine.

"Let's start trying," he whispered in my ear one night after a dinner he'd cooked for me. His warm breath tickled my ear; his hand migrated between my legs. We'd been the first of our friend group to do everything: engaged at twenty-one, married at twenty-two. We were twenty-five, and children were the logical next step.

He waited for my response, his eyes trained on my face, the way only David had ever looked at me. Like I was deserving of worship. My hesitation melted under that gaze. A thought fizzled in my head, like a snuffed-out fire: *I'm not sure I'm ready.* It was just nerves; of course I wanted a family with David. It was something we'd talked about and planned for.

That night, we started trying, and for the weeks that followed, I walked around with a newfound fragility, imagining the cells multiplying inside me. But the ensuing pregnancy test was negative, bringing with it a mixture of disappointment and relief.

"We'll try again," David said, his lips finding my neck. We did, and when my next period was late, I peed on a stick and held my breath as two lines instantly formed.

I surprised David by wrapping up the stick inside a tiny onesie I'd seen at a baby boutique in town. His expression had been one of awe. His mouth had dropped open and his eyes had crinkled at the corners. "Really?" He'd pulled me into the tenderest hug. I'd dipped my chin into the crook of his shoulder. *I have everything*, I'd thought as tears filled my eyes.

And I did have everything. Until a few months ago, when it all started to come undone.

When we arrived at the Oakery Estate for the wedding, Josh and Michelle left to join a group of teenagers, other students from St. Helena High. I waited for David to lead me through the crowd. He was an extrovert but had found ways to accommodate me when he sensed I felt shy or awkward. Tonight, his hands remained firmly in his pockets.

"You look good," I told him. It was true: at forty-two, David was still sandy-haired and square-jawed, with no hint of the paunch that inflated the waistbands of other men cresting into middle age. If anything, he was only becoming more handsome with each passing year.

"You too," he said quickly, without looking at me. My dress was pale green silk, the hem tailored perfectly around my high-heeled sandals. David had barely glanced at me since I'd put it on, even though I'd chosen it with him in mind. He'd always loved when I wore green, commenting on how it brought out my eyes.

"I'll be right back," he whispered in my ear before retreating into a well-dressed throng of men in black tie and women in elegant long dresses. I made small talk with some of the other guests, my fingers wrapped tightly around the stem of a champagne flute. When I saw Michelle's father, Rodney, and his wife, Jen, I waved. Jen made her way over and draped me in a hug.

"You look beautiful," she said, patting at her tight updo.

"So do you," I replied. Jen was Rodney's second wife, and younger than me—in her midthirties, if that. David and I had known Rodney casually before Michelle and Josh started dating. He'd been a winemaker for even longer than we had owned the Golden Grape, and when Michelle and Josh became a couple, David and I made an effort to get to know the family better. We went on a few double dates and learned that Michelle split her time between Rodney and Jen's home and her mother's—Sylvie's—house. Sylvie had never responded to my voice mails asking to meet for coffee: the few times I'd met her in person while dropping off Michelle, she had been aloof. Jen had drunkenly called her a snob once, and I wondered if she was right.

"I feel like this hairstyle was a mistake—it looks like a goddamn helmet," Jen said with a tipsy giggle. "Where's David?"

"Around somewhere," I said, a nervous laugh catching in my throat.

Over the last three weeks, I'd looked at David differently, studying his face for a truth he wasn't telling me. Ever since I'd found a receipt in his jacket pocket while getting our dry cleaning ready, for a small, expensive restaurant in Sonoma we'd been to several times, but not recently.

"We should go back to Sonoma," I'd said absentmindedly, the receipt curled in my hand. We hadn't been for a proper date night since Kieran was born nine months ago, and we'd both been strained over the summer, feeling more like coworkers than husband and wife. "Maybe a weekend away. We can get a sitter for Kieran. It would be good for us, don't you think?"

David had been in the shower. The sound of the water pelting down exaggerated his pause before he responded. "Yeah. Sounds good. I haven't been there in years."

My fingers had closed around the receipt. Until that moment, I had assumed it was for a business dinner. Later, I would open it and analyze the dishes ordered—two appetizers, two meals, a shared bottle of chardonnay—and picture David, seated across from another woman, his foot bumping hers under the table. I almost confronted him, but I could already hear his excuse: *Oh yeah, I forgot about that. Memory must be going with my old age.*

Now, the receipt was in the beaded purse that hung at my side. I was afraid that if I couldn't find it, it would be as if I had imagined its very existence.

It was ridiculous, the idea of David cheating on me, and something I'd never once considered in our two decades of marriage. It was ridiculous, until I remembered what the last few months had taught me. That I didn't know everything about my husband.

David sat beside me as the bridesmaids made their slow walk down the flower-strewn aisle, as the organ swelled in preparation for the bridal chorus. He rested his hand on my knee as everyone watched the bride approach her groom, her tawny hair covered by a long veil. The groom was who I focused on: how his expression changed as she neared, tears collecting in the corners of his eyes. His hands clasped in a knot in front of him. The rapid rise and fall of his chest. It was all there, so much bald emotion, almost too intimate for a crowd.

I cast a sidelong glance at David. He met my eyes, but his smile—so familiar I could have memorized it, down to the striations around his denim-blue eyes—came a beat too late.

We left the reception when the dancing began, the scent of sunbaked grapes filling the air. Napa's climate made the wine. The heat of day swelled the grapes with sugary ripeness, while the night balanced them with acidity. It was early in the season; the grapes for the sparkling wines would be picked first, followed by the whites a few weeks later. The reds needed longer to mature, and our cabernet sauvignon took the longest.

Josh stayed behind with Michelle. He said he would get a ride home with a friend. I worried about him constantly, but what I never admitted was that I worried more about what he might do than what someone might do to him. Josh had a tendency to become sullen when things didn't go his way, his mood snapping like an elastic band. And he'd been quieter than usual, ever since the last week of junior year. After the seismic shift in our family.

David didn't speak to me on the drive home. It wasn't like him to have nothing to say, but it felt like we'd been in a stalemate for several weeks. Tension bubbled in my chest, tightening the space between my ribs. I wanted to ask him about the receipt, about all the other business dinners I was suddenly questioning. I wanted to ask him so many things, but once those questions were out in the open, everything would change.

"Here we are," he finally said when we pulled into the long driveway leading up to our home, a converted farmhouse on the southeast corner of the Golden Grape. He got out of the car and headed toward our front porch, leaving me to follow. Once upon a time, he'd insisted on opening car doors for me, but it had been a long time since he had made those gestures.

I trailed behind him, taking in the familiar white wooden clapboard and wraparound porch. This was the house David was raised in. He'd originally given me his enthusiastic blessing to renovate and make it our own. But whenever I tried, he became incredibly nostalgic, and I'd be left feeling guilty for wanting to change anything.

As soon as the babysitter left, David came up beside me in the kitchen, his hand migrating to my lower back. His mouth dropped to my ear, his fingers tracing a trail up my spine. It was the kind of gesture that used to make me melt into his arms, but I stood stiffly. David didn't seem to understand that my affection couldn't be turned on and off, like a piece of machinery.

"We need to talk," I said.

He didn't want to talk, so he did what he always did to avoid it. He snaked up the hem of my dress and reached for my underwear, which he tugged down as he braced my body against the wall, his lips dropping kisses down my bare shoulder. His fingers rubbed against me, creating an unpleasant friction that he somehow took as an invitation to slip inside.

It would have been easier to go along with it, so that David went to bed satisfied and our stilted sense of equilibrium hummed along. But the less aroused I felt, the more enraged I became. The same nagging suspicion that had been collecting in my gut over the past few weeks felt impossible to ignore.

Finally, I pulled away. "You said you hadn't been in Sonoma in years."

"What are you talking about?" he said, genuine confusion in his voice.

I turned to face him, pulling my dress down. "Sonoma. Your last business dinner there. It was last month, but you said you hadn't been there in years."

He wasn't expecting the confrontation. I saw the surprise on his face, the slight panic in his eyes. "Bev, I don't remember every single time I travel for work. I must have forgotten. What's the big deal?"

"I know you better than anyone, David. I know when you're lying."

"I'm not lying." He rubbed circles into his temples. "Why are you so wound up?"

My voice trembled. "Are you cheating on me?"

He turned toward the granite counter, hunching forward on his elbows. "Am I cheating on you? Bev, are you serious?"

"Don't lie," I said. "Look me in the face and tell me the truth."

For a long moment, he didn't turn around. But when he did, he wasn't rattled or upset. His expression was calm, completely unreadable. "We haven't had sex since—well, in months. You've pulled away from me, and you barely talk to me anymore. It's like you're punishing me."

"Don't bring . . . *that* into it," I said, practically choking on my words. "This is about you and me. No—this is about you, lying to me. And you, pretending certain things never happened."

"Why do we need to dwell on it? It's over, and I'm the one trying to move on. Bev, you've become totally unavailable to me. It's like I'm living with a stranger."

"So you're cheating on me," I said, the force of it making the air leave my chest.

David pinched the bridge of his nose. "Is it any worse than what you've done to me? I have needs too, and they haven't been taken care of in a very long time. I'm not even talking about sex. You've shut me out of your life."

I mentally traversed the last few years of our relationship, David's heartfelt pleas for another baby, my arguments against having one. It felt like starting over from scratch, setting the clock back another eighteen years. Giving up on the plans we'd put in place: leaving the vineyard more often, spending more time overseas. We were only forty-two, and it was about to be just us again. Some people thought we'd given up our freedom by being young parents, but there was an upside: we would also be young empty nesters.

Then we'd had Kieran. I had seen things from David's perspective: it was our last chance to have another baby before we were too old, and didn't I owe him that? I'd psyched myself up, convinced it was a good idea. My sister, Camille, and her then-husband Paul were trying too, and even though she lived in Santa Barbara, knowing we could be pregnant at the same time helped bolster my excitement. Camille and I talked daily about it, but then I conceived after only a month of trying, and Paul changed his mind about children.

Now Kieran was almost nine months old, and things had been good, minus the fact that motherhood at forty-two felt entirely different than it had at twenty-five, leaving me constantly exhausted and forgetful and overwhelmed. My body had refused to snap back. And while David helped with Kieran when he could, sometimes it felt like he didn't understand how much I had to juggle to even function. My work at the winery, plus the invisible labor at home. The multiplying laundry. Visits to the pediatrician. Wakeups at night, sometimes hourly. Parenting babies and teenagers required different parts of me. Parenting both at the same time required too much.

*You can take some time off from the winery, you know,* David had said, and he probably genuinely thought he was being helpful. But I didn't want to give that up. I wanted to feel productive; it wasn't enough to simply be *needed.*

When he'd suggested we hire a nanny to help with Kieran, I balked at that too. Camille and I had been left with babysitters and family friends so often that our mother's retreating back, the bony knobs of her spine, was something I still pictured. I didn't want my own son to feel that too.

But despite a few bumps, David and I still would have made it through Kieran's first year virtually unscathed. We would have looked back and missed the same chaotic days from which we longed to escape. Time would have erased the stress and fatigue. We would have made it, had Josh not come to us that day in mid-June, his lower lip wobbling. *Something happened.* Tear-blurred eyes, protestations of innocence. The heated arguments that followed, and David's obsession with preserving appearances. Giving him the cold boulder of my back instead of snuggling into him at night.

"Are you fucking someone else, David?" I said now, enunciating every painful word.

He reached for my wrists, the anger leaving his face. "Let's sit down and talk rationally. We have a lot of things to discuss."

"No." I yanked my arms away before he could touch me. "We're not talking about anything until you answer my question. Are you having sex with another woman?"

In his silence, the slow ticking of the wall clock seemed too loud.

"I slept with someone else," David finally said, his blue eyes trained on mine. "I admit it. But only one time. It was a weak moment. You must understand why. The way you've withheld from me."

"Oh, it's *my* fault?" I shouted. "I'm the one who made you do this?"

David rubbed his eyes. "I'm not saying that. I'm just saying—we've both screwed up. Before now, I've been a good husband, Bev. I've given you everything you needed—"

"And now you've taken it all away!"

My scream took us both by surprise. David looked like he was afraid of me, and maybe I was afraid of myself. As the full weight of the betrayal settled in, I wasn't sure whether I wanted to physically hurt David, or sink into a sobbing heap on the floor and never get up. *My family.* David knew how much it meant to me. He knew what I had gone through as a kid. He knew I had done everything I could to stop history from repeating itself.

"We can fix this," David said, putting out a tentative hand. "We can work on us—"

I turned away from him, opened the fridge, and pulled out a bottle of chardonnay, momentarily, crazily, imagining the meaty *thwack* it would make against David's skull. "Who is she? Do you love her? Does she love you?"

When he spoke, it was practically a whisper. "Do you?"

I dropped my gaze to the floor, which had been tiled neatly with marble—my only real mark on the home we'd shared for so many years. I'd insisted on replacing the worn hardwood, which David had said I could do, only to later grumble that the house felt like it lacked its natural character.

"I can't look at you right now," I said, a ribbon of steel in my voice. "I think you should go. I need time to think, and I can't do that with you around."

His hand hovered above my lower back, but he pulled it away before it touched me. "You want me to leave? I'll spend the night at a hotel—"

"No." I wrapped my arms around my chest. "I can't be near you right now."

"But the harvest—I need to be here. And the kids. What will you tell them?"

The kids. Their questioning blue eyes. Then: the incident. The hurt in those eyes. David's own gaze, hard and stormy. My anger surged.

"The *harvest*, David? That's what you're thinking about right now?"

"It's our life's work," he said quietly.

I couldn't find a way to put the crushing disappointment I felt into words, so I took another shot at David. "Maybe you should have thought about your *life's work* before fucking another woman. Who was she, David?"

"Nobody you know," he said carefully. "I didn't know her either. I was there for work, but I stopped at a restaurant—I was hungry, and then I had too much to drink."

The chardonnay cold in my hand. The bottle of chardonnay on the receipt. Had she chosen the wine, or had he? When we'd first started dating, I loved watching David taste wine: the way he closed his eyes, bobbing his head ever so slightly like he was listening to music only he could hear.

I knew, rationally, that David wasn't more concerned about the harvest than he was about our marriage. But I had also recently learned exactly how far David would go to protect his family, and the reputation of our vineyard.

My voice was steady, even though I felt anything but. "You need to leave right now."

"I'll go," he said, fear deepening his voice. "But, Bev—you haven't been the same since what happened in June . . . You know we made the right decision, but I feel like you've been blaming yourself for it, and you've closed yourself off."

"It has nothing to do with that," I spat out. "This is about you."

"It's about us," he said. "We've both made mistakes."

"I never would have cheated on you."

"There are worse things," he said.

I watched him walk out the door. He paused briefly on the porch, like he wanted me to stop him.

I waited for the tears to come, but they never did. Instead of sadness was deep regret. I'd trusted David to keep me secure, but I had never felt less safe.

## Three

# June

Prospect Heights, Brooklyn
September 2022

**KYLE AND I ACT FAST** in the weeks following our engagement. Due to a last-minute cancellation, we can have our first choice of venue—the Wythe Hotel in Brooklyn—for the last weekend of October. I picture our reception in their elegant courtyard, with all that exposed brick and the twinkling lights we'll string over a long rectangular table. Our wedding will be small—only immediate family and close friends. It feels fast, but we've been together for so long that the cancellation seems like a sign that we're meant to be married quickly, surrounded by the people who have always been there for us.

It's Phoebe's idea to take engagement photos for us, even though we don't have a wedding website or traditional invitations—since the guest list is so small, we've reached out to everyone individually. "You'll still want to look back and show these to your kids someday," she insists, and the more I think about it, the more I like the idea of having this ephemeral time in our life immortalized. She also connects me with a local florist, and Kyle hires a DJ off a recommendation from one of his colleagues. My mom takes me shopping for a dress, which we find at the first boutique and buy off the rack, exactly my size. All the pieces click together seamlessly.

The only item we still haven't figured out is our honeymoon, but we've discussed several potential destinations. I surprised myself when I suggested Napa as a possibility. Josh grew up on a winery in California, and he was the one who encouraged me to open a bar of my own. Maybe I'm finally ready to make new memories in a place connected to him.

After the shock of Josh's death, I took solace in my ambition and poured myself into my pipe dream, scouting locations for the natural wine bar I was determined to open, daydreaming about the wine list and securing funding. Grape Juice—a small brick space with stained glass windows in Cobble Hill—finally opened seven years ago, and is one of my proudest accomplishments.

But while I was thriving professionally, my sadness hadn't gone away. Phoebe gently suggested I needed a hobby and reminded me of how we'd met—in our first year at Cornell, during an ill-fated attempt at intramural tennis. We'd both been laughably bad and mutually decided to quit after a couple of weeks, our friendship permanent in a way our athleticism wasn't. I knew she was right: it was time for me to do something for myself.

After a reluctant Google search, I decided to try out tennis lessons at the Prospect Park Tennis Center. Just like in college, I was terrible at first, but I enjoyed the aggression I could let off each week, the satisfying whack of racquet against ball, the rewarding ache in my muscles afterward. I started doing weekly doubles matchups, and one evening, there was Kyle, with his curly brown hair, wire-rimmed glasses, and a soft-spoken voice that belied his blistering backhand.

Josh had been gone for almost four years, and I was approaching thirty-four. My dating life had gone nowhere, but I had also barely tried. With Kyle, I found I gravitated toward his quiet confidence, the way he listened instead of always talking about himself. After catching each other's eyes for weeks, we found ourselves paired up on the court, and I realized I was excited in a way that made me feel both hopeful and guilty in equal measure. After our game, we talked for almost an hour. He told me he had been an avid tennis player as a teen at camp but had gotten away from the sport since then.

When he asked if he could call me sometime, I gave him my number.

On our first date, I learned that he was the same age as me—thirty-three. He seemed too perfect to still be single, but I quickly gleaned that he'd been laser focused on establishing himself in his career, and that he wasn't a fan of dating apps or flings: he was a relationship person, just like me.

I didn't tell him I was a widow until our third date, on a long walk through Prospect Park with take-out coffee. It was the first time I'd told the story without coming close to tears, reciting it the robotic way everyone else had told it to me. *It was an accident, a tragedy, but eventually I had to move on.*

When I said it like that, I could almost start to believe it. I was miles away from the woman I had been at the funeral: wild-eyed, unwashed, practically feral. I could finally see myself how others must have seen me in the weeks after that awful day, as someone unhinged and broken down by grief. When I knew Kyle better, I told him about that version of myself, and how in the weeks and months that followed Josh's death, my brain often tricked me into thinking I saw Josh in random places. But I left out my theory about Josh's last text message, instead explaining Josh's death in almost painfully clinical terms: *He drowned.*

Maybe it really was that simple. I was the only one who thought it wasn't. Maybe this is what it felt like to finally move on.

Phoebe is waiting by the Boathouse in Prospect Park when Kyle and I arrive, her camera bag beside her, the sun gleaming off her shiny black hair. She hugs me tightly. Kyle and I decided not to have a large wedding party, but his cousin Matt will be his best man, and Phoebe will be my maid of honor. I was hers when she married her husband, Peter, an investment banker she'd met online after dating a string of noncommittal men in our years after graduating Cornell. Now, they have their daughters Brooke and Brodie, who are three and four, and during the pandemic, Phoebe quit her job as a dietician to pursue her passion for photography. She specializes in milestone moments: weddings; maternity photos; and newborn sessions, sleeping babies curled up and blissfully unaware as their little heads are topped with crocheted hats and tiny flower crowns.

"I'm thinking we take the photos on the bridge first," she says. "The sun won't be in your faces, and I think the way it's hitting the water, it'll look really beautiful."

"You're the expert," Kyle says, wrapping his arm around my shoulders.

"I'll try to have them touched up and sent to you before you guys leave," she says as we make our way to Lullwater Bridge. "You're heading out on Friday, right?"

"Yeah," I say. For the past three years Kyle and I have taken our annual fall trip to the Catskills, where we rent an Airbnb and spend our days hiking, the trees scorched with brilliant red and yellow leaves. "But no rush. Seriously, thanks for talking me into this. I guess I didn't think of taking photos."

"Why not?" Phoebe says. "This needs to be celebrated."

"I know," I say. "I just—" Phoebe meets my eyes and nods. She understands. Most of our friends who wanted to be married did so by their midthirties; at almost forty, I'm the oldest bride in the group, and clinging to typical wedding rituals feels wrong somehow, even though it shouldn't. Besides, I've been married before.

"I didn't think of it either," Kyle says. "But I'm not very photogenic. Phoebe, you have to tell me if I'm making a weird face. People always say I look like I'm cringing. Including my own parents."

Phoebe laughs. She and Kyle have always gotten along. Her reaction to Kyle was entirely different from her attitude toward Josh. We argued more in the six months Josh and I were together than any other time in over two decades of friendship.

*You barely know him,* she'd said. *And I don't know—there's something about him I don't trust. He came on so strong.*

*You're just jealous* is what I couldn't say. Phoebe had been with Peter for almost a year by that point, and while she was ready for an engagement, he wasn't there yet. I wasn't even looking for love when Josh rocketed into my life, but our relationship became serious practically overnight. When we eloped, I didn't let her know beforehand—I kept telling myself I was waiting for the right moment—and when I did call her, she had been less than enthused. I knew she was hurt that I'd kept something so monumental from her and robbed her of the chance to be part of my wedding, like we'd drunkenly promised in college. She'd given me the cold shoulder for days, and then there was another, even more difficult call to make. Josh was gone.

Phoebe instructs Kyle and me to get into position on Lullwater Bridge. Beneath us, the green-tinged water is placid, a family of ducks scything a path to the shore. The trees around us are just starting to redden. Phoebe arranges us in the center of the bridge and tells us to forget she's there. I lean into Kyle, my hands pressed against the chest of his brown suede jacket, my ring winking in the sun. His smile goes all the way up to his eyes.

"I love you," he murmurs, like he's actively trying not to move his mouth. I start to laugh, pulling his face down to mine for a kiss.

"The photos are supposed to be candid," I say, linking our hands together. "You're allowed to move your lips. We can talk."

"I look like a robot, don't I?" He pulls me closer and gently dips me backward, his face relaxing. "Is this better? I guess it's practice for the actual wedding. I don't want the cameras to catch me accidentally grimacing while we say our vows."

"I promise I'll try not to make my vows cheesy enough to make you grimace."

I smile as my fiancé kisses my forehead, as Phoebe clicks away with her camera. I'm immediately swept back to my wedding day with Josh and the photos we took with his digital camera, his long arm outstretched to capture our sweat-shiny faces, cheeks flushed with sun and excitement. By the time I had them printed, he'd been dead for two months. They were so painful to look at that I left them in their envelope instead of framing them the way we had once talked about. Josh, handsome and alive; me, the happiest I would ever be. At least, until Kyle came into my life, proof that the universe wasn't as cruel as I'd once thought.

We walk from the bridge to the Cleft Ridge Span, my favorite archway in the park, and get into position at the mouth of the arch, its regal underbelly rising above our heads. We stand apart from each other, with our hands interlocking, and when I smile, it's real. It has taken me a long time to get here, but there's nothing in my life to worry about. I own an amazing bar, Kyle is the perfect fiancé, and I have friends and family who love and support me.

"Now try standing back-to-back and reaching for each other's hands," Phoebe says. "Just switch places so June's ring isn't hidden."

We shuffle obediently, and I fixate on the greenery in the distance as Phoebe clicks, as my hands are warm in Kyle's, my back pressed against his. I watch a group of teenagers on the grass who are tapping on their phones. A little boy tries to fly a kite, but the anemic huffs of wind only let it hover briefly a few inches off the ground, despite his mother's fruitless efforts to help.

"Smile," Phoebe says. "And look up, just a bit higher."

I obey, and suddenly, past the little boy and his mother, past the lazy sprawl of teenagers, there's a man in a baseball cap, too far away to make out the exact features of his face. But for a split second, he's staring straight at me, his eyes boring directly into mine. I gasp, a panicked inhale so hard and quick that I almost choke on my own breath. I drop Kyle's hands, my body numb. The man turns away quickly, but not before I take in the sharp cut of his jawline and his familiar stance, arms crossed and chin tilted downward. If I were closer, I'd be able to see that cleft chin, those cheeks bracketed with dimples.

*Josh*, my brain sputters, but his name gets stuck in my throat. It has been so long since I said it—so long since I've talked about him out loud.

He's walking away, hands jammed in the pockets of his jeans. I'm vaguely aware of Kyle and Phoebe saying my name, but they sound far away, and before I can process what's happening, I start running toward the man, my heart pulling me in his direction like the magnetized needle of a compass, even as my brain stumbles to keep up. It's not Josh—logically, I *know* it can't be him—but there he is, joining the foot traffic of joggers and Rollerbladers and dog walkers, quickly swallowed up by a throng of students in NYU jackets. I lose sight of him, spinning in a dizzy circle, hoping to catch another glimpse. But he's gone.

*He was never there*, I remind myself, trying to slow my hammering heart. It's never Josh, not since he kissed me goodbye at an Airbnb in San Francisco and told me he would be back soon with breakfast. It was never Josh, even though after his death every man over six feet tall with wavy dark blond hair had me seeing things. Wild-eyed, I chased strangers down streets, grabbed sleeves and tugged on jackets like a kid lost in a department store. *Is it you?* I'd say, drunk on hope and hysteria, only to find myself in the cold crosshairs of a stranger's eyes.

Those days—the darkest ones—are behind me. I haven't seen *Josh* on the street in years, and I no longer leave my apartment both excited and terrified that I might stumble upon him. I stop and sit on a bench to compose myself, my breath coming in thready gulps, my blouse tacky with sweat. I remind myself of the mantra I learned in therapy: visualize and reframe the situation. I'm seeing him because my wedding is approaching, and subconsciously, I feel guilty, even though I shouldn't.

A sliver of irrationality stabs back. *But it looked just like him.*

*They all do*, I remind myself.

"June?" Kyle says, rushing over to me. "June, what's going on?" His eyes are worried, and behind him, Phoebe's face is a mask of confusion.

"I thought I—I'm so sorry." They're both waiting for me to come up with an explanation. My voice wavers, and I know I'm on the verge of tears. I don't want to tell Kyle the truth—there's no need to bring up Josh right now, when we've already had so many conversations about grief, the bigness of my emotions practically engulfing our relationship. I don't want to tell Phoebe either. Years ago, I would report my "Josh" sightings to her like scientific findings. *He was in Whole Foods. He walked past the bar. I swear, I saw him in Central Park.* Each time, she talked me down, her voice thick with sadness. *Junie, you know it wasn't him. I'm worried about you.*

"You look like you've seen a ghost," Kyle says, sitting down beside me, balling my hands inside his. And he doesn't know how right he is. I will the tears away, forcing what I hope is a placid expression onto my face.

"Sorry, I thought I saw an old friend," I say, slipping quickly into the lie. I shrug, pushing away a stray piece of hair. "It wasn't her. I guess maybe I finally need glasses. We can be one of those married couples who start to look alike."

Kyle might have bought the lie, but I can tell Phoebe doesn't. Her eyes probe mine.

"I think we're done anyway," she says, thankfully moving on. "I got so many good photos. Kyle, I have no idea what you're talking about. You're extremely photogenic."

Kyle gives her a sheepish smile. "Thanks. Only because you make me look good."

His and my knotted fists swing like a pendulum between us as we leave the park, and Kyle and Phoebe carry on a conversation about where to go for lunch before I need to get to the bar. They're carefree, happy. I should be too.

I huddle closer to Kyle, grateful for the warmth he gives off. While my love for Josh felt like a roller-coaster drop I couldn't control, my love for Kyle has been a slow build where I can comfortably set the pace. I lean against his shoulder, knowing he'll plant a kiss on the top of my head, and I promise myself that I won't do this again. That the next time I see *Josh*, I'll stop my brain from playing tricks on me, from dwelling on what I used to obsess over. *They never found a body. He's still out there.*

I let my fiancé's arm encircle mine, and take several deep breaths. I no longer believe in fairy tales, but I also don't believe in ghosts.

# Four

# Bev

**FROM THE SKY, ST. HELENA** is the slipknot in a long ribbon of land. The city is corseted tightly by mountains to the west and the east, the valley's warmth trapped like carbonation in our small bottleneck. It was because of geography that our wines were so ripe. Napa Valley was home to more than four hundred wineries, many of them small, family-owned ones like ours, and we each had our specialties. At the Golden Grape, we were known for our cabernet sauvignon, as rich and complex as the land itself. For the first few harvest seasons, we picked the grapes too early, the tannin grippy on the palate, its aftertaste arid. Wine doesn't forgive. Make an error, and an entire year goes by before the vines yield themselves to another chance.

I had finally learned the trick, which was not unlike the key tenet of parenting. Patience. I had to resist the temptation to pluck the grapes from their vines, so that the sugar and the tannin could collide and ripen, to create lush velvet on the tongue.

I also resisted the temptation to tell everyone what had happened and sully the perfect reputation David had worked so hard to uphold.

The reputation wasn't just his: it was ours, and as much as I hated to admit it, I was just as unwilling to crack its veneer as David was.

I told only one person about what David had done, an impulsive phone call in the wee hours of the morning when my lips trembled with sadness and rage. Camille arrived on Monday, suitcase in tow, even though I hadn't asked her to. I wondered, had I not made the call, if she would have sensed my emotional turmoil and shown up on my front porch anyway. It seemed to be the way with us, as it had been all of our lives. We could somehow intuit what the other was thinking. Just before she'd called to tell me she and Paul were getting divorced, I'd had an uneasy feeling in my stomach: the news had come as a shock, but only a partial one.

"You're not going to be able to do all of this yourself," Camille said, wrapping me in a hug. I sucked in the familiar scent of her: sunscreen, mint gum. "I can watch Kieran while you do what you need to do on the vineyard." She pulled away and shook her head. "David. For god's sake. I never would have imagined."

"I know." Her eyes, so similar to mine but less feathered in fine lines, were trained on me. Camille had always liked David. She and I had lived the same tumultuous childhood; sometimes I could still feel her sweaty hand tentacled to mine, both of us in my bottom bunk, breath hitching in our chests as the voices rose up from downstairs in angry peals. When I was at UC Davis, Camille was at NYU studying psychology, a brief stint she'd soon abandon for a less conventional life of travel and random jobs to fund it. *Apparently a lot of women subconsciously end up with somebody like their father*, she'd told me on one of our calls, and I'd laughed, even though the idea chilled me. Our father—Walter Jamieson, a renowned judge in Minneapolis, known for being calm and fair and methodical.

My mother was the reason he was so placid outside the household. He took out all his anger on her, and sometimes us.

The last thing I wanted was to marry someone like our father, someone who yelled and swore and spanked our tiny bottoms, spittle flying from his mouth like runny egg whites. Someone who stormed out, who slammed doors, who made the people inside his house tiptoe around his destructive temper. Someone who cheated.

It was like I'd let Camille down by telling her the truth about David, and I almost wished I'd never called.

"I feel bad that you came all this way," I said. "I'm sure you're busy—"

"I'm not," she said, following me into the house. "I could use the distraction. There's only so many times I can rearrange furniture in the apartment before I lose my mind. I need someone to buy the goddamn place so I can get the hell out."

I scooped Kieran out of his playpen. He hated napping, and his cheeks were blotchy and red from the promise of new teeth. I placed him in Camille's arms, and he seemed to settle into her. My sister was a natural with children, which made what happened with Paul even worse.

"No luck on the job search?" I said, even though I knew if there were, she would have let me know.

"I didn't come here to talk about me," she said, taking a seat on the couch with Kieran in her lap. "But *no luck* is an understatement. I've done a couple home-staging gigs, but I'm starting to feel like maybe I don't have a good enough reason to stay."

She knew what I was thinking. That she had gotten lonely traveling. She'd taught English in South Korea for almost a year before backpacking through South America, staying in hostels with people half her age. *I'm ready to settle down*, she'd said, and the universe had given her Paul. It was serendipity, we'd thought; but really, it was a cruel trick of fate.

"I know," I said. "But it's been nice having you a drive away, instead of a very long plane ride."

She leaned back, her green eyes—the very same shade as mine, but rimmed with her trademark dark eyeliner—analyzing me carefully. "Bev, you don't need to pretend. It's me. I know when you're lying."

"I know," I said. "But I'm just trying to keep it together. Everything is such a mess." The tears started to fall, running down my cheeks in thin rivers. "Maybe it's my fault. We aren't having sex, and after what happened with Josh—"

"That wasn't your fault. None of it's your fault. Don't go to that place where you blame yourself. You wouldn't let me go there, after Paul—so

I'm pulling you off that ledge." She fingered the ends of Kieran's downy blond hair.

"That was different," I said, blowing my nose into a balled-up tissue. "Paul changed his mind without telling you."

"So did David," she said. "He had an affair."

"He said it was just one time, and not an actual affair." Somehow, there was a difference. I could maybe understand a slip, but an affair—the lying, the sneaking around, the coordination to make that happen—was a different type of unforgivable. And it was so out of character. David was as renowned for being a wholesome family man, devoted to me and the boys, as he was for his aversion to any sort of risk-taking. Our investment portfolio was conservative; he didn't even like to branch out with what he ordered at our favorite restaurants. He was in the stands at every lacrosse game Josh ever played, and he insisted on hiring tutors outside of school, wanting our sons to have the best education possible. He made annual donations to a number of charities.

But I was starting to wonder if he did all that because he felt it was important, or because it was important for other people to see and hear about it.

"And you believe him?" Camille said. I could tell she didn't. Just like she didn't believe our father.

I shrugged. It was impossible to articulate, even to my sister, how much of a guiding light David's certainty about us and our decisions had been over the years. I had seen his face when he confessed to cheating: the panic, the remorse. It had hurt him to hurt me.

"If you're serious about staying—" I started.

"I'm staying," she said. "I've been wanting to visit anyway. I haven't been here in, what, two months? Kieran looks so much bigger already. I feel like I'm missing seeing him grow up." She kissed the top of his head.

"You're a lifesaver," I said. "Josh is at school right now, but he has a new girlfriend—Michelle—so usually after school she comes here, or he goes to watch her play tennis. They're pretty inseparable."

"Wow," Camille said. "Another girlfriend. He's growing up too. I was thinking of going to see—"

I closed my eyes. *He's growing up too.* I felt a hand ensconced in mine. A small hand, never the one to let go. The one to let go was always me.

Before she could finish speaking, I interjected, "I need to go run and shower. I'm sure David had appointments booked—I have to cancel them, or figure out what to do. I didn't think about it before kicking him out. I was just . . . so angry."

"Okay," Camille said. "Do what you have to do. I'll be hanging out with this little man all day."

I walked away, guilt making my steps heavy. Lately Kieran had been frustrating: I struggled to manage any sort of routine with him, and found myself counting down the hours until he was out of my arms, after which I would miss the feeling of him there like an ache. Sometimes he looked at me with his enormous blue eyes and I wondered if he wished he had a better mother. My supply was drying up; I no longer woke up with my breasts like cement boulders, milk dotting my nursing bras like Morse code.

Kieran was too young to realize David was gone, but what would his life be like if I didn't give David a second chance? He would never remember having two parents happy together. David and I had *been* happy together, legitimately happy and in love, for more than twenty years. Didn't we owe our baby that experience?

As I stepped under the showerhead, I trained my focus on the more practical aspects of marriage, which were less painful to think about. Once upon a time, naive and clueless about wine—the suburban Minneapolis household Camille and I grew up in had had giant six-dollar jugs labeled *white* or *red*, consumed almost solely by our mother—I'd asked David how we would make money living on a vineyard. He had laughed, that beautiful sound that never failed to bring a smile to my lips. *We don't make money. We make wine,* he'd said.

David had largely been the face of our business, maintaining relationships with restaurant clients and dealing with our sales and marketing. He made casual appearances on tours and wine tastings, the everyman in a baseball cap, handsome and self-deprecating. I remained largely behind the scenes, raising the kids, quietly studying the grapes like they were my own personal religion. David was right: we did make wine. But our wine also made us a very solid amount of money. Our sons had only ever known privilege, and as much as I hated to admit it, I'd grown accustomed to a certain way of living.

If David and I got a divorce, where would it leave me? The vineyard was in his family, and the idea of leaving it was a dull pain in my chest. This was the place we had been happy. This was where we'd made a family together. I was good at my job, and I loved it. David was right the other night: this was our life's work, in so many ways.

I stepped out of the shower, shivering under the steam.

I wished I'd never found that receipt.

I wished I'd torn it up and said nothing.

By the time I made my way out to our tasting room, a woman was seated there, her back to me. She was wearing a pale silk blouse, her hair down in loose caramel-colored waves. She turned when I entered the room, stood up, and smoothed her pencil skirt. Her eyes were dark brown, her lips full, and she looked familiar somehow, like I'd seen her before, but I couldn't place where from. A glass of red wine sat on the table behind her. To most people's naked eye, red wines might look indistinguishable, but I could pick out a merlot from a syrah without a second glance. The woman was drinking our cabernet sauvignon, across the heavy teak table from Marcel, our manager.

"Bev," Marcel said. "I just called the house. Do you know where David is? I can't seem to get a hold of him."

"He must've forgotten to tell you," I told Marcel as I strode over, my voice more confident than I felt. "David's gone to San Francisco for a few days to meet with some restaurant clients."

"During harvest season?" he asked, surprised.

I shrugged. "It was last-minute, and a good opportunity."

The blonde woman watched us with poorly concealed amusement. "Nobody is worse at communication than a man. It's the same everywhere in the world."

A small laugh escaped my lips. The phone rang, and Marcel excused himself to answer it, leaving me with the woman and her wine.

"Are you enjoying it?" I said, gesturing to the glass as she sat back down. "Or would you like to try another varietal?"

She swirled the glass gently, then brought it to her lips. "Once I know what I like, it's hard for me to branch out. I'm old-fashioned that way." She closed her eyes while she sipped. "This is robust. I'm getting hints of cedar, black currant, and plum. No, not black currant. Black cherry."

"I'm guessing you didn't just stumble in here by chance."

She smiled and offered me her hand. "You don't remember me, do you, Bev Jamieson? We've drank wine together before. Not like this, though."

She had used my maiden name. I squinted, as if that would help me see her more clearly. Suddenly I knew exactly who she was, and wondered how I hadn't known instantly.

"Emilia," I said, the nerve endings in my hand sparking as I took hers in mine. My mouth went cotton dry.

"You do remember," she said slowly.

I nodded as it all flooded back. Davis, with its extensive greenery, its bike trails and zigzagging creeks. The vineyard, the arboretum. The laid-back pace of my life there. Emilia's throat, layered in chunky necklaces, tilted back in a laugh. Her fingernails, painted black, resting on the knee of my frayed jeans. The echo of our voices in the dorm bathrooms.

"Did you know—" I finally managed.

"That this was your winery? Of course. I know you and David got married. It wasn't exactly a secret. Everyone knew you'd end up together. You're welcome, by the way—if I recall correctly, didn't I introduce you?"

She didn't sound mad. I realized she hadn't let go of my hand, so I slipped mine away.

"I've wondered about what you ended up doing," I said, dodging her reference to David. "You always loved wine so much. I mean, you taught me what I knew about it back then." I laughed. "Which we both know was very little."

Emilia smiled. "You were a good student."

The skin on my neck heated up.

"I'm a buyer now," she said. "That's what I'm doing here, actually. Hopefully I'll bring something very special back to my clients."

I pushed down a bristle of irritation. David hadn't told me that Emilia Rosser was a potential buyer for the Golden Grape. Buyers worked with restaurants all around the world, helping them find wines that matched their requirements. Usually, he kept me informed about new ones. Had he left me in the dark for a reason? No—he had no idea about the history between me and Emilia. He only ever thought we were friends.

"And what do you think of our wine so far? Is it special?"

"I think it's tricky," she said, leaning over the table. "As far as food pairings go, it would overpower a lot of dishes. It's too full-bodied for the restaurant client I was considering—they serve mostly seafood. Maybe with a meaty fish—grilled swordfish, or tuna. Otherwise, it'll just be too overwhelming."

"Yes." I stared at the pink dip of her Cupid's bow. There was something mesmerizing about how she spoke, and in her face I saw her nineteen-year-old self, the girl whose dorm room was across the hall from mine. She had been beautiful then, with her waist-length hair and peasant blouses, but time had only enhanced her appearance. I felt frumpy and plain in my T-shirt and jeans and pulled-back dishwater ponytail, my threadbare postpartum hairline.

"Which one's your favorite?" she said. "Which one means the most to you?"

"Nobody's ever asked me that," I said. "I mean, I've been asked which one is my favorite, but not why it means the most to me."

She bit her lower lip. "I want to hear Bev Jamieson talk about wine for a change."

"Well, you probably know David and I took over the winery from his parents when we got married. We've been here ever since." I paused. "I know what you're probably thinking—how could I end up making wine my life when I used to hate how it tasted?"

Emilia laughed, like I knew she would. We unearthed the same memory in silence. Me, pouring her Dixie cups of different red wines, indistinguishable to me but intimately known to her. Emilia, blindfolded as she sniffed and sipped from each, identifying the characteristics and country of origin, the variety and the year. Me, checking marks off a sheet. My heart pounding through the thin fabric of my halter top. Her wine-stained lips, dark red feathering in the corners. The way I memorized the elegant shape of her mouth.

"People change," she said. "I'm not surprised at all that you ended up loving wine."

"To answer your question, I hate picking favorites with the wines, because—this is going to sound stupid, I know—but it's almost like being asked which one is your favorite child. I've helped them all turn into what they became. The decisions I made created them. But if I had to choose—we make this viognier that's really beautiful." I didn't tell her why I decided to grow the viognier grapes in the first place. Because it was the only permitted wine grape for the French wine Condrieu in the Rhône Valley, a famous wine region in southern France and somewhere I'd long wanted to visit. It was my way of being there without actually being there.

She pushed away the cabernet sauvignon, a lone red drop trapped in the divot where the glass met the stem. "In that case, I think it's time we moved on to the whites."

I poured out three whites to start, our chardonnay, viognier, and pinot gris, putting a finger's width in each cup, and watched Emilia pull the chardonnay. She picked up the glass by the stem, looking first at the appearance, the pale yellow of caramelized sugar. Next, she swirled the glass, releasing the scent, then brought it up to her nose and inhaled deeply. I found myself breathing with her.

"This one surprises me," she said after her first sip, pursing her lips together. "It's big, but not too buttery. I can taste the hint of pear. There's just enough sweetness." Her eyes locked onto mine. "Usually, I find chardonnay so contrived now. The care just isn't there."

"We're very specific," I said. "The process—we only age it in certain oak barrels. I can show you later if you want."

"I'd love that," she said. "Look at us—now you're the teacher."

I felt my cheeks redden and suppressed a smile as I sat down across from her.

The viognier was next. It was a small-batch wine, one we sold out of quickly every fall, after people came for tours and unexpectedly fell in love with it.

"You're right—this one is very special," she said, easing forward. "It's almost spicy. The honeysuckle is beautiful. This is what I'd drink on a date. You know—the kind of date where you really like the person, and everything feels like it's full of possibility."

Between sips, Emilia told me about what she'd been up to since graduating from UC Davis. Like David, she'd been a student of viticulture and enology, but unlike David, she'd set her sights on becoming a sommelier rather than a winemaker. Once she found out that becoming a buyer would allow her to travel constantly, she knew she had found her calling. She was based out of New York but claimed to live out of a suitcase most of the time.

"I'm on the hunt for smaller wineries—hidden gems, like this place," she explained. "My clients are discerning. They don't want their menus full of factory wines, or wine made with some formula, instead of simple human care. I guess I'm the opposite of mainstream—I'm always looking for something different. I got into natural wine when I was in Jura, and I'm very interested in anything biodynamic and organic. It hasn't caught on as much here yet, but I'm hoping it will." She talked quickly, gesticulating often, the same as she did twenty years ago.

I wrinkled my nose. David hated the idea of natural wine—its funky taste, its volatility. He believed additives were necessary to create a high standard and a consistent drinking experience.

"I don't know about natural wine," I said. "It just looks . . . like cloudy grape juice."

"That's exactly what it is, and it's amazing. I'll convert you," Emilia said with a wink.

I wanted to keep the conversation going. It felt good, talking to somebody who knew me before I was Bev Kelly, before I was a winemaker and a wife and a mother. Somebody who'd seen me at my most raw and uncertain. Somebody who had been a listening ear as I unraveled the pain of my past. David had always tried to fix everything, but Emilia had let me unload, not offering any solutions, just her reassuring presence, sometimes a messy anecdote of her own that never failed to make me laugh.

"What have you been up to besides work?" I asked, pouring myself a glass of viognier. Her slim ring finger was bare, but I asked the question anyway. "Did you get married?"

Emilia shook her head. "No. I'm not sure I'm the marrying kind."

"Do you have any kids?" I wanted her answer to be no, which didn't even make sense.

"No kids. My ex wanted them—it was a deal-breaker."

"So what happened?" I asked.

"She broke it off . . . It was the best thing for both of us." Emilia leaned forward, propping her chin on her hands. A curl hung beside her cheek, and I resisted the urge to push it back behind her ear. "You have kids, though."

I nodded, wondering why the truth felt like a lie. She didn't ask for details—*Names, ages, boy or girl?*—for which I was grateful. Most mothers loved talking about their children. I heard the other winemakers' wives tell stories, their eyes shining with joy. I used to be the same way, collecting the compliments that seemed to follow us wherever we went. *You have your hands full. You have a beautiful family.* My hands had been full, but I had never felt less useful, less productive, less myself.

Now, I felt panic instead of pride when I thought about my sons. When I considered who I had been as their mother.

I took a long sip of wine and changed the subject. "We really fell in love with this land. And we were lucky, since David's parents owned the winery—they'd already made a profit and a name here, so we didn't have to struggle."

But we had struggled, of course. We picked too early—our cabernet retained the scent of unripe green peppers. We picked too late, the wines cloyingly sugary, a perfumed blast on the palate. We put too many additives in the wines—too much water, acid, enzymes. We failed to protect our wines, leaving them vulnerable to oxygen and yeast and bacteria. Still, I had good memories of those early years, of the possibilities, the late nights of conversations, the meals over candlelight. David's arm, puckering against my skin in bed, his fingers resting against the huge dome of my stomach. Things didn't feel perfect back then. There had always been a new problem to fix, but David lived for the challenge. The struggles seemed to bring out the best in us, highlighting how well we worked as a team.

"And you were in love," Emilia said, running her index finger along the stem of her glass, trapping my gaze like a butterfly between clasped hands. "With the land, I mean."

I nodded, and she leaned in closer.

"Can I tell you a secret?" she said. "This pinot gris might be my favorite. It's more subtle at first taste, but the longer it's on my tongue, the richer and more complex it gets."

There was a stirring in my stomach, like strings being plucked. We were close enough that I could see the golden flecks in Emilia's eyes. My breath was clenched in my throat like a balloon.

It was only when Marcel waltzed back in that I tore my gaze away.

"I'm obsessed with your wine," Emilia said, standing up and straightening the hem of her skirt. "I'll be in touch. Or if you want to call me—here." She slid her business card across the table toward me, but leaned over before I could pick it up, jotting what I assumed to be a personal number on the back instead.

"You never came back," I blurted out after she started to walk away, scratching the embossed surface of her card with my fingernail, grappling for something to say to keep her there. "You said you would when you left, but you stayed in France. Why?"

She turned around, a tiny smile on her lips. "You know me. I go with my gut. And with the wine, of course. It wanted me to stay."

"Wine can't talk," I said, suppressing a smirk.

"Maybe not," she said with a shrug. "But wine has always loved me back."

It wasn't the first time I had stared at her departing back, wanting to run after her. But there had always been a critical difference between Emilia and me. She was the loudest voice in a room, the most certain. And I was too afraid to speak up.

# Five

# June

Catskill, New York
September 2022

**THE SECOND TIME** I see Josh is outside Grape Juice, when I'm standing behind the bar, going over the details of an upcoming order before Kyle and I leave for the Catskills. I glanced up by chance, and there he was, with his baseball cap and stubbled chin, peering inside the window. I'm certain it's the same man from the park—same height, same sandy hair under his baseball cap.

Trish calls after me as I abandon my tablet and dart outside. "June, is everything okay?" But I'm already gone. Our stamp-sized patio is full of lunch patrons; in front of them are pastel-hued orange wines and sparkling pét-nats in glasses, along with the remnants of our locally sourced farm-to-table lunch fare on oversize plates. When I first dreamed up Grape Juice, I'd pictured this very scene: intimate, casual, people enjoying each other's company and the unadorned beauty of the wines I loved so much, my care flushed into every detail and decision.

But today, I don't feel the same pride in the scene, in my dream realized. I don't notice or care that this will probably be one of the last weeks it's warm enough to sit outside. I don't want to be here at all.

The street is packed with people. I look in every direction, not know-ing which way to run, so I stay put, squeezing my eyes shut and pinching my thighs, hating my brain for this emotional subterfuge. *Visualize and reframe.* I remind myself that I'm allowed to be happy—I'm *supposed* to be happy—and that I don't need to feel guilty for moving on.

Visualize and reframe. Josh isn't here. Josh isn't anywhere, and he hasn't been for a very long time.

The two-and-a-half-hour drive to the Catskills in our rental car goes by quickly, the scenery out my passenger-side window transforming as we get farther away from Brooklyn. I'm grateful for Kyle's hands at ten and two on the steering wheel, his out-of-tune voice as he attempts to sing along to nineties rock on the radio, the sun glinting off his slightly smudged glasses. I'm grateful for two days of just us and the woods, filled with hikes and the hot tub, touring quaint Catskills wineries, and Kyle cooking us dinner in front of a flickering fire in the adorable four-hundred-square-foot A-frame we've been renting on the third weekend of September for the last three years. I rarely want to stray from Grape Juice for longer than a weekend, and the trips Kyle and I take are always carefully planned ahead of time. A lack of spontaneity is something we share in common, leading me to wonder if I was only ever spontaneous with Josh because he was too.

Most of all, I'm grateful for the distance, for the change of place. This cabin is something that feels solely ours, mine and Kyle's, with no other memories attached. As much as I love New York City, I have nearly twenty years' worth of memories there, ever since Phoebe and I moved to Williamsburg together after college, where she was an art major and I studied viticulture and enology at Cornell's College of Agriculture and Life Sciences, imagining myself on a vineyard someday.

The pace and bustle of New York City was a far cry from the Con-necticut suburb I was raised in, from the homey Tudor where my par-ents still reside to this day. I think they assumed I'd go into academia or education, like them—my father taught high school math, and my mother was a professor at Trinity College—but I'd been fascinated by the hospitality industry since high school. As an only child of two self-professed foodies, I'd often tagged along with my parents on their dinner dates, and I loved being at restaurants, with their constant low buzz of chatter and beautiful flatware and clinking glasses. I was drawn to the romanticism of wine, the way it brought people together; the way it felt like the perfect fusion of fantasy and practicality, science and art. My parents had been surprised when I applied to the program at Cornell, but they'd supported me regardless.

I went straight from Cornell to managing wine operations for an upscale Midtown bar, and while there, I became interested in natural wine through a group of coworkers who had become fast friends. It was a movement that was gaining traction worldwide, and although I was dubious about the foggy appearance and unconventional aromas, I immediately loved the taste and how it made me feel, with its absence of additives.

"It's basically the definition of grape juice," my friend Miriam had said. "Like, what wine was supposed to be before all the interventions."

"Grape Juice," I'd repeated. "That would be a cool name for a bar."

Two years into my job at the Midtown bar, I met Josh at Miriam's engagement party. He was cradling a scotch on the rocks in his palm, his eyes never leaving mine. When I got up to get another drink, he followed me and stood behind me at the bar.

"Can I get an orange pinot grigio, please?" I said to the bartender. When I turned around with my drink, Josh was there, fixing me with a sly smile.

I gestured to the bar. "I'm done, if you're ordering something—"

"I have a drink already," he said. "I'm not usually a scotch guy, but they don't have any real wine here. That stuff smells like a barnyard."

I laughed. "And what exactly is 'real wine'?"

He put his free hand on mine, his palm cold from the ice at the bottom of his glass. I wasn't sure what to think: he was cocky, almost too confident, but I couldn't ignore the electricity that crackled between us. "We could get out of here and I can show you," he said.

"I happen to like this barnyard wine, actually," I said.

"You must not have had the good stuff before," he said slowly.

"Or maybe I need to show you," I retorted. "When you're hungover tomorrow morning and feel like garbage, I'll be up at seven on my way to the gym."

He nodded, biting his lower lip, his gaze moving across my face. "I'm Josh."

"June."

Two drinks later, it felt like we knew all about each other. I learned that Josh was an associate at a family-law firm, working under divorce lawyers, hoping to make partner and one day open his own firm to focus on helping low-income families. His initial cockiness was explained: he'd grown up on a winery, and living in that environment had never fully left him. He was handsome and smart and hung on my every word. I even got him to sip from my glass of orange wine and admit that it wasn't entirely unredeemable.

To my shock and delight, he pulled me into a corner for a kiss that took my breath away, a kiss that never stopped but continued into a cab, into the tiny walk-up he shared with a roommate who gratefully wasn't home. I was no stranger to one-night stands, but immediately, this felt different. We fit perfectly together. There was no awkward fumbling, no hesitation, no doubts.

Only later did I find out that Josh had come to the party with another girl but left with me. I never learned her name. It didn't matter anyway, not in the face of what we had.

The next morning, I called Phoebe and told her I thought I'd just met my husband.

"That sounds a bit crazy," she said, and I sensed both skepticism and bitterness in her voice. "You don't need to rush into anything." I knew she was sensitive to seeing our friends get engaged at a practically alarming frequency, especially since Peter wasn't showing any signs of being ready to take the next step with her.

But Josh and I felt almost chemical, our connection equally strong in mind as in body. We started spending every night together, and after three months, when his lease was up, he moved his meager belongings into my cramped Bed-Stuy studio. His impromptu proposal, on a ran-dom weeknight in that very apartment, was both surprising and not. Phoebe thought we were rushing, but we *knew*.

"I was thinking we could do Giant Ledge today," Kyle says, pulling me out of my trance. "There's still plenty of daylight left."

"Definitely," I say. The trail's five rocky ledges offer spectacular views of the Hudson valley, the treetops scorched a brilliant vermilion. I reach for Kyle's hand, blinking away the image of *Josh* in the park, *Josh* in front of my bar. I push past the thought of telling Kyle about it. Maybe he'd understand—he knows that once upon a time, I'd imagined that the man buying fruit at the bodega across the street was my long-lost husband—but the conversation would taint what's supposed to be our romantic escape.

Two's company, and three is a crowd. I force Josh out of my mind, focusing on the relief that here, Kyle and I are exquisitely alone. Here, nobody can find us.

After we're settled in at the Airbnb, we lace up our hiking boots, pack our day packs with water and snacks, and head out to the starting point for Giant Ledge. The parking area is busy: this is one of the most popular hikes in the Catskills, and for good reason. The climb will take us about four hours there and back. Our shared love of the woods is something Kyle and I bonded over, and hiking became an activity we pursued as a couple, at first seeking out routes closer to home, but also making a bucket list of hikes we wanted to complete together. Giant Ledge is one we love enough to revisit every year.

We pass by other hikers, Kyle letting me take the lead and falling into place behind me. At the first ledge, tents are pitched and people are talk-ing and laughing, an easy hikers' camaraderie. By the time we make it to the fifth, the sun is an orange solar flare, and we're the only two people here. Kyle wraps his arms around me and kisses the chilly edge of my ear, then pulls a small bottle of champagne from his backpack for us to share.

"We could have our honeymoon here, you know," he says as he pops the cork. "It feels like we're the only two people in the world."

I soak it in: his arms around me, the rolling red-topped hills below us, the slight sway of the trees in the breeze. It does feel like we're the only two people in the world, and the urge is there—to move on, to keep forming new memories together.

But on the hike back, my brain begins to self-sabotage, the visuals of Josh at the park, Josh in front of the bar, running through it like ticker tape. I can't stop picturing Josh in the trees, baseball cap obscuring his face. It doesn't even make sense. Josh never wore baseball caps: I'd joked with him, when his face became ruddy with sunburn in the California heat, that he'd look like a leather suitcase unless he started taking better care of himself.

*You need to take care of me*, he'd teased, and somehow it was the sexiest thing imaginable, Josh leaving himself in my care.

But I didn't take care of him. I never really had the chance to.

After dinner—creamy parmesan risotto with shiitake mushrooms, accompanied by a bottle of *col fondo* prosecco—we settle down next to the crackling fireplace, my feet tucked underneath Kyle's legs, both of us with our laptops out. When we were getting to know each other, we bonded over our mutual ambition, Kyle on a partner track at his private equity firm and me with Grape Juice, which was still in its tenuous first year of operations.

"I'll be about half an hour," Kyle says, stroking my ankle with his thumb. "Then I'm all yours."

My cheeks are warm from the alcohol and the fire. Truthfully, I'm supposed to be doing work right now—I should be tracking the numbers for last week, or checking in on the online rostering system Kyle set me up with to monitor the profit situation, and there are a few vendors I need to follow up with. But I find myself opening a new tab on Google and typing in *romantic honeymoon destinations*, not wanting Kyle to linger on the idea of honeymooning here in the Catskills—as much as I love it here, I want to do something new for us as a couple.

We fall into a comfortable silence. Kyle's thumb works in a circular motion around my ankle as I add *Napa* to my search and click through wineries, taking in pictures of happy couples strolling through green rows of vines.

I've been to Napa several times before for work, but there are so many wineries. Most of the ones I've been to specialize in natural wine, and we stock some of their products in the bar. Looking back, I got into natural wine at exactly the right time. The natural wine movement was hitting New York with a practically cultish force. Everyone suddenly cared about pollution—in the environment, in their own bodies. They wanted less interference, fewer ingredients, to know where their drinks were coming from. And I liked the immediacy of natural wine, the lack of pretension. It doesn't need to be aged: it's meant to be enjoyed right away, something Josh and I disagreed on. As impulsive as he was in life, he was traditional when it came to wine.

Josh and I didn't make it to Napa together. We were supposed to go—we were freshly married, and it was his idea to go there so I could get inspiration for the bar he was sure I would open someday. He wanted to show me where he'd grown up, even though the vineyard had long since been sold. But we made it only as far as San Francisco. That little Airbnb was the final place I would ever see him.

I cast off the thought of Josh. This is about me and Kyle, our first time in Napa together. It makes sense for us as a destination, as wine lovers. Generally, any vacation spot involving wine and hiking is a win for us. Just as we connected over our mutual love of the woods, we found out early in our relationship that we were both passionate about wine. The first time Kyle ever cooked for me, there had been an array of natural wine bottles on his countertop.

"I didn't know which kind, so I got them all," he'd said timidly. "I hope one of them goes with this casserole . . ."

"You didn't have to do that," I'd said, although I was touched by the gesture. "I don't just drink natural wines. I still like regular wine too."

"I have to be honest, I didn't even know what natural wine was before we met," he'd admitted. "I mean, I'd heard of it, but not what it really was. I googled it, but I got confused."

I loved talking about natural wine, educating people who were new to it. I told Kyle the same things I'd told so many curious new customers at Grape Juice. That what they were drinking was essentially fermented grape juice. That the grapes are grown without pesticides, with no additives, and with very minimal intervention during fermentation. That it is often unfiltered, leading to its sometimes cloudy appearance, and that its taste can be more volatile than conventional wine. That while more homogenized wine has become the standard, natural wine *is* technically the traditional way to make wine, dating back thousands of years.

Kyle had listened intently, and we'd taste-tested each bottle. The next morning, when he was clearheaded and hangover-free, he called himself a convert.

I smile at the memory, clicking through each winery that comes up on my screen. None of them feel quite right. As I keep scrolling, a timeline snakes through my mind. We'll go on the honeymoon directly after our wedding, and hopefully soon after, I'll be pregnant. I've downloaded a fertility tracking app on my phone. The idea that I could become a mother within the next year is both exciting and terrifying. But I'm ready. We both are.

I try to look at each potential location as a newlywed, rather than a wine bar owner. I'm looking for something romantic and special. Not necessarily anything for the bar. I scan the search results, seeing many wineries I've heard of but also plenty that are new to me. I click the next one on the list, the Backyard Winery, and notice the photos of the beautiful inn and spa on-site, immediately connecting to the intimacy and attention to detail, the way everything looks small yet perfectly maintained.

I navigate to the About Us section. *We're family owned, and anyone who visits will feel like part of that family. Our winery was founded on the idea that wine should be accessible to all, and being here, we hope you feel as at home as you do in your own backyard. These rolling forty-five acres are meticulously harvested with our own hands, which produce the wines that come from this land and reflect its special terroir. Come for a guided tasting with Sadie and Andrew Smith, and you'll never want to leave.* The photos show lush columns of vines, with metallic foothills rising in the distance.

I'm about to abandon the Backyard's photo carousel and place it on my list of potential destinations when the next image appears: a man and woman standing in front of a wall of wine barrels, presumably giving a tour. They must be the owners, the husband-and-wife team, Sadie and Andrew Smith. Sadie is petite and blonde, wearing jeans tucked into rain boots, smiling widely. It's the husband's face I notice second, the slideshow moving quickly enough that I almost don't see him at all. He's in his late thirties or early forties, handsome and angular, hair graying at the temples under his blue baseball cap, eyes creased with the effort of his smile.

I close my eyes, reopen them. *No. There's no way.* It's my brain playing games again.

The carousel moves on to a new photo, but I frantically click back and freeze the image on my screen, pausing on his double-dimpled smile. If he frowns—but he rarely ever did—the crow's feet would still be there. Those lines are my doing, according to him. *It's your fault I already have wrinkles*, he'd said, his fingers mapping my cheekbones, thumbing the bow of my top lip. *I can't stop smiling when I'm with you.*

Over my keyboard, my hand goes numb. My vision starts to blacken at the edges, my breath coming in quick, uneasy waves. I've had so many panic attacks over the last decade that my body has found its own efficient way to process them: silently, with almost no physical evidence of the mental turmoil bubbling under my skin. Kyle is still rubbing my ankle absentmindedly, his attention focused on his own laptop. He has no idea that not even inches away from him, I'm about to drown.

*Drown*: the same way Josh did, almost exactly ten years ago.

His body was never found, so there was nothing to bury, nothing left behind but his wallet and cell phone and keys for the rental car, sitting neatly inside his well-worn Chuck Taylors.

His mother, Bev, hadn't even been able to look at me during the funeral, her face a messy watercolor of tears and runny mascara. She didn't believe my theory about the last text I received from Josh. None of them did. There was nothing to suggest foul play, nothing to suggest anything other than my husband deciding to take a swim on a balmy morning at

Mile Rock Beach. A few witnesses had spotted him at the beach, pacing back and forth, staring at his phone. But no one saw him enter the water.

Eventually, I had to admit to myself that it wouldn't have been the most out-of-character thing for him to take a swim. Josh loved doing things spur-of-the-moment. Was our recent elopement and road-trip honeymoon not proof of that? Maybe he'd accidentally clicked the heart emoji or had spontaneously decided to add it.

Over time, I looked back on the day of the funeral, mortified by my behavior, and I accepted that I had to move on. That I'd been through the kind of tragedy people aren't built to endure. My husband, the love of my life, was dead, drowned, his body lost, and I had to accept that.

But it's his face I'm staring at on my computer screen. It's his image I frantically attempt to enlarge, his features blurred by pixelation. Not the Josh I married, thirty and lanky, still endearingly baby-faced, but an older version, the man he would have grown into, the one I would have had children and a home and Christmas traditions with.

*My husband passed*, I got used to saying, absorbing the *I'm so sorrys* from strangers without even hearing them. *My husband is dead.* A statement I had finally accepted. But here he is, with a different woman, with a different name.

Here he is, undeniably alive.

# PART II

# *Crushing*

After the harvest, the grape clusters are sorted for quality, and a decision needs to be made: whether to remove the stems or leave them on, depending on the structure of the grape. For white and sparkling wines, the skin and juice are gently separated by a mechanical crusher, the grapes minced finely enough to release their liquids. With red wines, the grapes are usually kept whole to create color and body. In either case, the result is the same, called the must: squeezed grape juice, ready to be made into wine.

Crushing, like its name implies, is a breaking apart to come back together.

# One

## June

Catskill, New York
September 2022

**I MUMBLE AN EXCUSE** to Kyle before shutting down my laptop and stretching my arms over my head. "I think I'm going to head out for a run."

"Right now? After the big hike we just did, and all the wine?" He's confused, and rightfully so. I should have come up with a better reason to leave, but we're in the middle of nowhere. I shouldn't be coming up with a lie at all.

"It's getting dark," he adds. Dusk presses against the A-frame's huge glass windows. We chose this place for the unfettered views of the woods and open skies, but now, panic sets in as I consider how exposed we are. Someone was watching me in Prospect Park; someone was outside Grape Juice. Someone who looks uncannily like Josh. He could be anywhere right now.

"I know. I just feel like I need to get out for a bit." I pull on a hoodie. "The food is sitting so heavy in my stomach."

He motions to close his laptop. "I'll come with you."

I shake my head. "No, stay and finish your work. By the time I'm back, you'll be done, and we can go in the hot tub."

At first, I don't think he'll listen, but he nods and squeezes my hand, giving it a quick pulse, before returning to his screen. I suck in a grateful breath, even as I feel like the worst kind of liar, the one who deceives by omission. But the last thing I want to do right now is explain to Kyle what is unexplainable even to myself.

I slip into my shoes on autopilot, and when I'm outside, I break into a run, darting down the trail until my lungs feel like burning bags of fire. The wind whips my face. The temperature is dropping, this afternoon's warmth receding, and the air I'm breathing in feels like something I could choke on.

I wish there were someone here with me who knew Josh, who I could ask for a second opinion. Maybe Andrew doesn't look that much like Josh, and it's my grief playing another cruel trick. I hold my breath and let it out slowly, trying to steady my heart rate and stop my imagination from careening away. They say everyone has a twin out there in the world, someone whose features look uncannily, inexplicably, like our own.

Yet Andrew Smith is a winemaker, in Napa Valley. Andrew Smith, identical—at least, in that photo—to my dead husband. Josh grew up on a winery in Napa and knew lots about wine. It was a mutual passion of ours, even though it sometimes felt like we were at odds. He hated the very thing I loved most about natural wine: that no two bottles were ever totally identical. He liked knowing what he was getting. Mostly, I didn't mind our little debates. Inevitably, we'd end up tipsy and in bed together.

"How can you drink something that leaves this behind?" he'd once said, holding my glass up to the light, where sediment blotted the bottom.

"They're wine diamonds," I'd said, referring to the nickname for the tiny crystals of sediment. "They're a sign there was very little intervention."

"You and your intervention," he'd said. "Wines need help to become better. They were designed that way. Same as people. The right person comes along, and then—" He lunged for my waist and his hands roamed up my rib cage as I giggled uncontrollably.

The winery where Josh grew up had been called the Golden Grape, and I'd googled it after we met, but it hadn't turned up any discernable results—there were several wineries worldwide that shared the name, and it had been sold before having a web presence was the norm for wineries. Andrew Smith owns the Backyard, a different place, but also in Napa. I don't know what that means, or if it even means anything beyond a coincidence.

As I run, my feet thudding on the trail, I mentally collect more pieces of information. Josh's mother, Bev, didn't approve of me. I only met her once before we were married, and she'd called Josh away into the kitchen, leaving me in the living room with Josh's brother, Kieran, who had been around thirteen years old at the time, lanky and metal-mouthed. I could hear slices of their argument. I can still feel the teacup in my hand, the way I'd gripped the delicate handle for dear life.

"I love her, Mom," Josh had said. "She's the one."

Bev's response hadn't been warm and flowery. They'd gone back and forth, their voices lowered so that I could hardly hear. I made out a snippet: ". . . barely know her, and she barely knows you."

I hadn't expected her disapproval. Usually, I got along great with parents. I'd been excited to meet Josh's mother. He had told me shortly after we met about the shock of his dad's death, and I'd felt his heartbreak acutely. I got the sense that he was holding something back, but I chalked it up to his sadness over losing a parent unexpectedly. It was clear how important Bev was to him.

I was near tears as we drove away, certain I'd blown it with my future mother-in-law. Josh had fed me reassurances, his fingers creeping up my leg.

"She's just protective," he'd insisted. "She'll come around."

She never did. It was the only time I ever saw her while Josh was alive. That day, we decided to elope, and a week after that, he was dead.

My eyes are fixed on the ground, my feet dodging the tree roots that curl up like bony knuckles. Endless questions and theories race through my brain. The night Josh and I met, he'd come to the party with a girl. She was blonde, and he'd told me she was just a friend. I never knew her name, and can't recall her face.

I sense myself spiraling again, reading too much into one picture on the Internet, trying to create a connection that isn't there.

I consider sending the photo to Phoebe, with a lighthearted caption: *Doesn't this look a bit like Josh?* But Phoebe had been there for my darkest moments, my middle-of-the-night phone calls when I insisted I'd seen Josh on the street. She was so worried about me that at one point, she broke down in tears and called my mom. Now, she thinks I've finally moved on, and I don't want to make her return to the pitch-black place I used to live in any more than I want to go back there myself.

There's nobody I can ask. I haven't spoken with Bev in ten years, not since the funeral. My behavior there erected a brick wall between us. My wild, guttural sobs were expected, as were my gaunt face and wrinkled black dress. But when the empty coffin was lowered into the ground, I lost it, launching into a long, rambling speech about Josh not being dead, about the fact that he was still out there. I lashed out, leveling accusations at the people around me that they'd given up on him. My mom rubbed circles on my back as the sky swirled above us, but I still remember the horror on Bev's face as she hugged Kieran, shielding him with her body, like I was somebody she didn't recognize and couldn't contain.

I stop and lean against a rock, my body pressing into its coldness, and open a new window on my phone, then type *Andrew Smith, Backyard Winery* as I wait for the Internet to chug to life. The winery comes up in several search results: family-owned wineries in Napa Valley, boutique vineyard hotels, wine-tasting wedding destinations. But there are no image results for Andrew Smith himself. Social media doesn't yield any results either. It's the same for Sadie, like neither of them exists outside this one picture.

I became obsessed with drowning cases after Josh was classified as a drowning victim. In most cases, a body is found within two or three days. In almost all cases, a body is found at some point. It was a thought that haunted me, the idea that a swimmer or boater could come across Josh's body in an advanced stage of decomposition, a gruesome picture that flashed through my brain in nightmares.

The police didn't consider anything about Josh's death suspicious, because to them, it was a tragedy, a man who'd got caught in a riptide. The sea had been rough that day, the waves churning up sand like browned butter. Under those circumstances, nobody thought it was unusual that Josh's body wasn't found. Nobody except me.

The concerned faces in the crowd at the funeral were just a blur. I squeeze my eyes shut, trying to take myself back to that day, the small gathering of family and friends who came together for Josh. An image invades my memory: a woman on the fringe who I didn't recognize, standing just apart from everyone else, slight and blonde, hands in the pockets of her black trench coat. When she saw me looking at her, she'd turned and walked away, and she wasn't at the visitation afterward. I try to conjure her face and see only the face of Sadie Smith, the smiling winery owner. Had it been her? Had she been there that day?

My therapist has talked to me about this, about the ways I project my guilt. I convince myself of things that had never happened. I feel responsible for Josh's death because I let him leave that morning.

"I know you're loyal to your eggs Benedict," he'd said, pressing me against the white duvet, his hands clamping down on my wrists. "But I know this little café that makes these homemade donuts that'll melt in your mouth."

It was so early; the sun was only on the verge of rising. "Stay here," I'd mumbled, trying to pull him down on top of me.

"They'll be all sold out unless I go early," he had said before kissing me on the cheek and hopping out of bed with a devilish smile. "Stay hungry. I'll be back soon."

But he wasn't. And in the weeks and months after that terrible day, I found new ways to torture myself, coming up with new theories about what had really occurred. But eventually, I knew everybody else had to be right: Josh's death was a tragedy, not a mystery.

Now, all the doubt comes rushing back. Maybe his disappearance was neither a tragedy nor a mystery. Maybe it was a carefully laid plan.

I dial the number for the Backyard and press the phone tightly to my ear, but the call doesn't connect. I walk up the root-gnarled hill in front of me, holding my phone up to search for a connection. Finally, a bar of service appears, and the second time I call, a woman answers, her voice clear and light.

"Backyard Winery, how can I help you?"

I pause, my throat dry. Now that someone is on the phone—maybe even Sadie Smith—I have no idea what to say.

"I'm looking for Andrew Smith," I say quickly. Once I hear his voice, I'll know. There's no mistaking Josh's deep, almost slumbery baritone, the way it made all my nerve endings vibrate.

"I'm sorry, Andrew isn't in right now. If you'd like, I can leave him a message."

"No," I blurt out. "Do you know when he'll be back?"

The woman pauses, and when she speaks again, her voice has a slight edge. "I'm afraid I don't."

A crack sounds behind me, and I whip around, expecting a hiker, or possibly an animal. There's nothing in sight, not even a squirrel. *Josh*, I think suddenly. Just like it was Josh in the baseball cap, Josh on the website, Josh so many times before today. Josh, who loved me so forcefully that I could feel it in every fiber of my being. He wouldn't do something like this to me. He never would have left me.

"There you are," comes Kyle's voice as he appears on the trail behind me, making me jump and quickly end the call. "I got worried." He surveys me, concern in his brown eyes. "Are you okay?"

I force a smile as I pocket my phone.

"Sorry," I mumble. "I ended up having to take a work call. We were supposed to get a shipment of orange pinot grigio for a party and it didn't arrive on time, so Trish was freaking out."

I don't know where the lie comes from, or why I feel compelled to tell it. I've always been honest with Kyle. He has the kind of face that makes people want to tell him things, the same way he's truthful with everyone around him. I've told him all about Josh, and he has listened without pity or judgment. That's a quality I appreciate about Kyle: unlike most men, he can simply listen without feeling the automatic need to fix.

"No worries," Kyle says, wrapping his arm around my shoulders. "Should we walk back?"

I nod, falling into step next to him, hating myself for being stuck in the past. He's content, worry-free, and I don't want to spoil everything until I know exactly what's going on with Andrew Smith. This is Kyle's engagement too, Kyle's upcoming wedding, the first and only time he wants to do this. He has been patient with me for years, taking every milestone at my slow speed and never guilting me over it. If I show Kyle the picture of Andrew Smith and mention that there's even a chance he could be my presumed-dead husband, I know he will listen with an open mind, but I also know what he'll say, albeit gently. *It can't be.* And I don't want to hear that right now, not from him.

The only way to figure this out and move on is to meet Andrew Smith in person. Up close, I'm sure it will be clear he's not Josh. Then I'll be able to fully let go of the past and focus on my fiancé and the life we've built together, the one full of easy laughter and hikes and wine on patios and cheesy reality dating shows.

Kyle brushes a piece of hair off my forehead. I want to put the past behind me as soon as possible, but I can't exactly leave Kyle here to hop on a plane to Napa right this second. I need to come up with a different excuse, something that buys me time.

"When we get home, I need to head out to a few wineries on the Finger Lakes," I say, the lie gaining shape as I recall the unanswered emails in my work account, a few winery owners who wanted to set up meetings. "I'll just be a day or two. It's a really underrated wine area but I think it's about to have a moment." My body tenses as I wait for Kyle's reply.

"Sounds good. We're supposed to have that meeting with the caterer on Wednesday, but I'll see if we can push it off till when you get back."

I feel a small pit of dread start to open in my belly, the idea that I may be risking my own wedding to take this trip. I tamp the panic down and try to sound casual. "Oh yeah, I forgot about that. I should be home in time anyway."

"It's no big deal," he says, simple and sweet. "Hey, let's get back to the cabin so I can kick your ass at Scrabble. That is, if you're up for a rematch after last time . . ."

"If you're ready to get crushed," I say, managing a laugh. Kyle and I are far more competitive when it comes to board games than we ever were on the tennis court together.

I melt into his arms as we walk in sync, but I can't stop thinking about Andrew Smith on a winery in Napa with his beautiful wife. I picture them holding hands and walking down endless green aisles, popping grapes into each other's mouths like baby birds. My brain whirls like a broken compass. Do they have kids? Josh had wanted to be a young dad, young enough to kick a soccer ball and hoist giggling toddlers onto his shoulders.

I nuzzle into Kyle's jacket, not wanting him to see the deceit written all over my face. The truth is simple: I'm not over Josh, and never will be.

I'll always be a widow first and a wife second.

# Two

# *Bev*

St. Helena, Napa County, California
September 1999

**I SPENT THE NEXT COUPLE OF DAYS** distracted by the business of the harvest. The chardonnay grapes were days away from being ripe, their tiny window of time approaching. David usually made the call on when picking began, but in his absence it would be my decision, a fact that must have been eating him alive. Five or so years ago, when we'd made a wrong call on the cabernet grapes, it had somehow been my fault. *You insisted they were ready*, David had said quietly, our mouths souring on the overly tart wine, a wine we'd never be able to bottle and sell.

In his planner at home, I found his appointments for the week, meetings that I called to reschedule. Every female voice who phoned the winery asking for David made me suspicious. *Is it you?* I wanted to shout. *Are you her?* The more I thought about it, the more I wondered if he was with the other woman in Sonoma. If I'd kicked him out and sent him back into her arms. He hadn't attempted to call me, and I had no idea where he was.

Camille had so many questions about David. "You're sure it was only the one time?" she said, her eyebrows arched as she poured me a coffee, at home already, like she knew my kitchen better than I did.

"That's what he said. But I don't know if I believe him. I keep torturing myself thinking, What if this has happened since the start? And it's only now that he got caught?"

I reminded myself that he didn't get caught. I exploded on him with hardly any proof, and he confessed. He could have lied, and maybe I wouldn't have confronted him again. Did one slip mean he deserved to lose everything?

At my insistence, Camille went out for the day to check out some restaurants in town. She had been a foodie since college, and she used to have an active social life in Santa Barbara, where she and Paul had settled, but most of her friends had started as friends of Paul's, and he had inherited them after the split. I hadn't given up hope that she'd still meet somebody who wanted the same things she did. Children, a family. But we both knew her window of time to become a mother was narrowing.

"I can take Kieran with me," she said. "He's my little buddy now, aren't you?" Kieran looked up at her with a drooly smile. "Probably has better manners than most of the dates I've been out with too."

"That's okay. I need to nurse him anyway," I said. "But tonight, let me make you dinner and he can eat with us. If you consider it eating. It's mostly just tossing pureed vegetables across the room."

"Perfect. Food fight. It's a date."

When she was gone, I bundled Kieran into his stroller and walked down each corridor of the vineyard, plucking grapes and using a refractometer to test their sugars. *They're not ready*, my instincts said, the same instincts I'd ignored so many times when they applied to myself.

After quickly nursing Kieran, I deposited him back in his stroller and kept walking. I walked to the far southwest edge of the property, where the vines gave way to a pond, its surface a dark bronze under the midday sun. It was easy to overlook the thin black hoses that wove through the trellises like veins, easy not to see the practicality under the romanticism of winemaking. Before winemaking became my life's work and the vineyard my home, I didn't understand its mechanics, nor did I stop to think how the vines would be watered in the arid summer months. The pond was, in many ways, the Golden Grape's source of life, and the way we remained self-sufficient, storing the winter water for summer.

I fixated on its calm surface before I even noticed the girl sitting at its edge, her feet dangling in.

"Michelle? What are you doing out here?"

She turned around, offering me a warm smile. "Hi, Mrs. Kelly. My practice got cancelled, so I came over to see Josh. He wasn't at the house, so I took a walk and ended up here."

I knew Michelle was a talented tennis player. On one of our double dates with Rodney and Jen, Jen had drunkenly bragged about Michelle and how disciplined she was. *When I was her age, I was out smoking pot at parties*, she'd shrieked with her signature hyena laugh. *Not Michelle. Never Michelle.*

"Oh," I said, my brain spinning. "I haven't seen Josh this afternoon—I figured he was with you." I paused. "And please, call me Bev."

A frown crossed Michelle's face. "Must have been a misunderstanding. Sorry I'm randomly out here on your property. I can go if you want. There's just something about this place that I love. My dad's winery is a lot smaller. There's nowhere to hide." She laughed. "Not that I'm hiding. I don't know why I said that."

I sat down beside her, leaving Kieran sleeping peacefully in his stroller. Lately, he only slept on wheels: in his car seat, in the stroller. All the baby books heralded the importance of routine, of wake-time windows and consistency. The same parenting books I'd meticulously studied the first time around were collecting dust somewhere in our basement.

I had no idea what to talk to Michelle about. Josh's last girlfriend, before Michelle, was Abby, a petite brunette he'd been completely enamored with, until the end of the school year, when everything that happened made it impossible for them to remain together. *I hope you know I had nothing to do with it*, Josh had said matter-of-factly. *You know I'd never do something like that.*

I'd wanted to talk to David about it alone, the way we always did, making decisions together. But David had spoken before I could even open my mouth.

*Don't worry. I'll take care of it.*

And he had, with such efficiency that I wondered if I had imagined it all. He had called in favors, his voice cordial and calm on the phone in his office. He'd made things go away. He had protected our family. But he had never once asked me whose side of the story I believed, or considered that he might be defending the wrong person.

The boarding school brochures. My protestations. David's inability to hear me. He didn't see, didn't care, that the small, unquestioning little-boy hand had fallen out of my grasp, no longer trusting me to protect him.

I had wondered what would happen when Josh and Abby saw each other at school for senior year. But then I heard that Abby had decided to do her final year from home, and picturing her there—alone, not surrounded by friends—made my guilt go from heavy to suffocating. It wasn't until I found out the real reason for Abby not going back to St. Helena that I understood she didn't have friends anymore, and David's voice became even louder in my head: *She played a part in this too, didn't she?*

I'd watched Josh closely for signs of heartbreak that never came, and the very lack of it angered me in a way I couldn't articulate, because how could I want my own child to suffer?

Then Michelle had entered Josh's life. A fresh start, with somebody who was a better fit. Abby was out of sight, out of mind, almost like she had never been there at all.

"He's moving on," David had said when I tried to talk to him about my concerns.

"He's moving on too quickly," I said. "He should be alone for a while."

"He's seventeen, Bev. You want to try keeping him away from girls? Good luck."

"You were so quick to believe him," I muttered, just loud enough for him to hear.

His eyes lit up. "And you were so quick not to."

David didn't have a temper; he rarely lashed out. But his voice had all the fraught tightness of a tendon about to snap. He didn't want to talk about the incident. It was almost like he wanted to pretend it had never happened: even when it was just the two of us, he refused to be candid with me or deviate from the story we were telling the public.

"How are you?" I asked Michelle now. Whenever I asked Josh that question, he gave little more than a shrug. "How's tennis going?"

"Good," Michelle said. Her eyes were wide and pale blue fringed by dark lashes, her blonde hair shimmering across her strong shoulders. "Really good, actually. I got picked for this specialized training program next summer in Florida that starts after my regular camp. So, I'm excited for that. I'm hoping for a scholarship to college, but we'll see."

"That's amazing," I said. Josh hadn't mentioned the extent of Michelle's involvement in tennis, which was slightly surprising—except when I considered that he was seventeen, with his own life, and barely talked to me at all. It was almost like there was frosted glass between us, a fogged-up wall through which I could no longer see the towheaded little boy who once insisted on curling up in my bed because he was afraid of the dark.

Michelle's lips curved into a smile. "Yeah, it's exciting, but I don't want to get my hopes up. My stepmom thinks I should dream big, but my mom keeps telling me I need to have a backup plan."

"Your mom sounds a lot like mine. I wanted to be an art historian when I was your age, but she didn't think it was practical. I wanted to study abroad in Europe and see more of the art up close."

My mother, Dorothy, had been a beautiful woman when her face wasn't pinched in an angry scowl. She was a self-taught painter but had stopped making art when she had me and Camille, and as I aged out of the little-kid years, I often wondered if she resented us for the choice she made to be a stay-at-home mom. I never knew my parents' relationship was dysfunctional until I went to the houses of school friends and saw the small gestures of affection between their mothers and fathers: a hand on the waist here, a kiss on the cheek there. Walter and Dorothy barely touched. They were two cold fronts who became nuclear in close proximity.

Walter had treated her poorly: at first, their arguments had been well concealed, but as the years went on, they weren't as concerned with shielding us, and we learned to walk on eggshells to keep the peace. I wished I hadn't overheard Dorothy confronting him about a woman from his office—at almost nine, I was barely old enough to know what that meant, and could only crouch on the stairs, hands balled into sweaty fists on the balustrade, as he unloaded on her over the same avocado-green countertop where she prepared all his dinners.

I hated her for taking whatever he doled out, verbal tirades that twisted everything into being her fault. Walter's anger trickled down, and Dorothy was often its messenger to me and Camille, her frustration spilling over the smallest things. I hated him for taking our mother and turning her into somebody who scared me.

I didn't want to end up with a man like my father, but I wanted to become my mother even less.

"Study abroad. That's cool," Michelle said, pulling me back to the present. "Did you end up doing it?"

I shook my head, managing a weak smile. "No."

Emilia had left to study abroad, not me. *That's not a practical use of money, Beverly,* Dorothy had said. *We've already paid for you to go all the way to California for school.*

So I had stayed. For a while, Emilia had sent postcards of endless lavender fields and picturesque hilltop villages, of paintings by Van Gogh and Picasso and Cézanne. *Greetings from Provence. Wish you were here.* I still had them somewhere, but hadn't looked at them in decades.

A dimple appeared in Michelle's cheek. "Maybe I'll do something like that."

"You should," I said, trying to sound encouraging.

"Oh, there's Josh," she said, standing up and brushing off her denim shorts. I craned my neck and shielded my face from the sun, and spotted him walking toward us with his familiar gait—confident, assured, just like his father. I saw so much of David in Josh. As much as Josh would never admit it, he was a hopeless romantic, always happiest when he was doting on a girlfriend. And I'd seen how he treated his girlfriends, bringing them flowers and taking them on dates. I wondered, again, what had really happened with Abby. I shivered, despite the heat.

I could tell that Michelle was stopping herself from running toward Josh, the same way he resisted kissing her in front of me. Instead, he fiddled with his puka shell necklace, the one he always wore. "Sorry I am late. I stayed at school for that group project thing."

"I need to head back," I said awkwardly, standing and rocking Kieran's stroller forward. "Michelle, you're welcome to join us for dinner if you'd like."

"That'd be great," she said. "Thanks, Mrs. Kell—Bev."

"Is Dad back yet?" Josh asked.

"No," I said quickly. "He's still in San Francisco."

"Cool," Josh said, and the way his jaw tightened was almost an exact facsimile of his father's. How would he react if David and I were to get a divorce? Would David spin things to make me look like the one at fault? And would that be the truth? I had pulled away from him over the past months, our arguments more and more frequent. *Maybe we need to think about this*, I'd said, only to have David stare at me like he had no idea who I was. His rebuttal had been terse. *You're upset that I protected this family? What did you expect me to do?*

He never seemed to take Abby into consideration at all. Maybe the most chilling part was that I felt like he didn't care what had really happened, as long as it could all be swept away.

But the last thing I wanted for our sons was the tumult Camille and I had grown up within, the bombed-out shell our house became after every argument. I had been determined never to yell, never to physically discipline. My boys wouldn't live in fear.

Walter and Dorothy's divorce, when I was fourteen, should have been a relief. It was Dorothy who filed, citing irreconcilable differences. Walter accused her of tearing our family apart, but I was old enough to know he was more worried about his reputation than he was about me and Camille.

It should have been a relief: two conflict-free households. But the war hadn't been over. It had only changed arenas.

"He might be there a few more days," I said. Josh nodded, and he grabbed Michelle's hand, his large knuckles covering her small ones.

When I returned to the house, the phone was ringing. The caller ID said it was an unknown number. I closed my eyes, picturing David on the other end, with all the right words. Begging to come home. Desperate to repair.

But David only ever knew how to mend surface-level cuts so that they didn't leave scars. He had no idea how to fix the bones broken underneath.

# Three

## June

Napa County, California
September 2022

**IT'S JUST PAST TWO P.M.,** California time, when my flight lands at the Napa County Airport, a flight I charged to my business credit card. It's technically a business expense for the bar, coming here, and serves the dual purpose of concealing the trip from Kyle. Guilt chewed away at me the entire flight: I'd lied to both Kyle and my staff at Grape Juice, leaving everything that mattered to me on a whim.

As soon as I'm off the plane, I fight the urge to call Kyle and admit to where I am and what I'm doing. At the airport, I rent a car to drive myself to the Backyard Winery. My only mission is to see Andrew Smith in person and figure out exactly who he is, and I want to get it over with as quickly as possible.

I plug the address of the winery into my iPhone's GPS, which tells me the Backyard is a thirty-four-minute drive, mainly down the St. Helena Highway. My palms are damp, and nervous sweat is forming in the armpits of my blouse, making it tacky against my skin. I open my phone and send Kyle a quick message letting him know I've arrived. He kissed me goodbye this morning, thinking I was renting a car and heading upstate to Kettler Ridge Natural Winery, and here I am, multiple time zones and practically an entire country away from him.

Anxiety clenches my stomach like a fist as I start driving, and I watch the clock on my GPS as the number gets lower. Twenty minutes to the Backyard, then fifteen, then ten. I drive through Napa itself, the grape-studded sign greeting me: *WELCOME to this world famous wine growing region.* Vineyards crop up on both sides of the highway, green vines and stone buildings and rolling foothills in the distance. Normally, I'd be excited, but my nerves have made it impossible for me to notice much of anything.

It would be so much easier if I hadn't seen the picture of Andrew Smith. If his resemblance to Josh weren't so undeniable. I've revisited the photo almost hourly. My wedding to Kyle is on the horizon, my future finally ready to begin. But I'm feeling every emotion at once. Apprehension, terror, and—perhaps most frightening—the smallest amount of hope. The hope that I was right, and Josh is somehow alive, even though that would totally upend my life. Because it would mean that Josh left me on purpose—that he'd knowingly caused me a decade of pain.

My GPS tells me I've reached my destination, and even though I'm nowhere near ready for it, I ease the car into the driveway of the Backyard and pull into a vacant parking spot in the lot. The main building, as I already know from looking at photos online, has a stone front and a sunbaked path leading to the boutique hotel and spa. Behind the main building with the tasting room is a stamped concrete patio with a small fountain and several circular tables repurposed from wine barrels. There are people milling around, laughing and having fun, on what looks like a guided tour being led into the vineyard. I have to force myself out of the car on numb legs.

I stride into the tasting room, which is beautifully antiquated with stone walls and low tables, its earthy smell inviting. There are three women at one of the tables and an older man pouring wine into their glasses. He flashes me a smile.

"I'll be right with you," he says as the women look at each other and sniff their wineglasses gently, then break out into giggles.

A memory creeps unbidden to the surface of my brain. A date with Josh at a tiny Italian restaurant in the Village. He'd told me to swirl the wine, then sniff it, and then he'd put his hands over mine on the stem of my glass, the mere contact sending electricity down my spine.

*Your nose can pick up thousands of flavors*, he'd said, dipping his lips to my neck. *Your tongue, only four.*

I knew that already—arguably, I knew as much about wine as he did—but I kissed him, letting him believe he was teaching me something new.

*He's here*, I think, the hairs on the back of my neck raised, like those of an animal picking up a particular smell. Any second now, Andrew Smith could emerge from the vines. It's harvest season for the white grapes: Does he pick them himself? The Backyard's website spoke of the winery's dedication to traditional hand harvesting and machine-free processes. It sounds like they're careful about the interventions they use. Josh never came to appreciate or understand natural wine, despite my best efforts. But he knew so much about conventional wines that I can easily picture him on a winery—on *this* winery—gently tending to the grapes.

*How are you real?* I once asked him, because it felt like I was living in a fairy tale, and I was waiting for the other shoe to drop. He had laughed it off, silencing me with a playful *I'm not*, along with a wolfish smile.

"I'm sorry to keep you waiting," the man in front of me says now. He looks to be in his late sixties, with gray hair and deep laugh lines. "Welcome to the Backyard Winery. My name is Marcel, and I'm the tasting-room manager. Are you interested in having a tasting? We also run tours here—usually sign-up is required, but today isn't very busy, so you can certainly join the next one." He glances at his watch. "It starts in half an hour."

I return his smile, trying to match his friendly demeanor. "Thank you. Actually, I was hoping I could meet with Andrew Smith. I'm . . . I'm an old friend of his."

Marcel hesitates for just a second before answering. "I'm afraid Andrew is out of town on business right now. Is there something I can help you with instead?"

I shake my head, feeling both dread and disappointment. "No, I'm just here checking out wineries and thought I'd drop in and say hi. Do you know when he'll be back?"

"Unfortunately not. He was only supposed to be gone for a few days, but I believe he extended his trip."

I want to ask Marcel exactly where he is, but the question sounds too intrusive. Is he in Brooklyn? Was it him I saw in the park and in front of Grape Juice?

"No problem," I say. "Is his wife here? Sadie?" The idea of meeting Sadie Smith is, for some reason, almost more terrifying than seeing Andrew in person.

"She left to pick up the kids from school, but I'm sure she'll be back before too long."

*The kids.* He says it casually, an afterthought, but the effect is shattering.

"The kids," I repeat robotically. "Um, I haven't seen them in years. How old are they now?"

Marcel gives me a quizzical look. "Declan is fourteen, Ariana's eight, and Mila . . . she turns three in a couple months. How did you say you know Andrew and Sadie?"

My legs are fixed to the ground, my body in a state of gluey paralysis, where I have no idea what it will do or what words will come out of my mouth. It's almost a relief: Andrew can't possibly be Josh, because it would mean he had children before he even met me. That would mean every conversation he had had about wanting to be a young father was something that had already happened, which is impossible.

"I'm just an old friend," I say, my voice trailing off. Marcel is looking at me expectantly, waiting for me to say something else, and I manage to mumble something about wanting to go on the wine tour.

"I'm actually getting married soon," I add, making sure he sees my engagement ring. "My fiancé and I are considering Napa for our honeymoon."

"Wonderful," Marcel says. "I hope you love it here."

I busy myself before the tour starts by looking around the tasting room, at the bottles of wine on mahogany shelves, at the Backyard's sophisticated black-and-gold label. I take notice of the dates on the wine bottles: 2014, 2015, 2018—years I spent practically numb. On a small gallery wall are framed photos of the vineyard throughout the years, a few featuring Sadie and Andrew, but even when I stand on my tiptoes and squint, they're not close-up enough for me to make out Andrew's facial features with any degree of certainty. In fact, the more I stare, the less Andrew looks like Josh at all, and for a panic-soaked moment, I realize the earlier resemblance was likely just another cruel trick of my brain, and this entire trip was probably a waste of time and money.

As I fixate on the framed photos—the winery's sun-warmed stone buildings, the verdant hills in the distance—I recall conversations where Josh had described the place he grew up, the Golden Grape. I can't think of any specifics that would tie that place to this one. I glance over at Marcel, trying to figure out a way to ask him without seeming suspicious, but he's pouring a flight of wine for a young couple, and the ornate wall clock lets me know that the tour is about to start.

The tour is led by a woman named Nadia, who has curly black hair in a ponytail and flawless dark skin, and is probably in her early thirties. She leads our small group into the vineyard, pointing out the grapes and how the winemakers know they're ripe. She's charismatic and knowledgeable, and I nod and smile with everyone else, playing the role of wine neophyte.

"What are these for?" one of the other people on the tour, a short blonde woman in a denim jacket, asks, pointing to the black irrigation lines.

"Great question," Nadia says. "They're a crucial part of the irrigation system. We need to store our winter water so that we can irrigate the vines during our hot, dry summers."

I turn around, using my hand to shield my eyes from the sun. Every trellis is meticulously maintained, and maybe it's just my imagination, but I feel Josh here. It's easy to picture him crouched in the vineyard, his hands on the grapes.

"We'll continue along—feel free to take as much time as you like.

Our next stop will be to the fermentation room and the barrel room, and you'll get a glimpse of the lab too."

On the southeast corner of the vineyard is another building—a house, a yellow-sided two-story with elegant pillars and a white fence that closes it off from the rest of the land.

"Is that part of the winery?" I ask Nadia.

"Oh, not exactly. That's where the owners live."

"Andrew and Sadie?" I blurt out.

She nods. "Yes, their family lives there."

My pulse quickens, my stomach twisting. I stare at the house, picturing the beautiful family that inhabits it. And as the sun hangs low in the sky, burning a hot trail across my vision, I see a curtain flutter in one of the upper windows, a fast enough movement that I can almost convince myself it didn't happen.

I've spent ten years trying to convince myself that something didn't happen the day Josh disappeared. And now that I'm here, I'm more unconvinced than ever.

# Four

## Bev

St. Helena, Napa County, California
September 1999

**I SHARED SOMETHING IN COMMON WITH MY HUSBAND:** I was good at pretending like things had never happened. I tried not to think about Emilia Rosser and how I had felt seeing her again. I had no idea if she'd contact me, but I carried around her business card in my wallet, every now and then pulling it out to study her embossed name, the phone number she'd jotted above the work one. I considered what would happen if I called the number. Had she put it there because she wanted me to? Was she here for another reason besides wine?

I pushed away the thought. I let myself be distracted by Camille, by her booming laugh and dry humor. She often followed me into the vines as I took measurements leading up to the pick, toting Kieran around and burying kisses into his chubby neck. She knew I didn't want to be alone. It had happened before: the first time I'd given birth, after David and I came home from the hospital. I had no idea what I was doing, and I sensed I was about to screw it all up. Camille had been living in New York at the time, and she flew to Napa and slept in our guest bedroom, cooked meals, and even washed my hair as I recovered from my

C-section, my incision itchy and inflamed. She sat in silence with me as I cried, free-flowing postpartum tears I didn't even fully understand, tears that frustrated David, who seemed to always be working on the vineyard, unhelpful for anything he couldn't immediately fix.

When Kieran was born, Camille was living in Santa Barbara, and having her closer was an immense source of comfort. She'd been there at the hospital, rubbing my shoulders and applying pressure to my back while I was in labor. At home, she'd dropped in with coffee and meals, offering to hold my colicky baby so I could get some sleep. David and I had been to Santa Barbara to visit with her and Paul numerous times before their divorce, and those were some of the happiest times in our marriage. The way he tended to me in public; the way his hand always seemed to find the small of my back, his fingers humming with electricity.

But things were different after Paul told Camille he didn't think he wanted kids anymore. Before they were married, they'd had discussions about family, especially because they met in their late thirties and didn't have the luxury of time. Paul had been open to it, even though he'd spent much of his life indifferent. He said Camille had changed his mind—that he'd wanted a family with her. But then when the time actually came, he balked.

I knew Camille felt betrayed by his admission that he wanted a child-free life after all. I assumed that after her divorce from Paul, Camille would return to her nomadic lifestyle—she had no roots in Santa Barbara—but she seemed stuck. He'd given her the apartment in their divorce settlement, and it had become her albatross.

*Don't worry about me*, she often said, a joking tone in her voice during our calls. *I'm always going to be fine.*

I'd admired how she had handled everything, but I saw the joy in her eyes when she played with Kieran, engaging him in a way I never seemed to have the energy for. She would have been a better wife, a better mother, than I ever was to David and the boys. Camille got down on the floor with them, the same way David did after a day of working on the winery. They both made it look so easy, to sink to their level, to lose themselves in the tumble of the kids.

I could handle the baby phase, its mundanely predictable rotation. Eat, change, rock, sleep. It was the stage that followed that I struggled with most. Preschool. Childhood. Play. *Watch me. Watch this. Watch me, Mommy.* I rarely crouched down to become part of their world. I realized, too late, that I was subconsciously waiting for them to grow into mine.

"There was a woman here looking for you," Camille said when I came into the house after being in the vineyard, helping the pickers with their haul. "She was kind of wandering around. Really pretty—blonde hair. Emilia, she said her name was?"

"Oh, yeah," I said, offering one of my grape-reddened hands to Kieran, who turned away from me and into Camille's arms.

"Who is she?" Camille asked. "Why does that name sound familiar?"

"She's a wine buyer. I wonder if she came back here to put in an order. I know she liked what she tried." I paused. "And she sounds familiar because I knew her in college."

"Wait," Camille said, pushing her hair—the same light brown shade as mine, but cut in a tousled bob, whereas mine hung listlessly past my shoulders—behind her ear. "You don't mean—the Emilia who you—"

I nodded. "Yes. That Emilia."

"She just randomly showed up here, after all this time?"

"She and David have been in touch about wine. He was supposed to meet with her the other day but obviously wasn't here to do it."

"And David doesn't know about you and her?"

I shook my head. "No. I never told him. I didn't feel the need to." I thought back to my conversation with Emilia in the tasting room. I'd felt invigorated, like I had been taking a holiday and was being the best version of myself with the change of scenery.

I stood up, reached into my purse, and grabbed my wallet, Emilia's business card inside. I wanted to call her. If Emilia placed an order for one of her clients, it would be something to tell David about when he returned, proof that things could run just fine in his absence.

"I'm going to call Emilia," I said. I brought the business card into the kitchen and dialed her number from the landline before I could talk myself out of it.

For some reason, the throaty cadence of her *hello* when she picked up made me forget what I was about to say.

"Emilia? Hi. You left me your business card, and my sister said you were here looking for me today. Is there something I can help you with?" I cringed at the overly formal tone of my voice, and a pause stretched interminably on the other end.

"Who is this?" she finally said. My cheeks heated up, and I tried to stammer out my own name, but then her soft laugh filled the air. "I'm kidding, obviously. Of course I know who it is. Hi, Bev Jamieson."

"Do you want to try out any more of our wines? Because I'd be happy to set up a tasting—"

"I was actually thinking you could taste some other wines with me," she said. "I came back looking for you, but I met your sister instead."

"She's staying with me for a bit, to help with the kids while David is . . . away."

"That's nice of her. Anyway, I'm in Stags Leap, staying at the Blossom. I was just about to get some dinner."

I paused. "So you want to—eat dinner with me?"

"Yes," she said, matter-of-factly.

"Why?" I asked, before I could stop myself.

"Because I'm hungry?" she said with a laugh. "And we have a lot to catch up on, don't we? I mean, if you're game for cheating on your own wines with a different winery."

I swallowed, silence lingering between us.

"I'm hungry too. I'll see you soon." I hung up and went to ask Camille if she could watch Kieran, a question I already knew the answer to.

The Blossom—the nickname for Blossom Estates Winery—was palatial, with thick walls hewn out of gray stone and turrets designed to give it the look of a medieval castle. I instantly felt out of place when I showed up in their tasting room. I was wearing a wrap dress, with my hair in a high ponytail, but my clothes didn't fit me the same since having Kieran, loose in some places and tight in others. I'd nursed Kieran before leaving him with Camille, and my breasts felt shrunken and deflated. I saw

Emilia first from the back. Her blonde curls were fanned out across her shoulders; a black leather skirt hugged her hips. She turned around when I entered the room, and closed the space between us, grabbing my hands.

"Look at these," she said, rolling my wrists so that my palms faced up, my fingertips inky from touching the grapes, from bringing them to my mouth to check for ripeness. "I noticed them the other day. I pictured you using them. All the magic you've made with your wine hands." She cocked her head. She ran her index fingers along mine as if they were seams, and I fixated on her manicured nails. "My hands—they're for presenting bottles with a flourish. Pulling corks. Pouring perfectly." She paused. "Enough about hands. I don't know why I'm even talking about this. Am I nervous? Please, tell me to shut up."

"Don't," I said with a weak laugh. "I've always hated my hands. How they never look clean. I have all these calluses, and I'm sure I'll get arthritis from all the vine-pruning work."

Two garnet-colored glasses appeared on the bar in front of us. I followed Emilia to a pillared patio and sank onto a stone bench across from her. At least two hundred acres of vineyard stretched until it disappeared into the spiny haunches of the mountains.

"We all have flaws," she said as her blouse slipped down her shoulder. "My scar from falling out of a tree when I was eight. Remember? I tried to tell you I'd been in a bar fight."

"Ha. And I told you mine was from a bike crash, and you assumed I meant a motorcycle, not a Disney-princess bike." I tipped up my throat, knowing that the tiny milk-white scar was almost imperceptible unless someone was really looking.

"My badass biker chick. Your throat has so much character."

I laughed. "But really, it bled a lot. The whole thing was very dramatic. Camille was screaming, and I was just gushing blood from my throat, thinking I was going to die."

"Well, thankfully, we both survived, and now we're here together. I want to know everything about living on a winery. Waking up with the grapes right there. Tell me about it." She leaned forward, her brown eyes fixed on me.

I told her first about the climate, which was almost perpetually warm and bright, besides the occasional fog that the sun burned off as it crested the foothills. I talked about Napa, its Michelin-starred restaurants and abundance of festivals, especially around harvest time, always something to do and see. I explained how my favorite work was my interactions with the environment itself, the hands-on parts. The testing of grapes, collecting fruit samples, checking pH and sugar levels. The hush over the vines when it felt like I was the only person in the world. Emilia seemed to hang on to my every word.

"I always knew you'd end up with an interesting life," she said. "The way you used to talk about art—remember all those conversations we had? I'd teach you about wine, and you'd teach me about art. We'd be up till, like, three in the morning. Now you've taken over my role."

I laughed, but my cheeks started to flush.

"Now, this place—it's really legendary. A lot of people say it put Napa on the map. Its cabernet defeated the top Bordeaux at the Judgment of Paris, 1976. Although maybe you know that already," I said.

"I did know that," she said. "A real David-versus-Goliath situation." Her smile wavered. "David. So he's still on his business trip?"

I swirled the wine around in my glass to release the aromas, then brought it to my nose and inhaled deeply to avoid answering her. When she showed up a few days ago, she'd said she kept in touch with David over the years. Why hadn't she kept in touch with me?

"Black currant," I said. "Black cherry. And I can smell plum."

Emilia mimicked my sequence, but it was imbued with her own grace, her movements precise but artful, almost like I was watching a dancer complete a familiar routine. I used to love watching David sniff wine, but over the last few months, I'd been fixating on the clinical way his nostrils flared when he inhaled. Watching Emilia was practically hypnotic, how she gave her whole face to the act, closing her eyes and pressing her lips together. I was suddenly nineteen again, in a dorm room, trying to make sense of my feelings.

"Ripe plum. Not baked. And there's a hint of licorice in there too. Something else. Blueberry." She brought the glass to her lips.

"Sometimes I think it's ironic how you wouldn't have met David if not for me."

I wasn't expecting her to take us back into the past. But she wasn't wrong. Emilia and I had lived in the same dorm freshman and sophomore year, and she and David had been in the same viticulture and enology program. The fall of junior year, before she left for study abroad in Provence, she'd invited me to a party one of her classmates was hosting, and it was there that I met David.

By then, I knew my feelings for Emilia were more than friendly, but I'd never acted on them until the night before she left. I was afraid to. My sexuality confused me. I'd had boyfriends before, and had never thought of girls as more than friends, but Emilia was different. I had pictured how her lips would feel against mine. I'd imagined us going further. I'd wondered if she imagined it too, or if that version of us only existed in my head.

"Me too," I said.

My attraction to David had been instant: he was handsome and flirtatious, with his shaggy hair and twinkling eyes, the kind of person who vibrated energy and charisma. I hadn't expected him to notice me, but he came over immediately and introduced himself. He spoke with his hands, always gesticulating. He liked to touch. It seemed like part of him was always grazing part of me, and the way he clung to my every word made me feel singularly important. When he left to get us drinks, I watched him, not wanting him to touch anyone else, to give his undivided attention away.

*I think he likes you,* Emilia had said, bumping my hip with hers. The smile that had played on her lips looked weird, like she wasn't happy at all.

"I mean, maybe you would have met anyway," Emilia said now. "The universe has a way of pushing people together when it's meant to be."

I drained the rest of my glass, the wine going straight to my head.

"Why are you really here?" I asked Emilia, raising my eyes to meet hers. "Why now?"

"Because I had an appointment with David," she said. "That's the truth."

"That's all?" I said, my voice practically a whisper.

Her silence answered for her. And maybe it was the wine, or my rage toward David, or my anger at myself for driving him away. But on the breezy patio, where Emilia and I were the only two people on a Thursday evening, I closed the distance between us and pressed my lips against hers, petal light, as if my mouth were an open *O* against a mirror. It felt like a homecoming, a wormhole to the past, another life I could have lived.

She responded, slow but urgent, her lips circling mine, and the place I felt it most was in my chest, like my heart was splitting into pieces, splinters of it exploding like shrapnel from my rib cage. I squeezed my eyes shut. Her hands migrated to my hair, her fingers light spokes against my scalp. I pulled away, forcing myself to end something that I wanted to last much longer. I was afraid to look at her, but when I opened my eyes I saw that she was still fixated on me.

"I'm sorry," I said, even though I didn't mean it.

"You said that last time," she said. "You weren't sorry then either."

"I don't—I mean, I'm married," I said, looking around to see if anyone had noticed us. What was I thinking? People knew me and David. They knew the Golden Grape. Napa was a lot of land, but it was small in many ways. How many people already knew about David's indiscretion? He would be humiliated if people thought our happy family was broken, but it would kill him if we actually were.

"You don't kiss other women, or cheat on your husband?"

I soured on her use of the word *cheat*. It shouldn't be cheating when David did it first.

"Both."

Emilia whispered in my ear, sending a shiver down the knobs of my spine. "I won't judge. And you know I won't tell."

The two of us in her dorm room as I helped her pack for Provence: all the words unsaid. I wanted to tell her to stay. I wanted her to ask me to go with her. The tears that had leaked out of my eyes in the dark. Her fingertips on my cheeks.

I pushed away thoughts of the past. Regret wouldn't change a thing.

"I want to see you again before you leave." I reached for her perfectly manicured hand and watched it twine between my fingers, my ruddy wine hands. "I just—I've thought about you so often over the years. I wondered if you thought about me."

She paused. "I did. Of course I did. But I thought if I reached out, you might not want to talk to me . . . I couldn't take the chance."

I didn't respond because I didn't want to lie to her. Would I have risked unburying all the old feelings, had David not cheated first?

"I'm not a cheater. David slept with someone else," I said, the shock from hearing the words out loud reverberating through my body. "He confessed recently, and I kicked him out. He said it was only once, but now everything is such a mess."

Emilia's mouth twisted into a grimace. "So this is about getting back at him?"

"No. No, that's not it at all. That has nothing to do with you." I couldn't articulate the complex emotions David's betrayal had wrought.

She smiled sadly. "I can't be your revenge, Bev. Just like back then, I couldn't be . . . whatever you needed me to be. I thought you and David were happy."

My face was flaming. "Did you?"

Again, she was silent.

I stood up. "I'm sorry. I need to get back. You know—the harvest and all. But I hope you enjoy the rest of your time here." I turned around and maneuvered through the other tables, not wanting to look back.

"Bev—" she called. "I'm just trying to be honest—"

My vision was tear blurred as I ran away, as I got into my car and drove back to the vineyard and the beautiful life David and I had built and destroyed together.

## Five

# June

St. Helena, Napa County, California
September 2022

**MOST WINE TOURS END IN THE TASTING ROOM,** where the people who've stuck around get to sample the wine they've just learned about. I stand with my companions, swirling a glass of cabernet sauvignon under my nose before sipping. It's the kind of big, bodacious wine Kyle adores, the tannin swelling perfectly under my tongue without being chalky. If I weren't pretending to be somewhere else, I'd bring him home a bottle. I can taste the care in this wine. With a shiver, I think about the man who might have made it.

I don't savor the wine, or spit what I don't want into the spittoon so that I can safely drive back to the airport. Instead, I down the contents of my glass and ask for another.

"Are you enjoying this?" Marcel asks. "It's our most popular blend."

I nod. "It's delicious." It has been a while since I drank conventional wine at a bar, but this one leaves a silky aftertaste. A smile fights its way onto my lips. The Backyard would be Kyle's idea of wine heaven.

But when I think about Kyle, I feel incredibly guilty. I need to tell him where I really am, but I'm terrified he'll see this as a sign that I'm not ready to get married, or that his proposal sent me careening back into the past. He has been patient to an almost impossible degree, and I think I've always been secretly afraid that, eventually, his patience would run out.

I watch the entrance to the tasting room like a hawk, desperate for any sign of Sadie Smith but terrified to actually meet her face-to-face. If that really was her husband in Brooklyn, did he tell her he was going all the way to New York for his business trip?

My phone starts to vibrate on the table beside me. It's an incoming video call from Kyle, and panic sets in instantly. It won't flag any suspicion if I don't answer it—he would just assume I'm busy working—but I want to hear his voice, to be anchored to the feeling of home. I pick up the call and hold the phone close, reminding myself that he's not going to know that the tasting room in the Backyard isn't the same as the tasting room at Kettler Ridge.

"Hi, sweetie," I say as his face fills up my screen. His chin is prickled with stubble, his hair partially obscured by his Dartmouth hoodie. He's sitting on our sofa, the gray sectional we picked out together. The tears spring to my eyes unbidden. If I were there, we'd be drinking wine together, and a board game might be scattered on the table in front of us. Or I'd be nestled under his arm as a reality dating show played on the TV, which we'd barely be able to hear over our running commentary about the contestants, whose lives and journeys we become embarrassingly invested in. I miss Kyle's dry humor; I miss the well-worn hoodie I tease him about that he refuses to get rid of, and the way his hair curls on his neck when he misses a haircut, and even the indents on his nose that his glasses leave behind.

"Hey, Junebug," he says. "How's it going there?"

I shrug and paste on a smile, holding up my wineglass with my free hand. "It's going well. I know I said I might be back tomorrow, but there are a couple more people I'm talking about meeting with. I might be an extra night here . . ."

"That's cool," he says, leaning back into the sofa. "All good here. I even cooked tonight. I made that gnocchi recipe you got from Phoebe.

And look what I'm drinking with it." He holds up a stemless glass filled with a hazy liquid I recognize as a natural riesling.

"Nice," I say, trying to stop the tears from welling up. Kyle loves testing out new recipes, even when they end in burnt disaster. He's always doing considerate things for me, things that bring us closer together. And I'm doing something that will push us further apart. "I miss you so much."

"After one day? I must be pretty great," he says, forcing me to smile.

"I guess you're okay. I was just . . . thinking about our honeymoon, and that we should plan the details soon."

Now it's his turn to smile. "That sounds perfect. Now that most of the wedding stuff is taken care of, it's a good time to figure that out. Are you still thinking Napa?"

I nod, wondering how he would react if he knew I was there already.

"Yeah, I think so." I chew my bottom lip. "I should get going, but I'll call you tomorrow, okay? I love you."

"I love you too. I'll try not to have too much fun without you. See, this is why we need to get a cat—someone to listen to me when you're not here."

"We're not getting a cat," I say with a grin. "A dog, maybe . . ."

It's an ongoing debate between us, not being able to decide on a pet. But we still send each other links to shelter animals we see on social media and dream of adopting them all, despite our busy work schedules.

When we hang up, I look around the room with renewed motivation. Wherever Andrew Smith is, if he was looking for me, he's going to know I'm here. And his wife can't stay hidden for long. Somebody was in that house, and even though I didn't see her face, I bet it was her.

Nadia is behind the sleek bar area, retrieving clean wineglasses for a trio of women with blonde hair and bridal-party sashes. I wait until she turns around before asking my question.

"Do you know if there's any vacancy at the hotel?"

The boutique hotel at the Backyard, I'm told, is a new addition, only five years old, affectionally referred to as the Barn. Nadia lets me know that it was Sadie's idea to convert an old barn into an area to accommodate guests, with six units spread out over two floors. All the rooms are occupied except one, on the ground floor, which has a two-night minimum stay. I swipe my credit card, hoping the second night won't be needed. The room itself is small but chic, all bleached wood and minimalist design, with sliding doors leading onto a small terrace overlooking the vineyard. When I comment on the decor, Nadia tells me Sadie designed it herself.

"She has a real eye for this stuff," she says. "She's very creative. I sometimes wonder why she's a winemaker when she's so good at other things. But she loves this place. This land—she loves it like one of her kids."

"Her kids," I repeat. "Yes, from what I've heard, they have three? That must be a real handful."

Nadia shrugs, rocking from one foot to the other at my door as she passes me the key. "Yeah. I have no idea how she balances it, but she does. She's a great mom."

"She really sounds like it." I pause. "I'd love to meet her. I actually got engaged recently, and I'm here in Napa to check out possible wedding venues."

Her forehead furrows slightly. "By yourself?"

I know I need to cut back on the questions. Maybe the desperation to find answers is laced in my voice, making me sound manic instead of casual. But I can't afford to waste any time. "My fiancé is working, so I'm here scouting a few places that might work for us. We love the idea of a smaller venue, and something family owned."

"We do beautiful weddings here," Nadia says. "It's another thing Sadie is passionate about. She loves love."

"She and her husband—Andrew?" I say, trying to make his name light on my tongue. "Have they been together for a long time, then?"

She nods, her springy curls bouncing on her shoulders. "Yes, basically forever. From what I've heard, it was love at first sight. I swear, they have entire conversations without even opening their mouths. They're that in sync. I don't know—I mean, between you and me, I've been with my boyfriend for three years, and he still has no idea what I'm thinking most of the time."

I spare a polite laugh, but my stomach sags like I've been punched. It sounds exactly like what I had with Josh. Love at first sight, our own unspoken communication. But if Andrew is really Josh, have I stalled my life for the past decade mourning a man who didn't even exist?

"I need to get back," Nadia says. "But you can call the front desk if you need anything at all. And Marcel will be in the tasting room at the bar until around ten, in case you want a drink."

I sink onto the bed when she leaves, my pulse drumming erratically. As much as I want to close my eyes and fall asleep, I force myself to stand up and fix my hair in the bathroom and head back to the tasting room. Maybe Marcel will be able to help me piece together whatever puzzle is struggling to take shape in my head.

Dusk has settled in, and the vineyard is almost eerily quiet, the blackened foothills standing in the distance like watchful sentinels. The walk from the Barn back to the tasting room takes less than two minutes, but I spend the entire time thinking someone is watching me, my body and brain as jumpy as a spring. What if Andrew, in his baseball cap, were to emerge from the shadows? I'm sure he knows every hiding place this land has to offer.

Marcel is rinsing glasses behind the bar when I enter, the block heels of my boots scuffing on the stone floor.

"Hello again," he says. "Miss . . . Emery, is it?"

I nod, my neck suddenly hot. When I checked in, I had to use my business credit card, my name in ribbed gold: *June Emery*. Now, I'm relieved my name has no tie to Josh. I never legally changed it after we got married, and I was June Kelly for only that one ephemeral week.

"I'd love a glass of chardonnay. I didn't get to try it earlier."

"Of course." He pours the pale liquid, which is the shade of clarified margarine, into a delicate glass and passes it across the bar to me. "Let me know how you like this one."

I swirl the wine and give it a quick inhale before letting the first sip touch my lips. It's not a traditional chardonnay, overly oaky and dry. It's complex, with teasing hints of butterscotch and lemon peel, almost like a hard candy that would dissolve on my tongue if I let it.

"You drink that like someone who knows wine," Marcel says, watching me with curiosity. "Are you a winemaker too?"

"No," I say quickly. "I actually own a natural wine bar, in Brooklyn." I regret telling him as soon as the words are out of my mouth, but since he has my name anyway, it would be easy to look me up and find Grape Juice. As easy as it is to find Josh's obituary online, the one where he's survived by his loving wife.

"Natural wine. That's wonderful," he says, looking genuinely impressed. "I love the stuff myself, although Andrew would disagree. You're friends with Andrew, you said? Did you meet him through wine?"

*Through wine*, as if it were a matchmaker, bringing us together. *Andrew would disagree.* Just like Josh, never appreciating the taste.

"Something like that," I say. "He might not even remember me, though. It's been so long. I almost forget what he looks like." I laugh, hoping it sounds casual. "I don't suppose you have a photo of him to jog my memory?"

Marcel narrows his eyes. "No, I don't. I'm one of the last dinosaurs who doesn't have a cell phone."

"How long have you worked here?" I ask.

"Too long," he says with a dry laugh. "My whole life, it seems."

I'm grateful for the easy segue into the next question I want to ask. "I was noticing the different awards earlier. I was under the impression that the Backyard had been family owned for generations, but the awards and photos only date back a certain number of years. Did I get that wrong?"

He looks surprised but recovers quickly. "Well—it used to be a different winery before Andrew's time. Back then, it was called the Golden Grape."

My breath catches in my throat. The Golden Grape.

The winery where Josh was raised.

I can still hear Josh's voice in my head, telling me that it shut down when his parents retired. Josh never talked much about what his dad was like before he died, and I never pressed the issue.

"Did you know of it?" he asks, obviously noticing the shock on my face. "It's probably before your time."

"No," I say with a shrug. "Doesn't ring a bell."

There are so many things I want to ask Marcel, but there's a heaviness in my chest, a panic threatening to overtake me. I don't want to explain how I know the Kelly family. I don't want to say that, for one short week, I was one of them.

"I'm really hoping I'll get to see Andrew before I have to leave," I press gently. "Do you have any idea when he'll be back?"

This time, when Marcel shakes his head, I get the sense I'm not the first person who has asked. "Andrew has to travel a lot for business. I'm not sure when we can expect him back. But Sadie—she's usually out with the grapes in the morning, especially during the harvest. She's very . . . hands-on, I suppose you'd say. A perfectionist."

It's a quality Josh had liked about me, one he jokingly needled me for. *You never let anyone help you*, he would say, pouting his full lips, when I got out of bed in the morning and instantly hopped onto my computer. *You should come back here and play hooky*. Occasionally, I'd had to bite back my annoyance that he didn't understand my dedication to my job, but I knew it was because he wanted me so badly.

"Maybe I'll get to see her tomorrow," I say, raising my glass to drain the remaining wine.

Marcel nods. "She loves to greet guests. Andrew, he's a bit more soft-spoken, as I'm sure you know. So smart, but very quiet."

I smile in return and nod, but he sounds nothing like the Josh I married. If something had happened to Josh—if he had had to disappear and become Andrew because he was in trouble with the law, or on the run from someone dangerous, and he couldn't tell me—it would make sense for him to hide from guests on purpose, letting his wife be the face of the winery. Or—a deeply unsettling thought—I'm not the first woman he has done this to. Maybe he was afraid someone would recognize him, someone from his New York life.

Or maybe I'm spiraling again, and there's an explanation that makes sense besides Josh faking his own death to hide out in the very place where he was raised.

I might not be able to meet Andrew Smith, whoever he is, tomorrow. But instead, I'm going to make sure I meet his wife.

## Six

# *Bev*

St. Helena, Napa County, California
September 1999

**CAMILLE WAS STILL AWAKE WHEN I RETURNED HOME,** sitting on my sofa, wrapped in one of my robes. Kieran was asleep on her chest, and a bud of annoyance flared through me—she never wanted to put him down, even though I made it clear he needed to get used to sleeping in his crib. I couldn't hold him all the time the way she wanted to. Maybe it was less that I was annoyed, and more that I was jealous. Being with children brought out the best in Camille. Her tenderness, her joy. It brought out the worst in me. My impatience, my irritation.

I loved my sons. But I suspected that I was a better person when they weren't around, and that they'd become better people without me. The thought used to storm my brain in the early years of my marriage. I imagined the horror David would feel if he knew what I was thinking. I pictured him leaving me, moving on with somebody who was a natural mother.

"What's wrong?" Camille said as soon as I stepped into the kitchen. "Did it not go well?"

I couldn't lie to Camille—she always knew when something was wrong. I didn't even bother trying.

"It was fine, but . . . I did something stupid," I mumbled, pulling a bottle of chardonnay out of the fridge—the same bottle I opened the last night I saw David. I was equal parts heady and humiliated. The kiss—the electric softness of it, the way it felt like taking my first breath after being starved for air—was blunted by what had come after it. And I couldn't blame Emilia for rejecting me, especially after what had happened in college.

"What did you do?" Camille asked as I sat down beside her, handing her a glass of wine.

"I accidentally kissed Emilia. Except it wasn't an accident. I wanted to kiss her. Not because I wanted revenge on David, but . . . because I just did. Maybe I have for a very long time."

Camille nodded. "Oh," was all she said, but she didn't look the least bit surprised.

I realized in college that I was attracted to both men and women, but it was the one thing about myself that I'd never told David. I'd been honest with him when it came to everything else—including my parents, even though I was embarrassed by my dysfunctional family when his parents had been happily married for almost thirty years. I couldn't bring myself to be totally open about my sexuality. Aside from Emilia, my friends were all straight, and I was scared I'd push David away if he knew I wasn't.

Camille was the only person who knew what happened between Emilia and me the night before she left for Provence, when I'd gone to her dorm room to help her pack.

Emilia had opened a bottle of red wine—a malbec, she'd said—and we finished the entire thing as she tried on bell-sleeved blouses and corduroy miniskirts, deciding what to bring. We'd both been laughing when I flopped down on her bed beside her, and my hand automatically curled into hers, sadness suddenly unfurling in my chest. We'd been friends for two years; we'd been almost inseparable, and now she was leaving.

Maybe it was the wine, or maybe it was the flirtation that had always underscored our friendship. Or maybe it was the fact that she was leaving and this might be my only chance. Our heads were both on her pillow, and it was I who leaned in, I who kissed her first, the plushness of her mouth igniting my nerve endings. She kissed me back. I climbed on top of her, sucking in a breath, and let my hand rove up her shirt. But just as quickly as it began, I ended it. There was Provence: she was going, and I was not.

"I'm sorry," I said, but I wasn't.

"I'll be back, you know," she said, propping herself on her elbow. "This isn't goodbye forever."

A few weeks after she left, her absence a persistent knot in my stomach, I ran into David while I was out grabbing coffee. "Bev, right?" he said, later confessing that he hadn't wanted to sound like he'd remembered more than just my first name, even though he'd been thinking about me. We ended up talking, which turned into a walk around campus, which turned into a late dinner. Emilia's words echoed in my mind. *I'll be back, you know.*

I convinced myself that what I felt for David was stronger. When I was with him, life felt safe and uncomplicated, like I could jump from any height and land softly.

David had made sense as a boyfriend, and I'd felt immensely lucky to have him. The physical attraction was immediate, and we shared an equal degree of emotional chemistry. His moods were stable. He had a plan for his future. We had entered each other's lives at the exact right time. David had dated a few girls in college, but nothing serious; I'd dated a couple of guys, but had questioned everything after that night with Emilia in her dorm room. David almost felt like a sigh of relief. He had won my heart, yes, but also my lungs, and that was somehow more important. He made it easier to breathe.

David and I were asleep in bed together in my dorm room when the landline on my desk rang. It was two in the morning, and Emilia was on the other end, tinny and far away. She had been in Provence for three months, and I'd been hearing from her less and less.

"Bev?" she said. I hadn't heard her voice in so long. My chest capsized. She was supposed to return in April.

"Hey," I whispered.

It was the whisper that must have given me away. She knew I wasn't alone.

"Look, Bev—I'm sorry for not saying anything sooner, but I really love it here. I've decided to stay. I'm going to put my degree on hold and work here for a bit. I'm learning so much, and just being immersed in everything—it's truly a dream."

"Wow," I said, a lump in my throat. David stirred in my bed, his arm reaching for where my body should be.

"You could come, you know," she said. "The school year is over soon. Why don't you fly out here, and I'll introduce you to my friends, and . . . I just think you'd love it here, Bev. All the art—it's just so you."

I squeezed my eyes shut, tears collecting in my lash line. Part of me wanted to be frivolous and impulsive, like Emilia. I could book a one-way ticket. I could choose to go. But I knew I wouldn't. My parents wouldn't approve, and I couldn't afford the trip on my own, and most of all, because of the man quietly snoring on my pillow, his face bathed in moonlight. He had given me everything I wanted, and he deserved a girlfriend who did the same.

"I'm sorry—I can't. I'm seeing someone . . . It's serious." I didn't tell her it was David. She didn't ask.

"Oh," she said. The hurt in her voice pained me too. "That's great. But . . . if you ever change your mind, I'll be here," she said, and those were the last words she spoke to me until three days ago in my tasting room.

"That's it?" I said to Camille now, my pulse still racing. "You don't have anything else to say about it? Just 'Oh'?"

I could tell she wanted to roll her eyes. "Look, Bev. I just think you should be careful. You haven't seen Emilia in, like, twenty years, and you have a family. This isn't like you . . . I think you and David need to figure out what's going on before you move on to someone else."

"Well, he didn't afford me the same courtesy," I muttered.

"I know," she said. "But that doesn't make it right." Her lips grazed the top of Kieran's head. "And don't take this the wrong way, but have you considered that part of this might be about punishing David?"

"No," I said, even though I wasn't so sure at all. Kieran burbled in Camille's arms, stuffing his fingers in his mouth.

"He called here looking for you," Camille said. "Tonight. I told him you were out. When I answered, he thought I was you. He sounded miserable."

I pictured the scene—David in a dark hotel room, the phone cradled to his ear. I tried not to care, even though part of me was on autopilot, instinctively wanting to comfort him.

"What did he say?" I asked.

"Just that he'd try back again later," she said.

I could picture what would have happened had I been home to answer the call. David would have pleaded with me not to hang up, to hear him out. His voice would have been thick with emotion. *Bev, I screwed up*, he'd say, a proclamation of his guilt. *Things will change if you let me come home.*

And if I relented—if I told him to come back—nothing would change. David's indiscretion would be glossed over, and our marriage would be improved for a while, our issues invisible beneath the surface, buried far enough down that we could convince ourselves they didn't exist. David would pull the same magic tricks he'd used with the school administration to make the problems go away, and sweep the evidence off our pristine floor.

Until another argument summoned them out of the depths. To keep the peace, I'd swallow my resentment until I was too heavy with it to move or fight back.

Camille's face softened. "Look—if you and Emilia reconnect and decide you really want to pursue things, I'd fully support you, you know that. I know how much you cared about her. But you have to work through things with David first."

"I know. And anyway, I doubt I'll see her again." A shiver crested my skin as I remembered the look on Emilia's face, a mixture of longing and apology.

Camille stood up slowly. "I'll go put Kieran down, okay? Then I think I'll head to bed. Turns out this whole taking-care-of-babies thing is pretty tiring. They're needy, huh?"

I smiled with a rush of gratitude that it wasn't all as easy for her as she made it look. "Yeah, it's not always what it's cracked up to be."

"Oh," she said, pausing at the stairs. "I told Josh it was okay if he used my car to take Michelle out on a date. He was dressed in a button-down shirt and had some flowers for her—it was adorable."

"That's fine. Thanks for letting me know." I normally would have smiled at the image, but it made me uneasy. Michelle, by the pond, talking about her future, so certain about where she fit in the world. So much like me at her age. Josh, never used to hearing the word *no*. I was afraid one of them would end up hurting the other, the way most teenage relationships played out, the love so intense that neither party saw the end coming. And Abby was in the back of my mind: Abby, who had changed everything for our family and who had been irrevocably changed by us. Not just changed, but broken.

I wouldn't give Josh advice about Michelle. What had I said to him, when Abby hadn't been at the house for a few days and I'd asked him how she was doing?

"She's been busy," he'd muttered, dropping his voice, a rare moment of vulnerability coming out. "Maybe too busy for me."

"I'm sure that's not true," I'd said. "Can you do something to show her you care? You know her so well. Girls like it when you show them you've been paying attention."

His eyes had lit up, a smile crawling across his face. "Maybe you're right," he'd said. "I know her so well."

I shook off the memory, how his words had almost sounded like a threat. He had never indicated how close they were to the edge. Was it possible he had twisted my words into a weapon, or was it just another example of me saying the wrong thing at the wrong time?

"And one other thing—Kieran said *mama*." Camille could barely suppress her grin. "I mean, he probably thought I was you . . . but I swear, my heart cracked in half."

"That's great," I said, taking in her smile, which looked equal parts elated and guilty.

I watched her ascend the stairs with my sleeping baby, whose first word hadn't even been directed at me. Camille had spent a lot of time with him over the past few days, more quality time than I had in weeks. Maybe he was just babbling and finding his voice, not assigning meaning to his words. Maybe he genuinely did think she was me. I waited to feel the gut punch of regret for not being there, but it never came. Instead, I felt happy for Camille. She had been talking to him nonstop. She had worked for it. She'd made Kieran the focal point of her days, and how many times had I thought of him as an obstacle instead?

When I was pregnant with Kieran, I did everything I could to get excited for a new baby, and sometimes it worked. David painted the nursery pale green and put the crib together himself. We'd chosen intentionally gender-neutral decor. *I think it's going to be a girl*, he had said, because he thought we'd finally be having a daughter.

Thinking of that version of David—soft, excited, his eyes crinkling at the corners—weakened my resolve, and I fought the urge to find out what hotel he was at and tell him I was ready to talk, ready for him to come home. Maybe it would be for the best. We had so many memories between us from the past two decades: Who would gain custody of those, if we were to separate? Would everything we had built be for nothing?

But I had missed his call, and I convinced myself it was for a reason.

The landline rang just as I closed the fridge door, the sound of it making me jump. I raised the phone to my ear, pressing my hand into the counter, expecting it to be David calling back.

But it was Emilia on the other end.

"I'm sorry about tonight," she said, her words coming out in a tumble. "I feel bad about where we left things. I didn't mean to be so harsh."

"Don't worry about it." I managed a small laugh. "I got caught up in the moment. You were right. It's all too complicated."

"Maybe," she said.

I paused. "I should get going—"

"What would you say if I told you I was in your vineyard right now?" she said.

"What do you mean?" I held my breath in my throat like a bubble.

"I was thinking about when I left for Provence. How much I missed you. It's totally insane, but I once considered getting on a plane to fly back and surprise you. What did I think was going to happen? Anyway, obviously I never did, but I always wondered—would it have changed things?"

"I don't know," I said, my mouth dry. I had imagined going to Provence and seeing Emilia, walking hand in hand with her as we explored cobbled streets. Sometimes I could have sworn I saw her in a crowd on campus, her blonde hair streaming down her back.

"I'm sick of wondering. I took a cab to your place, and I'm walking back by the pond. It smells amazing out here. I think the chardonnay grapes are ready to be picked."

"I don't know if they're ripe yet," I said.

"Maybe you should come outside and find out," she said.

I sensed there was nothing left to say, only something left to do, a decision to make. I knew that if I did go outside, I'd be crossing a line I could never come back from. A line David had already blown past.

"I can't," I said.

The receiver trembled in my hands as I put it back in the cradle and drained the rest of my wineglass. Everything was moving in slow motion. I headed up the stairs but paused as a memory came flooding back: David shrugging into his oversize flannel jacket and heading out to tend to some business, forgetting to say goodbye. The same excitement he'd reserved for me, now given solely to our vineyard—or so I'd thought.

I rushed back down the stairs. Emilia was probably gone, but that didn't stop me from slipping into my shoes and pulling the front door closed behind me, then breaking into a run when I reached the vines, their green tentacles stretching into the distance. David and I had broken the family we'd created, the one we'd sacrificed so much for. David wanted my forgiveness, my love, but I wasn't sure I could give him either.

I didn't see Emilia, but there were a few pickers who remained stationed at the vines, shearing the excess from the trellises. Their heads followed me as I ran down each aisle, as my legs burned with the exertion. Emilia was gone, and the moment had passed, almost like a dream.

But there she was, striding toward the pond with her shoes dangling from her fingertips, twilight fuzzing around the ends of her hair.

"You're still here," I said when I caught up with her.

"The grapes are ready," she said, gesturing to one of the trellises. "Look at how perfect they are. This beautiful yellow green."

"On this side," I said, taking in the grapes, the swollen softness from the vines that had pumped them full of sugar, the process of *veraison* transforming them from the hard little berries they were less than two months ago. "These ones get the most sun."

She closed the gap between us. Her hands were instantly all over me. On my face, in my hair, on my waist. And in the same spot where I'd taken Brix measurements two weeks ago with my husband, I sank to the ground with the woman who'd introduced us.

"Someone could see us," I murmured, aware of the remaining pickers preparing the vines.

"Then we better be quiet," she whispered, her lips soft against my clavicle.

It felt different but the same, kissing Emilia. But as she unwrapped my dress, my skin broke into goose bumps in the cool night air.

"I've never . . . with another woman," I said. "You're the only woman I've even kissed." I didn't tell her how often I'd thought about doing more with her, how I'd touched myself as I imagined it.

Emilia pulled back briefly, and I put her hand on my stomach, her finger just above my C-section scar, which was silvery and white. "I've thought about the night you kissed me so many times," she said.

"Me too. It was the last time I felt that sure about anything." It was a truth I was afraid to even admit to myself, and I didn't allow it to linger long between us.

"We should—go somewhere before we get caught," I said, my eyes searching out somewhere we could be alone. The barn near the edge of the property, the tall wooden structure where the boys sometimes hung out with their friends. "Follow me."

She trailed behind me, and we both broke into a run. Suddenly, I felt as giddy as a teenager again, overrun with hormones and excitement.

Maybe we were being watched, but in that moment, the anticipation was so intense that I didn't care.

As soon as we were inside, Emilia's hand snaked under my dress and up my legs, where her thumb pulsed against the outside of my underwear. I leaned back against a bale of hay and stared at the vaulted ceiling, then let my eyelids flutter shut as darkness pressed softly against them.

Emilia moved slowly. She pulled down my underwear gently and her fingers made contact with my skin and unfurled inside me. When I opened my eyes, I was brought back to my last conversation with David. The way he had yelled that he was never even allowed to touch me anymore.

I forced myself to stop thinking about David. I didn't even think I was capable of being aroused like that, my body being played like an exquisite instrument. Emilia's fingers worked faster and faster, her thumb rubbing against me, and when she brought her mouth down to meet her hand I caught fire, crying out.

I didn't know how long we stayed there after, my body trembling. And I was desperate to touch her, to make her feel the way she'd made me feel, but a sound, a crackling from outside the barn, made me leap up.

"That was—" I started as I pulled my dress down, my legs still shaking.

"I know," she said, preempting my sentence.

It all felt so reckless, letting my body govern my brain, and shame threatened to flood over me. But in the muted gray of the barn, Emilia's own face looked peaceful, even though there was a hint of sadness in her dark eyes.

"I know this can't go anywhere," she said. "But maybe there's a reason we met again, after all this time."

I nodded, lacing my fingers through hers. I let myself believe what she did: that we were temporary. It was what I had told myself so many years ago, whenever the thought of her flared into my mind, disrupting the stability of my life. I had forced myself to believe it then, but I wasn't so good at pretending anymore.

# Seven

## June

St. Helena, Napa County, California
September 2022

**MY PHONE STARTS TO RING** when I'm still asleep. I didn't set an alarm, and outside my window, the sky is dark. Yesterday's events crash into me like an anvil—the knowledge that Andrew Smith is a father, and the fact that the Golden Grape is the Backyard—and I almost want to bury my face in the pillow and not have to confront the truth. But the ringing doesn't stop, and when I reach for the phone with sleep-fogged eyes, I see that the caller is Kyle. It's a FaceTime, which I pick up, blearily rubbing my face.

"Hey, Junebug," he says. "Sorry to bother you. I just wondered—the caterer called me back, and said she doesn't have any availability this week outside of our appointment tomorrow morning. Do you think you'll be back by then?" I can see that he's at his office, his meticulously organized bookshelf behind him.

"Tomorrow—that should work, yeah. Sorry, I'm just waking up. It's so early."

The words are out of my mouth before I can take a second to think. The clock on my phone says it's just past seven California time, which means it's already ten in New York.

His brow furrows slightly. "I guess you had a late night?"

It's not suspicion in his voice, but something akin to confusion. I'd messaged Kyle after getting back to my room last night, only around eight California time. At home, Kyle knows I'm a night owl. The nature of my job has made me one, along with the years of nightmares and insomnia after Josh's "death."

"I couldn't sleep," I say. "Just being somewhere new, and away from you. I tossed and turned for hours."

His expression mellows. There's a slight shadow on his face, which tells me he didn't shave this morning. I picture his morning without me, and how quiet it must have been. Kyle is a person who likes the rituals of a relationship, the small everyday moments. He loves drinking coffee together on the sofa before work, both of us scrolling through the news on our phones. He never forgets to kiss me goodbye before leaving for the office.

"I had a crappy sleep too," he says. "I figured I'd like having all of the space, but turns out I like it better when you sprawl all over and take up my side of the bed." He laughs. "Your room looks nice. What's that picture of on the wall behind you?"

I turn around quickly, the air leaving my lungs. It's an aerial photo of Napa Valley, one I'd stared at last night, picking the Backyard out of the patchwork and marveling over exactly how much space there is in the world for a person to hide in plain sight.

"Just a view of the wineries," I say, moving the camera back to my face. "Hey, I should get going, but I'll call you later, okay?" I do the math. If I'm out of here by dinnertime, I'll be back in New York in time to sneak into bed with Kyle.

His mouth forms a wide smile. "Sounds good. Go do your thing. I love you."

After we hang up, I'm not sure whether I want to laugh or cry. But I have a renewed motivation to find Sadie Smith and learn more about her. And I need to find out when her husband is coming back. I can't wait around for him forever.

·　·　·　·

Sadie isn't out in the vineyard communing with the grapes, like Marcel had suggested she might be. The woman at Josh's funeral enters my thoughts. I remember her black trench coat and how it was tightly tied around her small waist. I'm sure she hadn't been at the visitation, and I wish I could better trust my memories from that day to determine whether it had been Sadie or someone else.

I walk the rows of vines in my leggings and sneakers, past pickers shearing plump clusters of grapes into collection baskets. The sun is yolk yellow in the sky overhead, the morning chill starting to dissipate. It's going to be a beautiful day, but I won't be out enjoying it.

I wander toward the tasting room, but it's not yet open for the day. I pull on the locked door, then back up against it, staring into the distance. That's when I see the house, with its wraparound porch and ivied siding. I realize, as I take in the details, that it's the exact kind of home Josh had described when we talked about our future. He'd even mentioned a wraparound porch, a recollection that makes my stomach curdle. I hadn't realized he wasn't just daydreaming—he was describing the house he grew up in.

The man I'd married was kind and generous, his charisma rendering him larger than life. Yet it felt like the two of us were nestled inside our own little nucleus. Now, I'm forced to grapple with the truth: Josh didn't *want* me to know about the rest of his world.

I watch the windows, confusion gripping my stomach in a vise. Are Sadie and her children inside right now, enjoying breakfast? Josh used to flip pancakes as theatrically as possible, without the use of a spatula. I loved how playful he was. It was part of what made me know he'd be a great dad one day.

If he is Andrew Smith, he was already a dad the whole time.

I start heading toward the house, like I'm a marionette being pulled by an invisible string. I know it's ridiculous. It's not like I'm going to knock on the door and demand that my husband come out. But I need answers, and my time is running out.

I'm passing by the brick structure that houses the barrel room when I hear a muffled voice. It sounds like a woman. Nadia, maybe, but when I walk around the side of the building, nobody is there. I try the door, not expecting it to open, but it does, and I'm inside the dimly lit room, the thick, humid scent of fermenting grapes swelling inside my nostrils. The barrels are stacked to the ceiling, narrowing from the base like a cheerleader's pyramid. Natural wine isn't aged in a cellar, so in many ways, it's the opposite of what the Backyard is doing. The wines I serve at the bar are all about immediacy, while the wine in these barrels needs to mature before consumption.

"Excuse me, what are you doing here?" The sharp voice pulls me out of my trance, and I jump back from the barrel I'm standing beside. A woman emerges from the shadows, her blonde hair in a perky ponytail, her petite figure obscured by a knit sweater and loose jeans tucked into rain boots.

I'm face-to-face with Sadie Smith.

Her eyes don't leave mine. She looks around my age, maybe a bit younger, one hand resting on her slim hip with an iPad in her other hand. She doesn't look old enough to be a mother to a teenager, but I suppose if Josh and I had gotten pregnant, I could have a ten-year-old by now.

"I'm sorry," I sputter. "I'm staying at the Barn, and I guess I was just exploring. I had a tour yesterday and got to see this place, and the door was open—I'm sorry. I shouldn't have come here."

Sadie studies me, and her posture relaxes, her gaze softening. My nerves defray along with her. She believes me—that I'm a guest, that I'm excited about wine. "It's okay. I get it. You just wanted to see where the magic happens—I don't blame you. Do you want a sample, since you're here?"

"Are you sure?" I know that the wine in those barrels is gestating like a baby, and that every time the barrel is opened, the wine is exposed to air. But Sadie extracts a wine thief—a tube-shaped tool that lets her dip into the barrel—and injects a small pour into a glass.

"This is the chardonnay," she says. "I'm sure Nadia would have mentioned this on the tour, but we still use oak barrels for several of our wines. We've moved into some stainless steel for the wines that require less complexity, like our riesling—wines that don't need the addition of the oaky flavor, or in the case of reds, which don't need the softening effect oak has on tannin."

I sip from the glass. "It's delicious," I say, the simple answer from someone who doesn't know wine. I won't tell her the truth. That, at first, it's a bit astringent on my taste buds, but the longer I hold it in my mouth, the more the flavor mellows, releasing its sweetness like a caramel apple.

"I'm Sadie," she says warmly, extending her hand. "Hopefully you're enjoying your stay so far. What brings you our way?"

"I actually got engaged recently." I flash my left hand in front of me, as if the ring is the proof I need. "I was in Napa visiting friends and thought I'd check out some wineries that do weddings. I saw some beautiful photos on your website." I bite the inside of my cheek, waiting for her reaction.

"That's wonderful," she says. "Congratulations. That's a beautiful engagement ring."

"I like your ring too," I blurt out, and instantly wish I'd said nothing. She's not wearing an engagement ring, but a plain gold band.

"This?" She waves her hand; I can tell she's a bit confused. "I have a nicer ring at home, but I work with my hands so much that it's not really practical for me to wear it."

"Have you been married for a long time?"

She nods. "Yes. Sixteen years, actually. It's crazy how the time flies."

I seize the opportunity to bring Andrew into the conversation. "And you run the winery with your husband, right? I love that it's family owned—those are the kinds of businesses I like to support."

She gives me a tight smile. "Yes, it was Andrew's idea for us to take over this place. I actually knew almost nothing about wine before I met him, and he introduced me to it gradually, until I really fell in love."

"With him, or the wine?" I joke, but she doesn't laugh.

"Both, I suppose," she says with a shrug. "I feel like I'm always learning something new. About the wine, that is."

"You mentioned you took over this place. Did you buy from a previous owner?" I say, pressing the subject but unsure if I trust Sadie enough to say the rest. "I can't imagine anyone wanting to give this place up."

"We took over from Andrew's parents," Sadie says, her face expressionless. "Sometimes change is a good thing. And sometimes there's no other choice."

I suck in a sharp breath. Andrew and Sadie inherited the winery from Bev and David Kelly, the same winery Josh told me had changed hands long before we met. There are so many things I want to say to Sadie, but none of them even make sense in my own head.

"Where is Andrew now?" I settle on saying, my words coming out blunter than I intended. "I mean, is he working here today too?"

"He's out of town on business," she says. "But anything you need as a guest, I can help you with."

The edge in her voice is unmistakable, a thread of steel wool under her friendly smile.

All the questions I wanted to ask her dissolve on my tongue. I consider what would happen if I spilled everything to Sadie, brandishing the screenshot I'd saved from the Backyard's website. *I saw your husband's picture and he looks identical to my former husband. Do you see the resemblance? Was it you I saw at his funeral?*

But it's too insane to say out loud.

"I'm sorry, but I need to get going," Sadie says. "I have an event off-property. I'm sure I'll see you around later today, though, if you're planning to stay? I can have Nadia show you some of the wedding and honeymoon packages we offer." She pauses, and when she speaks again, her voice is soft but forceful. "Of course, there are so many wineries in the area, so I understand if you're shopping around."

I nod, setting my glass down. "I'd love to talk to Nadia."

I follow her out and watch as she walks briskly toward the house, her ponytail lifted by the light wind. My pulse pounds in my ears, and her last words echo there like a drumbeat. *I understand if you're shopping around.* A throwaway statement, maybe—or a polite way of asking me to look elsewhere.

# Eight

# *Bev*

St. Helena, Napa County, California
September 1999

**THE NEXT MORNING, I VENTURED INTO KIERAN'S ROOM,** where he was still sleeping soundly, then headed downstairs, tightening the knot of my robe. My body buzzed with the memory of Emilia. I wondered if she was thinking about me too. I wanted to see her again, even though it still hurt me to think about betraying David. Even though he had already betrayed me.

I found Josh in the kitchen, hunched over the newspaper, sipping from a mug of coffee. In profile, he looked so much like his father that I almost did a double take.

"Good morning," I said as he turned around. "Thanks for making coffee."

"Aunt Camille did," he said. "She was up with Kieran earlier. She said she was going into town to get groceries." His eyes dropped back to the newspaper, and I noticed the dark circles ringing them.

"Is everything okay? Camille said you went out with Michelle last night. How did that go?"

"It was fine," he said, offering up no other details.

"Is she coming by today? She can stay for dinner again—"

"She has practice," he said shortly. "Says she can't miss it."

"Well, tennis is important to her—" I started, but he cut me off.

"It's our two-month anniversary, though, and it's just a practice. I thought she'd want to celebrate on the actual day. But I guess since I took her out last night, she thought that was the celebration." It was a rare burst of emotion. Josh barely spoke to me unless I initiated the conversation.

"Oh," I said. "I'm sure you two will work it out—" I stopped myself from saying anything else. I decided that no advice was better than bad advice.

"Of course we will." He fixed me with his blue eyes, and I saw a side of Josh he rarely allowed me access to anymore, a reminder that he was sensitive and easily wounded. "We love each other, Mom."

"Wow," I said, the admission catching me by surprise. "Love. I mean, it's so soon, and at your age—"

It was the wrong thing to say. His nostrils flared. "You weren't much older than me when you met Dad."

His words felt like a slap across my face. David had been so different from other twenty-year-old boys, so much more mature. But he had done the same thing my father did to my mother. He had cheated.

"I just want you to be careful, and take things slow," I said instead, making him roll his eyes. It was a benign statement that meant nothing. I suddenly wished David were here. He always said the right thing. Authority came easily to David, in both work and parenthood, while I was constantly searching for the adult in the room before realizing it was me.

"Sure, Mom," he said, somehow slinging *Mom* like an insult. When Josh had been entering the toddler years, I'd heard *Mama* nonstop from his perpetually needy mouth, dual syllables that seemed to carry on like a song stuck on repeat. It morphed into *Mommy*, soft and sweet and questioning, a little boy with jam-stained dinosaur pajamas and damp ringlets clinging to his neck, always instinctively reaching for my hand to curl snaillike around his own, except my hands were always full. The final iteration, *Mom*, was as incisive as a stab wound.

•   •   •

When Camille returned from the store, she told me she wanted to take Kieran to the library in town for a baby playgroup she'd seen a flyer for. I gratefully accepted the offer, and after I dropped them off, I drove straight to the Blossom and nosed the Escalade into a vacant parking spot. A shivery sensation flooded my body as I thought about Emilia's face under the moon, the giddiness of rushing to the barn where we couldn't be seen. It was like my nerve endings had lain deadened for decades, and had sparked back to life.

Mingled within the excitement was the guilt. There was work to do at the winery, and I should have been with Camille and Kieran, taking my sister around Napa, spending time with my son. And there was David, lodged in the back of my mind. The mystery of what he was doing, where he had gone, why he had ruined everything.

Emilia wasn't in the tasting room, or milling around like I'd pictured she would be. I walked around the winery looking for her, but she was gone. I was brought back to UC Davis all over again: Emilia's vacated dorm room. The lyric she slipped under my door the morning she flew to Provence, scrawled in her loopy cursive. *But I'll be back again.* It was from a Beatles song; Emilia had loved John Lennon. When he was murdered a couple of years later, I'd thought of her immediately.

The song was unusual and tragic, lacking the popularity of other Beatles hits, but it was Emilia's favorite, making recurring appearances on the cassette player in her dorm room as she swayed with her eyes closed. Later, I'd gone over the full lyrics, wondering if Emilia had been trying to tell me she loved me every time she played it. If she had been trying to tell me for a long time, and I'd failed to hear her.

My lower back broke out in a sweat as I returned to the driver's seat of the Escalade, ready to admit defeat, before I heard my name.

"Bev?"

I practically jumped. Emilia strode toward me in a pair of cropped black pants, her hair in a loose bun.

"I should have called first," I said apologetically. "I just thought . . . I don't know what I thought."

She draped her arms over the window frame. "I have a meeting in an hour, but . . ." She peered into the Escalade. I glanced back with her and saw what she was seeing. Kieran's empty car seat. "I forgot you had another baby. David mentioned it, but . . . Bev Jamieson, with kids." She shook her head, smiling wryly. "I remember when you said you didn't want any."

I remembered saying it. I remembered believing it. I had been stubborn and idealistic, and had been adamant about putting myself first, the way my mother never did. I'd wanted to travel the world, not remain in one place forever.

"Kieran. He's nine months old . . . He's so sweet." There was a squeezing sensation in my chest. Kieran really was such a sweet baby, and I needed to spend more quality time with him. "What else did David tell you about our family?"

She shrugged. "Nothing I didn't already know."

I didn't want to think about what else she might already know—but no, David wouldn't have told her anything that would sully our family's reputation. Suddenly, I didn't want to think about anything. I didn't want to think about the questioning blue eyes, the hand falling out of mine, the spirit I'd been about to break.

"Your meeting is in an hour?" I said hopefully, and her eyes flickered up to me, her head tipping in the tiniest nod.

We walked up the stairs to her suite in silence, and I followed Emilia into the palatial bedroom. The door had barely closed before I pressed her against it and kissed her mouth; her cheek; her ear; her throat, the delicate milky skin there. I traveled down her breasts, unbuttoning her silk blouse, teasing her nipple with my tongue, savoring the little gasps that came out of her mouth. Sex with David had been regular but perfunctory, dwindling from twice a week to once before it ground to a total halt.

I unzipped Emilia's pants and let them fall on the floor at her ankles. This was one of the fantasies I'd had about her: undressing her, unwrapping her like a gift. Everything about Emilia was soft, even softer than I'd imagined. I gently parted her legs and took my time exploring her: with my mouth, with my fingers. Her fingertips migrated into my hair, massaging my scalp as a low groan escaped her throat.

Afterward, she made us tea in the kitchenette of her suite, and we brought it out to the patio, where we watched the spiraling trellises of vines stretching into the southern sun.

"I wasn't sure if I'd see you again," she said, at the same time I opened my mouth, my own awkward question tumbling out.

"So, do you have anyone you're seeing back in New York?"

She laughed, soft curls falling out of her messy bun. "No. It's difficult with how often I travel. And I guess I just haven't met the right person yet—someone who made me want to settle down."

"I settled down with the right person," I said. "And we still managed to fuck it up."

Her eyes were downcast. "Do you know who David cheated with?" She paused, her lips forming a rosebud shape. "If you don't mind me asking."

I shook my head. "He said I didn't know the woman, and it happened only one time."

"Are you going to divorce him?" she asked.

"I don't know."

"I know you came from a broken home," she said, bringing her teacup to her mouth. "But coming from one is better than living in one."

"But their divorce didn't make it better," I said. "Camille and I became their little messengers. They'd fight over us. Use us to pass along information to make each other jealous. The idea of doing that to my kids . . ." I rubbed my face in my hands, my skin stretching taut. "I've done everything possible to not turn into my parents."

"You haven't," Emilia said, reaching for my hand. "You're a great mom. I can tell by how you talk about them. And I know you love David."

I did love them, but that love wasn't enough to make me a great mom. Thinking about my roots—the rotting soil of my dysfunctional family—only exacerbated the distance between loving somebody and actually being good for them.

"I thought about you after graduation," I said, meeting her eyes. "I heard that you moved to New York, and that you had that sommelier job lined up. I wanted to get in touch, but I didn't know what I would say. David and I had just gotten engaged, and I was happy, but I missed you."

Emilia smoothed my wrist with her thumb. "Why do you think I kept in touch with David? He was my friend, and we had wine in common, but we also had something else in common."

"Me," I said.

"You."

Emilia looked at me with a mixture of empathy and curiosity. She took my hand in hers, cradling my fingers in her palm. I read her expressive face. Maybe she wasn't lost after all.

"Do you think David wants to make things work with you?" Emilia said.

I shrugged. "I think so. Before this, I thought he'd do anything for me."

I had friends whose marriages had ended. Camille's had ended too, her heart broken. I'd listened to their stories, aching for the hurt they felt. But I had never once felt afraid that David would do the same to me. Never once had I questioned whether our marriage would meet the same fate. David and I knew everything about each other. We spoke our own shorthand. We were older, but no less in love; our love had mellowed into something deliciously warm and comforting, a climate I hadn't imagined ever changing.

But he had either believed Josh about Abby or just wanted the problem gone, and I didn't think the situation had been quite that simple. I had iced him out, pushed his brochures for boarding schools back at him in a huff. We'd had shouting matches I was sure the boys could hear, and I had sobbed afterward as the rage subsided. I was more like Dorothy than I wanted to admit.

In the aftermath, my relationship with David had been like a pond that had frozen over, going from deep to shallow before icing over completely. We skated around the surface, and any time I asked the wrong question or made a probing comment, another hairline crack forked out, threatening to plunge us both under, to a depth that would burst our lungs.

After Emilia left college, I chose a life with David. I loved my life with David, but maybe my feelings for Emilia had always been there, dormant but still existing underneath. Maybe I had always wondered.

"Tell me what you're thinking," Emilia said.

"I'm thinking," I said, "that maybe you were right about the universe pushing people together when it's meant to be."

## Nine

# June

**AFTER BREAKFAST, I SIT DOWN** with Nadia on the little patio area behind the Barn and let her show me the wedding packages the Backyard offers. She flips through each photo on her iPad, describing their wine pairings, their farm-to-table catering services, even the names of photographers in the area. I smile and act impressed, but what I'm really watching is Sadie's house. My seat at this table offers an unobstructed view of her navy-blue front door. She had mentioned an event off-site today, and about ten minutes ago, I watched her exit that door in a hurry, her children filing after her: two blonde girls, the older one holding the toddler's hand, and a lanky teenage boy.

Now, I'm biding my time to make sure she doesn't come back, and to ensure nobody is watching before I make my way into the empty house.

It's a crazy plan. I'm not someone who knows how to pick a lock, and there are probably security cameras, maybe even the kind that would alert Sadie on her phone if someone encroached on her property. It's for this very reason—that I know my chances of getting caught are high—that I've already packed my belongings into the rental car, ready to leave quickly when I have the answers I need. The idea of breaking into the house came to me shortly after my interaction with Sadie. There was something unsettling about her face, a hardness in the set of her jaw. She was hiding something.

"Moral of the story is, whatever you want, we can do," Nadia says, forcing my attention back to her. "We're super relaxed about weddings around here. We've done big outdoor ceremonies, but ever since the pandemic, we've also seen a lot of the smaller micro weddings, and we had one ceremony right in the tasting room. You can walk around and try to imagine where you see yourself. The whole vineyard is yours."

I smile, trying to appear light and carefree. "I love it here. I noticed during the tour that there's a beautiful pond—have you ever done a ceremony back there?"

Nadia's face instantly darkens, but she recovers quickly. "No, not yet. But, I mean, all the decisions are up to you."

Anxiety tightens my chest. I want to keep her talking, hoping the conversation will careen into some of the answers I need, but her attention is diverted by her ringing phone. "I'm sorry, I have to take this, but I'll be here later if you have more questions."

I nod and watch her walk away, grateful she's given me the perfect opportunity to be alone. I don't know how long I have until Sadie returns, and I need to get into the house before she does. I grab my purse and start strolling toward the vineyard.

I'm not alone as I move from row to row. There are vine pickers stationed above containers, carefully snipping bunches of grapes and sifting through them to avoid sunburned fruits and vine rot. None of them pay me much attention, and I quickly make a beeline for the house, my gaze darting around to make sure nobody is watching. The clock on my phone tells me it's almost noon.

The gate creaks as I slip inside. I don't see any security cameras, but that doesn't mean they're not around.

I don't expect the door to swing open when I pull on the knob. It almost feels like a trap: How could Sadie have left without locking her door? But then I remember the teenager who was the last one out of the house, his eyes focused on his phone.

*It's now or never*, I tell myself as I step inside and close the door behind me, my chest practically ready to capsize. Taking a deep breath, I raise my eyes to the first thing in my line of vision. I'm standing on a well-worn mat in a small foyer, and directly beside me is a gallery wall.

I forget how to breathe. I'm face-to-face with the life I could have had with Josh, in photo form. The largest one is a tall canvas panel, the kind of professional family portrait that is Phoebe's bread and butter, everyone barefoot in denim, kids bracketed by loving parents. Sadie is holding a blanket-bundled baby, and her smile is a joyous beam. Her loving, square-jawed husband has an arm protectively around her shoulders—protective, but never controlling—and his eyes bore into me, still stormy blue even in blown-out pixelation.

I sink to the ground, tears blurring my vision, my breath coming in sharp gasps. As much as I might have secretly hoped that this was all a coincidence, these photos are undeniable. They're the essence of Josh, every angle and every facial feature. Andrew Smith and Josh Kelly are one and the same. My husband is alive.

I don't know how long I remain there, a shattered shell, before standing up on numb legs and following the canvases through the foyer on some sadistic impulse into the living room, where they form a happy-family trail, the road map of Andrew and Sadie's life. There they are in a maternity photo shoot, Andrew's hands cupped around Sadie's belly as she stands ethereal in a cream-colored gown, their eyes locking with what I can tell, even from here, is genuine affection and love. There they are in front of the trellises, everyone laughing, nobody looking at the camera, a candid moment of glee. There they are on the beach, holding hands, so young—even younger than when Josh and I met. I slump over again as I get dizzy and out of breath.

Josh isn't dead.

It's what I wished for ten years ago—but I didn't wish for it to look anything like this.

I force myself to keep moving, and when I stand up straight, I'm in front of a mantel buttressing a stone fireplace. There are two snow globes on the mantel's edges, framed photos lining the space between them, and the blood chills in my veins when I see who is in one of the photos. Bev Kelly, Josh's mother, on what looks like a pier, holding her granddaughters on her lap, one on each knee.

So she knows Josh is still alive, and she's obviously a part of his new life. Bev, who never approved of me. *You've said that before, Joshua. You barely know her, and she barely knows you.*

I had strained my ears to hear more of their conversation that day. Snippets of their voices had carried into the living room, especially Josh's as he became more heated. Kieran, sitting next to me on the couch, had warmed to me instantly; he was telling me about a new video game, inviting me into his world like he'd known me for years, and I felt bad for not giving him my full attention.

"—not pregnant. But when you know, you know, and I know." He sounded defiant, and my heart swelled.

" . . . don't go," the muffled response had been. ". . . a healthy relationship . . ." I couldn't make out the rest of her sentence.

"I'm in love." Josh's reply was loud, assertive, but I could tell he was defending himself. I listened for the reply, but I couldn't make out anything beyond whispers, and one tiny sentence fragment.

". . . she doesn't know . . ." Her last rebuttal was clear and firm. "She deserves to know everything about you."

Josh emerged from the kitchen and sat down beside me. When he raised my hand and kissed it, he was smiling. On the drive away from Mill Valley, I tried to suss out the root of Bev's hesitation. Why didn't she think our relationship was healthy?

"She's questioning us," I said, feeling like a rebellious teenage girl in the face of a practical parent, not the almost thirty-year-old woman I was. "Do you know why she's so doubtful?"

"She's not doubtful," Josh said, without hesitation. "She's just a worrier. She was worried we're moving too fast. That's all. It was nothing personal." But his jaw was tight.

"She didn't like me," I said, my mouth curling into a pout. I hated how much it bothered me, but I'd just met my future mother-in-law, and I desperately wanted her approval.

"She does," Josh assured me.

"I heard her say something about how I deserve to know everything about you. Don't I already?"

Annoyance crossed Josh's face. I rarely ever saw him bothered by anything.

"Of course you do," he said. "You know me better than anyone."

Not more than half an hour later, he pulled over on the side of the highway, his blue eyes trained intently on my face, a wild spark within them that, by then, I recognized. "What are we waiting for? I'd marry you today. Let's do it, right now."

"Are you serious?" I gaped at him. "What about having our families and friends there?" I hadn't even started looking at wedding dresses, or thinking about venues, or preparing for any of the traditional bridal rites of passage. All I had was a Pinterest board I'd been casually adding to as I saw my friends get engaged and married. Above all else, I'd visualized my loved ones in attendance. I knew my mother—and Phoebe—would be devastated to be left out.

But Josh was convincing. It would be so romantic. We didn't need a show. We'd save the money we would have spent on a big ceremony and use it to travel together. And maybe I was afraid that if I said no, the bubble would burst.

Ultimately, I saw his vision, and that's why we turned the car around and ended up getting married on a beach in Santa Barbara, barely six months to the day we met. We'd found an officiant who lived in town after a quick Google search, not giving any thought to witnesses or signing a license. We'd worry about the legalities another time. Our loved ones would have to understand.

I walk deeper into the house, even though at this point, I don't know what I'm looking for. Andrew Smith doesn't exist. He's Josh Kelly. Or maybe Josh Kelly was the one who never existed at all. There's a soul-sucking finality to everything, a delayed shock that I won't let myself feel until I'm somewhere else.

I'm not sure what pulls me toward the stairs, besides a tiny voice in my head telling me to keep going. There are school photos of the children lining the walls. The two girls are Sadie's spitting image, but the teenage boy's resemblance to his father is uncanny. Was he too young to remember the six months his dad was gone from his life, or did Josh make up an excuse? Did he come home with a souvenir, telling him Daddy had been on vacation?

When I reach the top of the stairs, I venture down the hall, past three bedrooms. The first is sloppy, with a tangled plaid bedspread and rock-band posters, the obvious habitat of a teenager. The second has a pink canopy bed and a net of stuffed toys hanging from the ceiling. The third must belong to their youngest, with a vintage rocking horse in the corner and cubist paintings of farm animals framed on the walls.

The biggest room, at the end of the hall, belongs to Sadie and Andrew, a four-poster queen bed against the far wall, probably because the room isn't quite large enough to fit a king. There are nightstands on either side of the bed. Josh always slept on the right, so I open that drawer, expecting to find something of his, but all I see is a tube of L'Occitane rose hand cream. The nightstand on the other side—Andrew's side, apparently—holds a charging block and a case containing a pair of reading glasses. Josh had perfect twenty-twenty vision. Has his vision degraded in middle age?

I leave the room, blowing out a frustrated breath. My phone vibrates in my purse, but I ignore it. Adrenaline keeps me moving forward, even as my instincts tell me I should leave before I get caught.

A half flight of stairs takes me up to a third-floor loft, a small room with low ceilings. It looks like it's being used as an office, tidy but cramped, one of the walls slanting dramatically into a triangle to accommodate the dormer window. I sink into a desk chair and click the keyboard mouse, firing the desktop screen to life. But I don't have the password.

I need to leave this place—this house, the Backyard, Napa—and go home, and figure out what I'll tell Kyle, Phoebe, my parents, everyone. Will I go to the police? If so, what will I say?

I begin to rifle through the contents of a filing tray, a last-ditch effort before giving up and leaving the house. There are different printouts pertaining to the winery, papers likely awaiting organization. I glance at each one, not even knowing what I'm looking for.

Until I find it.

My blood runs cold, a deepening chill collecting at the base of my spine.

**COBBLE HILL WINE BAR GRAPE JUICE A TRIBUTE TO LIFE AFTER TRAGEDY**

It's an article about me.

Andrew—Josh—has looked me up. He knows about my bar—about my life. It really was Josh whom I saw in Prospect Park and in front of Grape Juice.

I fold the paper in half and shove it into my purse. I'm about to stand up when there's a tap on my shoulder. My heart races, and a deep male voice asks:

"What are you doing here?"

# Ten

## *Bev*

St. Helena, Napa County, California

September 1999

**THE NEXT DAY, WHILE CAMILLE WATCHED** Kieran, Emilia and I spent the afternoon together in her suite at the Blossom. We rarely left the bed, even staying there to share a vintage bottle of roussanne, which tasted floral and herbaceous. It was irresponsible, shirking my duties at the winery, but home felt like the last place I wanted to be.

I purposely lost track of time, having taken off my watch and left it on the nightstand. Emilia went down on me for what felt like hours, until my hips bucked uncontrollably, my fingers tangled in her hair, each wave of the orgasm stronger than the last.

We lay together after, the ceiling fan doing slow laps overhead as Emilia mimicked its motion, tracing lazy circles on my stomach. It wasn't just sex, even though Emilia did things to my body that I never thought possible for a body to feel, like all my skin was on fire at once. It was the easy, playful conversations, no topic off-limits, the way we fell naturally back into teasing each other, the same way we'd done in college.

"I'm still terrified of heights," Emilia confessed. "Remember how we talked about driving up to the Sierra and doing a climb? Yeah, that was never going to happen."

I nodded. It had been a plan we made, one that never materialized.

"I still hate cooking," I said. "And I'm a winemaker who can grow grapes, but not a garden. I have a black thumb. I kill almost everything I touch."

"We're just a bunch of contradictions," Emilia murmured with a laugh.

She opened up about her journey to become a sommelier after returning from Provence, and her struggle to be taken seriously in a male-dominated industry. "I've sat for the master sommelier exam twice," she said wistfully. "But I failed both times. I guess I shouldn't feel too bad—there are less than eighty master sommeliers in the world. It's like a club I'm desperate to join that doesn't want me."

"Fuck them," I said, making her smile.

She told me about the best wines she's ever tasted—a Brunello di Montalcino from Tuscany, ruby red and silky with dark fruit and wild herbs; a trousseau from the French region of Jura, less renowned and more obscure, but with a mouthwateringly juicy palette. She described the places she'd been in evocative, sensual detail, making me feel like I was there—but more, making me desperate to go there myself.

"I should have gone to Provence too," I said, thinking about that night in my dorm room, Emilia on the phone, David in my bed. Two people I loved, but only one I'd ever said it out loud to.

I watched her lips move, taking in every gesture she made, entranced by how she spun the details of her life since I'd last known her—ordinary to her, but foreign to me. I tried not to think about David, but he slunk into my thoughts regardless. When Emilia spoke, it was like shining a spotlight on my relationship with David and the life we'd built, the resentment that had built up like scar tissue over the last few months. There were so many things I loved about David. His kindness, his big laugh, his pride when he talked about our kids. His work ethic. The dark blue jeans and flannels he wore. The way his hair grew long around his ears if he didn't cut it every four weeks.

I'd loved his parents, Millie and Joseph, too. Millie, who always brought a homemade casserole when she came to visit; Joseph, who'd launch the boys up on his shoulders. They had passed away within months of each other, Joseph from a heart attack, Millie from an aneurysm. David had wept, and I'd held him in our bed, letting his tears soak my pajamas. He was certain they had been so in love that Millie's body hadn't wanted to exist apart from the man she had adored for almost five decades.

Their marriage had fascinated me—but it was also a marriage from a different time. Millie served her husband his meals without complaint. She was content to raise David and run the household while Joseph ran the winery. Millie was endlessly compliant; if ever she was unfulfilled, none of us knew it. Is that what David had expected from me? Did men seek to marry a woman like their mother?

And had I led him to believe that type of marriage was what I wanted? Maybe it had been what I wanted. When I was young—after Emilia left— all I'd wanted was somebody who wouldn't leave me alone. Somebody who would take care of me. And there was David. He was exactly who I needed at that time in my life, and my life had grown around him like skin surrounding a healed wound.

But I had changed. What did I need now?

I tried not to think about what would happen when Emilia left again, but it was hard not to imagine. She was leaving for Naples next week and told me about the wineries she'd visit there.

"The olivella grapes—there's nothing like them. You'd be in heaven." She paused, her eyes flashing as they met mine. "You know, you could come with me, if you wanted." She said it lightly, a throwaway comment, but just like two decades ago with Provence, I knew she wasn't joking.

"I want to," I blurted out. "I can't, but I want to."

She arched an eyebrow. "You'd even consider it?"

I shrugged. "Yes. No. I mean, I can't take off without having things figured out here, but . . ."

"I know," she said gently.

We were both quiet as Emilia refilled her wineglass. If I even breathed, I knew it would break the spell. Emilia moved first, brushing her lips against mine. I could taste the wine on her tongue as it slipped into my mouth. David crept back into my head, my husband as a young man standing at my door with carnations, his eyes glimmering with hope. He'd asked me to be his girlfriend so quickly, leaning into commitment the same way most boys went out of their way to avoid it. He'd been encouraging about my classes, had even proofread essays for me and made helpful suggestions about projects.

Emilia pulled away, her voice breathless. "This might sound like a cliché, but it's the same thing I tried to tell you back in college. You need to do what makes you happy. Not what makes somebody else happy. Otherwise, you'll lose yourself."

*I already have*, I thought sadly. Parts of me were like dead leaves, an untended vine, its grapes shriveled into puckered raisins. Emilia had blown sunshine and life into the dust-covered places. When had I gone away? I was happy—until three months ago. Until four weeks ago. Or was it only comfort, disguised as happiness? In hindsight, I could see what I was blind to back then. That my personality had faded, like a garment put through the wash too many times.

And in a surge of anger toward David, I said something bold.

"I want to go to Naples," I murmured in Emilia's ear, my hand cupping the soft skin on her hips. "Maybe I should have gone to Provence too."

Emilia smiled, leaning into my warmth. "You should go everywhere, Bev."

When I got home, Josh and Michelle were at the kitchen table, textbooks in front of them—such a wholesome picture that I couldn't help but relax. They didn't hear me come in. I watched Josh lean toward Michelle and kiss her cheek. My smile fell when I heard what he said next.

"I don't think you should talk to him anymore. He obviously wants to fuck you."

My body tensed. He sounded cold and possessive.

"He's my friend," Michelle said. Her voice was timid. I sensed that this wasn't the first time they were having this argument. *Fight back*, I wanted to say.

For a second, I was afraid I had actually said it, because suddenly they both looked up in tandem. If Josh was surprised to see me standing there, he didn't show it. He twisted his puka shell necklace methodically.

"Hi, Mrs. Kelly," Michelle said.

"Hi, Michelle. It's just Bev," I said.

"Bev," she repeated. "Sorry, I keep forgetting."

"We were just studying for calculus," Josh said. "Aunt Camille took Kieran for a walk." He stretched his arms over his head. "Dad's still not back. Isn't this a bit long for him to be gone?"

"He has a lot of people to meet with."

"Usually he calls when he's gone," Josh said. "Has he called this time?"

I nodded like a bobblehead. "Yes, late last night. I'm sorry I forgot to tell you." I turned to Michelle, eager to change the subject. "Michelle, do you have any matches coming up? Has your coach said anything else about the summer?"

Her eyes flashed with something like a warning, and her gaze landed immediately on Josh, a wordless exchange so quick that it would be almost imperceptible to anyone not paying close attention. But I saw it.

"Um, no updates," she said, turning back to her page and doodling a spiral in the margin with her pencil. "But Josh and I were actually thinking of going backpacking next summer. Before college starts."

"Backpacking," I repeated. "I didn't know you wanted to do that, Josh."

"I was going to talk to you about it," he said sheepishly. "I was hoping you'd think it was a good idea. For the culture and stuff. You and Dad backpacked after college."

"You're not even in college, though," I said. "Where would you want to go?"

He shrugged, his broad shoulders rising. "Europe, probably. Italy, or France. We'll see." His fingers wrapped around Michelle's. Michelle remained laser focused on her page, almost like she was actively trying not to look at me.

"That's exciting," I managed, my mouth cotton dry. "What about the training program in Florida, though?"

Michelle's posture stiffened. "I haven't decided on anything. It's still early."

I walked to the fridge and opened the door, letting the cold air chill my body. I'd prided myself on Josh being a gentleman, on being the perfect, respectful boyfriend, just like his father. But ever since last year, he'd seemed moody and restless, never entirely happy.

I should have been worried about Michelle breaking his heart. But I was far more concerned about what Josh might do to her if he didn't get his own way.

## Eleven

# June

St. Helena, Napa County, California
September 2022

**I TURN AROUND SLOWLY,** terrified to see the man behind me who just tapped my shoulder. But as he comes into focus, I realize he isn't a man at all, but Josh—*Andrew's*—son, Declan. I've seen him in the photos on the walls, but in person the resemblance is a new wave of shock. He has his father's square jaw and cleft chin, the same slate-blue eyes and floppy hair.

"Who are you, and why are you in my dad's office?" Declan asks, his voice laced with suspicion.

My tongue feels too big for my mouth, sluggish and incapable of spewing out an excuse. "I'm, um, a decorator working with your mom. I was measuring the rooms. She said I could let myself in and out. I didn't know anyone else would be home."

Declan furrows his brow, which makes him look even more identical to his father.

"Wow, again? She and my dad just renovated last year," he says, pulling an iPhone out of his pocket. My breath hitches in my throat: he's going to call Sadie and tell her I'm here.

But he doesn't make a phone call. His eyes are fixated on the screen, on a message there that he swipes away. "Um, don't tell my mom you saw me here. I'm supposed to be in school."

I hold in my sigh of relief. "I—of course. I'm heading out anyway. I have all the dimensions I need."

As soon as I'm down the stairs and out the front door, I pick up my pace, until I'm almost running to the parking lot. My purse flaps at my side and my brain threatens to short-circuit from what I found in the office.

I unlock the door to my rental car, get inside, back out of my parking spot, and nose the car onto the highway. I need to get as far away from the Backyard as I can. My hands are shaking so hard that I can barely keep the car on the road. I pull off to the side, jam my hazard lights on, and put my forehead against the steering wheel in an attempt to center my breathing.

The details of the last day I ever saw Josh rush to the surface, a morning so deeply embedded in my memory that it has become part of my DNA. The cloudlike pillows on the king bed in our Airbnb, the way Josh pressed me against the comforter, his breath tickling my ear. I was famished: we'd had sex twice and stayed up to watch the sunrise, and it was his idea to go and get us breakfast. He'd glanced at his phone to check the time—it was ridiculously early, but the sunrise had been worth it—and said he'd be back soon with the homemade donuts. We had plans that day to drive into Napa to visit some wineries. That night, we were due to have dinner with Bev in Mill Valley. He told me he wanted to show me where he grew up.

My chest heaves, and bile crawls up my throat. I'm dizzy and nauseated and heartbroken and angry all at once.

If Josh didn't send that final text from his phone—if someone else did—his hand must have been forced, a new life he suddenly had to step into because something in his old one had gone terribly wrong. That might be easy to believe, if not for the fact that he had already been with Sadie before me and had children with her. I'm torn between wanting to defend Josh, because I know he couldn't fake the way he loved me, and bitterly hating him for hiding so much about his past—and his present.

And there's another question that needs to be answered: Does Sadie know about her husband? Does she know what I know—that he's actually two people?

I can't keep this in anymore, can't carry it on my own. I pick up my phone with the intention of calling Kyle, but instead, it's Phoebe's name I click on in my contacts list, Phoebe who knew Josh and was there at my rock-bottom worst.

"Hey, Junie, I was just thinking about you," she says, her face filling up my screen. Her hair is in a messy bun on top of her head, Brooke and Brodie's playroom in the background, the girls sprawled on the floor looking at books. "I thought maybe we could do a couples' dinner this weekend, when you're home from the Finger Lakes. Kyle told me you were there, but you're back tonight, right?" She squints at the screen. "Are you okay?"

"Josh is alive," I blurt out as the tears start to fall. I explain it all to her, the words spilling quickly from my mouth. "He was in Prospect Park the day you took our photos. That's why I ran off. I saw him, and he knew I saw him, and he ran away. And I saw his photo on this winery website, and came here to find out the truth, and now I have proof he's alive."

Phoebe's face morphs into an expression of shock. She stands up and moves out of the playroom, her lips pursed. "What are you talking about? You need to slow down."

"I'll explain it all later, but I saw him, Phoebe. I saw him in the park, and he has a wife and kids here, and he printed an article about me, and his wife says he's on a business trip, but I don't believe her." I stop to take a breath. "He's here. Josh. He lives here."

"Calm down," Phoebe says, motioning with her palm. "You actually saw Josh? And where is 'here'? Where are you?"

"Well, I didn't see him yet, not here," I say. "But it was him in the park when you were taking our photos, I'm sure of it. And he was outside the bar last week, obviously watching me."

"June," she says, her voice gentle. "You've said that before. Did you actually see him in the park? At the bar? Did you see his face?"

"Well—not exactly, but I now have proof it was him." I can feel myself losing steam, doubt creeping in. "There were family photos in the house . . ."

"Where exactly are you?" Phoebe says. "You need to come home, and we can figure it out from here, okay? Come over. I'll make us tea and we can talk about everything."

"I can't," I say weakly. "I'm in Napa. Josh is living at the winery where he grew up."

"You're in Napa? Kyle said you're up at the Finger Lakes."

"Please don't tell him. All I know is that Josh is still alive, and he's married to this woman named Sadie, and they own a winery, and all the pieces are clicking together. Josh grew up here—at this same winery. Something forced him to leave me."

"Are you trying to say that he faked his own death? June, I love you, but do you realize how crazy that sounds?"

"He's here, and he was looking for me, or else he never would have come to Brooklyn." I pause. "And I've been having these flashbacks. Sadie—she was at Josh's funeral, I'm sure of it. And remember the party where I met Josh? He was with a blonde woman at first. He didn't say they were together, but it could have been her—I need to find out what's going on."

Phoebe pauses. "What you need is to come home. Kyle and I will help you through this. You know we will. We love you." She smooths the skin on her forehead. "June—look. You and Kyle are getting married soon, and you feel guilty about moving on, so your brain is playing tricks on you. But you of all people deserve to be happy. Do you hear me?"

I push back. "This isn't about guilt. It's about figuring out the truth."

"We all loved Josh," Phoebe says. "But—"

"You didn't," I spit out, the venom taking me by surprise. The admission hangs between us, and she looks down. She doesn't want to meet my eyes and confirm it.

"I was just looking out for you," she says with a sigh. "All I was going to say is, you can't just go digging into his past. Nothing you can do now will change that he's gone. Promise me you'll come home."

"I promise," I lie.

When we hang up, my panic rises. I can't return to the Backyard, and I can't go to a police station, ranting about my dead husband who isn't actually dead at all. But I can't go home yet either.

Suddenly, it dawns on me that there is one place I haven't been, one other person I can talk to about Josh.

Her voice floats through my head, as clear and disapproving as the day I met her, part of a conversation I was never meant to hear. *And she barely knows you.*

She was right about that.

*A mother knows best.* And no mother knows better than Bev Kelly.

# Twelve

# Bev

St. Helena, Napa County, California

September 1999

**THE HEAT OF THE DAY** pressed against my back as I walked the rows, taking in the bare vines. The chardonnay grapes were picked this morning under my orders, after a series of meticulous Brix measurements to test sugar levels. They'd then be sorted and prepared to move through the crusher, where its cylinders would work rhythmically to remove the stems, then break the skin and release the juices. I wondered what David would think about me making the decision without him. Two calls had come in yesterday, both of which I ignored, from numbers I didn't recognize. David wanted to talk, but I wasn't ready to listen.

I walked absentmindedly between the bins, staring at the grapes I tended like babies. Wasn't this what I wanted? It wasn't just David's dream. I loved the winery, loved the process of creating something that could be bottled and enjoyed. Wine was what I knew. If I ended my marriage—if I told David it was over, and started spending more time with Emilia—would I regret it forever? Camille was right. I had a family to think about, sons who relied on me.

Camille had listened to me speak with a high degree of skepticism. "I think you're playing a dangerous game," she had said last night, the two of us cross-legged on the sofa as Kieran crawled on the rug. "You fall for people too easily, and you change yourself to make them happy. Even if you don't realize you're doing it. It's like you're afraid to make them upset."

"Maybe when I was younger," I said. "I see it now. But this is different. I feel—more like myself, somehow. I'm seeing Emilia again tomorrow."

Camille raised her left eyebrow, the identical way I knew that I sometimes raised mine. "Okay, but I think you're using her to escape, and it's not a permanent solution to anything."

I paused before telling Camille the rest. "She's heading to Naples after this. I was thinking of going with her—if you were willing to stay a bit longer and watch Kieran."

She frowned, and I knew I had gone too far. "Are you serious?"

"I am serious. It's not like I'd be taking off forever, just for a week. I didn't know how long you planned to stay here, and you've been such a huge help with Kieran . . ."

Camille rubbed her temples. "But he's your son, Bev. And this is your winery. What about David? You've been avoiding his calls—that's what you do when you don't want to deal with something." She looked at me imploringly. "You both hate conflict so much, but sometimes you just need to have it out."

She was right. If I shone a black light on my marriage, I would be able to see the phosphorescent bursts where David and I both retreated from conflict. The times I'd been annoyed at him but chosen to let it slide; the times he'd looked at me with frustration, but rearranged his face into a more temperate expression. *Nothing is wrong.* And in our defense, it rarely ever was. We didn't fight, didn't take low shots at each other like my parents had. But maybe we had veered too far the other way. Our arguments were so infrequent that when they happened, they felt catastrophic.

"I know I'm being selfish," I said. "It's not that I don't want to be here." I reached for Kieran's dimpled hand and held it loosely in mine. "But lately I've wondered about what would have happened if I'd gone to Provence with Emilia instead of staying because of David."

"I get it," Camille said. "But just remember that the grass isn't always greener somewhere else. I know David did something terrible, and I'm not telling you to forgive him—I don't know if I could. But you have the boys. And this place that you love so much."

"I know," I said. Kieran pulled his hand away and palmed a wooden block instead. I couldn't explain to Camille how it felt like the things right in front of me were already slipping away.

"Josh is at a tough age too," Camille said. "He acts grown up, but he needs you. Especially after last year. They—they all need you, Bev."

I didn't want to think about Josh. He had once been so much like Kieran—innocent and cherubic, giggling joyfully over the smallest things. I blamed myself for turning him otherwise. After all, I had been the primary parent. Did he sense the whole time that motherhood hadn't fit me right? That when he tried to get my attention, my mind was elsewhere? Maybe the main reason I enjoyed working on the winery so much was because it took me away from who I was around the kids, allowed me to be a person with her own purpose.

I was always waiting for whatever phase the boys were in to pass. Toddlerhood, preschool, childhood; *It'll get easier*, I'd told myself, except it never did. Things only got different, and only when they got different did I desperately want them to go back to how they were before.

"I don't like the way he acts with Michelle," I told Camille. "I'm afraid their relationship is getting too serious, too fast. He was talking about backpacking through Europe with her. They've only been together for two months."

Camille shrugged. "Honestly, he's almost eighteen, right? He's not a kid anymore. I went backpacking not much older than him. So did you. And I'm not sure what you mean about Michelle. He's very sweet to her."

But the comment didn't bring me any relief. Just like I once had blinders on when it came to David, Camille had tunnel vision when it came to her nephews. She couldn't see their faults, and nothing I could say would convince her otherwise. And it wasn't like I was going to bring up my concerns about my own son to Michelle—she would be even less receptive to a conversation about her boyfriend coming from his mother. How would I even start?

And lurking underneath, like sediment at the bottom of a wine barrel: the thought that maybe I was the one with the problem, the one who refused to stop picking at suspicions. Maybe David had been right the whole time about Josh's involvement in what had happened to Abby, and my inability to let it go was what had driven him away.

I met Emilia at the Blossom again. From there, we spent the day visiting different wineries, sun-warmed hours that passed in a blink, one long conversation I never wanted to end. Camille's words of warning all but evaporated in my head. It was as if the past twenty-two years hadn't transpired at all.

I let my pinkie finger migrate toward Emilia's as we walked, and I pulled her behind the brick wall of a cellar, slipped the straps of her dress down her shoulders, dragged my lips down her body. Her laugh was light and airy; I wanted to bottle the sound when she was gone.

By the time we reached the last winery of the day, my head was fizzy with a combination of alcohol and anticipation. I rarely drank so much while breastfeeding Kieran, but I didn't want to say good night to Emilia. I wanted to wake up beside her the next morning, and the next morning after that. My grip on her hand tightened as our remaining time together dwindled. She leaned down and whispered in my ear, her breath warm on my neck.

"Remember we're out in public, and if someone here knows you, they're going to wonder what you're doing holding hands with another woman."

"I don't even care," I said defiantly. "David cares more about our image than he does about me." Guilt emerged with the words, because I didn't actually believe that. Maybe I wanted to believe it, because it would have made the choice easier to make.

Emilia sighed. "I know you guys are going through a lot, but I also need to be honest with you. The way David talks about your family . . . he loves you and the kids a lot."

It was the last thing I wanted to hear, but Emilia had always been fair, never wanting to conceal something just because it was hard to digest.

"I know. I need to talk to him and figure it out. But we're here to-gether now, so let's make the most of it, okay?"

She nodded, but there was sadness in her eyes. "Okay."

I led Emilia into the vineyard, where we stood still together. I lost myself in her kisses, in the hummingbird beat of her heart. I put my hand between her legs, my own body made weak by the breathy sigh she made. She whispered my name, and my head was full of fire as my mouth started to descend down her neck.

"Bev," I heard again, except this time it wasn't coming from Emilia. I pulled away, tucking my hands in a ball behind my back, my heart threatening to crack through my ribs. And when I looked up, I was star-ing at Michelle, who was wearing jeans and a hoodie, her hands in her pockets.

"Michelle," I stammered. "What are you doing here?"

Her eyes flitted from me to Emilia. "Um, I live here. This is my dad's winery."

My head spun. How had I not realized we were at Younger Broth-ers? In my drunken, infatuated state, all the wineries had blended to-gether. What would Rodney Young, or Jen, think if they saw me here with Emilia? Rodney and David played poker together once a month with some of the other winemakers; I knew they all talked.

"I—this is my friend, this is—"

"Emilia." She stepped forward, nodding at Michelle. "Look, I'll give you two a minute, okay?" I watched her wander away, her hair in a loose tumble down her back.

When Michelle and I were alone, I grappled for an explanation, but I knew she'd seen us. Panic lit me up. Would she tell Rodney? Or far worse, Josh?

"Michelle, if you could keep this to yourself . . . nobody knows I was here tonight."

"Don't worry," Michelle said. "I won't tell anyone. My dad's out at some dinner thing anyway."

I forced myself to meet her eyes, even though I wished the ground would swallow me up, and she must have wanted the same.

"Thanks," I said. "Look, all of this is very complicated, so I appreciate you not saying anything."

She tapped the toe of her sneaker on the ground. "I figured it was complicated."

I wanted to ask her what she meant by that, but my face was burning, my chest marbled with anxiety. Michelle's eyes were darting for an escape.

"I should go," I said, starting to walk in the other direction, back to the parking lot toward our shuttle. But something made me turn around—maybe it was knowing I wouldn't get another moment like this with Michelle, one where embarrassment made us both nakedly vulnerable.

"Michelle," I said. "You should go to Florida next summer. Focus on yourself. Europe will be there later, and if Josh really cares about you, he won't want you giving anything up for him."

"I—okay," she said, confusion written all over her face, but when that melted away, there was something else in its place. Understanding, maybe, or even relief. But she didn't say anything else, and I didn't hang around longer.

In the moment, I was glad I spoke up. But when it was already too late, the same way it had been too late with Abby, I wished I hadn't said anything at all.

# Thirteen

# June

Mill Valley, California
September 2022

**A REVERSE ADDRESS LOOKUP** for Bev Kelly turns up no results, nor does a Google search for her name. I don't have a phone number for her, and I have no idea if she has moved over the past decade. She could be living in a different state, a different country, even.

I try to remember the house Josh took me to when we visited Mill Valley so long ago. We had been so inescapably giddy about our engagement and had taken a road trip to surprise our parents with the news. Mine had been shocked but had welcomed Josh into the family. Bev had been decidedly colder.

Little details of the house in Mill Valley flit into my memory. The white exterior, bordered by bright gardens, a hobby Josh told me his mother got into after her retirement, when they moved away from the Napa area. The inside, all vintage charm and cluttered with family tchotchkes.

Josh had attended Berkeley and told me he had visited home on weekends often, easily able to commute. I rack my brain for the address of the house but can't even recall the name of the street. I start to panic without any direction to go on. Then I remember Josh had been at the gym early on the morning we visited, and he'd emailed me the address, asking if I could drive. I never delete any of my emails. I open my email on my phone and navigate into the folder labeled *Josh*. And after taking a few moments to load, there it is. *Mom, 10 Summit Avenue.*

I plug it into my GPS now and am told I'll arrive in exactly one hour and twelve minutes.

The drive passes in a blur, the vineyards that pattern both sides of the highway rising into parched foothills and trees. The closer I get to my destination, the more terrified I am about what I need to say to Bev. *I know Josh isn't really dead—when did you find out he wasn't?*

After Josh died, Bev had softened to me, and we'd found solace in our shared mourning. But when I'd started ranting my conspiracy theories at the funeral, I could sense her sympathy morph into frustration and horror. The funeral was the last time we'd ever seen each other. There was nothing linking us together afterward. Until today, my last contact with her was an email six months after Josh died, apologizing for my behavior at the funeral. It was something my therapist encouraged me to do, a phone call I needed to make. I took the easy way out and sent the email instead. I'd been drunk on my grief, and the idea of hearing Bev's voice was too heavy to bear. Her response had been short. *No need to apologize. It's a hard time for everyone.*

My fingers grip the steering wheel so tightly that my knuckles turn bone white. Bev should have been the one apologizing to *me*. She knew how much I loved Josh, and she never once tried to contact me after learning he was alive.

I arrive in Mill Valley shortly past two o'clock. I park on the street outside the house, somehow relieved that it looks the same as it did in my memories. The landscaping is immaculate, with delicate pink sumac and yellow-eyed asters.

My panic rises as I walk up the flagstone pathway leading to the front door, and my hand is a sweaty fist when I knock. At first, there are no signs that anyone is on the other side, and I wonder if maybe Bev isn't home, or if she really has moved over the past decade. But then I hear light footfalls. The door swings open, revealing a petite gray-haired woman, her smile falling as soon as she sees my face.

"June," she says, the one syllable of my name landing like a dull thud between us.

"Hi, Bev," I say.

My former mother-in-law looks almost exactly like I remember her, except with more lines around her eyes, more white in her hair. She's thin and elegant, her skin burnished by the California sun, her eyes pale green behind a pair of tortoiseshell glasses. The shock on her face mirrors the fear in mine.

"I'm sorry to just drop in, but I was in Napa, and I need to talk to you. Is it okay if I come in?" My voice is steady, somehow so much more assured than I actually feel, and I have to fight to keep the accusation out of it.

"I—well—I suppose so," she says, her mouth still slightly agape. "I'm so surprised to see you here. We haven't talked in . . . well, in such a long time." She inches the door open. "I wasn't expecting company—I was just about to do some gardening."

The house looks different than it did when Josh and I came here. She has renovated, replacing the older flooring with shiny bleached hardwood, the wall paint now a muted gray. The vibe is beachy and re-laxed. Kieran's video game console is gone; the last time I looked him up, he was in college and doing some backpacking. Bev is an empty nester now, which must be difficult, given the way Josh used to talk about her warmth as a mother.

On the wall is a black-and-white sign that reads *Family is everything*. Despite the sentiment, or maybe because of it, I shudder.

"We can sit outside," Bev says as I trail behind her through the sunny home and onto a deck overlooking a backyard resplendent with flowers and plants. She gestures to the plush patio furniture, and I sink onto a chair while she goes to the kitchen to make lemonade. I briefly check my phone. One missed call from Kyle.

She returns with the lemonade, a pitcher and two ice-filled glasses, and perches on the chair across from mine, like she's afraid to sit down. I suck in a short breath, then force myself to speak. Once, I'd been so eager to impress my soon-to-be mother-in-law; now, it's taking all my resolve not to lash out at her.

"I know you're wondering why I'm here. I think there are some things we need to discuss."

Her smile is tight. "You're in town for work? Business for the bar?"

I try to conceal my surprise that she even knows about the bar. She must have looked me up after Josh was gone, kept up with my life—the same way Andrew Smith had.

"Yes. Well, sort of. I'm here looking at some wineries. I actually just got engaged last month, and we're looking at possibly getting married out here." I watch her face carefully. Her gaze flickers to my ring finger.

"That's wonderful," she says. "Congratulations. You deserve to find love again. Josh would have wanted that."

I purse my lips, not wanting to think about what Josh would have wanted.

"The thing is," I say, "I know Josh isn't really dead."

Her expression sags, her eyes hooded and sad, and she opens her mouth to speak, but I cut her off.

"I'm not actually here on business. I found a website for the Backyard Winery. And I know Josh is alive, and that he's living there as Andrew Smith. He's married to a woman named Sadie, and they have a family. But you know that already."

The truth hangs between us, as thick and impenetrable as steel. Bev's eyes dart around, like she's looking for an escape route. Her hands tremble in her lap.

"It's—it's not what you think," she says. "It's really not. Josh is dead, June. I'm sorry for what you've had to go through, thinking he wasn't. What you think you saw wasn't Josh."

"Cut the shit, Bev," I say, my voice laced with venom. "Your picture is on their mantel at the Backyard. How long have you known?"

"June," she says. "There is a man at the Backyard who looks identical to Josh, and that's because he *is* identical to Josh. Josh has a twin brother."

The world starts spinning around me. Forming a sentence seems impossible, but I force myself to cobble my words together. "Josh doesn't have a twin. Come on, Bev."

Bev gets up and pads back inside the house, and momentarily, I think she doesn't intend to come back. But when she returns, it's with a photo of two floppy-haired teenage boys standing side by side without touching, their arms crossed, both of them gangly, their features slightly too big for their faces, but with the promise of handsome to come. One of them is wearing a puka shell necklace. Bev is standing to the side, dwarfed in height by both of them.

"Josh and Andrew," she says. "I promised Josh I'd never tell you about Andrew, but here we are."

"I saw Josh in New York," I say, unable to stop staring at the photo in front of me. "Just last week. He was watching me in Prospect Park, and again in front of my bar. Are you telling me it was Andrew I saw?"

"Andrew hasn't been watching you," Bev says. "I'm quite certain he hasn't traveled to New York. And he and Josh hadn't spoken for many years by the time you met Josh."

I finally manage to snap my gaze up. "What do you mean, you promised Josh you wouldn't tell me about him? Josh and I told each other everything—he never could have left out his twin brother."

"Josh asked us not to mention Andrew to you. He didn't want everything being dredged up all over again. When Josh died, the boys hadn't spoken in over ten years. Even when their father passed—that didn't bring them together." Bev looks into her garden, into the beautiful rainbow of flowers, and her shoulders slump, the light breeze blowing her sleeve against her clavicle. "What happened was an accident," she mutters, as if she's in a trance. "A tragedy."

*An accident. A tragedy.* Words I've heard so often that they've lost all meaning.

"An accident? What kind of accident?" I probe, unmoving in my seat. "Are you talking about what happened to Josh, or something else?"

Bev's faraway expression snaps back to me, like she doesn't realize what she has said. "It's in the past, and that's where it belongs."

I press her, not ready to move on. "But whatever it was . . . you're still in contact with Andrew. I saw your picture at his house. What was it that made Josh hide his brother? What did Andrew do?"

When Bev speaks, her voice is sharp. "Who said Andrew did anything? Sometimes bad things happen, and there's no logical explanation. They just do."

I sense that extracting any more information from her will be challenging, but I'm here, and I can't give up. I piece together the details I have so far. There was an accident, and it caused the estrangement between Josh and Andrew, something bad enough for Josh to conceal his brother's entire existence. The Josh I knew was loyal and loving. He adored his family. It would take an unthinkable betrayal for him to excise his own twin from his life.

And there's only one type of betrayal I can think of.

"Did something come between them? Or . . . someone?"

I can tell by Bev's tense posture that I've struck a nerve. I point to the photograph on the table. "They were, what, sixteen here? When did things fall apart between them?"

Bev takes a long sip of lemonade. In those few seconds, I sense her brain whirring, trying to come up with a response that will get me to stop asking. She must be protecting Andrew. Whatever he did, it was bad enough for Josh to turn on him, but not for his mother to cut him off.

"Andrew went away to boarding school for his senior year. We felt like it was the best thing for both of the boys, having some separation."

I sense from the stiffness in her words that she doesn't believe what she's saying.

"Why didn't Josh want me to know about Andrew?" I ask. "Please, Bev. It's important for me to know."

Bev opens her mouth, but my phone's ringtone cuts off whatever she was about to say. I go to silence it, and see that it's Kyle again. His texts flash across my lock screen, and I quickly swipe them away.

**June, what's going on?**

**Phoebe called me.**

"Fuck," I mutter under my breath, panic flaring up. I know I should call Kyle—I need to call him, to explain and reassure him—but more than that, in this moment, I need to focus on what Bev is telling me. I put the phone on vibrate, and choose my past over my future.

"Why, Bev? Why didn't Josh want me to know?"

"He wanted to tell you on his own terms," she says, exhaling slowly. "I encouraged him to be honest with you. But none of it is my story to tell. Josh was my son, and I'm not going to betray his memory."

We lapse into stonewalled silence. She has all the answers, but she's not giving them away. As frustrating as it is, I can see where Josh got his loyalty, and it's strangely comforting, that a part of him lives on in his mother.

I ask another question, pulling us closer to the present, unsure of how Bev will react. "Where was Andrew, on the day Josh died?"

"At the vineyard," Bev says. "He didn't take it well, hearing about Josh. In spite of everything, he still loved his brother. I think he held out hope for a reconciliation."

I try a different entry point. "Andrew took over the winery. And he changed its name and, apparently, his last name. Why does he go by Smith?"

"It's his wife, Sadie's, maiden name," Bev says, finally latching on to a question she's willing to answer. "Before Andrew proposed to Sadie, her father was diagnosed with stage-four colon cancer. They knew he didn't have much time left. It was important to her to honor him. Andrew understood that. And he was . . . eager to rebrand. Put his own spin on things."

My heartbeat is in my ears. There's so much more Bev isn't telling me, and so much Josh kept from me on purpose.

My phone vibrates. Another call from Kyle. With each missed call, he slips further away. I can't let this visit leave me with more questions than answers. "Why would he want to rebrand the winery? Wasn't it a family-owned business for generations? Was it because of the accident you mentioned? Did it happen at the vineyard?"

Bev scrapes her chair backward, its legs screeching against the stone. I've said too much, my rapid-fire questions scaring her away.

"I'm done talking about this, June. I've learned that nothing good will come from living in the past, and you should too." She meets my eyes, her gaze watery but focused. "Josh wouldn't want you dwelling there."

It's almost a threat. I stand up, wanting to shake Bev's frail shoulders, needing more information to spill out of her. But it's clear she has locked herself up like a vault.

I follow her to the door. I home in on the anger, a much more productive emotion. In New York is a fiancé who would do anything for me, and an hour and a half away is a woman who knows more than she's letting on. And somewhere out there is Andrew Smith.

If Andrew is looking for me, he knows where to find me.

"Bev," I say as we pass through the kitchen. "You never wanted me to marry Josh. What exactly was it about me that you didn't like?"

She doesn't answer me, doesn't stop walking until she's at the front door. When she turns around, her mouth is pressed in a firm line. "There was never anything about you I didn't like, June. All I wanted was for everyone to be careful."

I nod, accepting her lie. And the last thing I see before exiting her home is the mantra displayed in black letters on her sunny living room wall.

*Family is everything.*

## Fourteen

St. Helena, Napa County, California

September 1999

**I TOSSED AND TURNED** in bed that night. Michelle could tell Josh about what she saw, and then I'd be the villain to my children, to David. But something Michelle had said nagged at me. *I figured it was complicated.* What exactly did she mean by that?

In the morning was the crush. The white grapes had already been sorted for quality, their stems removed. From there, the mechanical crusher compressed the grapes to release their juice and separate their skins. I watched the cylinder squeeze the grapes, sucking their skins off, leaving the must behind—the flavor for the wine itself. Normally, the crush was one of the most satisfying parts of the process, but I couldn't help but see myself in the machine, rotating between the cylinders, crushed under the weight of the decisions I'd made and the choices yet to come.

"I always wondered why they called it a crush, when you like someone," David had once said, early in our relationship, the two of us cramped in my dorm room bed. "It sounds violent, don't you think?"

"It is," I'd teased. "It feels like all the air is sucked out of your lungs."

"I feel like the air is easier to breathe with you around," he'd murmured. It was the kind of romantic sentiment I was used to hearing from David, but his words had still leveled me into contented silence. I'd liked how his body was wrapped around mine, the warmth of his arms around my bare chest.

I stood beside the machine, feeding it destemmed grapes, hypnotized by its mechanical hum. After I stopped cranking the crusher, I went back to the house, but as soon as I opened the front door, I could hear the phone ringing. When I saw the 805 area code, I answered it, my pulse racing.

"Andrew," I said, the two syllables of his name twisting my voice with emotion.

"Hi, Mom," he said.

It had only been a month since I'd seen him—one month since David and I drove him to the lime-grassed campus of the Dunn School in Los Olivos, his possessions packed neatly into three suitcases. David had been nervous on the drive—I could tell by the tight grip of his hands on the steering wheel, even as he hummed along to the radio—and I had spent the hours tamping down tears. It felt like we were abandoning Andrew, as much as we tried to sell the virtues of the school to him—the beautiful setting, the top-notch education. *You're such a smart kid*, David had said. *You'll fit right in. It'll be a fresh start.*

In the rearview mirror, I'd noticed Andrew wince. He never should have needed the fresh start. When he was gone, I still felt his hand in mine, the warm weight of it. His nervousness to start school as a kid, the constant tug at my side. The blue pools of his eyes. Later, his voice, froggy with puberty, asking me to check over his homework. He took such care, such pride, in everything he did.

So many times since we'd left him at Dunn, I imagined him dropping my hand and deciding to hate me.

"How are you?" I said carefully. "How is it there? I've been thinking about you, but you said you didn't want us to call right away . . ." Andrew had told us before he left that he wanted to be the one to make contact—that he didn't want us checking in before he had time to settle.

"I didn't," he said. "I'm fine. Classes are good. It feels kind of like home, actually. With the vineyards all around."

My mouth formed a wobbly smile, but a tear slid down my cheek. David was the one who had made all the arrangements for Andrew to attend. He had pulled strings with the friend of a former client in the admissions office, and I had been equally grateful and repulsed by his cool head under pressure, his ability to sweep the mess under the rug. When I learned that the Santa Ynez Valley was literally in the school's backyard, I had felt a warped degree of relief, imagining Andrew looking out of his window and seeing vines climb into the distance, just like I was at home. I pictured us gazing into the same setting, telling myself it would feel like home to him.

David had tried to assuage my doubts about it all. *He's a gifted kid, Bev. He'll do better there. The public school system wasn't serving him well. He has a bright future—we don't want this following him around.* Even when it was just the two of us, he hadn't wanted to talk about the real reason. To him, the lie had become the truth.

"That's great," I said. "We miss you here. I miss you."

"I know," he said. "I do too. But I'm doing well. And it was good to see Dad."

"What?" My heart dropped like a stone.

"Yeah. Dad was here . . . Didn't you know? He said he was on a business trip. He just stopped in for a bit. He told me you wanted to come, too, but couldn't get away."

Everything I couldn't say burned in my throat. David had covered for me, the same way I was covering for him back at home. When I kicked him out, he hadn't gone to be with some mysterious mistress that my imagination had conjured up. He had gone to see our son, the son who might still be under our roof had I gotten my way.

"That's right," I said, choking up. "I love you, Andrew . . ."

"I know, Mom. I love you too. How is Kieran? I miss him."

"Good," I said, nodding as the tears crested my eyes. "He's good. Getting bigger."

"And Josh?" he said.

"Good." I was surprised he'd even asked about Josh. Josh had never once asked about Andrew.

"I'll see you at Thanksgiving," he said. "It'll be good to be home."

After we both hung up, I cried in earnest, sinking down onto the kitchen floor with sobs racking my body. Even though it had been a short conversation—a normal one, with no audible resentment on his end—I wondered if he sensed my immense guilt and understood the real source of it. Andrew was always perceptive, wired into my moods and sensing my shifting energy. Had he been around after I made David leave, he might have asked, *Mom, what's wrong?* and I might have broken down and told him.

The boys had always been opposites, the balance between them uneven since they were born: Andrew had needed a short NICU stay to be hooked up to a CPAP machine because of his weaker lungs, while Josh got to come home with us right away, a separation that filled me with agony. Even before birth, Josh had been the bigger twin, the one siphoning the most nutrients from the placenta. Andrew's growth had been a constant source of worry to the doctors. Almost an entire pound separated them when they were pulled out of me, and the gap had only continued to grow.

But Andrew and Josh were also identical in so many ways. Once Andrew had caught up in size, when they were still babies, I'd had to draw a blue dot on his heel to tell him apart from Josh, but as they aged, there was a softness about Andrew that Josh lacked, less in body than in mind, like he wasn't born with the hard armor the world would require of him—a hard armor that Josh seemed to wear like it weighed nothing.

After I finally forced myself off the ground, washed my face, and put on mascara for a meeting I'd forgotten to cancel, I did what I was good at: I compartmentalized. I stopped thinking about Andrew and all the ways in which I had failed him. When Camille came in the door, her cheeks flushed after a walk with Kieran, I nursed my baby and told Camille that yes, she could bring him to a playgroup, and no, I hadn't thought any more about David or Emilia.

It wasn't until I returned home from the meeting that I saw the flowers on the front porch. They were pale pink, with silky petals. I couldn't identify what kind they were, but Camille would be able to when she returned. I suddenly pictured what would happen when David came home. Camille would leave and go back to Santa Barbara. She'd sell her apartment and spin a globe with her finger to pick the next place she wanted to live, and she'd be gone. The thought was devastating. I loved having her with me, having her feel like part of my immediate family.

I knew Emilia had left the flowers, and that she must be somewhere on the property, ready to surprise me, which made me smile. I brought the flowers inside, placed them in a vase, and set them on the kitchen table. As I stared at them, I made the decision. I would go to Naples with Emilia. The harvest was almost over, and Marcel was more than capable of running the Golden Grape in my stead. Camille could stay and care for Kieran and make sure Josh was okay. Maybe this was my midlife crisis and I would return with the urge out of my system. I'd return and be able to be the wife and mother my family needed me to be. The version of me they deserved.

I padded upstairs to our bedroom, where I began pulling open drawers and taking out perfectly folded clothes. I didn't know any specifics about Naples—its climate, its terrain—but I could picture myself there with Emilia, the two of us exploring vineyards and each other. It wasn't Provence at twenty, but maybe it was our do-over.

My clothes were lined up on the bed: small piles of dresses I hadn't worn in years because I'd deemed them impractical, along with jeans and T-shirts, my usual everyday wardrobe. I would need a new suitcase. The only one I owned was the size of an overnight bag, but I wouldn't be gone longer than a few days, maybe a week. I couldn't be away from Kieran for much longer than that. I'd need to pump breast milk, or could I wean him before I left?

I'd have to let David know I was going, which meant I'd need to answer the phone the next time he called. I would finally need to tell him what was on my mind.

The knock was soft, so soft I barely heard it. I had left the front door unlocked, and footfalls in the foyer heralded her arrival.

"I'm upstairs," I called down, a want unfurling inside me.

I listened as she ascended the stairs, patches of color blooming on my cheeks, humming as I added a sun hat to the pile on the bed.

"Going somewhere?" said the voice at the door, a voice that definitely didn't belong to Emilia. When I whirled around, David stood in the doorway, clad in dark jeans, shoulders broad under one of his trademark flannel shirts. Panic haloed my entire body.

"David," I said in a breathless squeak as my husband entered the room.

"Bev," he said, his dimples pronounced in his cheeks. "I think it's time we talked."

## Fifteen

# *June*

Mill Valley, California
September 2022

**I CALL KYLE AS SOON AS** I'm back in the rental car, FaceTiming him with shaking hands. He picks up on the first ring, his face contorted with worry.

"June, what the hell? Phoebe called me and told me you're in Napa. What's going on?"

I feel the sting of the betrayal, even though I know it wasn't fair to put Phoebe in that position.

"She said you're seeing Josh again. June, he died. He's dead. You need to accept that. What are you doing there? What's going on with you?"

Kyle's voice brims with panic. Kyle, who manages stress better than anyone I've ever met. Hearing him unsettled and knowing it's my doing floods me with shame.

"I'll explain everything," I say. "I should have just been honest, but I didn't want you to think that me coming here had anything to do with me not wanting to marry you, because it doesn't."

"Why would I think that?" he says, pinching the bridge of his nose, his glasses riding up. "I've always been—I've always understood what you were dealing with after what happened with Josh. But I thought you trusted me enough to let me know what you're going through."

I trusted him before, and I need to trust him now. I suck in a breath before launching in, telling him the entire story, starting on the day Phoebe took our engagement photos. When I get to the part about Josh's twin, he cuts in, his eyes narrowing in confusion.

"Wait, a twin brother?"

"I know it's crazy. But that's what his mother told me. After Josh died, I thought I was seeing him everywhere, as you know. It turns out, I was right. Kind of." I squeeze my eyes shut. I feel like I'm viewing the world from underneath a heavy blanket. "He kept so much from me."

Kyle's shoulders rise. "How is it possible he had a twin brother you didn't know about? I don't get it."

"He never wanted me to know Andrew—that's his brother's name. Josh's mom told me they were estranged. And she mentioned an accident but wouldn't say anything else. It sounds like Andrew was at boarding school, but Josh wasn't . . . I think Andrew must have done something terrible for Josh to keep him from me."

"Well, have you seen Andrew? Has he seen you?"

"No, he isn't here, but I went to the winery and met his wife. I asked her where he was, and she told me he was away on business. But I think Andrew was following me in Brooklyn. I found a printout in his home office about my bar."

Kyle rubs his chin with his hand. There's stubble on his face, and he looks exhausted. "You went inside their house, June? With who?"

"I just . . . went in."

"You were snooping around in someone else's house?"

He looks at me like he doesn't know me. He's right: I've gone too far. Again. And all because I still just can't accept the truth—that my husband simply drowned in the ocean. And on top of everything else, I know there's a chance that acting like this could make Kyle call off the wedding, scared that he doesn't know me at all, scared that I'm not ready to get married again.

"I just want to find out why Josh kept his brother from me, if it has anything to do with what happened to him."

"But Josh drowned," he says. "It was an accident."

Logically, I know this is true, and yet, I can't back down. I won't.

"What if Andrew . . ." My voice trails off, because I don't know how to finish the sentence, but Kyle must know how it ends.

Kyle sighs, his lips flattening into a thin line. "I'm worried about you, June."

I blink back tears. I've lied and omitted so much from Kyle over the past week, and I know if I'm not honest from this point on, I'll lose him.

"I just need a bit of time," I say.

"Time for what? What are you going to do?" Kyle asks. "Is our wedding putting too much pressure on you? Are you having some kind of a breakdown?"

"I'm not, I swear—marrying you is all I want," I stammer. And it's true. Kyle took my twisted feelings and unraveled them, dismantling my theory that everyone only gets to have one great love in their lifetime and mine had come and gone. He doesn't believe in soulmates—the idea that there is only one person in the world perfectly suited for someone else. He's more pragmatic than Josh. And I love him for it.

"Okay," Kyle says, but it doesn't sound like he means it. "Look, I'll give you some space, but I think you need to let this go, June. Not for me, but for your own sake."

A tear slips down my cheek. "I just need to find out more about Andrew. About Josh's mom, and what really happened. Then everything will go back to normal. I promise."

"I'll cancel the caterer meeting," he says, looking down.

"No, go." My voice is shrill; I'm terrified that if he cancels the meeting he'll start canceling other things too. "We need to finalize the menu by next week."

His smile is tight, but he nods. "I love you, Junebug."

Relief floods my chest, even though it's short-lived and I know he might hang up and rethink everything. "I love you too." But now that

Kyle knows where I am and what I'm doing, I have renewed courage, a fresh motivation to find the answers I desperately need.

After we say goodbye, I drive down Bev's street and park in front of a random house, then pull out my phone and open Google. I search *Golden Grape Winery*, and predictably, nothing usable comes up.

For my next search, I'm more specific. I type in *Golden Grape Winery Napa + accident*. Again, nothing pertinent comes up, and I blow out a breath, feeling discouraged, weighing my options. I could drive back to Bev's house and demand more answers, but I know better than anyone that a person won't divulge more than they're willing to part with.

Bev had said, *It was an accident. A tragedy.* Maybe she was talking about Josh's death, but I don't think she was—she was remembering something that had happened between her sons.

*Golden Grape Winery Napa death*, I enter into the search bar, and this time, a different result populates: a link to a news article from the *Napa Valley Register* dated November 30, 1999: *St. Helena High student dead after tragic vineyard drowning.*

I click on the link, my heart thudding heavily, my brain stuck on the word *drowning*.

The article is short, and I read it in one breathless gulp.

> The body of Michelle Young, 17, of Oak Knoll, was found in a pond on the property of the Golden Grape Winery in St. Helena following a search party on Saturday. Young was last seen with friends at a gathering on the property Friday night. No foul play is suspected. A funeral and visitation will be held next week for Young, a talented student athlete who attended St. Helena High.

There's a yearbook photo of the girl accompanying the article. She's blonde and blue-eyed, with arched eyebrows.

I don't know how Josh or Andrew knew Michelle Young, but she went to St. Helena High, the same school Josh attended. And she's the same age. They might have been friends—or more than that.

Two accidental drownings.

And one common denominator: Andrew Smith.

# PART III

# Fermentation

Due to the wild yeast on grape skins, the must starts primary fermentation on its own. Yeasts devour the sugar in the grape juice, emitting alcohol and carbon dioxide. The natural must knows to transform on its own, but winemakers often intervene, killing the wild yeasts in favor of adding a particular yeast strain of their choosing, rendering the end result more predictable and, perhaps, easier to digest.

Once set in motion, fermentation does not end until every bit of sugar is spun into alcohol. There is no scientific principle for how and when this is done. Here, as in life, instinct rules.

# One

## *June*

Mill Valley, California

September 2022

THERE AREN'T MANY OTHER RESULTS ONLINE about Michelle Young's death, besides her obituary, with the details of her funeral and visitation. She was survived by her father, Rodney Young, and stepmother, Jennifer Young, along with her mother, Sylvie Mills, and two younger sisters. A memorial from St. Helena High attests to her athleticism, including her aspirations to become a champion tennis player.

I look up each member of her family but can't locate her sisters, Carrie and Darla—maybe they've gotten married, changed their last names. There are too many Jennifer Youngs to take the time to parse out which one could be Michelle's stepmother, and the only Sylvie Mills who might fit the description is apparently retired and living in Florida, according to a Facebook profile photo of a blonde woman on a beach in a sun hat.

Luckily, *Rodney Young Napa* churns up a valid result. He's a winemaker in Napa, or at least he was, at Younger Brothers Winery in Oak Knoll. I click through the photos on the winery's website. Rodney's picture is on the About Us page, beside another, slightly taller, gray-haired man. Rodney and Richard, who must be the two brothers behind the winery name. The other photos show a quaint, well-maintained vineyard. *Like our family, our wines have integrity and warmth, and are best enjoyed in the company of loved ones*, the website says.

I put my phone on my lap, my eyes darting to the car windows, where sunlight streams in. I'm alone on Bev's street—there's nobody around, nothing surrounding me except perfectly manicured houses and gardens, and yet, I can't shake the suspicion that I'm being watched. That somebody other than Bev knows I'm here.

I'm already so close to Napa. I could go back, make a stop at Younger Brothers and see if Rodney is there. Based on the website's photo, he looks to be in his late sixties, around the same age as my parents. Even if he still works on-site and I find him, what would I possibly say? *I need to know more about your daughter, because I think my husband died the same way she did, and neither of them was an accident.*

I lower my forehead to the leather steering wheel, my frustration mounting. The more I think about it, the more threatened I feel by Andrew Smith. He hasn't done anything to me—*yet*—but he has looked me up, knows where I live, and was obviously in Brooklyn to find me. But what he wants with me, I have no idea. He's estranged from Josh for a reason—he must have done something terrible, which could explain why he was sent to boarding school. Is it possible Andrew was involved in Michelle's death? And if that's the case, what if he also did something to Josh?

I navigate back to the first article about Michelle and zoom in on her photo, wishing she could speak and tell me her truth. Her lips are curved mysteriously, like she's holding in a secret. *What happened to you?* I silently plead.

When I scroll to the bottom of the page, I realize there's something I missed the first time around: a comments section, which I click to expand. Multiple comments populate, ranging from mournful to rage fueled.

**RIP Michelle, a beautiful soul lost too young.**

What were the parents doing while a girl drowned on their property?

I'm feeling sick about this

The tragedy of young people drinking without any parental supervision. This could have been prevented.

Her boyfriend is the one who killed her. Josh Kelly. Why am I the only one who knows he pushed her in, probably held her head under? He was the last one who saw her alive. I hope he rots in hell.

The last comment makes me break into a full-body chill. *That's impossible*, my brain screams, because I know Josh. I only knew him for six months, but I *knew* him. There wasn't a mean bone in his body, and even reading those words feels like a betrayal.

My hand tightens around the phone. I'm nauseated, and momentarily, I'm afraid I'll throw up.

Maybe Andrew wrote the comment, to avert the suspicion from himself?

I hover over the words, wanting more information about the person who wrote them. But the commenter is anonymous. Bev had been reluctant to part with any specific details. She could have told me about Michelle's death herself—surely she knows all about it, having lived at the winery when it happened. Was she protecting Andrew, or Josh, or both?

My brain circles around an explanation, but all I can come up with is that while this person did not really know Josh, they definitely cared about Michelle.

My back straightens against the seat as I type a name into my GPS: *Younger Brothers Winery*. Michelle's father might not even be there, and if he is, he might not want to talk.

But if the comment on that article proves anything, it's that there was someone out there who wanted Josh dead.

# Two

## *Bev*

St. Helena, Napa County, California
September 1999

**MY HUSBAND REMAINED STATIONED** in the doorway, his face both intensely familiar and suddenly alien, the tiny bags ringing both eyes, the cleft in his chin. My limbs refused to obey my brain, which didn't know what to command them to do anyway.

"David," I repeated, the only thing I could think to say.

"Are you leaving?" he asked, gesturing to the clothes on the bed.

"I was thinking about taking a trip," I stammered. "Where were you?"

"You asked me to leave," he said, his hands in his pockets, like he wasn't sure what to do with them. "So I went. I checked in on Andrew, then I stayed at a little hotel in Petaluma, just doing a lot of thinking. I tried calling you, but you probably know that. I wanted to give you space, but I couldn't stay away forever."

Seeing him standing in front of me made my resolve weaken, the memories of our marriage flooding back. He looked so apologetic, like he'd give anything for a second chance.

"What were you thinking about?" I asked, sitting on the side of the bed. He pulled the door closed and slowly stepped across the carpet, then took a seat on the opposite edge, far enough away that we weren't even close to touching.

"Us. Me. The things I've done. The way I've treated you." He spread out his hands—big hands, palms clean, not burnished with grape stains like they normally were this time of year. "I owe you an apology. My . . . indiscretion, it was bad enough. But the way I told you made it even worse. This isn't who I am. How did we get here, Bev?"

"I don't know," I managed, the fight sucked out of me, heavy sadness in its place. I'd imagined confronting David, but now with him next to me, I couldn't think of a single thing to say.

"I don't want to dwell on the past," he said. "We've spent enough time there. The night you asked me to leave . . . I tried to blame you. And that was just as bad as what I'd done. None of it was your fault. I'm sorry for everything, Bev. This isn't on you."

I stared at the carpet. It was exactly what I wished he would have said that night.

"I don't know if there's still a chance," he said, his voice small. "I just want us to love each other the way we used to."

My eyes teared up, but I couldn't seem to find my voice. How could I explain that I felt forked into two, between the path I'd traveled and the one I hadn't?

"You cheated on me," I settled on instead.

David's eyes were glassy. "It only happened once, and I swear that to you. I take full accountability that I fucked this up. If you need more time, I understand. But I just need to know—is there a chance?"

I weighed both scenarios in my head. If I left David, would Emilia be there for me? And would that be enough? Josh and Andrew would question whether their childhood had been a lie, and Kieran would grow up shuttled between two households, never remembering a version of his parents happy together.

David inched closer on the bed, gently moving my piles of clothes out of his way. His fingers tentatively stippled the skin on my arm. For better or worse, David knew me. We'd built a life together. We'd promised, in our vows, that we'd love each other until death do us part. And he

was taking accountability, asking for a second chance. His bald vulnerability was the most disarming thing of all.

"I should have listened to you," he said. "About Andrew. I went to see
him, and he seems . . . different. I really do think it's good for him, being
at Dunn, but maybe you were right about what happened . . ."

"It wasn't about being right," I said. "It was that you wanted to pretend
the incident with Abby never happened. You changed the story so that we
came across better. You didn't even consider that there was more to it."

"I just wanted to protect our family," he said quietly. "That's all I've
ever wanted to do. Maybe I didn't handle things perfectly, but I was
doing the best I could. I love you and the boys more than anything, Bev."

When he kissed the knuckles on my hand, I didn't stop him. When he
tilted my face toward his, I felt myself sucked into the familiarity of his
touch. I let him kiss me, my mouth responding on autopilot. I clamped
my eyes shut and retreated into my memories as David's lips trailed down
my neck.

The sound of footfalls in the hallway made me open my eyes. The
door had been pushed open, and Emilia was standing half in, half out, her
smile falling. I pulled away from David.

"Emilia," we both said at the same time, my voice remorseful and
David's confused.

The betrayal on Emilia's face was gutting, the way her soft features
seemed to harden. She shifted from one foot to the other.

"The door was open, and Marcel said you were here . . ." Emilia's voice
trailed off. I wasn't sure who she was addressing, me or David. "I'll go, and
give you some privacy. We can talk later."

"I just returned from my business trip," David said. "I'm very behind
on calls and emails, so I apologize . . . If you give me a few minutes, we
can meet in the tasting room."

"It's okay. I was just stopping by . . . I'll call you another time." Emilia
was already turning to go, and she didn't look back. Once she was gone,
I found my voice again.

"I met with her while you were away. I didn't even know you two
were still in touch."

"Well, I'd seen her at some events over the years . . . She mentioned in San Francisco a few months back that she'd love to stop by. I'm glad you met with her. How did it go?"

My mouth was dry. I compressed my time with Emilia—our beautiful, endless days—into the most boring answer. "It was good. She's interested."

"That's great," David said. "I forgot I was supposed to be seeing her—after I left, it was like my mind went blank. But you used to know her too. It must have been nice to catch up with an old friend."

I felt a pressure behind my eyes. I was going to cry.

David noticed. "What? Did something happen?"

I turned my sadness into anger, because I didn't want David to guess at the real truth. "Who was she? The woman you cheated on me with? Who was worth wrecking our marriage for?"

He rubbed his temples. "Do you really need to know? Wouldn't it just hurt more?"

"Tell me," I said.

David paused, hissing a breath through his teeth. I was afraid of what he was going to say, but suddenly desperate to hear it.

"Her name was Ashley. I don't know her last name. She was there, at the restaurant in Sonoma . . . sitting alone at the bar. Then the waiter brought me a glass of chardonnay, and apparently she'd sent it to me. I went over to say thank you, and we got to talking, and . . . I went home with her."

I nodded. I could picture the scene: David in a suit, the sharp way he dressed to meet with clients, so formal and handsome. Ashley, younger than me with ample cleavage, hanging on his every word.

"I was lonely," David said. "And I made the biggest mistake of my life."

For some reason, hearing the actual details of the story made it more digestible. Ashley was no longer a threat to our marriage. She was something David had needed to get out of his system. He had physically cheated on me, but what I had been doing all week with Emilia was so much worse. Though I never would have done it had David not stepped out first.

Maybe in a sick way, I was glad he had.

"Say something, Bev," David said, his voice pleading. "Do you hate me?"

I stood up and started walking toward the door, my nails biting into my palms.

"Where are you going?" David asked.

"I need to be alone," I said. I waited for him to argue, to follow me anyway, to try to put a Band-Aid on this, like he did with everything else. But maybe he really had changed, because he let me go.

I caught up to Emilia in the parking lot, just as she was getting into her rental car. "Wait," I yelled, jogging toward her. She stopped, the sun bouncing off the blonde crown of her head, and turned around, her eyes hidden behind oversize sunglasses.

"I was going to tell you that I wanted to go to Naples," I said. "I was packing. That's what I was doing in my room. I had no idea David was going to show up."

"But you knew he was going to come home eventually," she said. I saw my reflection in her lenses, my face elongated and distorted, my hair a mess. "What did you tell him?"

"That we had a meeting," I said.

She was silent, but a flicker of hurt spread across her face. An invisible electric fence had suddenly sprung up between us. I was choosing David all over again.

"I need to go," she said. "Goodbye, Bev." She gave me a small, sad smile and got into her car, and I watched her drive away, unsure if I'd ever see her again. *Don't go*, I silently screamed, wanting to run after the car and wave her down. But I remained statue still, my eyes burning with dust.

I wandered the vineyard, my brain racing with things unsaid. Hours ago, I'd been considering what my life would look like without David. I'd made him the villain in all of this, the one who'd betrayed our marriage. But I had been the one in the wrong, and I had just driven Emilia away for the second time because of my inability to admit what I really wanted.

By the time I made my way back to the house, David was chopping vegetables for a salad, Camille was feeding Kieran in his high chair, and

Josh was seated at the table, laughing at something his father had said. We were all one perfect happy family, minus Andrew's empty chair. We were a family who moved on. Just like we'd moved on after Abby. It would be so easy to go back to normal, to live in a world where David's affair and mine had never happened.

# Three

# June

Oak Knoll, Napa County, California

September 2022

**YOUNGER BROTHERS WINERY IS** located in Napa's Oak Knoll district at the southern end of the valley, an area known for its ideal growing conditions, where the temperature is regulated by the breezes from the bay. It's noticeably cooler here than it was when I left St. Helena. This is part of the beauty of Napa: the pockets of space that look so similar in photos but feel so different in person. Here, the growing season is longer and more leisurely.

I formulated my plan on the drive here, what I'll say if I end up seeing Rodney Young. I don't know whether he was the anonymous commenter, but in case he is, I can't reveal that I'm Josh's widow, or else he might ask me to leave. He needs to think I'm on his side and that I have no personal connection to Josh. Michelle and I would have been the same age, had she lived, and I doubt Rodney remembers every high school friend she had over the years. I'll pretend to be one of them, dropping by to pay my respects.

But as much as it makes sense in my head, my heart is hammering when I walk into the tasting room, which is small and dark, a musty heaviness in the air. I'm greeted by a woman around the same age as me, her dark hair pulled into a ponytail.

"How can I help you?" she says. She looks eager to have a customer: I'm the only person in here.

"I'm actually looking for someone," I say, trying to arrange my face into a casual expression. "Rodney Young? I used to know his daughter."

The woman's smile falls slightly. "Rodney's usually at the house. He's probably over there now . . . Is he expecting you?"

"Not exactly," I say. "But I was in the area and just wanted to say hi."

She shrugs, and for a panicked moment, I'm afraid she's going to tell me I should leave. Luckily, her attention is diverted by an older couple who walk in behind me, allowing me to slip out without further questions.

As soon as I leave the tasting room, I realize I have no idea where the house she mentioned is. But as I squint into the weakening sun, I see a small house at the southwest corner of the property, not big and beautiful like Sadie's, but older and run-down. The brickwork appears to be crumbling, parched ivy creeping up the sides.

I head toward it without allowing myself to consider how irresponsible this is. The only thing I know about Rodney Young is that he might have had a vendetta against the man I was supposed to spend the rest of my life with.

I knock at the door, tension gathering in my chest. It takes all my concentration to breathe normally. Nobody answers. Rodney isn't here, and I can't just lurk around, waiting for him to return.

But just as I turn to leave, the door opens, and Rodney Young stands before me. His forehead is creased with frown lines, his mouth is pulled into a scowl, and his bushy silver eyebrows are pointed downward, like he has spent most of his life in a perpetual grimace. But he's definitely the man from the website, minus the smile and affable grandfatherly demeanor.

"Yes?" he says, his voice sharp. "Can I help you?"

I speak quickly, hoping my excuse sounds less flimsy than it does in my head. "Mr. Young? I'm not sure you remember me, but I was a friend of Michelle's at St. Helena High, and I was in the area and wanted to stop by . . . just to say hi. It's been a really long time, but it would have felt strange leaving Napa without coming here."

He studies me with small, dark eyes. *He doesn't believe me*, I think, my fear spiking. It takes so long for him to speak that I wonder if I should just turn and leave.

"You look a bit familiar," he finally says. "I guess it's been so long."

"Yeah," I say, awkwardly stepping from foot to foot. "I'm sorry, if you're busy, I can—"

"You can come in, if you want," he says, cutting me off. "But you'll have to excuse the mess. It's just me here, and I don't keep great care of the place."

I nod, holding my breath in my chest, and follow him into the house. I pull out my phone and type a quick message to Kyle. *I'm at Younger Brothers Winery, meeting with Michelle's father. I'll text you when I'm done here.* I send the message, a last-minute contingency plan in case this goes awry.

I look up, taking in the framed pictures lining the walls of the hall-way. They're of Michelle and two other blonde girls who must be her sisters.

"Have a seat," Rodney says, gesturing to a brown leather sofa. "I'm not used to having company anymore. My brother sold his share of the winery back in '08, and that's the same year my wife left, so it's just me here now."

I feel like I should say *I'm sorry*, but I'm not sure what I'd be apologizing for. I sit down, and he takes a seat in an adjacent leather chair with overstuffed arms.

"Can I get you anything?" he says. "Coffee, tea?"

I shake my head. "No. I just wanted to come by—being here in Napa brought up memories of Michelle. I've thought about her a lot over the years."

He nods, his mouth moving like he's rolling marbles in his cheeks.

"You went to school with her?" he finally says.

"Yes. When she died—I'd never lost anyone close to me before." I chan-nel the way I felt after Josh died, the way it felt like I was drowning too.

There's something manic in his eyes, a rage that belies his frail stature. He must be around the same age as my own parents, but he looks so much older, as if his loss had aged him.

"She didn't just die," he says, and my chest tightens. He must register my confused expression, because he continues to speak. "She was murdered. Everyone knows that."

I think about the comment on the article. "Her boyfriend was always a bit suspicious to us. Josh." I feel guilty even using his name in this context, but I need Rodney to reveal more.

Rodney takes the bait. "Yes. Thought he had us fooled, always showing up with flowers and gifts. I knew what he was doing."

It sounds like my Josh he's describing, who never showed up empty-handed. I wait for Rodney to share more, but he doesn't. He taps his fingers on the arm of his chair. I need to work harder to get him to talk.

"He moved too fast," I say, drawing upon the comments that the people in my life had made back when we were together. "He came on so strong. We tried talking to her about it, but she wouldn't listen. She was in love."

I can tell this strikes a nerve with Rodney. His chin juts into a sharp nod. "She wouldn't listen to me either. Or any of us. She was skipping out on tennis to be with him—talking about going to college together. She changed when she met him."

"She did," I say. A silence falls between us. I don't know how to keep the conversation going, or what else to say without seeming suspicious. "Do you think—do you think she wanted to break up with him, and he did something to her?"

"I know in my bones that he did it. Michelle told me she was staying at her mom's house the night she died—and told Sylvie she was staying with me. I called around to her friends the next day when she never made it home, and found out about the party at the winery. The police interviewed a bunch of the kids who'd been there, and they all said the same thing. That Michelle and Josh had been fighting, and he was the last person to see her alive. Were you there that night?"

I cough into my hand and have trouble speaking for a moment.

"Yes," I say, venturing further out on my limb. "I was there. I saw that fight too."

"I heard her on the phone with him once—she was begging him to listen to her. Whatever he was saying back, I'd never heard her so upset. Then later on, the phone rang, and I picked it up. He started talking before he knew it was me and not her. He said, 'You only go to that camp because there's a guy who wants to fuck you.' I unloaded on him. Told him not to come near Michelle again. And he responded, so calmly, 'We'll see about that.'"

Even if I wanted to reply, I don't have the words. It wasn't true—Josh wasn't like that. Not my Josh. But I feign understanding, forcing myself to nod along.

"Michelle was a happy person," Rodney continues. "Until she met him. He didn't listen when I told him not to see my daughter again. The night of that party, he snapped. My daughter didn't drown in some freak accident. She was murdered."

My skin breaks into a chill. The words he's saying about Josh, my gentle, loving husband—I don't want to hear them. I certainly don't believe them.

When I speak, my voice shakes against my will. "I heard he died. Josh."

This time, Rodney gives me his first smile since I arrived, an expression that looks foreign on his face. "I heard that too. A drowning. Proof that karma exists in the world. That's the only reason I sleep at night, knowing he's not out there anymore doing the same thing to someone else's daughter."

My throat is dry. Even though I want to find out who killed Josh, I'm not ready to be alone in a house with the man who might have done it—a man with the ultimate motive. "You think . . . he would have done it again."

"I know it. People like that, they have a pattern. They don't stop. The whole family is crazy, if you ask me. My ex—Michelle's stepmother—she and I were friends with the Kellys. But Bev never even looked me in the eye after all that. I ran into her once, years later—some festival near Mill Valley. She acted like she had no idea who I was. The apple doesn't fall far from the tree."

Now, it's Bev's voice I hear in my head, the conversation she and Josh had in the kitchen. And Bev, earlier today, saying that bad things sometimes happened with no explanation. Almost like she was trying to convince herself.

"I never stopped following Josh's life," Rodney continues. "I heard he got married, right before he died."

"Oh?" I manage, shifting on the sofa. My palms are damp, and my chest is tight. I want to stand up and leave—to be anywhere but here. Rodney is looking at me differently, as though he sees right through me. He just admitted to following Josh. If he saw his social media, he would have seen my face. Did he follow Josh to the beach the day he died?

"The ocean wasn't on his side," Rodney says. "I guess the water knew the truth."

I go to stand up, knowing I need to get out of here as quickly as possible. There are other things I could ask Rodney—details about the relationship between Josh and Michelle, maybe—but right now, my fear outweighs my desire to know more. "I really should get going—I just wanted to pay my respects."

Rodney doesn't stand. He's still, like he has retreated into some dark place and is now suspended there. I wipe my hands on my jeans and head for the front door.

"I know who you are," he calls after me, sending a shivery blast down my spine.

I turn around when I'm at the door, even as my adrenaline urges me to get out, my heart throbbing hard enough to crack my rib cage. I ask the only question Rodney can answer honestly. "Were you the one who killed him?"

"No," he growls. "I would have loved to. But someone must have beat me to it." He turns to face me, still seated in his chair. "Count yourself lucky. He would have destroyed you the same way he did Michelle."

There's nothing else for Rodney and me to say to each other. With those parting words, I bolt out the door. I break into a run when I'm out-side, unable to get a deep breath of air. When I'm back at the rental car, I pull my phone out of my purse to text Kyle and let him know I'm okay, even though I don't feel okay at all. There's a missed call from him, and a text from half an hour ago.

> I know I said I'd give you space, but I'm really worried, June. I'm en route to JFK right now. I'll be in Napa tonight.

*I love you*, I write back with a gush of relief. His text doesn't sound angry, and he's getting on a plane, for me. Because he loves and trusts me.

As I nose out of the parking lot and head toward the airport to wait for Kyle, I weigh my options. I've come this far, and now I've dragged my fiancé into this mess. In a way, I have nothing left to lose. I could try to go back to Bev's house and confront her again, but what would I say? That I've been to see Rodney Young, and he thinks Josh was a murderer? That I know she's hiding something for one of her sons? If she's been covering something up for decades, she isn't going to let her guard down now, just because I'm asking nicely.

And as much as I try to tamp down my unease, there are the things Rodney said about Josh. He sounded so certain when he spoke about Josh's character—but it was like he was talking about a completely dif-ferent person from the man I married. Over the past handful of hours, I've found out that Josh lied to me—about his brother, about his dead ex-girlfriend. Was he afraid I'd love him less if I knew his dysfunctional family history? Or did other people see something in Josh that I didn't?

I blow out a breath. If Rodney didn't kill Josh, somebody else did. Was it someone who was there the night of the party—someone else with ties to Michelle?

My mind circles around the other obvious suspect: Andrew. Rod-ney said the kids at the party saw Josh and Michelle together before she died, but what if it wasn't Josh they saw at all? No matter what Rodney believes, Josh wasn't capable of murder. But I know nothing about his identical twin brother.

Still—how can I get to Andrew if I can't find him?

The answer comes to me in a flash. There's one person I need to talk to—the same person I was too afraid to question before. Someone who has known Andrew for decades and might have been at the party when Michelle died. Andrew isn't around to look me in the eye and tell me what happened between him and his brother, but someone else is.

His wife.

## Four

St. Helena, Napa County, California
September 1999

**THE MOST DISCONCERTING PART** of David being back was the way he acted like he'd never left. He had only been home for a couple days, but already he woke up at five in the morning. without the help of an alarm clock, and went straight into the winery to work. He ran tours, talked to guests, and tended to the red-wine grapes on the vines like babies.

Maybe I shouldn't have been surprised. I already knew David was skilled at shrugging off the messy truth. As far back as I could remember, he'd always greeted each new day with a smile and a good mood, any discontent dissolved overnight. His optimism had been contagious. But now he was forcing it, and I couldn't fathom how he was capable.

"Everything is the same as I left it," he said. He patted me on the back, then his hand began massaging my shoulder blades gently. "You did a great job while I was away." We were both skirting the real questions. Whether I could forgive him, and whether we had a future.

I almost wanted to tell him the truth: that I'd largely left the operations of the vineyard to Marcel and our other employees, trusting them to do what David rarely did. That I'd left Kieran largely to Camille. It was their work he was praising. But if I had told him that, I would have needed to explain where I had been.

Everything was the same upon his return, except me. David didn't know how being with Emilia had altered me. Emilia, who was flying to Naples this week.

But David watched me so closely, so tenderly, that it was impossible to get away to see her. He kept asking me if I was okay.

"We should plan a trip to visit Andrew," David said as we stood in the kitchen three days after his return, which was also the day of Emilia's departure. He grabbed a glass and poured himself water from the tap. "It really seems like he's doing well there."

"Sure," I said, willing him to go deeper, to say out loud the real reason Andrew was there, instead of pretending, even when it was just the two of us.

"We could bring the whole family," David said. "Make a road trip of it, stay at a hotel."

"No." My chin snapped up.

"The boys have to talk at some point," David said, putting down his empty glass and wiping his lips. "They're not going to ignore each other forever. Josh forgives Andrew."

"He actually said that? Josh said that?"

David nodded. "He said everybody makes mistakes."

David never listened to my suspicions about what happened. The only person who believed Andrew was me, and even my own conviction had wavered. *You don't know Josh like I do,* Andrew had said after we'd been called into a meeting with the principal at St. Helena. David had gently suggested that Andrew was jealous of his brother—but I worried he was afraid of his brother, and *I* was afraid of what would happen if they both remained under our roof.

*What about Abby?* I'd said, thinking of the poor girl whose life had been upended, imagining myself in her shoes.

*It's unfortunate, Bev. I feel for the girl, but she's not our daughter. We need to protect our sons.*

And we did, at the expense of someone else's daughter. I thought of

Abby often: how one photo had changed the trajectory of her life. One photo, purposely revealed by one of my sons. I had been a teenage girl once. Everything had felt like the end of the world. The smallest embarrassment at school—a trip on the stairs, food in my teeth, a tampon that fell out of my bag—had made me spiral into self-loathing. Where would I be now, had I been exposed back then the way Abby was?

*You know her so well.* Had my words somehow reminded Josh of the photo in his possession? That he did, indeed, know Abby so well, in body and in mind?

I wondered if he'd had any idea that Abby would fight for her own reputation. As humiliated as she'd been, she had attempted to put the blame where it belonged: on the person who'd betrayed her. But nobody listened. Her friends distanced themselves, like her scandal was contagious. Her parents were angry and mortified, but when they found her in the bathroom with a bloody line seaming her forearm, they realized how close they were to losing her and how badly she needed their protection. To them, home school was a way to save their daughter's life.

So many times, I had kept myself awake at night, picturing Abby hovering over the sink with a razor blade, crimson circling the drain. The tears in her eyes. The chest-bursting frustration that nobody would listen to her. Had she thought of Josh when she pressed down, imagining what he would do if she was gone? Had she thought of Andrew? Or had she thought of me, the woman who had helped to make her the sacrificial lamb for her sons' reputations?

"He'll be home for Thanksgiving anyway," I said to David now. Andrew would be home for a full week, which made me nervous. Would he and Josh continue to ignore each other, or would they fight? Both options felt equally toxic.

I tensed as I waited for David's rebuttal, but he didn't argue with me. He kissed my forehead. "I'm going to look at the cabernet grapes," he said instead, shrugging into a hooded sweatshirt. "Maybe do some leafing and suckering."

"I think it's too early," I said.

"You might be right—we'll see. I'm going to stop by the winery after and make some calls. Maybe you can go into town and pick up something for dinner? Something nice, for just the two of us."

"Technically, the three of us—Camille will be here too," I said.

David pursed his lips. "Actually, when I saw her this morning, she said she was visiting some friends tonight." He smiled. "Just like Camille, making friends everywhere she goes."

I tried to tamp down my disappointment. Camille was the perfect barrier between me and David, the third party mediating our stony silences. I had come to rely on my sister in so many ways. It was she, more than David, who I truly believed would do anything for me.

In suggesting I go into town, David had given me the excuse I was looking for. I needed to see Emilia before she left and make things right between us, and I hoped I wasn't too late. I bundled Kieran into his car seat and fastened it into the Escalade.

When I arrived at the Blossom, I lifted Kieran out of his car seat, where he was sleeping peacefully, his dark lashes casting shadows on his pale cheeks. He cried in frustration, and I jiggled him in an attempt to calm him down as I entered the lobby and walked up the stairs to Emilia's room. I knocked on the door but nobody answered; I banged again, hard enough to hurt my fist. She wasn't there, and fear filled my chest as I returned to the lobby.

"I'm looking for Emilia Rosser," I told the young woman behind the desk. "Can you tell me if she checked out yet?"

She scanned the computer in front of her. "Um, I'm not able to give information about our guests . . . you can always have a seat and wait, though?"

I shook my head. "I can't wait." Kieran started to wail in earnest, sharp peals that reddened his cheeks. People in the lobby turned to stare.

"She can't be gone," I said through gritted teeth. I turned back to the blank-faced clerk. "She needs to be here."

I retreated outside with Kieran, our tears falling in tandem. Emilia was gone, and I doubted I'd ever see her again. The feelings rising inside me were becoming a full-fledged panic attack, one that stole my breath as I attempted to clamp Kieran back into his car seat.

"Bev?"

I whipped around at the familiar voice.

Emilia was behind me, ethereal in a white sundress, her lips berry red. "What are you doing here?"

I leaned against the car door, relief making my knees weak. "I don't want you to go. I hate how we left things the other day, and—I'm sorry. I had no idea David was just going to show up."

Emilia's gaze was resigned. "We both knew he was going to come back eventually. It's not like he was going to disappear off the face of the earth. And you wouldn't want him to, anyway."

"That would make things a lot easier, though," I joked, even as my eyes filled with tears.

"That's your problem," Emilia said. "It always was. You hate making decisions. You're afraid to say what you're really thinking."

My first instinct was to defend myself, but I knew she was right. "I just didn't know . . . that it would all be so final. That one thing would lead to another, and now here I am. With the perfect life, but it doesn't feel perfect anymore. My kids hate each other, and they hate me, and I would hate me too."

Emilia's face softened. "They don't hate you. And I don't fault you. I remember David back in college. He's a good guy, and he took great care of you."

"It's true." My voice broke. "I tried so hard not to turn into my parents, to be a truly happy family. But I think I went too far in the other direction, especially with my kids. I never said no to them. I didn't discipline them, and I ignored bad behavior so many times to keep the peace when they fought. David liked to say 'Boys will be boys' and told me they'd resolve things on their own. Did David tell you about Andrew? About why he's at boarding school?"

"He mentioned boarding school," Emilia mumbled. "He just said Andrew was gifted."

I hated hearing the lie secondhand, even though it was the same lie I'd told others. I didn't want to perpetuate that lie with Emilia.

"It wasn't because he's gifted. It's because something happened with Josh's girlfriend, and David wanted to sweep it under the rug. I didn't fight for Andrew." But I hated fighting. It had taken me most of my life to realize that silence could be just as lethal.

"I can't tell you what to do," Emilia said. "I'm not in your shoes. I don't have kids to think about. I'm not going to pretend to understand what that's like as a mother." She let Kieran grab her finger, and his cries finally relented. "I've thought about you so often over the years, and I'm not going to forget this time we got to have."

She didn't need to say anything else. I knew this was goodbye, and I wasn't ready for it. She turned my palms face up and circled the wine stains with her thumbs.

I wanted to say more—to tell her I should have chosen her all those years ago—but Kieran started to wail again, a full-throttled cry, and I realized maybe it wasn't true anyway. If I'd chosen her, I wouldn't have my beautiful boys, my life on the vineyard.

"I should go," Emilia said. "I have to get ready for my flight."

"I know. I just—I'm going to miss you."

She kissed my cheek, her lips soft and yielding. "Maybe our paths will cross again, Bev Jamieson." I watched the swinging hem of her dress as she strode toward the stone stairs leading to her room—the room where we had shared so much.

I wasn't ready to go home. I didn't want David to smell Emilia on me; I felt guilty when I thought about how earnest he had been since returning home. He was willing to put in the work, to admit he had been wrong.

I stopped at the grocery store, since I was supposed to be picking up something for dinner. I would make David's favorite meal—chicken cacciatore, braised in a sauce like the one my mother used to make, with peppers and onions and tomatoes and herbs, adding a splash of our own cabernet. It would be a peace offering. As I pushed the cart through the store, glassy-eyed and numb, I vacillated between picking up the items I needed and wanting to abandon the cart in the middle of the aisle to chase after Emilia. Kieran kicked his chubby legs; he was overjoyed to be doing something as simple as riding in a cart pushed by his mother. His grin, studded with four tiny teeth, anchored me.

As I entered the bakery section—I'd get some of the focaccia bread David liked, the kind adorned with olives—I saw a familiar figure, short and wiry. It was too late to retreat. I didn't want to see Rodney Young, but he looked up and saw me. I managed a smile, which he didn't bother returning.

"Hi, Rodney," I said, panic starting to pluck a string in my gut. He had always been friendly and effusive; we'd been in his home, had played cards at his kitchen table as blues music sounded from his CD player. He'd insisted on refilling our wineglasses, his cheeks ruddy and forehead shiny, persuading us to stay a little longer. But now, he was unsmiling and looked like he wanted nothing to do with me. Had he seen me and Emilia that day at his winery? Had Michelle mentioned something?

"Bev," he said, his voice curt.

"Good to see you," I said, waiting for his excuse for being so brusque—he was in a hurry; he'd had a bad day. But he spun on his heel, like he was getting ready to leave, a bag of hamburger buns swinging from his hand, before turning back to face me.

"I've always liked you and David," he said, and I braced myself for it, *He knows*. He knew about me and Emilia. He would tell David, and everything would be ruined. Would that be a good thing? Would I only be spurred to action if I lost everything?

But his next words surprised me.

"I hate to say this, but I don't want Josh around Michelle anymore."

I blinked, not expecting to hear that. I couldn't find the right words, so I goggled at him in stunned silence. "What—why?"

His expression darkened. "I just don't want your son around my daughter, and I'll leave it at that."

I watched him stride out of the store. Kieran chewed on the strap of my purse, his drool coating the leather. My cheeks flushed from the confrontation.

When I arrived home, I didn't mention it to David. We already had enough to deal with. And Camille was right: Josh was almost an adult. If he and Michelle were going through a rough patch, they would either fix it or break up.

For everyone's sake, I hoped for the latter.

# Five

# *June*

St. Helena, Napa County, California
September 2022

**WHEN I RETURN TO** the Backyard, the windows of Andrew and Sadie's house are lit up, glowing a buttery yellow. The evening chill has set in, so I wrap my denim jacket tighter around myself. I raise my hand to knock, but the door swings open before I can even make contact, leaving my fist suspended in midair.

"June, right?" Sadie says. Her hair is in a low bun, and there are red stains on her T-shirt, on her hands. *Blood*, I think, but I know it must be grape residue from the crushing and fermentation. "Is everything okay with your stay? Is something wrong?"

"No, it's all fine." In the turbulence of today, I almost forgot I'd booked a two-night stay at the Backyard; my room key was still in my purse. "Look, I'm sorry to just show up like this, but I was hoping we could talk. Could I come in for a minute?"

A line appears between Sadie's eyebrows, but she recovers quickly, her lips turning up in a polite smile. "Okay—I just put my youngest down for the night, and the house is a total mess, but . . . yes, come on in." There's a hesitation in her voice, like she's hoping I'll change my mind.

I follow her into the foyer and down the hall toward the kitchen, my eyes darting to the family photos on the walls, the ones that stunned me into disbelief mere hours ago. "You have a beautiful home," I say.

"Thanks." She sounds a bit strained, and I wonder if she knows I've been here before. "Please, take a seat." She gestures to the kitchen table. "I'm so discombobulated; this whole day just got away from me. Can I offer you a glass of wine? I sure could use a drink."

"I'd like that, thank you."

She reaches up to open a white cupboard above the countertop and retrieves two wineglasses. "We made a small batch last year with these mondeuse grapes as a kind of experiment. They're native to France and aren't grown here, but every so often, I get it in my head to try something new. I've been waiting to open this bottle." She faces me, uncorks the dark bottle, and pours us each a glass, then carries them over to the table. The wine is the color of dark cherries.

"Cheers," Sadie says, and we each sniff and swirl the wine in our glasses in tandem. I hold the first sip in the back of my throat like a breath. It's peppery and aromatic, a throaty blend of savory and sweet.

"It's delicious," I say.

"And you know wine," she says. "You own a natural wine bar. I looked you up."

"That's right. I—did you know who I was yesterday when we met?"

"I recognized you," she says, taking another small sip. "I couldn't figure out from where, until I realized you were Josh's wife, and I saw you at the funeral. I'm so sorry about Josh. It's terrible, what happened."

I sip my wine, feeling it go directly to my head. The woman in the trench coat, turning away. It had been Sadie. "Yes. It really was."

A silence hangs between us, hard and heavy.

She holds her wineglass under the light. "The funny thing is, I didn't even drink wine until Andrew introduced me to it after we inherited this place. His dad was trying to sell it for the longest time, but nobody wanted to buy, so Andrew came to him and told him he wanted to take over. I think David was relieved, honestly. From what Andrew told me, David loved this land and wanted it to stay in the family."

"I remembered your face from the funeral," I say. "But I didn't know Josh had a twin brother. I saw Andrew's photo on your website, and I thought—" It's almost too ridiculous to say out loud what I actually thought. That my husband had come back from the dead. That he was never dead in the first place.

Sadie's face softens, her eyes deep with empathy. "God, I'm so sorry. I can't imagine how awful that must have been. I know how I felt when I found out . . . No wonder you were looking for Andrew."

"You didn't say anything to me. At the funeral."

Sadie shakes her head. "I wasn't even supposed to be there. Andrew wouldn't go. He completely shut down. I'd only just found out Josh existed . . . I felt like if I couldn't convince Andrew to go, I at least needed to be there, to show that we cared. But I couldn't bring myself to say anything to you. I thought it was best I didn't. You were . . ."

She doesn't have to say the rest. I was hysterical. I was a wreck. What would I have said, if she had introduced herself, if she'd paid her condolences? If I'd found out about Andrew ten years ago?

"Anyway," Sadie continues, "when you showed up here and I realized who you were, I should have said something, but you were gone by then."

"I didn't say anything either. I wanted to, but I didn't know how. Until today, I had no idea who Andrew was. And I'd like to see him in person, because I want to talk to him about Josh." I feel the wine warming my insides. I haven't eaten anything since last night. "I'm staying here another night—my fiancé is arriving shortly." I wasn't planning to mention Kyle, but it feels like a form of protection.

"That's great," Sadie says. "And for what it's worth, I'm glad you found someone after what happened to Josh. That couldn't have been easy." She looks genuinely happy for me, her blue eyes on the brink of tears.

"It took a long time," I say. "It took me years to accept Josh's death as a random tragedy. I got a text message from his phone telling me he was going for a swim, and it just didn't feel like him. He used an emoji, which he never did." It sounds ridiculous out loud, even more so now than it did in the months after Josh died.

"I know," Sadie says, drumming her fingertips on the table.

My breath comes as a sharp inhale. "How do you—"

"Bev told me you went to see her today."

"She told you?"

Sadie nods, the insides of her lips stained from the wine. "She was worried about you. She and I talk almost every day. She called me right after you left."

"Oh. Okay . . ." I'm temporarily thrown off, irrationally annoyed that Bev and Sadie are so close, when she didn't approve of me as a daughter-in-law. But I force myself to refocus and move on.

"Look, I found out what happened here, on the vineyard, with Michelle. Were you there the night she died? The party at the winery? I know you and Andrew have been together for a long time . . . Were you in high school together?"

She shakes her head. "No, we met in college. I never knew Michelle. But why are you asking about her?"

"I'm trying to figure out who Josh was. The parts he never told me about. Did Andrew ever tell you anything about that night?"

"Not much," Sadie says. "Just that Josh was the last person to see Michelle alive, and that they were arguing. Andrew said Josh flipped out when he saw him talking to Michelle. Andrew didn't mean anything by it—he was home from boarding school for the weekend. But Josh had a pattern—he only seemed to want girls when somebody else was interested in them."

I think back to the first night Josh and I met. He'd been at the party with another woman, but I was there alone. I hadn't seen a jealous side. I'd been wholeheartedly swept up in the heady romance, the idea of love at first sight. We rarely had normal days. They were full of grand gestures. Our relationship was an amusement park ride, a carousel I never wanted to get off. It was thrilling, the certainty in Josh's voice when it came to us. *I'd marry you today.*

I shrug off the intrusive thought. "Boarding school? Josh never mentioned anything about boarding school." I don't say that Bev already told me about Andrew going there. I want Sadie to give me her own, unbiased version of events.

"Because he didn't go," Sadie says. "Only Andrew was sent away."

"Wait, what? Why was he sent away?" My head is spinning wildly. Bev had said Andrew was at boarding school, but the way Sadie phrased it made it sound like he was sent there against his will.

Sadie looks uncomfortable, like she wishes we weren't having this conversation. "There was an incident with one of Josh's girlfriends . . . Andrew got wrongly blamed for it, and that was when their relationship fell apart."

"What kind of incident?"

"It was so many years ago, June . . . Do you really want to hear all of this? I don't quite understand why this all matters."

"It does." There's an edge of desperation in my voice. "I know it doesn't seem relevant, but it is. I need to know who Josh was."

Sadie sucks in her bottom lip and briefly chews before letting go, like she's weighing how much to tell me. "One of Josh's ex-girlfriends had a nude photo that somehow got passed around the school. Apparently Josh had had it in his nightstand, and other than himself, only Andrew would have had access to it. Josh told everyone Andrew was the one who circulated it as some sort of revenge because he was jealous of Josh, but it was Josh who did it. He was mad because he'd heard from a friend that she was planning to break up with him, and he didn't handle rejection well."

"At least, that's what Andrew told you," I snap, immediately defensive. But Sadie doesn't snap back. Instead, she just looks sad and resigned. "What was her name? The ex?"

"I don't know," Sadie says. "Does it matter?"

I change course, sensing a shift in Sadie, like she's about to shut down. "Does Andrew think Josh was responsible for Michelle's death?"

Uncertainty clouds Sadie's face. "They were arguing. That's what he told me."

The panic I felt sitting across from Rodney threatens to return. I've been so fixated on finding out who killed Josh that I haven't let myself dwell long on *why* someone killed Josh. On whether it was an act of vengeance for something Josh had done—something that might have been even worse. I can't give in to those ideas. I'll get lost in the pitch black of them.

"When did you find out Andrew was a twin?" I ask, pushing the image of Josh and Michelle, Josh and another wronged ex, out of my head.

Her eyes take on a misty, faraway look, and she's silent for a moment. When she finally speaks, her voice is low. "Not until after Josh was dead. Andrew completely broke down when Bev told him the news. He told me everything. It all spilled out—the photo, boarding school, Michelle, Andrew thinking Josh might have had something to do with her death. I was shocked. I had no idea he had a twin, and apparently he wanted to keep it that way." She laughs bitterly.

"Josh didn't tell me anything either," I say, a small part of me grateful to be in solidarity with Sadie, given that she'd been kept in the dark too. "Everyone said we barely knew each other when we got married. But I really thought I knew everything about him."

Maybe that's what is bothering me the most. Not that he lied, but that he lied so easily.

Sadie's face clouds over. "Andrew thought not telling me was the best way to protect me. From what Andrew told me, and forgive me for saying this, Josh bounced from girl to girl, always chasing the next high. He wanted what he couldn't have. I think Andrew was afraid Josh would try to break us apart."

Hearing her tell the story that way—the way Andrew must have told her—sends a shiver down my spine. Sadie obviously believes it. Did Andrew lie to her to make himself look better, or was I on a familiar trajectory with Josh? Had he not died, would our roller-coaster ride have ended in a staggering drop? Rodney Young seemed to think so. I take another sip of my wine. My glass is emptying a lot faster than Sadie's, the wine hitting me harder than usual on my empty stomach.

But Rodney and Sadie are both biased. Rodney is a grieving father, and Sadie only heard Andrew's side of things. Maybe they misunderstood Josh. He had been a hopeless romantic—not chasing the next high but trying to find true love.

Suddenly, Sadie rises from her seat. "Mila's up. She's going through a sleep regression at the moment, and she's waking up a few times a night.

Terrible twos, I guess." She heads for the stairs, jogging when she reaches the bottom.

I hadn't heard Mila make a sound.

I remain in my seat, my mind racing. Andrew has obviously convinced Sadie that Josh was involved in Michelle's death, but the version of Josh she's describing is the complete opposite of the man I married. Josh was passionate, and he moved quickly, but that's only because he was sure about me.

Still—he lied about his past. Was he trying to protect me, or was it more about protecting himself?

A staticky sound comes from the counter, followed by Sadie's low voice murmuring something to Mila. I notice the baby monitor, the same kind Phoebe has, the one with a video screen. Kyle and I occasionally babysit her girls, so I'm familiar with how it works.

I stand up and turn the monitor's screen on, expecting to see an empty toddler bed, because Sadie probably picked Mila up to soothe her. But instead, I see a fully sleeping little girl sprawled on her back, curly hair matted to her face. And what I hear isn't Sadie comforting her child but Sadie speaking with someone else on the phone, in lowered tones.

". . . says her fiancé is joining her. What do I do?"

I hold my breath, turning up the volume as high as it can go.

"I'm going to say something," she hisses, then a long pause. "Fine, but you need to get here soon."

My damp palms clasp the monitor. There's a good chance she's talking to Andrew. Which means whatever he's doing, and whatever he wants with me, she's probably a part of it.

Suddenly, there's no noise. I frantically turn off the monitor's screen and place it back on the counter where I found it. I sit down at the table and scroll through my email on my phone.

"Sorry about that," Sadie says, sitting down across from me. "Look, June—I know we just met, but you seem like a good person, and I'm sorry for everything you've gone through. You're right that Josh kept Andrew a secret. But only because Andrew cut him out first. Andrew wasn't perfect back then either, but . . . Josh might have been truly dangerous."

I blink, my eyelids heavy. "What are you talking about?"

Sadie sighs. "I get the feeling you think Andrew is somehow involved in Josh's death, but I can assure you he wasn't. He spent a lot of time thinking it wasn't an accident, but eventually, he accepted the truth. And I think you should too."

My mind reels. I'm not the only one who didn't think it was an accident.

I try to stand up, but my knees buckle.

Sadie's kitchen goes fuzzy around me. I was right all along. Josh was murdered. But I don't feel any warped degree of relief that I wasn't crazy for believing it. Instead, panic lights my brain like a match as I sink to the floor.

My vision goes dark as my mind spins with what I've learned.

Josh was murdered, but he might also be a murderer.

# Six

# Ben

St. Helena, Napa County, California
October–November 1999

**I FELT EMILIA'S ABSENCE** like a wound in the weeks, and then month, after she left, but I threw myself into work at the winery in an effort to stop thinking about her. I still didn't know what to do about David. His indiscretion had become the one thing we didn't talk about anymore, and the more we avoided the topic, the bigger it became. I spent long hours outside, grateful that there was always something to do in the vineyard. As the temperature sank, I relished the cooler evenings, and on one of the few days when the sky graced us with a rainstorm, I stood with my arms outstretched, letting the drops spackle my face and clothes.

A week after Emilia left, I cried when Camille went home to Santa Barbara, even as she promised to come and visit again soon. She was holding back her own tears too. Kieran was down for a nap. She'd said goodbye to him already, a private moment I hadn't witnessed. He was far too young to understand what was happening, but when he woke up later and I picked him up from his crib, his eyes darted around, as if he sensed I wasn't the person he wanted to see.

Josh and Michelle continued at a steady equilibrium. When she came over, she was polite if a bit reserved, and from the outside, Josh was a doting boyfriend. I started to question my earlier doubts and tried to see him like Camille and David did. As a teenager, one with a good head on his shoulders, who was making the best choices he could. Rodney's words at the grocery store evaporated in my mind: he was an overprotective father and probably didn't want to let go of his little girl.

Whenever I wanted to pick up the phone and call Emilia—and I did want to, often, to recapture how I'd felt around her—I called a different number instead. Andrew, at the dorms. He seemed solid, and like he was happy with his fresh start. Either he was a master at avoiding the truth, like David and I were, or he really had moved on.

"How are you doing, Mom?" he asked one night, two weeks before he was due to come home for Thanksgiving.

"I'm—I'm fine," I said, clutching the phone tightly. "Why? How are you?"

He shrugged. "I guess I'm a bit nervous."

Tension coiled around my shoulders. "About what?"

"Coming home. It's just different now." His words were heavy with hesitation.

"It's not that different," I said weakly.

"I'm nervous to see Josh."

Josh rarely came up during our calls.

"He's your brother," I started. I didn't know how to finish. I couldn't force myself to lie.

"I didn't do what he said I did, Mom," Andrew said.

I wanted so badly to take sides. The two words would have been so easy to choke out: *I know.* But that was admitting to myself that the truly guilty person was Josh, and the only proof I had was my own suspicion.

"Let's move past it," I said, attempting to smooth things over. "You're doing so well, and it's Thanksgiving coming up, and we have a lot to be thankful for."

He paused. "I just need you to know that I'm not capable of doing what everyone thinks I did. Sharing that photo. I didn't even know it existed."

I nodded, my way of agreeing without saying a word. I pictured him on the other end, drumming his fingers on his denim-clad knee. Andrew fidgeted when he was nervous.

"You're not," I blurted out, because I had been silent long enough. "You aren't capable of something like that. You care about people. You're amazing, Andrew."

He didn't speak. He wasn't expecting me to say it, but the truth we were both skipping around hung heavily between us. If Andrew wasn't capable, that meant Josh was.

"Then why am I here?" he said in a small voice, suddenly sounding half his age.

I forced my sob back. I wasn't allowed to cry, not when Andrew was holding it together, in a new place, uprooted from his entire life.

"You'll have so many more opportunities there," I said, recycling the same lie David and I had used so many times.

David insisted on driving to the Dunn campus to pick Andrew up. I would stay home with Kieran, who had started hating his car seat the same week he learned how to walk, a milestone I felt guilty Camille wasn't around to see. He screamed every time I tried to strap him in, red blotches appearing on his cheeks. Somehow, when I wasn't looking, my baby was becoming more and more like a toddler, just two months away from his first birthday. I had wanted him to grow up, but I missed the baby he had been the second he wasn't there anymore. Only motherhood offered the unique pain of mourning someone right in front of you.

I changed my outfit three times, parted my hair in the center, then threw it back up in a ponytail. My breast-milk supply was almost depleted, and the more Kieran relied on solid foods, the less he fed from me, which was both a relief and a disappointment.

When David pulled up and Andrew emerged from the back seat, I was struck not by how he'd changed but how he hadn't. I had expected that he would look different, transformed by his time at the Dunn School in ways I wouldn't recognize. But he looked the same. He looked identical to the boy we had brought to the campus three months ago. He looked identical to his brother. His brother, who remained upstairs, with his bedroom door pulled tight, rock music throbbing from the walls.

"Mom," Andrew said, wrapping me in his arms. Both of my teenage sons had outgrown me years ago. They both used to tuck their heads into the crook of my hip when they got scared, when I dropped them off at preschool and they didn't want to be separated from me. David had called them my "barnacles," once upon a time, with affection. Now, my head could rest comfortably on their shoulders.

"I missed you so much," I said, my voice thick with emotion. I wanted the week to be perfect.

"I missed you too," he said.

It had always been Josh who took up more space, Josh who lifted weights and spent time in the home gym David had installed in our basement. But I realized that Andrew wasn't the same. He had changed. He'd been working out. He looked more like his brother than ever.

On Wednesday night, after I'd made his favorite dinner—beef stroganoff, which he barely touched—Andrew surprised me by saying he was going to meet up with a couple of his friends.

"I can drive you," I offered. "Just let me pack up Kieran—"

"Thanks, Mom, but I can walk," he said. "I could use the fresh air."

When he was gone, I knocked on Josh's door to bring him a plate of food—he hadn't come down for dinner, insisting that he had too much homework to catch up on, which I knew was a weak excuse to avoid sitting across the table from Andrew. I found him lying on his bed, staring at the ceiling with headphones on.

"Where's Michelle tonight?" I asked gently. She'd been spending time at the house more often than not, so her absences didn't go unnoticed.

I could tell I'd struck a nerve by the way his body tensed up, the mechanical way he removed his headphones. "Home, I guess. She had a tennis thing and wanted to go to bed early."

"It's good for you to have your own lives." It was the wrong thing to say. Josh sucked in a breath.

"I know that," he said. "I do have a life."

"Have you spoken to your brother yet? You can't avoid him forever."

He put his headphones back on. "Have you ever considered it's him who's avoiding me?"

After I left his room, I shrugged into my jean jacket and wandered outside to the vineyard. I'd been taking long walks at night as a way to distract myself from thinking about Emilia. In the company of the vines—now all but empty of their grapes, a leafy-green gold during the day, blackened and spindly at night—I let myself obsess over where she was and what she might be doing and who she might be meeting, my gut twisting from the absolute lack of control I had over anything.

As I passed the barn near the edge of the property, the tall wooden structure where the boys sometimes hung out with friends on weekend nights, I heard sounds, low and murmured. A series of breathy sighs; an occasional hushed laugh. Muted orange light dappled the grass, coming from somewhere inside the barn. I realized it was the flickering of candlelight.

I held my breath in my chest like a bubble. David was supposed to be in town for a meeting. He'd told me not to wait up. I'd believed him, but clearly, I'd been wrong to. Kicking him out changed nothing, and our tenuous peace—the way we carefully tiptoed around the affair, the small ways we had been trying to reconnect—was part of a carefully constructed front. He was still cheating on me, and I was about to catch him in the act.

My footfalls were quiet as I approached. I thought about making my presence known, throwing all of David's lies in his face like scalding water. That was what I wanted to do, but the closer I got, the more it felt like I was walking in on something forbidden. Like I was the intruder.

I stood at the broken barn door, hovering in the dark as I peered through a missing slat of wood. That was when I realized I was wrong. It wasn't David inside. It was Josh and Michelle, in a nest of blankets on the ground, candles surrounding them. He was poised on top of her, kissing her forehead tenderly, her arms wrapped around him, his back milk white in the moonlight.

I had long known Josh was sexually active. I'd found an opened box of condoms in his nightstand the year before, its number of foil-wrapped packets dwindling. But I had never been confronted with the physical proof of it.

Michelle moaned lightly. "Josh," she whispered, and I squeezed my eyes shut, not wanting to see or hear any more. There was nothing I could do that wouldn't totally humiliate everyone involved. I fixed my gaze on the ground as I quietly sidestepped away, trying not to alert them to my presence. I heard rustling and murmured words, and only as I shuffled back toward the house did the truth of it finally hit me.

I'd just spoken to Josh. He was upstairs in his room.

Which meant Andrew was the one in the barn with Michelle.

My limbs became rubber. My brain tried to manufacture an excuse. Josh could have lied about seeing Michelle tonight, then slipped out here. When I returned to the house, I'd see his empty bed and know he had somehow gotten out the door and into the barn without my noticing.

I needed it to make sense. Because if it didn't make sense, it meant Andrew had lied about meeting up with friends and had impersonated his brother in order to have sex with his brother's girlfriend, and that was a thought too sickening to fathom. Andrew wasn't capable of that deceit, of tricking Michelle like that. It would eat him alive.

But we had sent him away to Dunn. We had chosen to believe Josh's side of the story. That Andrew was jealous and troubled, and had lied about the photo of Abby. That he had intentionally circulated it to ruin something Josh had that he wanted. Was Josh's version the truth? Andrew had seemed so calm, so at peace, every time I talked to him on the phone. But maybe he wasn't moving on. Maybe he was biding his time.

When I got back to the front porch, my brain felt disconnected from my body. I almost didn't want to go inside, because once I did, I would have to acknowledge what I already knew to be true.

Josh was sitting on the sofa, watching TV, his socked feet drumming on the coffee table.

"Hey, Mom." His gaze was fixed on the screen as a laugh track blared out. "Don't give me a lecture—I've done all my homework for the break already."

"I wasn't going to," I said. My voice sounded tinny and unnatural, but he didn't seem to notice.

So I said nothing. Above all, it might have been an act of defense. I was worried about what he would do to his brother if he knew what Andrew had done, just like I worried about what he might have done had Andrew not left for the Dunn School.

In the end, it was all the things unsaid that ended up mattering most.

## Seven

# *June*

**I BLINK MYSELF AWAKE** in a room I vaguely recognize through filmy vision and stare up at a ceiling fan doing lazy laps overhead. My head lolls to the side. There's a crushing sensation behind my temples, nausea rising in my gut. The first thing I see on the nightstands bracketing the bed is a photo of a newlywed couple. Sadie and Andrew, baby-faced and youthful.

Everything comes screaming back. My conversation with Sadie in the kitchen. Her hushed tones through the baby monitor. The wine. I'd drank fast on a totally empty stomach, and combined with Sadie's version of Josh—a man possibly capable of murder—my brain had short-circuited, like it was trying to protect my own image of Josh at all costs.

My breath hitches sharply as I sit up too quickly. My body is sluggish and doesn't want to listen. Sadie had whispered to someone—to Andrew?—*You need to get here soon*, and that must mean he's on his way. What exactly are they planning?

I force myself off the bed and down the hall, my legs wobbly and uncertain as I descend the stairs. The first thing I see is the back of Sadie's head. She's at the kitchen table, tapping something into her phone, my empty wineglass in front of her. She stands up and turns around when she hears me approach, her face full of concern. "June. You're awake. How are you feeling?"

"I'm okay," I say. "Just embarrassed. I don't exactly know what happened. I mean, I drank on an empty stomach, so I guess that explains it."

"Don't be embarrassed," she says. "After you passed out, you were mumbling something incoherent—I helped you upstairs to lie down. Do you want something to eat? I can make something quickly—"

My mouth is cotton dry, and I'm humiliated with myself for causing such a scene. "No, that's okay. I'll grab something with my fiancé when he gets here. I should get going . . ."

"I hope it wasn't the wine," she says. "It was a dry wine. We fermented it longer to lower the sugar content. If I'm being honest, it was a suitcase clone, from a clipping I brought back from a trip to France. This batch was a total experiment, and it's our first time drinking it. Maybe it's way too strong."

"It's not your fault," I say, nausea threatening to rise up again. "Do you know what time it is?"

Sadie taps awake the screen on her own phone and looks at the clock. "It's just past nine. You weren't out for very long. And in case you were wondering, your purse is sitting over there on the sofa."

I walk over, grab it, and pull my phone out. There are two missed calls from Kyle and a text from fifteen minutes ago. *My plane just landed, where are you?*

I call him with shaking hands, and he answers on the first ring. "Kyle, I'm at the Backyard. I have a room booked here where we can stay tonight."

"I'm just waiting for a Lyft. Is everything okay?"

"Yes," I say quickly, aware of Sadie's eyes on me. "It's totally fine."

After we hang up, I turn and face Sadie. "My fiancé is on his way here, so I should go. Thanks for—" I gesture around, looking for an appropriate way to end the night. "For talking to me about Andrew and Josh. I know it's not easy."

"Don't worry about it," she says. "I hope you can make peace with what happened to Josh, just like Andrew did."

Her smile is friendly, but her eyes are sad.

"You said Andrew wasn't perfect back then either." I suck in a breath. "What did you mean by that? Were you talking about the whole boarding school situation?"

Sadie narrows her eyes. "No. I know how . . . guilty Bev feels about that. All I meant was that Andrew and Josh had a very complicated relationship, and I don't think either of us will ever fully understand it, since we didn't know them back then."

I force myself to ask the question. "Is Andrew really on a business trip?"

Her smile fades. "Of course. Where else would he be?"

"I didn't mean—I'm sorry. I'm still really lightheaded." I back toward the door. "Thanks again for the drink, and I'm sorry I passed out."

I make a beeline across the property to the parking lot, feeling her gaze on my back. Time seems to pass interminably slowly before I see headlights. My body melts with relief when Kyle exits the back door of the car, his well-worn gray weekender bag slung over his shoulders. I rush toward him and launch myself into him. He gives me a short hug back. Usually, Kyle's hugs are big and hearty, given with not just his arms but his entire body, and I love nothing more than melting into them. But there is a stiffness in his posture that leaves me unable to do that.

"Kyle," I say. "I'm so glad you're here."

"I got worried," he says. "When you didn't answer, I kept thinking, what if something happened to you . . ."

"I know. But nothing did."

"So now what?" Kyle says. "Where is this Andrew guy? If you think he's dangerous, wouldn't you want to get far away from his winery?" There's just a hint of exasperation in his voice, and his eyes are lined with fatigue.

"He's not here. His wife says he's on a business trip, but I'm not sure if I believe her."

"You said he was in the park and in front of your bar," Kyle says. "Think really hard. Was it actually him? Because it would be totally understandable if you thought you saw Josh, with our wedding coming up so soon . . ."

"It was Andrew," I say. "I'm sure of it. Let's go into the room and talk."

When we're in the room, with the door locked and the curtains tightly shut, we sit down on the bed, and I tell him about Rodney Young thinking Josh killed Michelle, and Sadie telling me what Andrew had said about Josh's pattern with girlfriends. When I get to the part about the baby monitor and passing out in Sadie's kitchen, Kyle's knuckles are white, his lips pressed together.

"You passed out in their house? You need to eat something. Let's go into town and get some dinner, okay?" He starts to stand up, but I tug on his hands, pulling him back down.

"I'm not hungry," I say, shaking my head. I'm not ready to explain why. That the other versions of Josh I've been introduced to have left me sickened, without an appetite. That I haven't just been hearing other people's words but absorbing them, like some kind of poison.

But Kyle knows me well enough that he senses the source of my unease. "It's a lot to process. You knew Josh as this amazing guy, but maybe he wasn't exactly who you thought."

I tamp down my annoyance. It's one thing for me to question what I've been confronted with, but it feels entirely different to have Kyle do the same.

"He *was* an amazing guy," I say, still programmed to defend him. Until I have proof otherwise, I need to remain loyal to the man I loved so much.

"Okay," Kyle says gently. "But it sounds like several people you've spoken to didn't think so. There could be some truth to what they're saying. I just want you to be prepared for that—you're saying you came here to find the truth, but that doesn't mean you're going to like what you hear."

A silence falls between us. "I do want the truth," I finally say. "And I think I'm getting closer to it. I know Michelle's death is tied to Josh's. Two drownings can't be a coincidence . . . can they?"

Kyle interlaces my fingers in his. "Maybe not, but how could you prove anything? You already talked to Josh's mom, and Michelle's dad, and Sadie. Who else is left?"

We both know the answer to that question: Andrew. But we can't get him to talk if we can't find him.

"There was another girl—Sadie mentioned an ex of Josh's who came before Michelle, but didn't know her name. Apparently Andrew got sent away to boarding school over a scandal involving a photo of this girl. If I can find her . . ."

Kyle blows out a breath. "What difference would it make? All of this was so long ago."

"I don't know, but if she knows anything—"

His eyes are full of concern. "June, you're not going to want to hear this, but we can get on a plane home right now. Head back to New York. Leave all this behind."

"And if Andrew shows up there again?"

"We'd report him to the police. File a restraining order. But being in his vineyard is just asking for trouble."

The adrenaline starts to drain out of me, replaced by a combination of dread and bone-deep fatigue. Who knows if Kyle even believes it was Andrew I saw? He thinks I'm chasing a ghost, and if I keep going, I might lose him. We've been together for six years, weathering the pandemic and job promotions and apartment changes and the question of my ticking biological clock and, of course, my past. Kyle has been so understanding, but he can't wait for me forever.

"I can't go," I say. "This is where I need to be. Just one more day—it's late now anyway, and you just got here. If Andrew doesn't show up by tomorrow, we can go."

"Okay," he says. "One more day, and then we need to go home."

I move my hand up to the nape of Kyle's neck, threading my fingers through his hair.

"You know this won't bring him back, right?" Kyle says softly.

"It's not about bringing him back," I say. There's a sadness in his eyes, and maybe that's part of this: he's worried I'm still in love with Josh, and that I'll never get over him.

Suddenly I feel the urge to prove it to Kyle, maybe even to prove it to myself, that I love him as much as I loved Josh. I press him onto the bed, climb on top of him, peel off his flannel shirt, and pull his T-shirt over his head.

I fumble with his belt and pull down his jeans, but when I lower myself between his knees, he stops me, even though he's hard against my touch. Instead of letting me pleasure him, he lays me down beside him and unwraps me like I'm some kind of exquisite gift, his touch almost painfully gentle. He leaves my shirt on, pulls down my jeans and my underwear along with them. His tongue presses against me, maddeningly soft. I come against his mouth, white-hot with want.

When my eyes are open, it's Kyle's face I see, but when I close them, it's Josh, as much as I wish he would go away. I open them fully, forcing myself to be present with Kyle, the man who loves me in a steady, reliable way. *Nobody will love you like I can*, Josh had said to me on our wedding night, and he was right, but the way Kyle loves me is the kind of love I need.

By the time he climbs between my legs, the eye contact is too intense, our faces almost touching. I let my eyelids flutter shut, and suddenly it's Josh's chest pressed to mine, his heart beating in wild tandem with mine. When he's inside me, I wrap my legs around his back, writhing underneath him, our bodies bucking wildly on the bed. I lift my hips, wanting him even deeper, wanting to be completely filled up with him. We change positions, and when I'm on top, I grind into him until we both come at the same time, Kyle moaning lightly.

*Josh*, I almost say.

"Kyle," I say instead. "I love you."

Kyle is quiet beneath me, almost like he knows it's not just us in the bed.

No matter what happens next, we'll be on our way home tomorrow, and unless Andrew shows up, I'll be leaving without learning the truth about Josh. But maybe I was never meant to know. Maybe there's not one truth but everyone's version of it. Bev's, where her beloved son went for a swim and got overpowered by the tide. Rodney's, where karma is real. Sadie's, where Andrew has no reason to want his brother gone. And mine, where someone else sent me a message from my husband's phone.

But I have no idea which version is real, and somebody might want to make sure I don't find out.

# Eight

# *Bev*

St. Helena, Napa County, California
November 1999

**I AVOIDED LOOKING DIRECTLY** at the boys the day after finding Andrew and Michelle together, my thoughts dark and troubled as I prepared Thanksgiving dinner. I was afraid that the truth would burst from my lips, and what would happen then? What would Josh do to his brother for sleeping with his girlfriend? I was disgusted with Andrew, and questioning whether Josh was telling the truth the whole time about the photo of Abby. He had blamed Andrew, and everyone had believed him—except me. But what was Andrew really capable of? Had I defended him to David, possibly at the cost of our marriage, for nothing?

*We need to do something, Bev,* David had said after we got the call from the school about the photo. *We need to make this go away.* I knew he wasn't thinking about just our family, but our winery. Our reputation.

My brain began filling with memories like a deep well.

The boys at six years old, drawing pictures of our family. Josh's had been scribbled hastily, Andrew's more detailed, his little forehead creasing in concentration. The next day, Andrew's photo went missing, and he cried. He didn't flat out accuse his brother of stealing it, but he didn't have to. I knew where the photo was long before I found the strips of paper crosscut in David's shredder.

*They're kids*, David had said with a shrug. *They need to learn to work things out.*

The boys at ten, running races down the corridors in the vineyard, timing each other with stopwatches. They both planned to run cross-country for the elementary school team. To my surprise, Andrew was the faster runner, but one day, he came back with a sprained ankle, claiming he didn't want to join the team after all.

*Accidents happen*, David had said.

The boys at eleven, twelve, thirteen. Every year, there had been something Josh took away from his brother, insignificant enough for me to convince myself nothing had happened—small enough, maybe, for Andrew to convince himself nothing was wrong. He never said anything against Josh. Sometimes he looked at me like he wanted to, like he was imploring me to read his mind. It was easier for me not to intervene.

But after the barn, I looked at those memories through a new lens. Maybe Josh had never done anything wrong, and it was Andrew who had lied to make his brother look bad.

I knew it was only a matter of time until Josh found out and Michelle discovered the truth, a gut-wrenching thought that I could barely let myself imagine. In my despair, I convinced myself there was a chance neither of them would ever know. Andrew would be back to the Dunn School after the holiday. The boys were safer apart from each other. Eventually, Josh and Michelle would break up. They were seventeen, and even if they claimed to be in love, their end was inevitable.

When Josh asked if a few friends could come over to hang out in the barn on Friday night, David heartily embraced the idea. It wasn't an unusual occurrence, the boys having friends on the vineyard on weekends, although less so lately, with Andrew away and Josh spending so much time with Michelle. We knew that drinking happened, but one thing David and I agreed on was that we'd rather they do it on our property than somewhere else where we couldn't check in.

"Andrew, you should join," David said when Andrew came downstairs for lunch.

"I don't think so," he mumbled.

"They're your friends too. I want you to get out there and socialize a bit. Okay?" David was insistent, so hopeful that Andrew could fit in before we brought him back to Dunn on Sunday.

Andrew looked up at me, the same way he had as a kid. Imploring me to say something. My smile was tight, my nod almost imperceptible. He glanced back down at his plate when he realized I wasn't going to take his side.

David was in a good mood the evening of the party, upbeat and jovial as he sang in the kitchen, chopping peppers and tomatoes for a salad. I rocked Kieran to sleep as I walked past the bay window in the living room, eyeing the throng of teenagers gathering on the property.

"It's more than a few friends," I murmured.

"It's no big deal. Let them be kids," David said. "Besides, with them out of the house, I thought we could talk. We haven't . . . really talked yet, and I think it's time."

"Okay," I said, Kieran heavy in my arms. I was afraid he wanted to do more than talk. David and I hadn't been intimate since he returned, with the exception of a few kisses, a couple of instances of curling up together in bed.

"I'm making that seafood linguine you love so much. Remember, from that restaurant in San Francisco? That cozy little Italian place. When my parents babysat the boys."

"Oh yeah." David was trying, but reciprocating his enthusiasm took every ounce of my energy.

I did remember the restaurant in San Francisco. Josh and Andrew had been three or four, and I'd finally felt like myself again. I had been in a great mood until David brought up the idea of having another baby, a conversation I was nowhere near ready for. I told him I wanted my tubes tied: our family was complete, and with the baby phase behind us, I wanted to focus on raising our twin boys. He suggested I might change my mind. I went to the bathroom to get away from him, and when I came back, he was apologetic.

"I ordered for you," he'd said, his hopeful double-dimpled smile a peace offering. But I had never wanted the seafood linguine.

I kept my eyes trained on the window. A car pulled into the driveway, and Michelle got out of the back seat, wearing a pink dress and a shrunken leather jacket. She wasn't smiling, and instead of heading to the barn, she made her way up the porch.

*She knows*, I thought, my brain racing. I slipped outside to meet her.

"Hi, Mrs.—Bev." She smoothed down the hem of her dress. She was nervous, but so was I. Somehow I managed to make my voice sound normal.

"Hi, Michelle, how are you?" So much was unsaid between us. Michelle had seen me with Emilia. I had seen her with Andrew. We both contained truths that would be devastating if said out loud.

"I'm okay," she said, still fidgeting with the pink fabric of her dress. "Actually, I need to talk to you about something—"

But before she could say anything else, David joined us on the porch, a dish towel slung over his shoulder.

"Michelle," he said, his voice big and booming. "Great to see you. I think everyone's at the barn already."

She nodded, her entire demeanor changing. "Right. I guess I should head over."

I wanted to reach out and grab her elbow, to tell her to stay, to hear whatever it was she was about to say. But she didn't turn around once as she headed to the barn.

David was waiting for me in the kitchen after I put Kieran down in his crib, a hopeful smile on his face. He handed me a glass of chardonnay. "Cheers," he said, clinking his glass against mine. "To new beginnings. To no more secrets."

I took a first sip of wine, the vanilla-spice taste settling on my tongue. I waited for the guilt to set in over my own secrets, but it never did.

"I was thinking," he said. "Remember when we were dating and I used to cook for you while you were studying? Except if I made seafood, it usually came from a can, since it was all I could afford." He paused. "All I ever wanted was to take care of you, and I messed it all up."

"You did take care of me," I said. David used to show up at my door with food he'd made for me, simple dishes like Hamburger Helper or garlic noodles, lovingly packed in Tupperware. If I was busy with schoolwork, he would give me a quick kiss and tell me he would call me later. He never did something because of what he might get in return.

"Maybe my problem was that I didn't let you do the same for me," David said. "I always wanted to protect you from all the bad things. But you were very capable on your own."

"I don't know," I said, rubbing my forehead. "I've been thinking about the past a lot, since . . . your indiscretion. About us."

David clasped his hands together. "You're doubting everything because of me. Because of what I did to you. And, Bev, cheating on you was the biggest mistake I ever made." His eyes became glassy. "I want to put our family back together again. What do I need to do to prove it to you?"

I chose my words carefully. "When you were gone, I started thinking maybe we'd be better off that way. Being separate. Maybe we've just grown apart, David."

He drummed his fingers on the countertop. "We can find our way back to each other. We always have. We have a baby to think about—we don't want him to grow up in a broken home. Look at the upbringing we've given Josh and Andrew. Doesn't Kieran deserve that too?"

*And look at how they've turned out*, I wanted to shout, but David would never see his sons the way I did. He was a great dad, playful and loving, but his relationship with the boys lacked the worn-in intimacy that hallmarked mine. It was so much easier for David, disappearing into the vineyard and returning home for the fun parts, while I warred in the trenches with our children, potty training and prying stubborn mouths open to brush molars and trimming tiny half-moon fingernails without clipping skin, mediating temper tantrums and shouting matches. *Father* was something David wore like a designer label; *mother* was a scar embedded in my skin.

"You didn't want to hear something negative about Josh. You silenced me, and maybe I wanted to punish you, because I know I pushed you away. Maybe this *is* a broken home."

Panic appeared on his face. "I'm the one who cheated. I'm the one who messed up. And I understand I have a lot to make up to you, but I'm willing to do that. I want us to be a family again. I want that more than anything." He paused. "What would happen if we separated? Josh and Andrew will be away at college soon, but we'd have to share custody of Kieran. Shuttle him back and forth. Your parents had problems, Bev. They put you and Camille in the middle, and that wasn't fair. But you're an incredible mother. We're not *them*. We're . . . us. Bev and David. David and Bev. You're the only woman I've ever loved."

I swallowed, my throat closing up. "You're the only man I've ever loved too." It was true.

David tentatively stepped toward me. "Do you think you could forgive me for what I did? I know it might not happen overnight, but with time . . . we can go to couples counseling. I'll see a therapist. Whatever you need me to do."

"David . . ."

He closed the gap between us, took my hand in his, and led me to the sofa, where I reluctantly sat beside him. He kneaded my fingers gently between his. "I know we can't start over, but we can make a go of this. We can be a family, a real family. I'm not excusing what I did or putting it on you, but I did try to talk to you about how I felt, so many times. It was one moment of weakness . . ."

I could feel it dissolve like wet tissue paper, my hatred toward David, the anger I'd burned with while he was away. And it wasn't like I could just relocate to some far-flung location and still share custody of Kieran. I knew that already. I was tethered by motherhood and obligation, bound permanently by love.

"Bev," he said. "Do you want to be with me or not?"

I couldn't discount all the wonderful years David and I had had together. Emilia was gone, and I hadn't heard from her in nearly two months.

I cleared my throat. "You're asking if I can forgive you, but will everything just go back to the way it was?"

"No," he said. "We'll go to therapy. I'll go to therapy. I'll work less. If you want to travel more often, let's go. I can give you what you want, Bev." His palm was hot on my leg. "It feels good to touch you. I want you to feel loved by me."

When he stood up and offered me his hand, I took it and let him lead me upstairs to our bedroom. I stood motionless as he slipped my dress off. His touch was tentative, like it was when we first started dating, when he wasn't sure what he was allowed to do, his fingers migrating from my breasts down below my belly button, between my legs, hesitant and questioning.

"Tell me what you want," he breathed in my ear.

It was impossible to articulate when I felt so torn in half. But I owed it to us to try.

"I want us to be real. To let go of the idea that we have to be perfect. To not be afraid to fight."

I watched the surprise wash over his features. He had been expecting me to say something else. "You never have to be afraid around me, Bev. I'm not going anywhere." He dragged his mouth down my stomach, tongued the skin of my inner thighs. I pulled him on top of me. I wanted to be as close to him as possible.

I felt him enter me, slowly at first, then picking up speed. As he rocked back and forth, his hand cupping my face, my thoughts wandered, but my body responded. The orgasm built. I was out of excuses to hate David. He had cheated, but so had I. He had slipped up once, but I'd done it on purpose so many more times.

"I love you," he whispered, and I wrapped my arms around his back, pulling him deeper into me as I came.

"I love you too," I said.

Afterward, I got dressed quickly, and we retreated to the kitchen. David served me seafood linguine by candlelight, his face more jovial and animated than I'd seen it in a long time. I tried to reciprocate, to give him the affection he wanted. And as we sat side by side, his ankle finding mine under the table, I realized I didn't have to try. It was like we had slipped back into the way things used to be—but a messier, more

honest version. I took his face in mine and pressed my lips to his, letting
my tongue slip into his mouth. I hadn't kissed David like that in years.

"Wow," he said softly.

It was I who climbed onto his lap, I who rocked against him and
initiated a second time. *We're going to be okay*, I thought. I had chosen this
life. It was the bed I had made, and it had always been comfortable.

After we finished, we were sitting on the sofa with our wineglasses
when Andrew walked into the house, kicked off his sneakers, and ran
upstairs.

"What's wrong?" I called out after him, but he slammed the door to
his room without answering. I was surprised he had even lasted that long
at the party. When I stood up to go after him, David rested his hand on
mine and stopped me.

"Let him go. Whatever it is, he'll talk to us tomorrow, if he wants to.
We have to give the boys space to breathe."

"Okay," I said, my lungs tight with panic. I felt trapped, unable to
intervene, but David was right. Our boys were practically adults, and we
couldn't force them to do anything.

By the time Josh came back inside, it was after midnight. David had
gone to bed, and I was washing the dishes from dinner. I tried to read
Josh's face, but there was nothing strange about his expression.

"How was the party? Has everyone gone home?" I asked, my voice far
more casual than I felt.

He nodded, giving me a small smile. "Yeah, it was good. We made a
bonfire, but don't worry, I put it out. I'm gonna head to bed now."

"Did something happen with your brother? He came in a while ago
looking upset."

Josh shrugged. "I don't know."

"Wasn't he at the party?"

"Not really. He kind of kept to himself."

The worry churned in my gut. "Has Michelle gone home?"

"She got a ride with someone." He grabbed a bottle of water from the
fridge and headed for the stairs. "Good night, Mom."

I watched him jog away, tall and handsome. I wondered how different he would have turned out if he'd had someone else for a mother. I pictured her, that woman. She wasn't my mother, with her passive-aggressive comments, her moods flipping like a switch. She wasn't me, too afraid of conflict to course correct. She was somewhere in between, and she would be doing a better job than either of us ever had.

I spent the next morning with the late-harvest grapes, Kieran in his stroller beside me. David wanted to wait to pick them, maybe even until the following week, but the number of birds we'd had hovering over the vines, curiously hunting and pecking, made me think nature was trying to tell us something. The grapes were beginning to shrivel, their purple skin puckering as their flavor sweetened. If we waited too long, there might not be any fruit left to collect.

I looked up to see David coming toward me and was about to tell him it was time to pick, but he spoke before I had a chance to.

"I just got a call from Rodney Young. Michelle never came home last night, and her friends don't know where she is. The boys say she must've gotten a ride home with someone. You haven't seen her, have you?"

Dread filled my body. Michelle had wanted to talk to me, and now she was gone. My instincts were telling me that something terrible had happened.

I answered David the only way I knew how. "No. I haven't seen her since yesterday."

## Nine

# *June*

St. Helena, Napa County, California
September 2022

**I WAKE UP KNOWING** that today is a ticking clock. I promised Kyle that if Andrew didn't surface, we would go home. And if I don't follow through on that promise, there's a good chance I'll lose Kyle. He would never give me an ultimatum unless he meant it.

But I don't know how to find Andrew. The only thing I can think of is what I'm already doing, which is waiting at his winery for him to show up. I need to know the truth about Michelle and what really happened the day Josh died. I need to know if Andrew was responsible.

After breakfast, Kyle and I walk the acreage of the Backyard together. We pass the pond where Michelle drowned, its shimmering black surface perfectly still. I try to imagine a body being pulled out of it—Josh's girlfriend. He must have been devastated, totally inconsolable. Despite the warmth in the air, my skin gets a chill. The image in my head changes—Josh feigning surprise when her body was found, the same way he pretended to be shocked when I threw him a surprise thirtieth birthday party.

"Do you really think Andrew is just going to show up?" Kyle says, gripping my hand tightly, forcing me back to the present. "I have a bad feeling about this whole place. There's something not right here."

"We'll go into town for a bit," I say, grappling to buy myself time. "We'll go see Napa, while we're already here. I'll see if we can get a late checkout."

After Nadia agrees to the late checkout, Kyle and I rent bicycles in St. Helena and ride them into downtown Napa, where we stop for lunch at a cozy restaurant with a rustic courtyard overlooking the Napa River and dine on coconut-fried prawns for me and braised pork for Kyle, our ankles knocking together under the table. It's a beautiful day, sunny and clear, with so many people milling around, including well-dressed tourists taking a moment to explore the town between winery visits. Instinctively, I look for a tall man with a baseball cap, Andrew Smith, in every group. I don't see him, but wherever we go, I have the creeping feeling of eyes on me. Maybe it's my imagination, or my nerves, or the fact that I'm both desperate and terrified to see the one person who knows the truth.

My phone goes off several times with messages from Phoebe. *Is everything okay there? Are you coming home?*

I'm still a bit annoyed with her for telling Kyle what I was doing, but I'm glad he's here, so I send a brief reply.

**All is fine, Kyle is here now, I'll fill you in when I get home. xx**

After lunch, we ride our bicycles back to St. Helena, stopping at a couple of natural wineries along the way, and by the time we return to the Backyard, our baskets are filled with wine bottles. But there's no Andrew Smith, and time is running out. Kyle keeps looking at his watch, and finally, he turns to me with a sad smile.

"June, we've had a good day, but we need to go home, okay? I was looking up flights out of here this morning, and there's one that leaves tonight at seven—American Airlines. I think we should pack our stuff and head to the airport."

Tears burn my eyes, but I nod. There are no other excuses. I know I can't back out.

"I'll book the flight," I say.

"I'm sorry you didn't find what you were looking for," he says, massaging my shoulders with his warm hands. "But I hope you got some closure."

When he goes into the bathroom and turns on the shower, I try to digest what he said about closure, and I realize I can't. It's not just because I don't like the version of Josh I've learned about, but because believing that version existed would erase everything I thought I knew. And I knew the real Josh, the Josh who was devoted and loving and supportive to a fault. Right now, it feels like I'm the only person who can do right by him—the only one who wants to know what really happened to him.

On the American Airlines website, I select the flight leaving Napa and landing in JFK tonight. When I'm at the seat-selection page, I can see there are only two available seats on the flight, and they're nowhere near each other. I click on them reluctantly.

The plan comes to me in a flash. This is the only flight from Napa to New York City tonight, and I have the only two seats at my fingertips.

I quickly purchase the tickets on my business credit card and file the email in a random folder. It's reckless, but I can't take the chance that Kyle won't go on the website himself. I can't take the chance that he might not believe me, and that his trust in me could be broken.

When he emerges from the bathroom with a towel around his waist, his hair still wet from the shower, I turn around and frown.

"The flight's fully booked, but it looks like there are other ones tomorrow. We could get one of those instead? I know it's not what we planned, but . . ."

"Oh." Kyle's disappointment is evident, but he doesn't question me, which makes me feel even guiltier for lying to him. "Okay, I guess we don't have a choice. Where will we stay tonight, though?"

"I'll see if we can get this room for another night," I say. "Then we could go somewhere for dinner?"

He shrugs. "I'm still on East Coast time—I'm pretty beat. Maybe we can just pick something up and eat here?"

"Sure," I say. "I can order takeout for us. I'll ask Marcel in the tasting room for suggestions."

As soon as I say his name, it dawns on me that he's the one person I haven't talked to yet who might have been there the night Michelle died, and a blip of hope rises up. When I asked him how long he'd been working at the Backyard, he'd said, *Too long. My whole life, it seems.* He worked here when David and Bev Kelly owned it. He knew the family.

I grab my purse from the suede bench in front of the window and slip into my shoes.

"Wait," Kyle says when I'm at the door. I tense up before turning around.

"Yes?" I ask, practically holding my breath.

"I just wondered—could you pick up some Advil? I forgot to pack mine, and I have a huge headache."

Relief floods my body. "Sure, of course. I'll be back soon."

I find Nadia in the small lobby of the Barn and explain that I'd like the room for another night, if possible. Luckily, there isn't a reservation booked until Friday, so I swipe my credit card to pay the additional charge. "What does your fiancé think of this place so far?" Nadia asks.

"He loves it," I say quickly, stuffing down my guilt for wasting her time. Even if we didn't already have a venue booked, there would be no way we'd ever get married or have our honeymoon here.

Marcel is in the tasting room when I arrive, standing behind the bar's gleaming wooden surface, a pair of reading glasses perched on his nose. The top button of his starchy white shirt is undone, and his vest droops off his shoulders slightly. The tasting room is full of guests sitting around tables with flights of wine, but Marcel meets my eyes and smiles warmly when he sees me.

"Miss Emery," he says. "It's wonderful to see you again. Can I interest you in another glass of chardonnay? I remember how you enjoyed it last time. Or do you have something else in mind?"

"Chardonnay would be great," I say, taking a seat on a vacant stool across from him. He places an elegant stemmed glass in front of me and pours the wine with an expert flourish.

"Actually, I was hoping to ask you a question. This is going to seem random, but—you said you've worked here for a long time. I found out a girl drowned in the pond after a party—were you there that night? Do you remember anything about it?"

His smile is replaced by a resigned sadness. "That was a long time ago, and I'm afraid I don't know very much at all."

I'm not willing to let it go, so I press him. "Please, it's important. Anything you might remember—I need to know."

He turns away, and for a second I think he's dropping the conversation, but he turns back and begins to speak. "I only remember the next day, when her father reported her as a missing person and came with the others to search the vineyard for her. Everyone was in a panic. And when they found her body—it was a very dark time for all of us. I don't think anyone expected her to be dead."

"I can imagine. How terrible." I swirl the wine in my glass. "Did you see her at the party?"

He shakes his head. "I didn't even know about the party. I was done for the day around dinnertime. We didn't have the inn on the property back then—that was Sadie's doing, converting the barn and changing things around here. Back then, with Bev and David, we didn't have overnight guests."

"Oh." I feel myself deflate, my last possible source of information having no information at all. "That makes sense. It's just so sad, what happened."

"It was terrible," Marcel says, nodding. "And I know how hard Bev took it. It totally wrecked her."

My chest tightens. Bev hadn't wanted to talk about that night, hadn't wanted me to know anything about Michelle. I had wondered who she was protecting, but was she really protecting herself?

"It must have been so traumatic," I say. "Especially for something like that to happen here."

"Yes. Business was rocky after. I worried about losing my job. I could have gone somewhere else, but Bev and David had become like family to me. I didn't want to leave them. They were good employers. But Bev—after the accident—she changed."

I frown, gripping the base of my wineglass. "What do you mean, she changed?"

Marcel looks at me with suspicion in his eyes. "I should go see if the other guests need anything."

"Please—I need to know."

His shoulders seem to cave inward, and I fear that he's going to start asking me questions instead of answering mine. But he starts to speak quietly. "She was just so upset over the tragedy. It was understandable— we all were. Bev, though. She almost turned into a different person afterward."

"Did she feel guilty?" I ask.

"We all did," he says. "Even if we weren't there. We were a family."

"You must remember when Andrew went to boarding school, then," I say, inching forward. "That must have been a big change."

This time, Marcel raises an eyebrow, and I know I've said too much. "How well do you know the Kellys, Miss Emery?"

I need to give him something, so I go with the truth, knowing I'll likely never see him again anyway. "I—I knew Josh."

At the mention of Josh's name, Marcel's expression softens. "I knew him too. He was so much like his father." I steel myself for another version of Josh I don't want to know, but Marcel goes in the opposite direction. "Confident. Assured. Always took the time to chat with me—with all the employees. He was a fine young man. He would have done great things."

"Yes," I say, tears blooming in my eyes, fighting the urge to reach across the bar and hug Marcel for believing in the same Josh I do. "He was."

"Out of curiosity, why are you asking so many questions?" Marcel says. "This all happened so long ago."

"After the last time we talked, I looked up the winery on Google," I say quickly. "You'd mentioned that it changed names, and I wanted to learn why." As he looks at me, his dark eyes probing mine, I wonder if I senses the connection.

Marcel is summoned away by one of the tables, so I pull my phone out of my purse. I have a message from a number I don't recognize, and the words make my entire body freeze.

**If you want to talk about what really happened to Josh, come to the house— alone.**

I stare at the text message, unable to properly breathe. I glance over my shoulder, my eyes darting around the room, which is busier now than when I arrived. Marcel is talking to a couple seated at a table, and there is a group of women down the bar from me, their gazes flitting between their phones and the emptying wineglasses in front of them. I'm momentarily paranoid. I've taken up too much of Marcel's time, and somebody has seen me asking questions.

If the message is telling me to come to the house, it must be from Sadie. Maybe she got my number from the hotel booking? But she wouldn't tell me anything yesterday. Why would she suddenly be willing to talk now?

The phone trembles in my hands, and the din in the tasting room hums along, glasses clinking and people laughing, everyone so happy and carefree. I think about Kyle back in the room, waiting for his fiancée to return with a meal, the same way I'd once waited for Josh in an Airbnb in San Francisco.

I stand up, leaving my unfinished glass of wine and a twenty-dollar bill on the bar, and make the walk to Sadie and Andrew's house on au- topilot, my stomach a mash of terror and nerves. The more I learn about Josh, the many versions cobbled together by the people in his life, the more I wonder if I did blindly love a man I didn't know at all. Josh and I had spoken about traumas from our past. I told him about losing my beloved grandmother to cancer. He told me about his dad's heart attack, and how it had left him devastated—the suddenness of it, the fact that his father had still been so young, the fact that he never got to say goodbye.

But he had somehow managed to omit both a twin brother and a dead girlfriend from his history—presumably some of the most forma- tive and important people in his life. Would he have told me eventually?

We'd been married after knowing each other only six months. We still had a lifetime to go.

As I stand at Sadie's doorstep, my heart is racing so fast that my entire body feels like one erratic pulse. I knock, waiting for Sadie to open the door, with some kind of explanation that will help all of this make sense.

But when the door creaks open, it's not Sadie who answers.

It's Josh.

## Ten

# *Bev*

St. Helena, Napa County, California
November 1999

**RODNEY YOUNG'S FIRST INSTINCT,** after hearing Michelle wasn't with her friends or at her mother's house or at our vineyard, had been to call the police. He'd told us a pair of officers came to his house and asked questions, and promised they'd investigate. But frustrated with how slowly they moved, he'd taken matters into his own hands and recruited a group of us to search for Michelle—me; David; the boys; Michelle's stepmother, Jen; some of Michelle's girlfriends who'd been at the party.

"She didn't say she was coming over here," he told me when he arrived, his tone accusatory. "She said she'd be at her mother's. Did you know she and Josh were still seeing each other?"

"I thought they worked things out," I mumbled.

David's eyes darted between us. "What do you mean?" he said.

I stared at the ground. I waited for Rodney to tell him about our exchange in the grocery store. But he turned to Jen and asked her to start coordinating the teens into groups for a makeshift search party.

"Sylvie's not coming," Jen said in a low voice. Rodney shook his head.

"Her own goddamn mother won't be here? What, does she have something better to do?"

"She's doing her own search," Jen said with a tense shrug. "Carrie and Darla are with her."

Rodney was not a large man, but when he was angry, he looked more imposing. I could tell Jen didn't want to deliver any more bad news. But I couldn't help but be annoyed with Michelle's mother, the woman who'd given birth to her. From what I'd seen, Sylvie was standoffish and cold. What kind of mother wouldn't join a search party for her own daughter?

Somebody might have wondered the same thing about me. What kind of mother shuttles her own son away to boarding school for something he didn't do?

We walked down each row of grapes, calling Michelle's name until our voices were hoarse. I lost track of how many laps we trod of the same ground, finding no traces of her. Rodney insisted there was nowhere else she could be. He wouldn't even listen to Jen's whispered thought that maybe Michelle was upset and ran away.

In front of our house, Rodney asked Josh and Andrew an artillery-fire round of questions. "What time did she leave last night? You must've seen her leave." He looked from one boy to the other, clearly unable to tell them apart. "You must have said goodbye to her."

"I did," Josh answered, his clipped tone not matching the fear in his eyes. "She said she was riding with a friend. I went to put the bonfire out and figured she got home."

But when one of the girls who had been at the party piped in to say Michelle had been crying, the entire mood shifted. "Maybe she went somewhere to cool off," she suggested, like she was trying to be helpful.

"Why was she crying?" Rodney shouted, but the teenagers remained quiet, eyes fixed on the ground. "I told you that you weren't welcome around my daughter anymore," he added, staring at Josh, his hand balled into a tight fist. For a brief second, I thought he was going to hit Josh, but instead, he stalked off in the other direction, tugging at his hair.

"Is that true?" I asked Josh as the group dispersed to keep looking for Michelle. I didn't wait for him to answer before launching into a second question. "Why did he not want you around Michelle?" I needed to hear his side of the story. I needed it to make sense.

"I don't know what he's talking about, Mom," Josh said. "I think he's so worried that he's taking it out on me."

I wanted so badly to believe him. But I'd seen Rodney in the grocery story. Heard his warning. Something had happened.

As our feet pounded the sun-bleached grass, the collective panic deepened, and I *knew*. I knew, instinctively, that something bad had happened. On some deep, cellular level, I knew there was only so much I would be able to do to protect my sons from the world, and to protect the world from my sons.

Maybe my whole life had been careening toward this inevitable moment. Starting with the terrified young woman who had stared dumbly at a black-and-white screen during an ultrasound, who had held her breath when a technician informed her that there were two, that it would be risky, twins sharing the same placenta, competing for the same nutrients that only her body could provide. When she found out they were both boys; when their kicks and punches from within made her feel like she was the enclosure for a boxing ring. When she was cut open on an operating room table, feeling spent as her sons were pulled out of her and held up over a screen, bloody red and screaming.

I had been shaking too hard to hold them until several hours after they'd been born, and when they were in my arms, I had stared at their tiny, scrunched-up faces, and I had felt love, but also panic. I wondered who they'd become, both because of and in spite of me.

"Michelle," I yelled again, but my voice barely registered as more than a whisper. We'd combed every inch of land, every building and hiding place double-checked. *She could be home now*, some of the friends started to say as they stood in nervous clumps, trying to ease the thickening tension. Andrew wandered in circles, and Josh kicked a rock with his shoe.

I squeezed my eyes shut, picturing Michelle. Her easy smile, the confident way she stood. The girl in the barn, giving herself to the wrong boy. The girl who sat beside the pond and excitedly talked about her bright future.

My entire body went cold and rigid. *The pond*, its surface dark as an oil slick, capable of concealing so much. We had combed every inch of the vineyard, but not underneath it.

I ventured back there after the teens in the search party scattered. I wandered the pond's perimeter. The surface was still and uninterrupted: no bobbing blonde head, no fan of hair across the surface.

But out of the corner of my eye, I saw something on the muddy edge, a flash of white. I bent down to reach for it, then coiled the object in my palm, knowing, without even looking, what it was. A puka shell necklace, just like the ones Camille had brought back for the boys from a trip she took to Mexico. Andrew never wore his, but Josh always did.

Rodney called the police again, insisting his daughter wouldn't have run away. Apparently he had been in touch with Sylvie, who had been searching for Michelle all day; she'd gone as far as the airport, checking the hospital, along with every hotel, every flight. There was no sign of Michelle anywhere. I pictured Sylvie in her Mini Cooper racing down the highway, her blonde hair streaming like a flag, like an older version of Michelle.

Rodney bluntly told the police, within earshot of me and David, that he'd forbidden her from seeing Josh. He said he didn't know she was seeing him anyway. He said there was nowhere else Michelle would be than our vineyard.

The cops showed up that evening when the air was just beginning to cool. They brought search dogs, whose wet noses twitched in the air. Besides the shrunken late-harvest grapes, the vines were nearly empty; the cabernet grapes had been the last to go. I wondered if the dogs could smell the remnants of their juices, the bloody ripeness of them.

But they must have smelled something else, because they led the police back to the place I suspected they would. The pond. I sat on the porch swing, rocking back and forth, a blanket over my clammy shoulders. I heard the dispatch come through the device on a nearby officer's waistband. *We found something.*

David and the boys talked to the officers, their voices rising up like plumes of smoke. Nobody saw me slip away, through the vines, my blanket dragging behind me like a ghost.

I arrived just as they pulled her out of the pond.

At first, when one of the police divers emerged with Michelle bundled against his chest, I let a ridiculous hope bubble up that she was still alive, and I waited for someone to start CPR. But when he laid her down on the grass beside the pond, I could see how wrong I was. Michelle was gone. Her hair was viscous like seaweed, her limbs somehow stiff and floppy at once, her pink dress suctioned to her body. Her head lolled to the side, a crimson gouge near her hairline, pale blue eyes open but unseeing.

My fist went into my mouth, and I bit it to stifle my scream.

I didn't realize, at first, that Andrew was there beside me, his hand on my back. A wail escaped his lips, followed by the retch of vomit leaving his mouth.

One of the police divers turned toward us. "Nobody's allowed to be here. This is a crime scene now. You two need to leave."

Every nerve ending in my body was on fire during the walk back, Andrew and I hand in hand, steadying each other, the puka shell necklace in my damp back pocket. It was the longest walk of my life. *I'll have to be the one to tell Josh.* The thought made me nauseated.

Even more sickening was the suspicion that he already knew.

## Eleven

# *June*

St. Helena, Napa County, California
September 2022

**"JUNE," HE SAYS.** His voice isn't the same—it's not silky or assured, but hesitant. His hands are dangling at his sides, like he's not sure what to do with them. I can't speak, can't stay his name, because logically, I know it's not Josh I'm face-to-face with but Andrew Smith.

The resemblance is so identical its dizzying. I can't help the tears, the way they instantly leak from my eyes. I sink down, unable to even support my own weight. Through my watery vision, I look up at him, seeing how the years have altered his face. He has the same double-dimpled smile and slate-blue eyes, his sandy hair still thick but graying at the temples. Same cleft chin and square jaw, same five-o'clock shadow, even though he probably just shaved this morning.

"I'm Andrew," he says. "Please, come in. I think we have a lot to talk about."

I follow him into the house, where he hands me a tissue and waits for me to wipe my tearstained cheeks. I'm feeling a heavy mixture of disappointment and foolishness. Of course he isn't Josh. It's Andrew. And he knows exactly who I am.

I back up, the fear finally kicking in.

"Don't be frightened," he says, placing his hands out, the way some-one might attempt to reassure a skittish animal. "Sadie let me know you were here. As soon as I heard, I knew I needed to talk to you."

"She said you were on a business trip," I say, waiting for him to nod his assent. He doesn't.

"It's a long story," he says slowly. "Will you sit down?"

"Where is Sadie?" I spin around, expecting to see her in the kitchen or living room. Out of the corner of my eye, I notice Andrew sidle back over to the front door and lock it.

"She went to drop off our son at a friend's house," he says. "Our girls are asleep upstairs. Come and sit with me in the kitchen."

I trail behind him. The hair at the nape of his neck is wavy, the same way Josh's used to get between haircuts.

I focus on breathing normally. Andrew wouldn't do anything to me with his children sleeping upstairs. But I don't know this man, or what he's capable of, only that he looks exactly like Josh, right down to the broadness of his shoulders and the coarse hair on his forearms. When he turns around, I want to freeze-frame his face, capture exactly what my husband would have looked like had he lived to forty, like those forensic police photos that show a missing person's age progression.

"I thought the text was from Sadie," I say, sitting across from Andrew at the kitchen table, the same table where Sadie and I sat last night.

"I didn't think you'd show up if you knew it was from me." The casual way he says it sends a chill down my spine, and immediately my mind goes to Josh's final text message—the one that I'm more sure than ever wasn't from him.

I'm careful with my words. "Sadie told me you don't think Josh's death was an accident either."

"I didn't. I spent a long time wondering. And a long time feeling guilty."

His voice is softer than Josh's. Josh was all confidence, all high volume and energy, the person in a room making everyone around him laugh. Andrew seems quieter, more reserved.

"Why would you feel guilty?" I ask.

"Because I was supposed to meet up with Josh the day he died. I'm the reason why he was at Mile Rock Beach."

I stare at him, panic rising under my skin. "You asked him to meet you there?"

"Well, he asked me if I'd see him, and I suggested that place. But he didn't show up . . . or so I thought, until later."

A chill creeps over my body. "But you were estranged. Why did he want to meet up with you?"

"We'd been messaging back and forth for a couple months. Sort of . . . getting to know each other again. When he told me he was in San Francisco, we agreed to meet up. I think we both knew that seeing each other would determine if we'd ever be able to repair our relationship."

"He never told me about you . . ." My voice trails off. "I didn't even know you existed, much less that you were messaging each other."

"He reached out," Andrew says. "It had been so long, but I had been thinking about him too. I was curious what he wanted. He seemed different—like he really had changed. We were both different people back then. Our mom wanted us to reconcile so badly—she was constantly telling me it wasn't too late."

If Andrew is telling the truth, it means during the months Josh and I were together, he was messaging the brother he'd never told me about. Was I the catalyst for wanting to repair the relationship? Was he planning to be truthful with me about his family once he had a chance to speak with Andrew in person? It's something I'll never know.

"I was in San Francisco with him," I say. "We'd just gotten married earlier that week . . . He told me he was getting breakfast, then he sent me a text message saying he decided to go for a swim. He sent a heart emoji with it. He never used emojis."

I watch Andrew's face closely, but his gaze remains on the table. "Nothing from that day makes sense. I waited for Josh for almost an hour. When he didn't show up, I was angry at myself for giving him a chance. Then my mom called the next day to tell me he was missing, and I knew something had happened."

It's almost surreal, imagining somebody besides me waiting for Josh that day. Andrew doesn't offer any more details, so I jump in to keep the conversation going.

"Sadie said you'd gone to boarding school. Was it strange, going away without Josh?"

I can tell I've struck a sore spot. He drums his fingertips on the table methodically.

"I didn't exactly go willingly," he finally says. "But my parents thought it was the best for all of us. Maybe it was."

I sense him slipping away from me, emotionally retreating, and I know it's only a matter of time until he shuts down and stops giving me more details. But I have one question I can't leave without asking.

"I know about Michelle—that she drowned here during a party. Is she the reason you and Josh stopped talking?"

Andrew brushes his hair off his face, a gesture uncannily like Josh's. "Yes. We already weren't really speaking, but after Michelle—there was no going back."

When his eyes rise to meet mine, they're so cold and hard. The household hums with quiet. *After Michelle.*

"What happened?" I ask, knowing the ultimate outcome but terrified of the answer.

We sit in silence for what feels like an eternity before Andrew speaks again. "Michelle was different from anyone I'd ever met. She was so sure of herself. Confident. Athletic. We had a couple classes together junior year, and I wanted to ask her out, but I was shy, and I didn't think she had time for a boyfriend anyway. She had too much else going on. But then I made the mistake of admitting to Josh that I liked her. He was with a girl named Abby at the time—he always had a girlfriend. I thought I was safe to admit it, so I said I liked Michelle."

"And what did he say?" I'm mesmerized by the idea of teenage Josh, a version of him I never knew.

"That I should ask her out."

Relief washes over me. It's what any normal brother would do—be supportive. But I know that isn't how the story ends. That it's not even close.

"I'm not sure what happened next," Andrew says. "It depends on who you ask. But there was this photo of Abby that got passed around school. A photo Josh took of her—one he kept in his nightstand. I knew it was there. He'd bragged about it. She was—it was a Polaroid. She wasn't wearing any clothes."

Heat fills my chest, and I'm awash with humiliation for Abby, whoever she is, the teenage girl this happened to. It's different, hearing the story from Andrew, than it was hearing it secondhand from Sadie. More personal, and even more disturbing.

"I got blamed for the photo," Andrew says, looking ahead, instead of at me. "I've had a lot of time to think about it, and I think Josh panicked and blamed me when he realized how out of hand it had gotten. I think he wanted to embarrass her because she was planning to break up with him and he didn't want her to get together with anyone else, but he didn't know the school administration would get involved. Somebody was going to pay for it, and I was the obvious choice. I knew the photo was there. I could have stolen it. My parents believed Josh. He was a good actor."

"Oh," I finally manage, wanting to defend Josh, but not wanting Andrew to stop talking. "That must have been so hard for you."

"Hard, yes. And cruel. Abby . . . she tried to hurt herself, and she never went back to our school. I didn't either. My parents came to me with the idea of boarding school for senior year. They tried to pitch it as a better education—I was doing so well in my classes and wasn't being challenged enough. But they made it happen fast. My dad was well known, and he got everything swept under the rug. The school never actually expelled me, and it never went on my record, but I had to live with it anyway."

"I can't imagine," I say, but it's Abby I'm saddest for, a girl I've never met but desperately wish I could comfort. "That sounds so difficult—for you, and your parents for having to do that."

He nods. "I always got the feeling my mom secretly believed me. That she had doubts about Josh. But she never told me that, and now he's dead, and she'll never say a bad word against him."

I need to bring the conversation back to Michelle, as much as it hurts having to hear about this version of Josh. But Andrew keeps talking.

"You don't want to listen to this, but Josh had a pattern with girls. Michelle was part of it. When I came back for Thanksgiving and he was with her . . . he rubbed it in my face. I could see how he'd changed her. He loved to taunt me, saying I'd die a virgin. And I snapped."

My body goes cold. I can picture it, Andrew's temper coming to life, his shoving Michelle's head underwater in a pond and trying to blame it on Josh, the same way he thought Josh had blamed the photo on him. The way he could snap any second in this kitchen.

"What I did was terrible," Andrew says. "But then it got worse."

"What happened?" I grip the edge of the table, my fingertips white.

"At the party where Michelle went missing, Josh was the last person to be seen with her. Her cause of death was drowning, but she sustained a head injury prior to that. The police thought she must have slipped and hit her head on one of the rocks that surrounded the pond. But did she really slip? I spent a lot of time thinking he either pushed her, or . . ." He trails off, obviously not wanting to say it out loud. "Did he do it? Or was he not even there?"

I pause; is he waiting for me to weigh in? I picture Josh with a rock in his hand, his unassuming girlfriend turning around, something I'm horrified to even be imagining. "Why would Josh hurt his own girlfriend?"

When Andrew speaks, his voice is thick with regret. "Because he found out what I did. I knew he was going to find out eventually . . . but at the time, I didn't care."

"What did you do?" I say, my pulse throbbing in my throat.

"Michelle and I—we slept together," he says, a pained expression on his face.

"So she cheated on Josh with you, and he found out?"

"Not exactly," he says, taking a deep breath. "But if it weren't for me, Josh never would have been so angry."

I'm afraid of what he'll say next. The version of Josh I've met since arriving in Napa doesn't align with mine at all, and yet, the fragments are being pulled together like magnets, forming an image I desperately don't want to see.

"I want to go," I say.

"I slept with Michelle," Andrew says, his gaze locked on the table, like he's too ashamed to look at me. "And I made her think it was Josh she was with."

I lean back in my chair, filled with equal parts disgust and fear. Still—why would Andrew admit to doing something so hideous if he wasn't telling the truth about everything else?

"I didn't kill her," Andrew says as he looks up, his eyes imploring. "But if Josh found out, did I drive him to a terrible act? Who wouldn't have cracked after hearing about that? I've regretted it every day of my life, but at the time, I was so angry. I had to make him suffer."

I stand up on autopilot. I need to get out of here. Josh was apparently the last person seen with Michelle at that party, but Josh and Andrew are twins, so who was really with her? And Andrew was supposed to be meeting with Josh on the day of Josh's death, leaving him with a better chance than anyone to have his revenge and kill Josh.

"You did something to him," I say, backing away. "And you were following me in Brooklyn—you were watching me."

"No—there's a reason," he says, his palms coming down on the table, wiry strength coursing through his forearms. "Yes, I was watching you, but not because I want to hurt you—"

I inch along the countertop, my hands behind me. One of them closes over a hard object. It's a wine bottle, the same one Sadie and I drank from last night, the small-batch mondeuse. I grab the neck of it, and when Andrew stands up and advances toward me, I bring it in front of me. "Don't come any closer."

"June," he says, his face full of concern and regret. "Please, don't go."

I stalk past him to the foyer and jiggle the doorknob frantically, but I can't get it to open. Andrew doesn't try to stop me, but he keeps talking. "Josh kept things from you. Please let me explain . . ."

I don't want him to explain. I move into the living room, where I see the sliding glass doors leading onto the walk-out deck. I unlatch the doors, slip outside, and run headlong into the dark night of the vineyard, my breath coming in short huffs.

When Andrew calls my name again, his voice is louder. "June!" he

yells, and I fish through my purse with shaking hands, desperately grasping for my key card. I run straight for the Barn, my footfalls heavy. I turn
around to glance behind me, but Andrew isn't following me.

Still, I keep running, even though I'm not sure exactly what I'm running from. I might be escaping a dangerous man. Or the danger could be
all in the past. Maybe the danger died alongside Josh, my kind, adoring
husband.

A man who might not have existed.

# Twelve

St. Helena, Napa County, California
November–December 1999

**MICHELLE YOUNG'S DEATH WAS** ruled an accidental drowning. It was the water that had killed her, the drowning that was her official cause of death. But the rocky ledge she'd hit her head on had been what made her drown in the first place. The autopsy showed a high alcohol level in her bloodstream. It all culminated in a tragic but predictable story. She had gotten drunk at the party, tripped, and smacked her head on the ledge, then passed out, sinking under without so much as a scream.

I wanted to believe it, but I couldn't stop wondering about the puka shell necklace hidden in my jeans pocket. I had known it was only a matter of time until Michelle found out what happened in the barn. Andrew must have known that too. Had Michelle mentioned the barn to Josh, the time she believed they'd spent there? My brain spun with theories I tried to expunge. I wanted to think the same thing David did: that Josh was innocent of any wrongdoing.

I watched Josh closely in the days that followed, wishing a puka shell necklace would materialize around his neck and put to rest my suspicion that the necklace in my pocket was his. I couldn't quite remember—had he been wearing it recently? He was always losing things, leaving them at school or around the house. Had he lost it by the pond weeks ago?

David and I were supposed to take Andrew back to Dunn, but I didn't want to let him go. I was suddenly terrified of what would happen with either of my sons out of my sight.

I cried on the phone to Camille, who had been visiting friends in Maine for Thanksgiving. But even though I was used to telling her everything, I left out the part where Michelle had wanted to talk to me that night, and that I never heard what she was going to say. I left out the puka shell necklace. I left out a lot. I knew Camille would just find a way to defend the boys anyway.

The Golden Grape closed to the public until we could figure out a reopening strategy. We were warned that there would be a lawsuit: Rodney was suing us for accidental death and underage drinking on our property. We hired a lawyer, at first unsure if Rodney had grounds for a real case. But he did. We would have to pay, although we weren't sure how much. David wanted to fight it—to protect us and our winery at all costs— but I had no fight left. I couldn't put a price on Michelle's life.

Five days after the party, Rodney Young turned up on our property, ranting and red-faced, spittle flying from his mouth. "Your son killed our daughter," he shouted. "I know he did it. I told him to stay away. I knew he was bad for her."

All I could do was cry.

"We are so devastated over Michelle's death. But this was a tragic accident," David said, cool and collected as ever, as I stood useless in the background, tears dripping down my cheeks. He spoke to Rodney not like a friend, a friend he'd gotten drunk and shared meals with, but like a pacifying father figure.

"This isn't over," Rodney said, putting his hands on David and pushing him backward. "Maybe you should ask your boy what happened to Michelle. Better yet, send him out here. I'll get him to talk."

In the end, Rodney finally got back in his car, his tires spitting up gravel as he sped out of the parking lot. Jen was waiting in the passenger seat. She wouldn't even look at me. Sylvie hadn't come by. I'd had flowers and a card delivered to her house. She never responded, and I didn't expect her to. The flowers had probably been tossed promptly into the garbage.

We deserved Jen's avoidance, Sylvie's silence. We deserved Rodney's wrath. Michelle had died on our watch. I walked around with the same nausea I'd had in my early pregnancy with the twins. Back then, I had ignored it because it was inconvenient, the same way I had ignored the warning signs as the boys grew up. Josh loved to win; Andrew was his built-in competitor. I should have stepped in more often. I should have disciplined Josh and defended Andrew, instead of telling myself they'd figure it out. Josh would mellow with age, and Andrew would grow more of a backbone.

Josh and Andrew had already given their version of events from the party to the detectives, glassy-eyed and shell-shocked as they made their statements. Andrew had left the party early and gone up to his room, a story David and I corroborated. People had seen Michelle upset, but nobody knew what was bothering her. Josh said he was busy putting out the bonfire and thought she'd gotten a ride home with a friend.

Neither of them mentioned the barn and what had transpired there. It would have given them both a motive to want Michelle gone.

As the days stacked up after Michelle's death, I avoided my sons. I could barely look at them, and our conversations were formal and stilted. Michelle hung heavily in every room, making it hard to take a breath. Whenever I brought her up, the boys both went quiet.

"I don't want to think about her like that," Josh told me. "Like she isn't here anymore. It hurts too much."

I could tell he was holding back tears. I let myself believe that the tears were of sadness, not guilt.

Josh and Andrew weren't speaking, but they weren't arguing either. If Josh knew about what had happened in the barn, like I suspected he did, I would have expected him to treat Andrew terribly. But instead, the boys completely ignored each other in the days that followed Michelle's death. It was like each was already dead to the other.

I needed to talk to someone, but David felt unavailable, the same way he had felt after Abby. He had gone on autopilot, compartmentalizing

Michelle's death as a tragic accident. I needed someone more removed from the situation—someone who wasn't afraid to be honest.

I didn't expect Emilia to answer. I had no idea where she was—New York, Naples, or somewhere else, maybe at a lush green winery on the other side of the world, tipping a dark-cherry Chianti into her mouth and giving a throaty laugh. But she answered on the first ring, her voice hoarse with sleep. "Bev Jamieson. I was just thinking about you."

"Why do you keep calling me Bev Jamieson? I'm Bev Kelly now."

I heard the smile her face was making. "Because you'll always be Bev Jamieson to me. The girl I met the first week of college, with the shearling coat and the adorable Midwest accent you tried so hard to hide. No matter how much you change."

I paused. "Did I wake you up? I wasn't sure where you were."

"I'm in Puglia. And it's like I knew you were going to call. I was at a winery today that has this red wine you'd be obsessed with. I was thinking about you and how much you'd love it."

"You could have called me," I said quietly.

"You know why I didn't," she said. We both knew. It was the same reason she had never placed a wine order from the Golden Grape. She was keeping her distance.

I sank onto the sofa and tucked my legs beneath my robe, her voice untethering me from my dark reality. "Something happened," I said, and I told her everything about that night, leaving out only the details about Andrew and Michelle in the barn and finding the necklace at the pond. I would carry my doubts to the grave.

"Oh my god," she said. "I'm so sorry, Bev. That's terrible. I don't even know what to say, except that I know you're blaming yourself—I can hear the guilt in your voice. And this was not your fault." I could practically feel her fingertips on my face, her silken touch.

"But if the boys . . . ," I started, unsure of how far I should go. "If she drowned because of something they did . . . I told you about Andrew being away at boarding school, and the week he came home . . . this happened." I tiptoed closer to the truth without bringing up the evidence. "I should have done something. If I'd been a better mother . . ."

"You're a good mother," she said. "I know how much you care about them. But your sons are their own people. You can't influence everything they do."

She didn't understand. She wasn't a mother and never would be. Emilia was free to live for herself, but it was because she didn't know the sacrifices demanded by motherhood. The gap between us had never felt wider.

"Do you want me to come over?" she said quietly.

"You're halfway around the world," I said, her soft words curdling the longer they sat in my ear. It was that easy for her to hop on a plane and make a change.

"Just say the word, and I don't have to be."

"No," I said, the syllable coming out more harshly than I'd meant it to. It wasn't Emilia's fault that she couldn't understand what I was going through. And it no longer felt like just me and Emilia. David was home, and we were getting back to normal.

"We can just sit like this," she said. "It's the next best thing to actually being together."

So we did. We sat in silence, and eventually, I was hushed to sleep by the faint sounds of her breath.

More than once after Michelle's death, David found Rodney Young creeping around the vineyard, half-drunk and ranting that the police had missed something. David walked him off the property, trying to calm him down, offering him coffee, asking him if he wanted Jen to pick him up. The final time, Rodney spat in his face and told him he would make sure the Golden Grape was razed to the ground one day.

"The police missed something," he yelled. "But my lawyers won't. And I won't. I'll never stop looking."

He wasn't wrong. The police had missed something. The puka shell necklace was hidden under our mattress. When I was certain nobody was around, I would bury it deep in the garden.

Even though I had disagreed with David about virtually everything since the incident with Abby, I began to understand, in my panicked fugue, his approach. He had believed his son, and did everything he could to protect him. He believed the best of those he loved. And we didn't have any concrete proof that Josh had been involved, just like we had no proof now. I told myself the police would have found out if something was awry, and they had cleared both my sons of wrongdoing.

The more I thought about it, the more I questioned myself. If the necklace was Josh's, it could have fallen off at any point in time. Lots of boys at St. Helena wore puka shell necklaces. Andrew had one too—I'd just never seen it around his neck. Had he taken it to Dunn with him and left it there? When the boys were out of the house, I searched their bedrooms, opening desk drawers and digging through piles of clothes, but found nothing. The question of whose necklace was under my mattress would be another one for which there was no answer.

If Michelle had been upset after finding out about Andrew, it made sense that she might have had way too much to drink, trying to numb herself. If she had been disoriented, she could have stumbled to the pond and fallen in, hitting her head in the process. The chain of events made sense when I thought about it like that—as a chain, one link leading to the next. But in my head, it was looped and knotted. I was haunted not by certainty, but by the possibility that my sons could have been involved.

Still—what was the alternative? If I voiced my suspicions, I'd be irreparably breaking our family apart. Our family, which was already hanging by a thread.

"Our business is tanking," David said that night, pulling on his pajama pants in a frustrated huff. "My great-grandfather named this place, built it from nothing. It survived phylloxera because of him. And my grandpa kept it out of bankruptcy during Prohibition and the Great Depression. They never gave up, and I won't either. We can't let this ruin our legacy." His head was in his hands. I'd seen David cry only twice—when his father died, and then when his mother went shortly after. Family meant everything to him.

"A girl is dead, David," I said, my throat closing around that word: *dead*. Not just any girl—Michelle, a girl who'd had her whole life ahead of her. I didn't see how we, or the Golden Grape, could move forward.

"I understand that. And it's a terrible tragedy—I haven't stopped thinking about it. But Rodney isn't going to let this rest. He's out for blood, Bev." His forehead was creased, his undereyes pouchy. I knew how much David was dealing with: the phone calls, the threats, the ugly things he was trying to shield us from.

"We'll be okay," I said. I wanted to believe it.

His body shifted, and he took my hands in his. His eyes were wild in a way I rarely saw, and I willed him to give me more of that wildness, more of his anger and fear. "Bev, I don't know—"

He was interrupted by a crashing sound from down the hall. I threw my robe on and followed David toward the source of the noise. When we got to Josh's room, Josh was on top of Andrew, his fist midswing. But no—it was the other way around, Andrew throwing the punches, Josh on the ground, his arms up in defense.

"You're a fucking liar," Andrew shouted, spit flying from his lips. "Did you kill her?"

"I didn't touch her," Josh said, his palms raised, his voice calm. "Just like I didn't touch you. I don't know what you're taking out on me, but my girlfriend is the one who died."

Andrew lunged again.

"Stop," I screamed, helping David hold Andrew back from his brother. "Stop, please!"

His fist whirled around with his body, and I didn't move out of the way in time. The blow grazed my jaw, landing there with a thud before sending me reeling backward.

"Mom," he said, the intensity leaving his features. "Mom, I didn't mean to—"

"This is unacceptable," David said, jerking on Andrew's arm. "Apologize to your mother, right this instant."

"Mom, I'm so sorry," he sobbed, his face crumpling. "I didn't mean to hurt you. But I think he brought her back to the pond . . . I saw them together . . ."

Josh pulled himself up and sat beside his bed with his sleeve obscuring a bloody nose. "Why don't you tell them what you did, Andrew? Why don't you tell them what you did to Michelle? You're sick. You're a mental case."

It was the most the boys had interacted in almost six months. I'd thought I wanted their anger out in the open so that they could deal with it. But I realized it was too big, too uncontrollable. There was no way to fix what was shattered beyond repair.

"Look at your brother's face," David said, rounding on Andrew. "You're lucky his nose isn't broken."

"I'm sorry . . . ," Andrew said, his voice quiet.

David went to speak, but I cut him off, knowing that if I didn't say something now, I never would.

"Were you involved? Did you do something?" I didn't address one boy or the other, leaving the question in the air for both of them to answer. David stared at me, his lips tightly pursed. He would have preferred I said nothing.

Andrew spoke first. "I didn't have anything to do with it."

"Well, neither did I," Josh said.

I glanced back and forth between the boys who had grown inside me, curled around each other like shrimp, kicking each other in utero, vying for the same source of nutrients. They had turned on each other. But I wouldn't turn on them. How could I condemn my sons without proof? They both denied it, so I would do the same.

"This is a difficult time," David said. "We're all struggling. But we need to get through this as a family. All of us together." He put his arm around my shoulders.

When we were alone in our room again, my body still quivering, David turned to face me in bed, his hand finding mine. "We don't want Andrew to fall behind this semester. I think it's time we bring him back to Dunn. It'll be good for him."

I knew what he meant. It would be good for all of us to get back into a normal routine. For the boys to have some space from each other.

David curved his body around mine, the same way he used to in my tiny dorm room bed. I sank into him. This was us: our most worn-in embrace, and we had found our way back to each other.

"They'll get past this, Bev. We raised them well."

It was easy for him to believe that, but I was having a harder time. Maybe that was every mother's fatal flaw. They never wanted to think a person they created could be capable of something terrible. Maybe there were nightmares, playing out occasionally behind their closed eyes, images easy to blink past and wake up from. But when they did wake up, they'd be able to shrug off the chill and move on, the bad dream forgotten.

David started snoring gently, his arms still tight around me. I couldn't sleep, instead torturing myself with what-ifs. What if I had defended Andrew, instead of agreeing to send him away? What if I had called Josh out on the way he treated his brother? What if I'd doted on them more as babies, instead of always wanting to be somewhere else? What if I'd played with them more as kids, instead of checking off their needs like another to-do list?

Maybe none of it would have made a difference, but maybe it would have changed everything.

## Thirteen

St. Helena, Napa County, California
September 2022

**I TAKE A DEEP BREATH** and stare at the door to our room before going in. There's a text on my phone from Kyle that I never responded to—*Are you coming back with dinner, I'm starving!*—and I know he'll be upset that I lied, that I haven't dropped this, that I'm never going to be able to move on.

But when I slip into the room, I'm met with the soft sound of Kyle snoring. My body tenses. I'm relieved that he's asleep, but afraid that when he wakes up, he'll be angry at me for ignoring his text and never showing up with the food. He must have figured out that I'd lied about where I was going, and if I lose Kyle's trust, I'm not sure what else I have left.

I lock the door and do up the chain, then double-check the sliding doors to make sure they're locked too, the curtains fully drawn. My heart rate hasn't slowed down. Part of me—the honest part—wants to wake Kyle up and tell him what happened. It's too late for us to get on the flight that was leaving tonight, but we could go somewhere else, somewhere far away from Andrew Smith.

I sink onto the bed, letting the adrenaline pool in my gut. Andrew had been desperate to unburden himself. He had obviously wanted me alone, and maybe I got out just before he could hurt me. But is that really what he planned to do? He hadn't threatened me. He'd only wanted me to listen, the one thing I wasn't willing to do.

Kyle's deep breathing fills the room, and I feel my eyelids start to flutter shut, my head getting fuzzy. I should have stayed and listened to the rest of Andrew's story. I came for the truth, but I wasn't ready to hear his side of it. He was at Mile Rock Beach the day Josh died. A couple of people had *seen* Josh there, pacing back and forth, but maybe it wasn't Josh they'd seen at all.

It's a question of who is the dangerous one—Andrew or Josh. I know which version I want to believe, but I don't feel so sure about anything anymore.

Suddenly, I hear a sound against the glass sliding doors, a light *rap-rap-rap. It's a tree branch*, I tell myself. A tree branch blowing in the wind. Except I was just outside, and I know it's a windless night, the air pin-drop still.

The noise lets up, but my nerves are on edge, and my limbs can't seem to relax, drumming fitfully on top of the comforter. I get out of bed and pad across the floor to the sliding doors, bracing myself as I part the curtains. There's nobody on the terrace, and nobody in the distance, the vineyard just barely visible under the light of the moon.

I place my forehead on the cool glass, steadying myself with several deep breaths, before pulling the curtains shut. Sitting on the suede bench, I open Google on my phone and type in Michelle Young's name again, and I reread the same article that came up after I had searched for a death at the Golden Grape yesterday. I click back out of it and scroll the Google search results, unsure what I'm even looking for. Something to absolve Josh, something that magically makes none of this his fault. But there's nothing, beyond the same smattering of articles I've trawled for the past two days.

I click on Michelle's photo again and use my fingers to zoom in on her face, pleading with her to tell me the truth: not Andrew's truth, and not her father's truth, but her own. But she just looks like a very pretty teenage girl, someone I might have envied back in high school, with her thin, highly arched brows and pale hair, her lips shiny with gloss.

*I'm sorry*, I think as I stare at her face.

I plug my phone into its charging block and get back into bed with Kyle, only to see the phone light up with a new text message the second my head hits the pillow.

The text is from the same phone number as before, from Andrew. But when I open it, there's nothing to read. It's a photo, of the girl I was just looking at: Michelle Young. She's hugging a boy tightly, their cheeks pressed together.

*No*, I think, the denial so instant and severe that my teeth start to chatter in tandem with my pounding heart. *It's not possible.* I've been under too much trauma and stress; my brain playing a sick game. If I look again, I'll see that it was an illusion.

But when I do force myself to look again, my fingers trembling on the screen, he's still there, cheek to cheek with Michelle Young. In the same photo as the girl my dead husband might have killed is the other man who vowed to love me forever, the other love of my life.

It's a baby-faced version of my fiancé, the man whose body is warm against mine. Standing next to Michelle on a tennis court is Kyle, smiling widely.

**PART IV**

# Clarification

Only after fermentation is complete can the process of clarification begin. Wine is siphoned from one barrel to another, with the goal of leaving behind the solids and dead yeasts that had remained in the fermentation tank. To help the process along, winemakers may add substances such as clay or egg whites to the wine, which cling to the unwanted solids and force them to settle at the bottom of the tank.

Once clarified, the wine is transferred to another barrel, where it will be ready for the final stage: bottling and aging.

It might look nothing like it used to.

# One

# *June*

St. Helena, Napa County, California

September 2022

**KYLE PARKER.** *MY KYLE* Parker, the one who asked me to marry him, the man sleeping peacefully in the bed behind me. The man who has been with me for six years. My brain frantically tries to justify a photo that defies logic. Kyle had nothing to do with Josh. I didn't meet him until years after Josh was already gone, and our meeting itself at the tennis center was pure chance. So many times, we'd marveled at our timing: I had needed a distraction, something to get me out of my apartment, and Kyle had wanted to return to his roots, to his love for tennis that he'd lost over the years. *I used to play a lot*, he'd said. *But I've gotten away from it.*

Maybe tennis wasn't the love he had lost.

I try to make it make sense. Michelle had been a student at St. Helena High with Josh—and Andrew, before boarding school. Kyle grew up in Pasadena and went to a totally different school. How would he have met her?

I feel the blood drain from my head, leaving me dizzy. *Grief is tricky*, Kyle had once said. *Don't feel like you have to act a certain way around me. Just feel what you need to feel.* It never occurred to me that he wasn't just being empathetic, but was instead speaking from experience.

A sob catches in my throat, breaking the silence. Andrew Smith wanted to tell me something tonight, and it wasn't just about Josh. I understand now: he had to earn my trust before he unloaded a story about my fiancé, the man I've been with for years.

He wasn't trying to harm me. He was trying to warn me, to tell me the truth about two people: the man I'd married and the man I am about to marry. I'm not the only link between them. Michelle Young is too.

The sound of rustling sheets makes me freeze. Kyle rolls over in bed. I hold my breath. I have no idea what I'll say to him if he wakes up. I don't know what it means that Kyle and Michelle were friends—or maybe even more than friends? But if he cared about her, that means Andrew wasn't the only one with a motive to kill Josh.

Except that scenario hinges on the certainty that Josh was the one who killed Michelle, something I still don't know if I can believe.

I stand up, stuff my phone in my purse, and slip into my shoes. I need to go talk to Andrew again, to find out everything he knows before Kyle wakes up.

I'm almost out of the room when Kyle stirs again. "June?" I hear him say, his voice heavy with sleep. But I don't stop. I pull the door shut quietly, then turn and walk the other way, in the direction of Andrew and Sadie's house, tears blurring my vision.

I'm approaching Andrew's front porch when I hear footfalls behind me. My shoulders tense up, my heart pounding.

"June," Kyle calls out. "Hey, wait. What are you doing? I texted you hours ago—what happened to you getting dinner? Where were you?"

I turn sharply and head for the vines, even though I know I can't hide here. Kyle jogs after me and catches my arm. "June, why are you running away from me?"

"I just needed to take a walk," I stammer. "I couldn't sleep. I'm sorry, but I want to be alone."

He rolls his shoulders, his gray Henley riding up. "Why? What's going on?"

There's fear in his eyes now, his brows furrowed. All this time, I thought he was just worried about me and our relationship, but what he was really worried about was my finding out the truth. He came here for me—but not really for me. He came here to convince me to go back home before I got too close to the truth about what happened to Michelle—and with it, the truth about what happened to Josh.

I pull my arm away from him and grab my phone from my purse. I wake up the screen and find Andrew's text, then hold it out toward Kyle. "You knew Michelle Young."

He opens his mouth, but no words come out.

"Who sent you that?" he finally says, his voice flat.

But I don't answer him. I can barely stand to look at him. I drop my phone back in my purse and turn around.

"June," Kyle says. "We can talk about this. I've wanted to talk about it, but . . ."

I start to walk away, needing to put some distance between us.

"Stop, please," Kyle says, walking behind me, but the closer he gets, the more I pick up my pace, until I'm running, his steps gaining quickly as I search for a place to hide, a place to escape, but there's nowhere in these orderly trellises. I know Kyle would never hurt me, but now all I can picture is his ferocious backhand cracking down on Josh's head. My breath comes in frantic waves.

"Did you do something to him?" I scream, turning around to face him, the bubble bursting in my chest, the ugly words along with it. "Are you the one who killed him?"

But he doesn't get a chance to answer, because suddenly we're not alone. There's someone else with us, someone who emerges from the shadows. Someone who has been waiting for this moment for a long time.

Andrew Smith.

I watch as his fist collides with Kyle's face. And I understand now that Andrew was in Brooklyn, but it was never me he was following.

# Two

# Bev

**OUR FAMILY WASN'T WELCOME TO** attend Michelle's funeral, but I went anyway, remaining in my car as the black-clad mourners walked down the grassy flat of the graveyard. Kieran babbled from the back seat. *Mama. Mama. Mama.*

In the weeks that followed, people returned to their lives. Josh went back to school, and David and I drove Andrew back to the Dunn campus, with the knowledge we would see him again soon for the Christmas holidays. We met up briefly with Camille in Santa Barbara before returning home. She promised she'd drop in and visit Andrew, take him for the occasional weekend lunch, make sure he was okay. I could tell she was worried about whether *I* was okay, but didn't want to ask in front of David. She had a potential buyer for her apartment and was visiting a friend in Australia in the New Year.

"If the world doesn't end, that is," she had joked, attempting to lighten the mood. The rumbling worry about Y2K had picked up steam as January encroached. I felt like my world had already ended; I couldn't bring myself to care about what the computers would do when the new millennium was ushered in.

All I could think about was Michelle and my sons, reliving the past in excruciating minutiae. If I'd told Michelle I knew about what had happened in the barn, she might have left the party so much earlier. I didn't get to hear what she came to the house to tell me. Every outcome I conjured up involved Michelle still alive.

Shortly before Christmas, David stormed into the kitchen in a huff, his forehead wrinkled in frustration. "Three contracts canceled," he said, tossing a sheaf of papers on the table. "Three restaurants that don't want to supply our wine anymore. It's Rodney Young. He's trying to blacklist us with his business contacts in San Francisco. He wants to make our lives a living hell."

*Aren't they already?* I wanted to say. Nothing at the winery had been the same since Michelle died. After we reopened to the public, fewer people showed up for tastings and tours. Rumors spread as quickly and as hot as the Santa Ana winds. *A girl died in their pond. A girl died on their property. They were in the house when it happened.*

The lawsuit was ongoing, though our lawyer thought we had a solid defense. We hadn't knowingly served alcohol to minors. The death on our property had been deemed an accident. But Rodney was seeking damages, and I didn't want to fight. I just wanted to pay what we rightfully owed. David insisted that doing that was akin to admitting we were in the wrong and would tarnish the winery forever.

"Thank god for Emilia Rosser," David said, staring at his clipboard. "She emailed this morning. A few of her restaurant clients in New York want to carry our cab sauv. Now, those are connections Rodney can't touch. She says she's coming back out here again next month to go over the contract and paperwork."

The mention of Emilia's name was like an anvil hitting me in the chest. I lurched forward and gripped the table with my hands. "She's coming back here? Let me see the email."

I scanned Emilia's words on the computer screen.

*Bev and David,* she began, *my clients have all been so impressed with your cabernet sauvignon. It's very special. Before I recommended it, I was afraid it would be overwhelming, but the longer I sat with it, the more I became overwhelmed in a good way. The aftertaste was the best part. It'll pair beautifully with their meatier fish dishes.*

"It's great," David said. "You must've done a hell of a job in your meeting with Emilia."

I broke into a laugh, tears collecting in the corners of my eyes. It should have been a happy moment—knowing Emilia was coming back—except I couldn't remember how to feel happy. My guilt held me in a vise grip, barely allowing me to breathe. My appetite was gone, and my sleep was fitful. I wanted to see Emilia, but I also knew I didn't deserve to get what I wanted.

When the landline rang the next morning after I dropped Josh off at school, I answered, and almost hung up when I heard Emilia's voice.

"Bev?" she said. "Are you there?"

"I'm here." My voice was tinny and small, like I was hearing it come out of someone else.

"What's wrong?"

"Everything?" I attempted a laugh, but it got stuck in my throat. "Everything is a mess, and I don't know if I'll ever feel like myself again. I just keep wondering, What's the fucking point?"

"What do you mean, what's the point? You're living your life, Bev—"

"That's the thing. I'm not," I said. "I was stupid to think things could be any different."

Emilia was silent on the other end. Somebody else might have hung up on me and my messy emotions, but Emilia wasn't somebody else. She didn't know me better than anyone, but she knew parts of me better than most people did.

"You aren't stupid," she said. "And you're not responsible for what happened. I know you think you are, but you're not."

"I just keep wondering . . . what if my boys were involved?" The words landed with a thud. The suspicion I kept coiled in my chest was out, and I couldn't take it back. I waited for the dial tone on the other end.

"Bev, that's . . . you don't know that," she said. "From everything you've told me, it was an accident—a freak tragedy. I'm not going to pretend I know everything about teenagers, but I do know a thing or two about blaming yourself for things, and about resentment. Even if you were a bad mother—and I don't think you are—that doesn't make you a bad person."

I couldn't help it. I laughed, even though it wasn't funny. I laughed as tears fell down my cheeks. "If I had done something sooner—if I'd paid more attention—none of this would have happened."

"You can't know that," she said. "Look, this might not be a good time to bring this up, but I'm coming back to Napa."

"I know," I said as the front door banged open and David strode in. I wiped my cheeks and forced myself to smile. "Um, I should go."

"You can't talk," she murmured. "I know. But you can call me anytime. I might not understand everything, but I'll listen."

After I hung up, David came up behind me, and he kneaded his fingers into my shoulders. "I know the last couple months have been hell, but these deals with Emilia are good news, Bev. We can do this. We can stay afloat and piece this family back together."

I almost believed him. But the truth was, I didn't deserve David any more than I deserved Emilia. What I deserved was to stay in the cage of my own making forever. I would give up battering at its bars.

I waited for December to inch to a close. For the world to possibly short-circuit after New Year's Eve. Andrew came back for Christmas with Camille, who would be spending the holidays with us. The vineyard became a brilliant ombré of shades of green, yellow, and burnt orange. Normally, we would string lights and garlands studded with holly berries up around the porch, but nobody felt festive enough to make it happen. I walked through my days in an anesthetized fugue, going through the motions of motherhood without feeling a thing.

Christmas itself was resigned and somber. Josh and Andrew were rarely in the same room together, and I didn't hear them speak a word. Neither David nor I tried to make them. We both sensed that the chill between them was better than the alternative. Camille fried up ribbons of bacon and flipped pancakes on Christmas morning, buoying the house with her off-key singing and stories about the places she was going to visit in Australia, and I tried to laugh along, even though the tightness in my chest made it hard to breathe. Being around the boys was driving me to a dark place, one where I imagined what they might do next, fatalistic scenarios that left me in the unrelenting clench of a panic attack. What if something happened to Josh's next girlfriend? And the one after that? How many coincidences could we accept?

Worse than the anxiety was the guilt that followed. How could I think such terrible things about my own children? Did they sense how I felt toward them, the sick fusion of love and fear? Would it drive them down an even darker path, knowing their own mother had doubts about them? They deserved better.

On New Year's Eve, I was in bed before midnight; David had wanted to celebrate the new millennium and the fresh start it symbolized, but I didn't see the point. The year 2000 rolled in unnoticed while I slept. Everyone who had expected the world to look different when the clock struck twelve was confronted by the reality that nothing had changed.

I was relieved when Andrew went back to Dunn the first weekend in January. I was relieved that Josh didn't have a new girlfriend already. The distance made it easier to breathe. But Emilia would arrive in a matter of weeks, and the anxiety quickly crept back.

I was afraid to see her. We hadn't talked since our last conversation on the phone, and I was worried about how she'd look at me, now that she knew the darkness that really lurked under the surface. I was scared that our connection would be gone. I was equally scared that it wouldn't be. Things were finally good with David. We had moved on. He had slept with another woman once, but I had done so much worse. I was the one with more to atone for.

The days dragged interminably until Emilia's visit. I tried to focus on other things: on Kieran, on the winery. But my heart had started a count-down that my brain was never not aware of. Ten days. Six days. Three days. The jittery anticipation, the last-minute visit to the hair salon. The careful selection of an outfit.

I repeatedly told myself it would be just business with Emilia; I rolled that resolution over and over in my head. The last thing I needed was more complications in my life. But as soon as she walked into the tasting room, her pink lips barely suppressing a smile, I felt it all over again, that sensation of infinite plummeting, the warmth of knowing I would be caught at the bottom.

"Emilia," David said, extending his hand. "So nice to see you again."

It was surreal, the two loves of my life in the same room. In person, it was just as confusing as it was in my head. I loved both of them in different ways. David was air, Emilia fire.

She returned his handshake and moved on to me, enveloping me in a hug that lasted a beat too long, her air kisses lingering on my cheeks. "It's so great to see you both."

I barely remembered what she said about the deals, because I was too busy fixating on her nearness, on the way her body shifted in her seat, on the graceful precision of her fingers. I needed to be alone with her. If I spent time alone with her, I would know.

When David went into the vineyard after dark, I told him I was going out to meet friends. The lie gnawed at me, especially when I saw the relief on his face. He wanted me to have more friends. He thought a more active social life would be good for me.

I drove myself to the Blossom. Emilia was in her room alone, waiting.

"I wasn't sure if you'd come," she said, lingering at the door.

"I wasn't sure either." I stepped closer, savoring her sweet perfumed scent. "I don't really know what I'm doing here. I shouldn't be here. But I needed to see you, alone. My life is supposed to be getting back to normal, but I keep thinking about you. Us. What it would be like, being together for real."

"It is real," she said, reaching for my hand. "If you want it to be."

I took her hand. I let her lead me into the room. I was the one who kissed her first. It felt like I couldn't not kiss her. I didn't think about how I was betraying David. I wouldn't let myself go there. Maybe that was the moment I realized my love for her was here to stay, even if she wasn't. But I didn't say it. My love was never good for anyone.

.  .  .

In the months that followed, Josh inched closer to finishing his senior year of high school at St. Helena, and Andrew at the Dunn School, where he excelled in every subject. There was talk of a summer internship for Andrew, an idea I wholeheartedly supported. Josh was in and out of the house, often with his friends; there was a new girl I sometimes saw waiting for him at St. Helena, a headband pushing back her thick dark hair. I didn't want to know her name. I didn't want to know anything about her.

Just as the boys had avoided each other, I sensed Josh avoiding me, connecting only on a surface level. Sometimes I caught myself staring at him, but when our eyes met, he'd quickly look away. I didn't know what I was more afraid of: that he could read my mind, or I, his. Every time I thought about having a real conversation, Michelle's memory intervened. Instead of opening up, I turned away.

But most of the time, he acted lighthearted, happy, well-adjusted. He was a normal teenage boy, one who showed resilience after going through a trauma. I was the problem, not him. I was the one still living in the darkness, and I hated myself for wanting to drag him back there with me.

David and I hummed along, our arguments few and far between. As soon as the lawsuit was settled and we quietly paid Rodney what he had been looking for, David seemed more carefree, more optimistic, like a weight had been lifted. He talked about taking a trip together. We were having sex more regularly, and he was helping out with Kieran. The last of my breast milk had dried up, and David liked to mix bottles of formula and feel useful. He liked to take Kieran into the vineyard, guiding him as he toddled on his dimpled legs and pointed to the grapes. When I watched them, I thought about what a nice family they made.

While David wasn't keeping any secrets from me, there was one I still kept from him. My calls with Emilia, which had gone from sporadic to almost daily. I was able to be vulnerable with her in a way I couldn't be at home. David was so determined for us to move on, and it felt like I was the one anchoring us in the past. Emilia became the outlet for everything I couldn't say to David.

No topic was off-limits, and she listened intently each time my guilt entered the conversation, which was often. I told her about Michelle and how frequently she was on my mind, about the dreams I conjured for a future she'd never get to have. Emilia never tried to change the subject or lighten the mood. She let me feel, and in processing those feelings, I finally sensed the bloodier parts of myself suturing closed.

But my healing came at a cost: guilt mingled with relief. I hated what I was doing to David: keeping secrets, carrying on an emotional affair with another woman. Splitting myself in two. I was one person with David: his loyal, hardworking wife, ruled by logic and common sense. With Emilia, I was somebody else, the real and messy self I'd long tried to contain.

On Emilia's next visit, late in the summer—almost a year to the day she came back into my life—the mood between us shifted. In her room at the Blossom, we sat side by side on her bed. She wouldn't touch me first; she wouldn't disrespect my marriage. But I was the one who leaned in. I swept her hair off her neck and planted kisses on her collarbone. My lips found hers, the kiss wide and engulfing. I ached for her to touch me, but she shook her head as she stood up.

"There's something I have to tell you," she said, pacing at the foot of the bed. "I got a job offer, at a winery in Croatia. They're building a resort, and they want me involved from the ground up—designing their wine list, talking to clients. It's a dream job. And I'm going to take it."

"Croatia?" I stammered. "That's amazing, but—I thought you hated the idea of staying in one place."

She sucked her top lip into her mouth. "I know, but things change. And we can't keep doing this, Bev. I can't keep doing this. What are we, exactly? We spend hours talking to each other, but you're still married, and if this is never going anywhere . . ."

"It's complicated with David," I said. "You know that . . ."

"I know our situations aren't the same," she said, grasping my hands. "You don't have the same freedom I do. But if you ever changed your mind—if you ever wanted to try something different—you could come with me. To Croatia."

I pictured us there. I pictured us everywhere. I opened my mouth to tell her I couldn't go, even though I wanted to. But what came out was "I love you. I think I have for a very long time."

There was surprise in her eyes. I had said it first; I had said it out loud. The confusing thing was that I still loved David too. If Emilia hadn't existed, I might have been perfectly happy with David forever.

"You need to make a choice," she said softly. "And I can't make it for you."

I saw her on one side of a scale, David and the boys on another. One side heavy with history and obligation, the other light and unburdened. There was love on both sides. And my sons, no matter what they had done, were a part of me. I had carried them, I had raised them, and their sins were mine.

"I know," Emilia said, as if reading my mind, giving me a sad smile. "You don't have to say it. And maybe it was unfair of me to ask, but I needed to let you know it was an option. Back in college, I always regretted not telling you how I felt before I went away."

"You did tell me," I said. "Your note. The Beatles lyric. I knew what you meant."

I watched a tear roll down her cheek, leaving a saltwater trail.

After I got into my car, the unmade choice still hanging between us, I had to force myself to drive down the highway so that I wouldn't head back into the Blossom and tell Emilia I would go with her. When I arrived back at the Golden Grape, I let myself hunch over the steering wheel and cry. I'd need to collect myself before I went in the house, or else David would ask me what was wrong, and what would I tell him?

But before I could even dry my tears, a car pulled up beside me—a blue Mini Cooper—and a woman stepped out, only vaguely familiar through my glassy vision.

"Bev Kelly," she said. "I need to tell you something."

And then I finally learned the truth about my husband.

# Three

## June

**THE BLOW PUSHES KYLE BACKWARD,** leaving him clutching his jaw with his hand. When he sees the source of the impact, fear flickers in his eyes. He stands back up to his full height, looking from me to Andrew as Andrew circles him like he's prey.

"Look, I'm not sure what you think is happening here, but I'm just talking to my fiancée," Kyle says, raising his hands in either defense or surrender. "I know you're Andrew Smith. June said she saw you watching her in Brooklyn. If you're following us, or if you want something with her, you can take it up with me."

Andrew's eyes are vacant, and for a second, I think he's going to turn around and leave. I stare at Kyle, who is now standing with his fists clenched by his sides, like he's preparing to throw a punch back if he needs to. It's completely out of character. Kyle isn't capable of hurting anybody. He doesn't even kill spiders that he finds in our apartment; instead he uses a wad of tissue to deposit them on the balcony. But obviously Josh isn't the only man who has lied to me.

"I got your message," I tell Andrew. "I know what you were trying to tell me. But please—I need to ask him myself."

Andrew is breathing heavily, like he wants to intervene. But instead, he nods curtly, giving me the space.

I turn to face Kyle. "Did you know who I was when we met? Has our entire relationship been some kind of sick revenge for what happened to Michelle?"

Kyle rubs his jaw with his hand. "I didn't know who you were. Even when you talked about your husband Josh, I didn't put it together. It's not like you showed me photos or anything, and you didn't tell me his last name. I didn't go to high school with Michelle. I only saw her at tennis camp every summer. We weren't even friends, more like acquaintances with tennis in common."

I so badly want to believe him. "Did she talk to you about Josh? Did you ever meet him?"

"No," he says, a thin sheen of sweat on his hairline. "No, and no. I just heard . . . rumors."

"What kind of rumors?"

"About Josh. Michelle was close with the girls from camp, and the summer she was with Josh, I heard a lot of people talk. Her friends were worried about her. Somebody knew another girl Josh had dated, and there was this nude photo scandal that involved Josh and his twin brother, and her friends were trying to warn Michelle about Josh."

"Did she listen?" I ask, already knowing the answer. Did I listen, when everyone warned me about getting married too fast?

"I never saw her again after that summer. At camp the next year, everyone missed her . . . It just wasn't the same anymore. The girls were going on and on about Josh. About how he must have done something, because she couldn't have just drowned."

When Andrew finally speaks, his voice is measured. It's clear that whatever he's about to say has been marinating for a very long time.

"I overheard Josh and Michelle arguing a couple of days before she died. About a boy from camp who wanted to hook up with her. He'd apparently called her after camp was done?"

"It wasn't me," Kyle says, visibly surprised. "I didn't even have her phone number. I can think of a couple other guys who had a crush on her . . . and looking back, I'm sure part of me did too. But I'd never have acted on it, and I certainly didn't call her."

Andrew looks unconvinced. He turns to me, as if he hasn't heard Kyle at all. "After Josh died, I became obsessed with finding out who killed him. I spent hours on the computer. I looked up everything—everyone from Josh's life, and then from Michelle's, because I felt like they had to be connected. Two drownings—how could they not be? There was a photo of Michelle and Kyle on the camp's website. I remembered his name—Kyle Parker."

"It was one photo," Kyle says. "What motive would I have to hurt your brother? You think I'd kill a person based on some rumors?"

A small burst of relief. He's right. It sounds so far-fetched, and Kyle is a person who thinks everything through.

"I wouldn't have thought about you again," Andrew says, his eyes focused on Kyle. "But then my mom mentioned June's wine bar to us, and Sadie looked it up. She found June's Instagram." He turns to me. "That's when she saw the pictures of you with him. I didn't think anything of it, until I saw his name. It sounded familiar, and I couldn't figure out how, until I googled him and remembered. Michelle's friend from camp, engaged to my dead brother's widow."

"I know it's a huge coincidence," Kyle says. "But like I said, I never even met Josh, just like I've never met you, until today. Were you following June, in Brooklyn?"

"No," Andrew says. "I was in Brooklyn, but I was trying to find you. Because there was no way it was a coincidence. Josh's death, your connection to Michelle, your relationship with June. I was figuring out how to approach you, but then you flew out here . . . so I came home."

I level my gaze at Kyle, tears collecting in my eyes. "You knew Josh was a twin. You knew there were rumors about him. And you never told me." Kyle knew things about Josh that I never did.

Kyle stares at his hands. "Look, by the time I found out Josh Kelly was your husband who died, we'd been together for a couple of months and I didn't want to bring him up and wreck things. It felt like we were finally making some progress together, and if I told you what I knew . . . I thought you might freak out and break things off."

He's right. I would have found every reason not to believe him. It would have been Kyle's word against my dead husband's. Josh wasn't there to defend himself, and I would have taken his side. But still: Kyle isn't someone who lies by omission, no matter how hard the truth is to hear.

"Besides," Kyle continues. "My connection to him was barely there. I'm telling the truth about Michelle. I only knew about Josh Kelly from some rumors, nothing more. I agonized over whether I should say anything. It was torture—should I tell you and be honest, or not tell you, and spare you the hurt? For all I knew, the rumors weren't even true."

Tears start to blur my vision. I want to speak but don't even know what to say.

"I put it out of my head," Kyle says. "Who was I to wreck your memories of your dead husband? And what if you told me to go away? I was already falling in love with you."

I wipe my eyes. If Kyle had been the first person to tell me about Josh and his past, things would have ended between us. But now I've been introduced to versions of Josh from multiple people, and it's my version that doesn't fit with theirs. Which means Josh was either lying to me, or lying to everyone else.

I force myself to speak, even though defending Josh no longer comes automatically.

"Josh sent me a text message that morning he disappeared that I've always suspected he never actually sent himself. You didn't know me in the months after Josh died, but I've told you, I was a mess. What I didn't tell you were my theories about his death. About that text message. He used a heart emoji. He hated emojis."

Now I'm thinking back to the thousands of texts Kyle has sent me over the years, the thousands of heart emojis he's used.

Andrew steps in, his voice clear and calm. "I already told June that Josh and I were supposed to meet up that morning. I kept it a secret, even from Sadie. She had no idea, back then, that I had a twin. But Josh wanted to see me. When they found his things at the beach, I just never bought that he went for a swim. Still, I wasn't going to try and prove otherwise—I hadn't talked to him for so long; I knew nothing about his life. But after I saw you and June together on her Instagram, I started figuring it out."

Panic has made my limbs rubbery. I do the math: sometime after Josh and I started dating, he reached back out to Andrew. He hadn't told me about Andrew sooner because he didn't want to risk dragging his messy past into our new relationship. I felt that way with Kyle at first. I wanted the relationship to be fun and carefree. I never wanted to burden him. But because I loved him, I let him carry some of the load.

Maybe Josh was scared to tell me, or embarrassed about his dysfunctional family. Maybe it wasn't about covering something up, but about being afraid of what I'd think. Afraid I'd run away. Maybe he would have told me eventually, but now I'll never know.

My eyes burn with angry tears. I never considered that the same burden I shouldered was also weighing Kyle down. He had once mourned a friend, and I was mourning the man who might have killed her.

"I'm sorry," Kyle says, looking at Andrew with pity in his eyes. "But I had no idea who June was when I met her—that Josh was her dead husband."

"I tried to believe Sadie when she said my brother drowned, that it wasn't anybody's fault," Andrew says. "Everyone was willing to accept that it was just a big coincidence that he died in the water, the same way Michelle did. That they both drowned."

He puts a hard emphasis on the word *drowned*. My gaze flickers to Kyle, and his mouth is quivering, like it's an effort to keep it shut.

"You've been through a lot," Kyle says. "It's terrible, what happened." He reaches for my hand, but I pull it away.

"It is terrible," Andrew says. "For years after Michelle died, I blamed Josh. I was convinced he'd done it. But as time went on . . . I realized how angry I was back then. I was looking for somebody to blame. Josh was the reason I got sent to boarding school, and I hated him for it. But it doesn't mean he killed Michelle. I had no proof, and when he messaged me all those years later, it made me wonder if maybe I was very wrong."

"Look, I've got nothing to hide," Kyle says. "Do you want me to prove I wasn't in San Francisco when Josh died? Because I can."

Andrew steamrolls over him. "I spent a lot of time wishing Josh was dead too. He *was* dead, to me, for over a decade. But when he actually died, I couldn't have prepared myself for what that would feel like to really lose him. There was so much I never got to say to him."

He turns and speaks directly to me, as if Kyle isn't even here. His eyes are wide and imploring, the same eyes that had looked so calculating when we were alone in his kitchen. I know he feels guilty for his own role in his estrangement from Josh. And most of all, for the horrible, unforgivable way he deceived Michelle.

"There's no way it was a coincidence, or an accident."

"June," Kyle says, dueling for my attention. "I should have told you from the start, but I had nothing to do with Josh's death. I know I fucked this up, but please, believe me."

I want to take Kyle's outstretched hand, get in the rental car with him, and drive away, but that would mean that I definitely believe him—that he's innocent, and that Josh is guilty. It would mean I've spent the last ten years wondering how my life with Josh would have looked—exciting, passionate, deliriously happy. It would mean admitting that my fantasy was nothing but a lie.

I can't bring Josh back from the dead. But I also can't move on with the person who might have put him there.

"Is it true?" I ask Kyle. "It was only ever rumors?"

"It's true," he says, his jaw quivering. "I swear. Andrew has the wrong idea."

"No," Andrew says, shaking his head. I can see the defeat on his face. He needs this connection to make sense in his own brain, the same way I need it to be a coincidence.

"I'm sorry for your loss," Kyle says, reaching out to Andrew. "If you want, we can talk about this—or June and I can just go . . ."

Andrew extends his own hand, and for a second, I think he's going to take Kyle's in a handshake. But instead, he shoves Kyle to the ground. I stand rooted on the spot, unable to move. Andrew and Kyle grapple with each other on the ground, Kyle's fists swinging, but then Andrew is on top of him with his elbow across his throat, and I'm powerless to make a noise, or do anything. All I can suddenly picture is Kyle on top of Josh in the water, holding him under. Kyle, sending one last text from Josh's phone to the wife he knew was waiting.

Then the sound of a woman's scream makes my entire body go cold.

# Four

# *Bev*

St. Helena, Napa County, California

July 2000

**I STORMED INTO THE HOUSE,** rage emanating from my body. I wanted to physically hurt David. I pictured myself pushing him down the stairs; I imagined some kind of accident on the vineyard. I wanted him to suffer.

He was upstairs, getting dressed after taking a shower. His smile fell when he saw my face.

"Sylvie Mills," I spat out.

From the look in his eyes, I could tell he knew that I knew everything.

"I can explain—" he started, but I cut him off.

"You told me it was one time, with somebody I didn't know, when you were in Sonoma. You said her name was Ashley. Turns out, it had been going on for a year, David. A *year*, with the mother of your son's girlfriend. And how many others before her?"

"Josh wasn't even dating Michelle," he stammered. "If he was, I wouldn't have—"

"Like that makes it better somehow? God, David." I thought about the details he'd peppered in. Ashley, in Sonoma, a woman I'd envisioned so many times I could see her in my head. I had forgiven him based on a scenario that never happened. David, my safe place, not safe at all.

"Did Ashley even exist?" I charged on. "Or was it Sylvie the whole time?"

"I panicked," he said.

"You made promises," I continued, my voice trembling. "To Sylvie. You told her you'd leave me to be with her. You told her you were in love with her. And she believed you, the same way *I* used to believe you. You never stayed at a hotel in Petaluma after I made you leave. You went to see Andrew, sure—but then you went straight back to Sylvie."

"Bev, I don't want to be with her. I broke it off with Sylvie months ago. It was a huge mistake, and I didn't tell you because there was so much going on—"

"Like her daughter dying on our vineyard? David, the woman is completely broken." The image of Sylvie in the parking lot, her body practically skeletal, puffy bags under her eyes, would haunt me for years. Was Sylvie the reason why Michelle had wanted to talk to me the night she died? Had she seen her mother with David, and tried to warn me?

I stood tall, even as my body sought to cave in. Michelle had been upset that night. There was something she needed to say to me, and maybe it wasn't about my sons, but about my husband. Maybe David and I were to blame, our affairs trickling down, the knowledge of it polluting Michelle. She was just a teenage girl, and she never should have had to carry that weight.

No matter which way I spun it, Michelle was dead because of our family, and that was something I didn't know how to live with.

David sat down on the edge of our bed, his head in his hands. "I messed up, Bev. I already admitted to that. I said I'd go to therapy. I'll do whatever it takes. But things between us were so bad—"

"Don't even think about putting this on me," I said. I opened my mouth again, wanting to humiliate him as badly as he had done to me. I wanted to tell him about Emilia, that I'd realized his love might not be enough.

I didn't yet know that it was the one time when staying quiet would save my life.

"Give me another chance," David said, looking up at me with glassy eyes.

"Was there ever an Ashley?"

David's silence did all the talking for him. Such careful details, conjured out of his imagination.

"Please, Bev. We can get through this. For us. For our family."

I stepped away from him. "This family is broken."

"We can fix it—"

"No, David, we can't." I paused before the next words tumbled out, letting them take on the right shape, impossible to misinterpret. "I want a divorce."

It wasn't what he expected. The word lingered between us, enormous and terrifying. It wasn't about punishing David, because we were both guilty. It was about acknowledging that we were two broken pieces, and we no longer fit together to become whole.

David rebounded from the shock and kept fighting, like I knew he would. "We're husband and wife, Bev. For better or for worse, in sickness and in health, till death do us part."

"It's too late," I said, heading for the door.

David was quiet for a long time, his fingertips clutching his knees. Maybe he finally saw it. The people who suffered because of the vows we'd made each other. The wreckage underneath the perfect couple we were so good at pretending to be. It was my turn to break the cycle.

"Is this really what you want?" David called after me, his voice lullaby soft.

I thought about what I wanted. Once upon a time, I'd wanted David, but time had pronged us apart. The incident with Abby had shown me how different we were, and Michelle's death had compounded it. David and I had both tried so hard to neutralize the damage, but it had never gone away. It seeped into us, poisoning our marriage. All we had done was make the mess impossible to clean up.

Without turning around, I responded, "Yes."

# Five

# *June*

St. Helena, Napa County, California
September 2022

**I TURN AROUND. SADIE IS** the source of the scream, and she pulls Andrew off Kyle, whose face has been bloodied by Andrew's fists.

"Hey," she shouts. "Andrew! Let go of him!"

At her touch, or the sound of her voice, Andrew stops, staring at his reddened knuckles like he isn't sure what he has done. Kyle winces, pressing his hand to his nose, and staggers to a standing position. I want to comfort him, to take care of him, but I can't bring myself to move closer. I'm afraid to choose a side because I'm afraid I will choose wrong.

"I'm not letting him go," Andrew says, staring down Kyle like a predator hunting its prey. "He's the one. He's the connection. It has to have been him."

"Andrew," Sadie says, reaching for his hand, which he yanks away. "We don't know that. We don't know anything for sure. Without proof— what exactly were you going to do? You need to let this go."

Kyle's gaze flits from Andrew to me. "I didn't kill Josh. You know I'm not capable of killing anyone, June."

"You're lying," Andrew says.

Kyle keeps talking. "Think about it—how many places can you play tennis in the city if you're not part of a private club? By the time I figured out Josh was your husband, I made the decision not to say anything. I chose to keep the rumors about Josh from you, which also meant not telling you he was a twin. You were mourning him, and I didn't think it was fair to throw all of this doubt on somebody you loved so much."

He pauses for only a second, but in that second, I see myself when I met Josh, bored with my life, bored with my lackluster job. Josh swept in and filled my world with color.

*She deserves to know everything about you.* I hear the words Bev had spoken to Josh, her skepticism. Maybe she hadn't disapproved of us, as I'd always believed. Maybe she'd just been trying to protect me.

"The world isn't that small," Andrew says quietly. "It can't be."

"I can prove where I was the day Josh died," Kyle continues. "I would have been in Manhattan, working fourteen-hour days at the firm. I didn't take any trips to San Francisco. I was thousands of miles away."

None of us say anything, so Kyle keeps talking. "I didn't tell you about Michelle, or Andrew, because honestly, what was the point? Josh wasn't coming back. All you had left of him was six months of great memories. Who was I to take that from you?"

Our eyes lock. He's not wearing his glasses. They must be on the nightstand in our room. Without them, even with his battered face, he looks younger, and so earnest, like this confession has almost broken him. And in him I see the man who has loved me for six years, who has been everything I thought a partner should be. Kind, funny, caring. But now it's like flipping a coin and seeing the other side.

"I believe you." As I say it, I realize it's true. "But I don't know if I can trust you again."

Even if the choice seems like it should be easy for me, it's not. Kyle has felt like a safe place for so long, not just a partner but a best friend, someone warm and considerate. The kind of relationship I always told myself Josh would have wanted me to be in. But what do I know about what Josh would have wanted? There are some truths I'll never be ready to hear. I can see Kyle's side of things, his reasons for not revealing those truths.

But that doesn't change the fact that he'd lied by omission, the same way Josh had. He chose to keep me in the dark.

Josh never got a chance to screw up with me. Had we been given time, we might have figured out that we weren't actually compatible. I'd held him up on a pedestal for years, comparing every other man—even Kyle, sometimes—with a larger-than-life ghost.

I take a step forward to Kyle, but Andrew gets between us. "He was there, I know he was—I just can't believe it's all a coincidence."

"I'll prove it. Look through my old photos. Old emails. I had no communication with Josh Kelly at any point. Everything I heard about him was through rumors." He pauses. "I didn't even know he died until I met June."

"I don't believe it," Andrew says. "It can't be . . ." His hands are balled tightly, his jaw tense, his face warped in anger. My adrenaline surges. I don't know what he'll do next, and it's the uncertainty that scares me most. What is he capable of doing to Kyle? To us?

But instead of physically lashing out, he droops, his eyes dimming as his shoulders curve inward, as if the live-wire electricity were abruptly exiting his body. A mumbled noise comes from his mouth, but I can't make out what he's trying to say.

"Andrew," Sadie says carefully, placing her hand on his back. "It's over. Let's go home."

He shakes his head and crouches to the ground. There are tears on his cheeks, and a sob rips its way out of his throat, a violent sound that breaks my heart.

"I thought . . . ," he manages. Sadie sinks down beside him and wraps her arms around him. Briefly, her eyes meet mine, and I can see the weight she has carried too—trying to keep her husband from sinking under, from giving in to the darkness. I had thought Sadie just wanted me to go away, and maybe she did. Maybe all she wants is to move on from this, from her husband's theories about the past that won't do anything to change the future. Maybe it's something she and Kyle have in common, carrying the heavy burden of a loved one's guilt.

When Andrew lets Kyle and me walk away without following, I know that he never intended to do us any harm. He has no evidence that Kyle is guilty of anything, just like he had no proof that Josh was involved in Michelle's death. Suspicion will never be fact. And I don't think Andrew is capable of hurting anyone.

I glance back at Andrew and Sadie, who are still locked in a tight embrace. Each of us has a different version of Josh Kelly, the one man who could explain everything. The one person who could clear the air. But he's not here to do that, so we need to learn to breathe without him.

## Six

# *Bev*

Mill Valley, California
July–November 2000

**AFTER TELLING DAVID I WANTED A DIVORCE,** I rented a bungalow in Mill Valley, a small town in Marin County. Camille had sold her apartment and was traveling in Thailand but cut her trip short to come back and be with me. She was my lifeline during that time, after David and I sat Josh down and told him we were separating, and drove to Los Olivos, where Andrew was working at his internship on a vineyard there, to tell him in person. We had planned exactly what we'd say to them: a sterilized version of the truth—that we had grown apart, and that they deserved parents who were happy, even if that meant separate houses.

They took the news as well as could have been expected, although I saw the sadness in their eyes, the thoughts they wouldn't say out loud. It was the most identical they had looked in as long as I could remember. With a heavy sadness, I realized our divorce might cause the rift between them to grow, with no united family front anchoring them together ever again.

I thought back to the day my parents broke the same news to me and Camille. We'd sat with our fingers entwined, my sweaty palm searching for a grip on hers. I'd felt her sigh of relief in tandem with mine. But Josh and Andrew had never been close the way we were.

Since David would remain at the Golden Grape—it was his family's winery—Josh would live primarily with him until he left for college, which was our attempt to keep things as stable as possible. For the rest of the summer, I saw him on weekends. I would never admit it, but the time away was freeing for me. I didn't have to see his face every day and be reminded of all the ways I'd failed him, and all the things I'd do differently if I could.

They left for college at the end of August—Josh to Berkeley, Andrew to Stanford. They'd gotten into top-tier schools. As I watched my sons, both of them tall and handsome, walk across the stages to collect their diplomas, I realized there were some things I had done right as a mother. David and I hadn't failed them completely. They were disciplined, hardworking boys. Their futures were bright, either because of or in spite of us.

But any sense of accomplishment was soured when I considered how much of their academic success had been engineered by David. The tutors, the private lessons; making sure nothing had gone on Andrew's record about the incident at St. Helena. Their paths had been cleared, but at Abby's and Michelle's expenses. The tears that collected in my eyes at their graduation ceremonies weren't out of happiness, but out of a conflicted fusion of pride and deep sadness.

David and I remained amicable, sharing fifty-fifty custody of Kieran. I had him four days during the week, and David the other three; I became familiar with the drive from Mill Valley to Napa, the lolling, serpentine route punctuated by foothills and wineries. We'd both agreed we didn't want the divorce to get messy. David didn't do messy. Deep down, I knew he hadn't given up hope that we'd reconcile. That I'd start to miss him and would change my mind.

And I did miss him. I missed *us*. The idea of us, the one I'd held on to for so long, that I would have held on to so much longer had his affair not pushed me down a different path. I had been with David for more of my life than I had been without him. I missed the Golden Grape and the built-in sense of purpose it provided. I didn't know what the second act of my life would look like.

October sneaked up on us, full-fledged autumn in the valley, vineyards stained russet and gold, the summer heat burned off in favor of a chill that refused to recede. When I dropped Kieran off for his time with his father, I saw the cabernet reach the end of its fermentation, and I felt the loss of the winery like an ache. The dead yeast cells, with no sugar to feast on, died out and sank to the bottom of the barrel, and the wine was racked into a new container. I stared at the leftover sediment, realizing that I, too, had nothing left to feast on here, nothing feeding my starved spirit.

So many times, I thought about calling Emilia and telling her David and I had separated. Camille kept encouraging me to get in touch with her—she knew me better than anyone, and she knew I was still in love. But I talked myself out of making that call. Maybe I was afraid of Emilia's reaction—that it wouldn't change anything between us, because I was still rooted here, and her life was so far away.

I did speak to my divorce lawyer, Bradley, a few months into divorce proceedings, about the possibility of me moving overseas and retaining custody of Kieran.

He looked at me over his wire-rimmed glasses. "Would it be for work?"

"No," I answered. My career was a sore spot. I could have easily found work on a different vineyard, or even studied to become a sommelier, with my decades-long experience working with wine. But it felt like a betrayal to the Golden Grape, and I wasn't sure how to reconcile those feelings.

I couldn't tell him the truth. After all, no judge would agree to let me take Kieran to another country and deprive David of custody just so that I could chase after the woman I loved. And I couldn't—wouldn't—leave Kieran to grow up without a mother.

"You and David have joint custody," Bradley said. "In this case, it wouldn't be in Kieran's best interests to have him uprooted from everything he knows."

He wasn't trying to make me feel guilty, but I still felt the weight of his words. It wouldn't be in Kieran's best interests to take him away from this life.

"It'll be okay," I told Kieran, and he gave me a smile, his tiny white teeth showing. "It'll be okay," I repeated. Lying to children is easy. They trust we are telling the truth.

Whenever Kieran cried at night, it was Camille who heard him—I slept through it. During the days, I stared into space as he played in front of me. I tried to push Emilia out of my thoughts, but found myself dwelling on so many what-ifs, imagining what we'd be doing right now if we were together.

I napped with Kieran one afternoon, my arm wrapped around his little body. Sometime while I slept, he had wriggled out; I startled awake when I heard him cry. He had fallen out of bed and bumped his head on the floor, and blobby tears rolled down his red face. I picked him up and attempted to rock him, kissing the spot where a bump had begun to rise, but he wouldn't settle.

"What happened?" Camille asked. Kieran turned in the direction of her voice and reached out. I let her take him from my arms.

"We were sleeping, and he rolled out," I said.

Camille sat down beside me with a sniffling Kieran in her lap and rested her head on my shoulder, her presence the same warm security to me that it had always been. "Kids fall. It happens."

But it didn't happen with Camille. It didn't happen with David. It only seemed to happen with me. Every bump, every injury, every scar.

"I talked to my lawyer," I blurted out. "I thought maybe . . . I could move away with Kieran. But it's not possible." My conversation with Bradley had been two weeks prior, but it felt like two years.

"You don't need to move away, Bev. Things are going well here, right? With you and me and Kieran?"

"But you have a life too," I said. "It's not your responsibility to stay here for us."

"I'm not," Camille replied. "This is where I want to be. And Kieran seems happy. Look, there's no bruise or anything. He's fine, Bev."

He was fine, but I wasn't. Because without the distractions I was used to—the fast pace of the winery, and juggling the boys' schedules—the same intrusive thoughts I'd denied entry were floating around untethered. As much as I loved Josh and Andrew, the nagging worries I had about Michelle's death wouldn't go away, no matter how hard I tried to push them down. I wanted to talk about it—to know what really happened—but I knew they would deny involvement, just like they already had. My questions would only make my sons feel like their mother didn't believe them—a thought that broke my heart.

I stared at Kieran. The sweet, innocent toddler in Camille's arms, his cheeks stained with tears, deserved so much more.

Motherhood could be done without sleep, without energy, without money or status. But it could not be done without heart, and my heart had been broken by the job. My boys needed someone who would believe them unconditionally. Someone who wasn't living with a dark, festering tapeworm of doubt. Someone like Camille, who could still see them as wholly promising and good. The ambiguity over what had happened that night, and the unavoidable certainty of what I'd seen in the barn, was sending me over the edge.

"I need to find a way to make this work," I finally said.

"We will," Camille said, reminding me that we were a *we*, that I wasn't alone in this. "We're going to figure it out."

I didn't believe her. But when Camille said something, she meant it. I should have known better than to underestimate my sister.

It was almost a month later—on a random Friday in early November, with Camille out picking up groceries—when the doorbell rang. Kieran was in his high chair, his jam-smeared hands splayed on the tray, his feet sticking out of his dinosaur pajamas. He was going through a growth spurt and would need a new pair soon. I didn't answer the door. I hadn't made any friends in Mill Valley. It was undoubtedly a solicitor, and I was wearing my threadbare sweatpants, idly circling job ads in the newspaper spread across the kitchen table.

Camille had gotten used to constantly being around me and Kieran.

She had helped me to babyproof the bungalow, and she automatically bought Kieran's favorite foods at the grocery store. The longer she stayed, the guiltier I felt. Camille did so much for me. She needed to be living her own life, going on dates and having fun, instead of always focusing on us. It was time for me to start looking in earnest for a new career, and possibly a house of my own—one where I could put down roots, but still close enough to David that the custody arrangement wouldn't be impacted.

The doorbell rang again, and I walked over, preemptively annoyed at whatever sales pitch I knew I was about to hear.

Instead, I opened the door to Emilia, who was standing on the doorstep of my rented bungalow in boots and a long skirt, her skin burnished with a golden tan. I blinked repeatedly. She couldn't actually be here. She didn't know where I lived, had no way of knowing where I was.

"Hi," she said, her lips curling into a smile.

"You're here," I said, tears clogging my voice as I tried to catch my breath. "I thought you were in Croatia."

"I was," she said. "I mean, I am. But I needed to see you."

"How did you even find me?" I said. I didn't wait for her to answer. "Camille called you."

"She did," Emilia said, fiddling with the strap of her purse. "Can I come in?"

"Of course," I said dumbly. She followed me into the house, trailed after me into the kitchen, took a seat at the table, and folded her hands in front of her. I took in her manicured fingernails, and the dam burst behind my eyes.

"God, I've missed you," I said, closing the gap between us and pressing my lips against hers. I almost wished the desire were gone because it would have made things easier. But it felt even better than it did before. Our kiss was electric with sadness and anger and elation and everything in between.

I broke away, a sob surfacing. Kieran clapped his chubby hands, then smacked them against his tray, grinding Cheerios into dust on the plastic.

"Are you moving somewhere?" Emilia said, gesturing at the newspaper on the table.

"Eventually," I said. "This isn't my place—I'm just renting it. I can't stay here forever. I guess Camille must have told you about me and David . . ."

She nodded. "I had no idea. I thought you would have called me and told me yourself."

I reached for her hands. "I wanted to, but I didn't see the point. It wouldn't change anything. You have your life, and mine is very much still here, as much as I wish it wasn't. I even talked to my lawyer . . . I wouldn't be able to uproot Kieran like that."

Emilia's reaction wasn't one of resignation, as I'd expected. Instead, there was a knowing gleam in her eyes. "What if you didn't have to?"

"I've gone over every scenario," I said. "David would never give up his custody, and I don't want him to. Kieran is doing so well with our arrangement . . . Moving here to Mill Valley was a big enough adjustment."

Emilia knelt in front of me, squeezing my fingers. "Are you happy here? Is this what you want, Bev? Or do you want something different?"

"You know what I want," I said carefully.

She ran her finger along my collarbone, a velveteen heat rising under my skin. "There might be one scenario you didn't consider."

"Trust me, I've considered them all, and there's no way."

"Bev Jamieson," she said, her smile slow and deliberate. "There's always a way."

As Kieran babbled in his high chair, Emilia sat down beside me at the kitchen table, our knees touching, and told me her plan.

## Seven

# June

**WHEN WE'RE BACK IN** our room, packing up to leave, Kyle does prove to me where he was when Josh died. An old album on his Facebook shows him tagged in photos with coworkers at a brunch in the West Village on that same morning.

"I was telling the truth," he says gently. "You can look through my whole phone. My computer. You can talk to anyone I know. I wasn't there when Josh died. It breaks my heart that you think I'm even capable of that."

"I don't," I say, sinking onto the bed, my head in my hands. "But you have to see how coincidental it is, and the fact that you never told me you knew who Josh was . . . I know why you didn't say anything, but I still don't like it."

He moves toward me, like he wants to wrap his arms around me, but he hangs back at the last moment.

"I didn't know who Josh was," he says. "That's the point. If I'd actually known him . . . I would have said something. I'd only heard things, and it felt better left unsaid."

"I know you were afraid of scaring me off, but I would have listened to you, Kyle. I trusted you. I—I *trust* you." The weight of it takes me by surprise. I do trust him, even now. Maybe even more than ever.

I turn away and shove a wrinkled cardigan into my bag. The could-have-beens feel like a series of bloody scabs, picked over before they could heal. Josh could have been a father; he could have been a lawyer. We would have been celebrating our tenth anniversary this year.

But maybe our love story wouldn't have turned out that way.

I'd always gone along with Josh's ideas, loving his spontaneity and lust for life. But did he love me because I was easily malleable, desperate for adventure? Even the idea of opening a wine bar had been his—that it would be a natural wine bar was mine, but the initial seed had been Josh's.

I don't know what I believe—if Josh got into trouble in his teen years but wanted a clean slate with me, or if he was capable of so much worse than I ever could have imagined. I'll never know for sure, but what I do know is the love that's in front of me right now. I thought Josh was the love of my life, and he was. But here is Kyle, who gets to be with me for the rest of mine, if I let him.

"We can't pretend it didn't happen," I say, pulling my suitcase closed and zipping it up. "But I understand why you kept it from me."

I blink back tears, and this time, when Kyle approaches and puts a tentative hand on my shoulder, I lean into his familiar embrace. The man who taught me I could love again; the person who helped me believe in second chances.

"You can choose how you want to remember Josh. But it shouldn't be at the expense of your future. No matter what kind of person he was, I don't think he would have wanted you to throw away something great."

For some reason, I think about Bev Kelly and how she must have felt after Michelle died on her property. If she was caught between defending and condemning the boys she loved. Or if she has only ever lived in tortured denial.

Will I continue to do the same?

Everyone was right. Ten years ago, I did marry a man I hardly knew.

This time around, I did everything differently. Where Josh and I were fast, Kyle and I went slow. Where Josh and I sprinted, Kyle and I walked at our own pace.

If the two great loves of my life have taught me anything, it's that the amount of time you spend with a person means nothing. Because no matter how many questions you ask, you'll only ever see the parts of them they allow you to see. The rest stays buried.

"No more secrets," I whisper to Kyle.

"No more secrets," he repeats, and I'm brought back to a beach in Santa Barbara, my eyes ringed with a reddening sunburn from my snorkeling mask, Josh beside me in the sand, his hand creeping up my leg.

"Tell me a secret," I'd said playfully, and he hadn't even flinched.

"You already know everything about me," he had deadpanned, fixing me with his double-dimpled smile, which was almost blindingly white. "You know me better than I know myself."

I'll still mourn Josh Kelly, the man I loved at first sight and quite literally ran off into the sunset with. But more than that, I'll mourn the version of Josh embalmed in my memories. Because I'm not sure that person existed for anyone else but me. If not for a random click on the Backyard's website, I might never have known who Josh used to be. Just like I'll never know for sure whether he killed Michelle, or if someone killed him in revenge. They're questions I'll have to live with, ones I have to accept might never be answerable.

But there is one thing of which I'm certain. There isn't just one person for everyone. Two men promised to love me forever, and I've made the same promises to both. Two great loves, ones that forever changed me. One is gone, and one is still here, his arms wrapped around me as my head rests on his shoulder, right where it belongs.

# PART V

# *Aging*

After the clarification process is over, winemakers can immediately bottle the wine or give it additional time to age. Aging can occur in various places—bottles, barrels, tanks. There's great freedom in aging, as winemakers can choose whichever method they prefer.

Regardless of how a wine ages, and for how long, the end result is the same. Wine, like life, is meant to be enjoyed.

# One

# *Ben*

Finikia, Santorini, Greece
August 2023

**IF YOU LOOK CLOSELY,** you can see it. A scar, on the underside of a milky throat, just beneath the thin stretch of skin. It started as a pink gash but is now silvery white, a gathered burst that resembles a stretch mark. Someone would really have to know where to look, and nobody ever did. It's a nice fiction, that we know the person we marry better than anyone, but the truth is that we know the person they want us to know.

I stare down the hillside into the rolling blue of the Aegean, pulling my pashmina tightly around my shoulders. It gets cool here at night. Never cold, but cool enough to need an extra layer. My skin has adapted to the climate, browning a bit in color, like a toasted marshmallow that has bubbled in the heat. The air is salty, and I can smell the cherry tomatoes I've been growing, thick-skinned and sun-warmed. Tomorrow, we'll pick them for a salad.

My phone vibrates in my hand. I smile at the photos that come through. They're from Camille, screenshots from June's Instagram account. *Thought you might want to see these*, she writes. I scroll through the images. June and Kyle in a Brooklyn park, his hands cradling the dome of her stomach, her eyes closed, but her smile relaxed and genuine. A close-up of their entwined fingers forming a heart over the baby bump. June by herself, tossing her head back in a laugh. June with her head bent, like she's communing with her unborn child; Kyle in the background, grinning wildly.

They look happy. More than that—June looks absolutely joyful. Even though part of me is sad she didn't get to have this same future with Josh—married life, babies—I'm still happy for her. Josh treated her well in their short time together. Maybe David and Camille were right, and he was never the problem at all.

My wife sweeps down beside me, her long tunic wrapping itself dramatically around her legs. She places two small glasses of honeyed vinsanto wine on the table, one in front of me and one in front of herself. Our only ritual, the only shred of routine, is that we have none. Our days are spontaneous and unplanned. Sometimes we take a sailboat out, and others, we walk through the terraced vineyards near our home, down steep alleys and stairs that hurt our aging knees, and we bike the countryside, baskets filled with tomatoes and green cucumbers that will later turn yellow. We make love, and we grow wine grapes, both of our hands now stained. I've taken up sketching and painting; a few pieces of my art are on display in the local galleries we frequent, a small connection I share with my late mother. I drink the natural wine Emilia has taught me to love. When she told me my life, our life, could be better than I even let myself imagine, she wasn't lying.

We had traveled the world together, but it was Santorini—with its whitewashed Cycladic architecture and volcanic beaches, the sapphire basin of the caldera—that gave me a shivery sensation, a full-bodied knowledge that this was where I belonged.

"Oh, that's wonderful," Emilia says when I pass her the phone. Her hand rests on my shoulder. "She looks radiant."

"She really does."

"Kieran went down to that bar in Oia again," Emilia says. "There's a girl he likes. Maybe he's in love. Anyway, don't expect him home tonight."

I shake my head and give a soft laugh. "I never do." I worry about my baby, but not the same way I had worried about Josh and Andrew. He isn't a baby anymore: he's a grown man, one who was raised lovingly and well. He has been to visit me several times when he's been on summer break from college, and he's here for another two weeks.

I enjoy his company immensely: sitting with him on the terrace, having genuine conversations, hearing about his life and telling him about mine, watching his easy smile and round blue eyes. He's still finding himself, but he's happy and free-spirited and, above all, loved.

Emilia sips her wine as her hand migrates to my face and slips under my jawline. She knows about the scar, the one from a bike riding accident when I was a kid: Camille plowing into the back of my new princess bike with hers, sending me flying over the handlebars and onto the asphalt. The shock had knocked the wind out of me, leaving me gasping for air. I'd landed on a rock, which had managed to scrape my throat like a fingernail.

I remembered David once, in our early days, navigating the terrain of my throat with his fingertips, a path they'd take hundreds of times. He must have noticed the scar, but never asked for the story. That was David: always keeping things light, never wanting the gore.

When my first ultrasound showed two babies, identical twins sharing the same placenta, David had to sit down. *Twins. I wasn't expecting that,* he said as we both processed the shock. But I shouldn't have been surprised. Camille and I had grown up in matching outfits, getting mixed up even by people who knew us and constantly being stopped in the street by total strangers. *You should get them into movies,* one woman had said, handing my mom her card and introducing herself as a casting agent.

My mom never called her. We weren't interested in performing anyway. Not yet. Our performance of a lifetime was still decades away.

David didn't understand, and even I didn't at the time. I didn't realize that twins do run in families, but on the mother's side.

Emilia's hand rests lazily on mine as we both stare into the distance, at the sun, a bright ball in a reddening sky. She stretches out her legs and tips her face back.

*I need to find a way to make this work,* I had said to Camille all those years ago, and I hadn't, but she had figured out a way to change everything. Most people don't get a do-over. I had been on a different path before Emilia came back into my life.

The idea had been Camille's. I never would have thought of it, but she was the mastermind of the two of us. She always had a plan for herself. She was ready to have a family. To settle down, to raise children.

"Hear me out," Emilia whispered to me the day she showed up at my rented bungalow, the two of us huddled at the kitchen table. "What if you came with me, and Camille—what if she stayed, as you? Just for a few weeks, maybe a month."

I laughed. "That's crazy. And I'd never ask Camille to do that."

Emilia paused. "What if it was her idea?"

It made sense, in a way, after I got over the initial shock of it. Camille loved my boys like they were her own, with a fierce devotion and natural maternal instinct. Her adoration for Kieran was unparalleled. When I approached her about what she and Emilia had talked about, a tiny smile played on her lips.

"Being with the boys—getting to help you raise Kieran—that's all I want. To be someone's mother."

"You can still meet someone and have a baby," I said.

"It's too late for that. Even if I met someone now . . . it's not going to happen." She didn't look sad, just matter-of-fact.

"Well, you can adopt," I said. "You could have your own family."

"But I already do," she said. "Your boys—they're my family too. My blood. This is for both of us. I'd put everything into raising Kieran. I'd make him my whole life. And you know how much I love Josh and Andrew—I'd be there for them too. Forever."

"You're always traveling," I said. "I didn't think you even wanted to stay in one place."

"I can still travel," she said. "We can have the best of both worlds."

We were both quiet. She put her hand on mine.

"I've figured out a way for you to be in two places at once. Take the chance."

I spent the next week in a fitful sleep, trying to figure out if I could actually do it, if I could really leave everything behind and let my sister step in to help raise my son. *It's irresponsible*, I thought at first. *It's selfish*. It felt impossible to leave him for a month, but more impossible to stay.

"Everyone will know," I said, but Camille didn't think so, and she proved it to me. One day, when it was just her and me and Kieran at the bungalow, she dressed in my clothes, air-dried her hair like I did, put on the Burt's Bees lip balm I always wore. She opened her arms for Kieran, and he toddled into them.

"Mama," he said in his tiny little voice, and those two syllables broke my heart open.

The rest of the logistics were almost too easy. David and I barely had any contact anymore. My life was in Mill Valley, not Napa; I didn't see any of the same people. After Michelle's death, I had no friends. Our fellow vintners we had spent years growing close to wanted nothing to do with us. And Camille was a wanderer: she had random jobs, never a long-term career, and with her apartment sold, nothing tethered her to one place. When I was with Emilia, she would be here in Mill Valley, and when I was with Kieran, she could travel on her own.

What really made up my mind was the panic I felt about seeing Josh and Andrew again, when they'd be home for the holidays. I loved them so much, but that love was no longer enough. They deserved somebody who believed in them the way Camille did. It was as simple as it was complicated: I doubted my sons too much to properly protect them. Camille only ever thought the best of them. She was the right person to keep them safe—and more than that, she *wanted* to.

It wasn't that my boys didn't bring out the best in me, because, in many ways, they did. They had made me a more sensitive person, softer and more patient and empathetic. It was that I didn't bring out the best in them. I would never stop picking at the scabs of the past, never be able to let us move on. Michelle would never not be on my mind. Whether she was upset that night because of my sons, or because of David and her mother. Whether her drunken state was what led her to the pond, or if it was something—someone—else.

The arrangement worked well for the first few years. We switched off every couple of months, but the more time I spent with Emilia in Croatia, the more devastated I was to leave her. I started staying for longer stretches; a couple of times, Camille brought Kieran to visit us, and we kept up the ruse that Camille was his mother, I, his aunt.

Camille and I both knew a clock was ticking. Kieran was almost five, and we would no longer be able to get away with switching. He would know the difference, or one of us would inevitably slip up—he had school, friends, activities, a routine. It was becoming too much to handle. Josh and Andrew were adults now: they had graduated college, with jobs and lives of their own, and we saw them less and less. But Kieran was the one who intensely deserved not just *a* mother to raise him, but one who would give him everything.

"What do you want to do?" Camille asked gently, and as much as I loved Kieran—and I did love him, so much that it made me want to burst— I knew the answer. We were both happier being the other. And thus, he would be better off with me as his aunt, still a part of his life, though from a distance, and Camille as his mother, the rock of his day-to-day existence. The decision had been made. Maybe it had been made a long time ago.

It would be plausible that Camille could uproot her life and move away to be with Emilia Rosser. They'd been in Napa at the same time; we could easily spin a story about how they met at the winery and kept in touch, falling in love over time.

We've been back to Napa and Mill Valley countless times over the years, Emilia and I: holidays and birthdays and lacrosse tournaments; weeklong summer vacations; Kieran's grade school and high school graduations; Andrew's wedding to Sadie; David's funeral after his sudden heart attack, which came as such a shock. And another funeral, for Josh—my Josh, the boy I should have protected. After his death, I fell into a very dark place. I'd questioned everything. Marrying David. Divorcing him. Giving up my family and the person I'd been as a mother. When Michelle had died, I'd been devastated. When Josh died, I couldn't ignore the feeling that the two deaths were tied together somehow, a chill I've never quite been able to shake.

On one of our phone calls—night my time, afternoon Camille's—my sister told me what David had said upon finding out *Camille* had decided to travel the world with another woman.

*I'm not surprised*, he'd said when she dropped Kieran off for his time with David and told him the news. *After Paul left, I wondered. Good for her.* Camille laughed when she told me the next part. *Emilia Rosser*, he'd said, shaking his head, a gesture I could picture so well. *It's a small world. Almost like we set them up.*

I smile, the evening breeze caressing my face, bringing with it the smell of bougainvillea. Bordering our traditional cave home are flower boxes, our unconventional garden where we grow sunflowers and geraniums, plants that thrive under the hot torch of the sun.

*Good for her.* It is good for me, this life, better than I ever could have imagined, even if it took me a long time to get here.

Josh's death will always haunt me, and so will Michelle's, because on some level, I feel like I could have prevented both. Between my visits home, Camille kept me apprised of what was happening with my sons. She was able to get Andrew to come home for Christmas, and we were both there when he brought Sadie home for the first time. The boys never reconciled before it was too late, but Camille maintained meaningful relationships with both of them. And I remained in their lives as their aunt.

I had witnessed Abby's humiliation, and lived the agony of Michelle's death. I had been consumed by those girls, the ones I thought my sons were responsible for hurting. But the women Josh and Andrew ended up with, Sadie and June, found true happiness with my sons. I'll never know if it was Camille's influence on my boys that made them better people. Or if they were already good people, and I was the one whose brain couldn't accept that accidents happened, that coincidences existed.

"It's getting chilly," Emilia says, the freckled skin of her arms turning to goose bumps. "I'm going in. Are you coming?"

"Soon," I say, kissing her hand.

Not many people would understand what I did, and even fewer would approve of it. Not because I chose to leave my husband, but because I chose to leave my children—because I wasn't capable of being the person they needed me to be. I went across the world in selfish pursuit of my own happiness, but the most maternal thing I ever did was put my sons' happiness first and leave them with the mother they deserved. I question my choices every day but always come to the same conclusion. Camille helped to restore Andrew's confidence, and maybe he wouldn't have had a family of his own if not for her. Maybe Josh never would have met June and wanted to settle down. Kieran, though—his was the life that bore the least of my fingerprints, only my DNA, and so far, he's thriving. I love that he visits me so often in Greece, even though he thinks of me as his aunt.

I can look at myself in the mirror now, at my sun-beaten cheeks and forehead thatched with wavy creases, my gray hair, my well-earned laugh lines, the brackets around my mouth, the way my lips have thinned and feathered. I can look at myself and see the road map of my past. And more importantly, I can see my future, can see the future for all of us, one where we're exactly where we are supposed to be. I can define what I want, and what I don't.

I've learned that secrets might be inevitable. In the past, I've kept them, believing it was in everyone else's best interests to stay silent. The secret I'm keeping now—the one I'll keep for the rest of my life—is for the people closest to me, but it's also for myself. The truth would destroy us all.

As the reddening orb of the sun drops into the caldera, dragging the night down behind it like a shade, I can't help but smile. It was painful to say goodbye to a vision of the future I had thought I wanted; in a way, it was like a death, but a necessary one. The past is always with me. But the present is where I live now, in the beautiful mess of it.

David was the love of my old life, and Emilia is the love of my new one. Here I am, proof that second chances exist. Proof that love can appear after loss, after tragedy. The view from here might not be perfect, but I never needed it to be.

# Epilogue

## Eleven Years Earlier
### September 2012

IT'S LATE SEPTEMBER, AND TONIGHT will be our first pick of the chardonnay grapes. I went out to see them earlier today, the touch of sunburn on their filmy yellow skin indicating it's time for them to leave the vine. In a matter of hours, when the air cools down, our picking crew will head out and fill containers that will be emptied into half-ton macrobins. The excitement, the frenzy, the sweet smell in the air: all reasons why I'll never leave this land, why there's nowhere else I'd rather be.

As has become my tradition, I take a pair of pruning shears, slice off the first bunch of grapes myself, and let them hit the bottom of my container. It's not a far drop, but every time they thud against the plastic pail, I imagine what would happen if they splattered on impact, the fall knocking the life out of them.

"Andrew," I say. "Want to test one?"

He's not paying attention. He's staring at his phone, again, fixated on his screen with an expression I can't decipher.

"Sorry," he mumbles. "I just need to deal with a bit of business here."

He thinks he's being subtle, the way he glances at his phone. He thinks I don't know what he's up to. Men never give quite enough credit to the women who know them best. Six years and a child into our marriage, and Andrew doesn't know that I've seen the change in him lately. His phone screen, always angled away from me; his eyes darting up to see if I've noticed. His sharp, dismissive *nothing* when I ask what's wrong.

But still, I ask him again, this time more forcefully: "What's wrong?"

He sighs and rubs his forehead, like I'm an inconvenience. "Sadie, I told you this already. Everything's fine. Please just give me some space."

He expects me to let it go, but I can't. I've seen friends cheated on by their husbands. Infidelity doesn't always look the same, but it has certain qualities in common. The short fuse, the long periods of needing to be alone, the sudden need for privacy.

I've asked him point-blank if he's cheating on me, and he's denied it. But still, the signs are there. Our sex life has been dwindling over the past few months. I'm approaching thirty, and pregnancy left my stomach permanently silvered in stretch marks, a shelf of flabby skin easy to hide in pants but on stark display in the bedroom. And Andrew, like the wines he's devoted his life to, is only getting better looking with age. He must notice the way women look at him.

After the pick, when Andrew gets in the shower, I go into his phone, something I told myself I'd never do. And there it is: a number I don't recognize, one without a name saved with it. I know exactly what that means. With my pulse in my ears, a sob wanting to wrench its way out of my throat, I ready myself for a long text message thread, for back-and-forth flirtatious banter. But whatever Andrew and the woman have said to each other has been deleted on Andrew's end, leaving only two messages. He has been careful to cover his tracks.

The first, from him: *Are we still on to meet tomorrow? Mile Rock Beach, but up by the viewpoint, Lands End trail, where we can be alone. 7 a.m. I'll make an excuse to leave, but I can't be gone long.*

*Why so early, are you so afraid someone will see?* says the response, and I picture the woman who must have sent it, who doesn't care about

Andrew's wife and family at home. Fury grips my chest, and I set the phone face down where I found it, ready to barge into the bathroom and confront Andrew.

But I stop myself. If I confront him now, he'll be able to come up with an excuse, or make me feel crazy—and this is not the first time I've accused him over the years. What I need is proof, and I know how to get it.

*Make it 6:30. No more messages until then, my wife's getting suspicious,* I write back before I can stop myself, and promptly delete the message, along with her last one to Andrew.

At dinnertime, Andrew predictably makes an excuse for leaving the next morning. "I have a breakfast meeting with a client. Bastard's still on New York time, so he wants to meet at seven. Just in case you're looking for me."

I smile sweetly, scooping up mashed potatoes with my fork. "That's fine."

The next morning, Andrew doesn't see me leave the vineyard. I'm always up before the sun, and he's still in bed when I slip into my rain boots and one of his old flannels. He will assume I'm out in the vines, and our part-time nanny will be with Declan. Nobody sees me get into my car and drive to Mile Rock Beach, where I park in the back of the Merrie Way parking lot and enter the Lands End trail. The hike leads to a lookout point, almost two miles there and back. It's a place literally off the beaten path, where nobody is likely to recognize him.

About half a mile into the hike is a sign for the Mile Rock Beach viewpoint.

When I finally get there, a thin film of sweat coating my back, I don't see a woman waiting. Instead, there's a man facing away from me, staring out from the lookout. I would know him anywhere. His wide-legged stance, his broad shoulders and sandy hair. But how did he beat me here?

He turns around, shock all over his face. But he tries to hide his confusion with a smile. He's wearing a shirt I've never seen before. He's dressed up for the occasion, even smelling like fresh cologne.

"Hey," he says, his eyebrows pulling together. He's looking at me like a stranger, like he doesn't recognize me. "You're Sadie."

"What do you mean, *I'm Sadie?*" I stammer, a curtain of white-hot rage descending on my body. "And how did you get here already?"

His forehead wrinkles in confusion. "I'm sorry, I don't understand—I didn't think you'd be here—"

I don't give him a chance to finish, to formulate an excuse. I want to scream at him, but more than that, I want to hurt him. My temper, long dormant, snaps like a broken bone. Andrew wrote his own wedding vows, and in them, he had promised to always be faithful to me.

He takes a step toward me, palms up, like he wants to pacify me, and it's that gesture—his desire to absolve himself—that makes me reach out and shove him. The motion sends him staggering backward, and he lets out a small yelp before tumbling over the rocky bluff. There's a sickening crack on the rocks below, a sound I know I'll never stop hearing. When I get to the edge, I scream. My husband's head is bent at an unnatural angle, his limbs heavy and unmoving. There's no blood—*how is there no blood?*—but he looks more like a broken marionette than a man.

"Andrew," I scream, scrambling for a way down, and finally locate a set of rickety stairs that lead to the beach, my legs like leaden weights as I descend. But by the time I reach his body, it's too late. There's no pulse, the skin on his throat already starting to cool. The fall must have broken his neck.

I lose the ability to breathe.

Our son is my first thought: Declan, our sweet, giggling boy who loves nothing more than kitchen dance parties with his mommy and daddy. I've killed his father, and I'll go to jail for his murder. The thought of Declan makes me act quickly, survival mode activated not for myself but, foremost, for him. He needs me.

Andrew needed me too. We built a life together. We said vows. It hasn't always been easy, but we loved each other deeply. I stare into his blue eyes, the eyes that used to crinkle at the corners when he smiled. Now they see nothing. I killed him. *I killed him.*

"I'm sorry," I choke out to Andrew, even though he can't hear me, and he'll never hear me again. I try to move his body, a carousel of excuses circulating in my mind. I could run back to the parking lot and try to flag someone down for help. *We were hiking, and he fell.* It's a believable excuse—but what if I'm wrong? What if an autopsy shows that he only would have landed at that angle if someone had pushed him?

And besides: he came here to meet someone, and she could arrive at any minute to disprove my version of events.

My hand hovers over his jeans pocket, where a bulge protrudes. I reach in and pull out an unfamiliar wallet and cell phone. Andrew still uses the same fake leather billfold I got him when we were dating; I've never seen him carry anything else. The cell phone is different too, gripped in a navy-blue OtterBox. I flip open the wallet, and the driver's license is the first thing I see.

But the name on the license doesn't belong to my husband.

*Joshua Patrick Kelly*, it reads, along with a New York City address, but with the same birth date as Andrew's. *June 25, 1982.* I hold my breath, unable to wrap my brain around what I'm seeing. Has Andrew created an entire alter ego to use for his affair? Does he have a second address, a second life?

But no—that's impossible. Andrew falls asleep beside me every night. His affair couldn't have taken him that far away. As far as I know, he's never even been to New York City.

I tap to wake up the cell phone, the lock screen picture of Andrew and a woman I've never seen before: young and pretty, with wavy light brown hair and a sprinkling of freckles over her nose. His arm is around her, and they're on a beach, flashing their ring fingers at the camera, both of them in matching gold wedding bands.

"What—" I start to say, blinking repeatedly, as if the image will somehow make sense.

Suddenly, a text message flits across the screen, from a sender named June. *Don't be too long—I'm getting hungry, and not for food anymore!*

I click on the text, realizing too late that it would show someone had read it. The phone doesn't have a passcode, and I stare at the message before navigating out of the text thread and into the main messages. The last message beneath June's is from Andrew. My husband.

My finger hovers over it, the puzzle pieces shifting into place before

I click on Andrew's name. And the screen is promptly flooded with the entire thread my husband had deleted from his end, a message history culminating in a planned meetup this morning. I scroll back to the beginning—almost two months ago—a timeline that coincides with the start of Andrew's secretive behavior and unexplained moodiness.

> I know you said you didn't want to talk to me again, but you're my brother, and life's too short for us to hate each other forever. I've found someone, I'm really in love with her, and I've changed. I don't want to keep secrets from her.

I sit back, clutching the phone, my breath coming in sharp waves. Andrew isn't cheating on me, hasn't been meeting up with another woman behind my back. He was talking to his brother, a twin brother, one I never knew existed. A brother he was apparently considering reconciling with. A brother, now dead on the rocks in front of me.

A rustling noise behind me makes me spin around. But it's only a bird landing on a tree branch. Still—it's a reminder that someone could show up any minute. Andrew will show up any minute, expecting to see his brother. Instead, he'll find his brother's dead body.

Unless there's no body to find.

He's heavy to haul off the rocks, and even heavier to move into the ocean. I take off his shoes and drag him into the churning surf by his ankles, willing myself not to vomit. I kick the sand back into disturbed disarray, stomping its surface like I'd once stomped on wine grapes, and momentarily, I watch his body bob helplessly, unsure if the tide is about to bring it right back to shore, like a cat bringing a maimed mouse to its owner. After a minute, it disappears into the brown spin of the water, and I'm aware that my fate rests completely with the tide. If it's strong enough, it'll take the body out with it. If it's too weak, Joshua Patrick Kelly will wash back ashore with a broken neck, and there will be questions to be answered.

Salt spray licks my cheeks, my own tears mingling with it. I started the day as a wife and mother, as a winemaker, and now I'm a murderer.

On the sand, Joshua Patrick Kelly's phone bleats. *You're not texting me back, you'd better be on your way with breakfast!* Another message from June.

I type out a quick reply with violently shaking hands, trying to conjure a message a loving husband might send; wipe the phone clean on my T-shirt; and place it and his wallet inside his Chuck Taylors.

**Decided to go for a quick swim first, be back soon** ♥

I picture her reading it and smiling. I don't stay long enough to read her response. How long will she wait for him? How long will she search for him once she realizes he's gone? I hope she finds a way to move forward, to live without answers. Her husband clearly didn't tell her what he was really doing this morning, but in death, he won't have to answer for his lie.

In life, we aren't so easily absolved. We all have our secrets—the ones we keep from everyone else, and the ones we keep from ourselves. Sometimes it's the people closest to us who are the hardest to burden with our truths, but they're the ones we need to trust will hear us when we tell them what we want, what we need. What we've done.

What will I say to Andrew when I see him later today? I won't confess what happened here—I *can't*—but I can do what felt impossible even an hour ago: Talk to him about our marriage, our life. Tell him what isn't working. Let him know what I need.

Joshua Patrick Kelly will be the last secret we keep from each other.

THE END

# Acknowledgments

**THEY SAY SECOND BOOKS** are the hardest to write, and in my case, this was very true. It took several false starts for this book to come together, and it wouldn't have been possible without the support of so many passionate, talented people.

Firstly, and most enormously, to my agent, Hillary Jacobson, without whom this book would not exist. Thank you for wading through many, many early drafts to get to the core of the story, for endless phone calls and incredibly thoughtful notes and critiques. I'm beyond grateful that we work so closely and efficiently, and for your continuous faith in me and my writing.

Thank you also to Lauren Denney at CAA for your sharp editorial insights, which were so hugely helpful. To Sarah Harvey, my foreign rights agent, and Josie Freedman, my film agent, for all your hard work to make *Till Death* a success. To my lovely UK agent, Sophie Lambert; to Ali Ehrlich at CAA, and everyone else at CAA and C&W Agency who played a role in this book.

I am convinced I have the smartest, most hands-on editors out there, the kind who push me to be a better writer and do not settle for anything less. Because of their investment in me, I have grown in so many ways. Carina Guiterman, Nita Pronovost, and Clare Gordon, thank you for such an unforgettable experience with this book. You were willing to wait for me to get it right, and you helped me take it to a whole new level when I did. I'm so proud of our work together, and I think the finished product reflects the time and attention we poured into it. You're the definition of a dream team.

At Simon & Schuster US, thank you to Sophia Benz, Danielle Prielipp, Emily Farebrother, Julia Prosser, Maggie Southard, Nicole Brugger-Dethmers, Ruth Lee-Mui, Beth Maglione, Jonathan Evans, and Jonathan Karp. Special thanks to Jackie Seow for handling the exquisite cover, which was designed by Jeff Miller of Faceout Studios.

At Simon & Schuster Canada, thank you to Kaitlyn Lonnee, Sarah St. Pierre, Rebecca Snoddon, Rita Silva, Shara Alexa, Alexandria Mc-Corkindale, and Jasmine Elliott. Jessica Boudreau, thank you for coming up with the idea for the wine bottle on the cover—a detail that I absolutely love!

At HQ in the UK, thank you to Emily Kitchin, Manpreet Grewal, Angie Dobbs, Halema Begum, Tom Han, Georgina Green, Fliss Porter, Angela Thompson, Sara Eusebi, Lauren Trabucchi, Hannah Lismore, Rebecca Fortuin, and everyone else who had a hand in this book coming together.

I would be utterly lost without my writer friends, who have been with me at every step of this journey. To my writing bestie Jesse Q. Sutanto: I don't think I would have gotten through the saggy middle without all your cheerleading (and our amazing retreat!). To the wonderful May Cobb, who has been a ray of sunshine at my lowest moments, and whose friendship I value so very much. Our Unlikeable Female Authors coven truly IS life, and I could not be more grateful that these two talented women are among my dearest friends.

To Darcy Woods, Samantha Joyce, Emily Martin, and Erika David, thank you for believing in me and being true friends through so much. To Amber Smith, for your thoughtful early read and all your ongoing support.

Endless thanks to the kind, generous members of the thriller writing community. Their work might be dark and twisty, but they are the nicest people you'll ever meet. Robyn Harding, Sam Bailey, Ashley Winstead, Ellery Lloyd, Eliza Jane Brazier, and many more. I'm so honored to be in your company!

I'm also grateful to have such an excellent support system in everyday life. To my parents, Denis and Lucy Burns, thanks for encouraging my dreams from a young age, and for so many other things which would take a whole other book to write down. My sister Erin Shakes, who is my favorite person to drink wine with. My brother-in-law, Jermaine Shakes, and Fiona, Malachi, and Naomi.

On the Flynn side, thank you to my in-laws, Jim and Doreen, and to Suzanne and Jimmy and family, and Kelly and Eric and family (Kelly, thank you for unknowingly lending your lovely name in this book!).

To my extended family, Burnses and Gibbs near and far, including Aunt Pat, Uncle Tom, Aunt Susan, Aunt Linda, and Brian: I love and appreciate you all!

I have amazing girlfriends in my life, the kind of friends where it feels like no time has passed when we get together. Special thanks to Lauren Badalato, Tory Overend, and Shirley Konu, for loving me even when I'm at my most frazzled.

Of course, support starts at home, and I'm lucky to have a lot of it in the form of my husband, Steve. Thank you for encouraging my career, finding ways to make things work, and tolerating me before my morning coffee. We had four kids in four and a half years, and our house is always loud, but also always filled with love. I wouldn't have it any other way.

This book is dedicated to my children: Astrid, Cullen, Delilah, and Briar. It is impossible to put into words how much I love you, but I hope you already know. I will always be your biggest champion, and you will always be my biggest inspirations.

Thank you to all of the booksellers, teachers, librarians, bloggers, Bookstagrammers, and BookTokers for being such passionate advocates for books and reading. I'm so grateful for everything you've done, and continue to do, to support my books.

I would be remiss not to shout out two things that were instrumental in the creation of this book: coffee, which I drink in copious quantities, and Netflix, which helped keep the kids entertained during those long, confusing pandemic days. In particular, I owe the Paw Patrol, Peppa Pig, the Octonauts, and Gabby's Dollhouse a debt of gratitude.

Finally, the hugest thanks to my readers: for your patience as I worked away at this book, and for being excited to read it. It's yours now. I hope it was worth the wait.

# About the Author

**LAURIE ELIZABETH FLYNN** is a former model who lives in London, Ontario, with her husband and their four children. She is the author of three young adult novels: *Firsts*, *Last Girl Lied To*, and *All Eyes On Her*, under the name L.E. Flynn. Her adult fiction debut, *The Girls Are All So Nice Here*, was named a *USA Today* Best Book of 2021 and has sold in eleven territories around the world.